ƒP

CASANOVA
IN BOHEMIA
{A Novel}

ANDREI CODRESCU

THE FREE PRESS
New York ❧ London ❧ Toronto ❧ Sydney ❧ Singapore

THE FREE PRESS
A Division of Simon & Schuster, Inc.
1230 Avenue of the Americas
New York, NY 10020

For information regarding special discounts for bulk purchases,
please contact Simon & Schuster Special Sales:
1-800-456-6798 or business@simonandschuster.com

Designed by Deirdre C. Amthor
Manufactured in the United States of America

10   9   8   7   6   5   4   3   2   1

Library of Congress Cataloging-in-Publication Data

Codrescu, Andrei.
Casanova in bohemia : a novel / Andrei Codrescu.
    p. cm.
    1. Casanova, Giacomo, 1725–1798—Fiction. 2. Bohemia
(Czech Republic)—History—1618–1848—Fiction. I. Title.
PS3553.O3 C37   2002
813'.54—dc21   2001051117

ISBN 0-684-86800-8

Membre de l'univers, je parle à l'air.
—Giacomo Casanova

Acknowledgments

The author is grateful, above all, to Giacomo Casanova who allowed himself to be channeled for the purpose of rescuing his image from the likes of Federico Fellini and other unfair or rancorous assassins of his character; praise the author's soul mate, the living Laura who kept watch on the barque of his prose and steered it away from shipwreck more than once; hail the battered graces of Venice and Prague; and note also that this author is unapologetically grateful to his own life for setting him on fire more times than he can remember.

CASANOVA
IN BOHEMIA

On the fifth of June, in the year 1798, a body believed to be that of Giacomo Casanova, self-styled Chevalier de Seingalt, was buried in the graveyard of Dux Castle in the kingdom of Bohemia, in the presence of his last patron, Count Waldstein, his nephew, Carlo Angiolini, who had traveled from Dresden, and an assorted retinue of servants, most of whom had done their utmost to make miserable the last years of his life. Among the small group of mourners stood a woman named Laura Brock, who, though no longer young by the standards of that time, was nonetheless in the full bloom of womanhood, and radiated the certainty of a still firm body that knew its pleasures and its power. She alone knew the bittersweet secret of the passing of the man whose remains were being so perfunctorily disposed. As she listened to the ridiculous sentiments (all lies, really) of the priest delivering the eulogy, she suppressed a smile, and remembered the first time she had entered the library to serve Signor Casanova a cold supper of melon and ham.

1

"The cook must belong to that race of men, born in the North and soured by the East, for whom food is something to be endured rather than savored," quipped the old man in French, a language he felt sure the serving-girl couldn't understand. The ham was exceedingly fat and was flanked by a lump of red sauerkraut topped by a shriveled half potato. Certainly not what he had in mind when he had ordered it. What he had in mind was thin prosciutto wrapped around slices of ripe yellow melon. Ah, what he had in mind and what surrounded him were like sunlight and shadow.

He was dressed in a brilliantly colored Chinese silk robe embroidered with gold dragons, and wore a red wool cap over his wig against the dampness and cold that were a permanent feature of the castle. "And where," he continued, "did he find such a beautiful woman to abuse with his bad moods? Undeserving bastard!" He then gazed at her so long and so suggestively that she felt she could slap him.

Instead, she had answered him in competent, though oddly inflected French, "If Monsieur Librarian wishes his ham warmed, that can be arranged without making an enemy of the cook." She did not mention that among her duties she was required to serve and to please Hans Gelder, the cook, who was in all respects exactly as the Chevalier de Seingalt had described him. Laura Brock was neither innocent nor silly, and knew well the sound of hollow compliments, but if the old man assumed that she would serve him as she, of necessity, served Hans Gelder, he would wait a long time as far as she was concerned. The cook, though brutish and fat, was only thirty years old—the librarian looked to be at least one hundred!

Oh, how she had underestimated the old goat! Sitting in front of her in his ridiculous, old-fashioned wig was the most famous seducer in Europe, a man who at one time had made himself unwelcome in more than a dozen countries. Jealous men had hidden their wives and daughters at the mention of his name. Or so she had been told by Gelder when she asked what the curious Italian gentleman had done before becoming librarian at Dux. In truth, after she had gotten to know him, she learned that Gelder's description of Casanova, unlike Casanova's description of Gelder, was not in the least accurate. There was something boyish about the old man, almost innocent, though he was without doubt a devilish charmer.

"My dear fraülein, I did not mean to offend you or the cook," Casanova declared, recovering quickly from the surprise of her French. *"De gustibus non disputandum.* I still maintain that you are a beautiful woman. I see also that you are not a simple maid. I believe, in fact, that you know how to read and that this library is not an entirely strange place to you."

At this Laura blushed in all sincerity. He had somehow discerned what she had been at pains to conceal for the eight months she had labored in the service of Count Waldstein. She had been taught to read by her father, the minister of a small country church in the village of Würzburg, Bavaria. At seventeen she had entered the service of Baroness Stefania von Helmund, who had taken a liking to her, arranging for French lessons and loaning her books, only some of which were moral or instructional. They would discuss Laura's reading in the Baroness's great baldaquin bed, from which the ailing and elderly Baron had been absent for many years. Often they wept for their heroes and embraced in sympathy with imperiled lovers, hoping that by imitation they might save the fictional characters from their literary fates. But only a few years into her service fate had intervened, and the Baroness had died unexpectedly in childbirth, a mysterious occurrence that baffled the impotent Baron most of all.

Rather than return to her village, where her father hoped she would marry a local farmer, Laura found employment, and a certain freedom, at Dux. Count Waldstein seldom visited his country estate; the servants had the run of the place, and after becoming Gelder's occasional mistress, Laura Brock could do as she pleased. It pleased her to read, in secret, books from the vast Waldstein library. So when the new librarian appeared, Laura had volunteered immediately to serve him. If he was a strict old man who didn't approve of a servant reading, she would put sleeping drafts in his wine. It now appeared that drugs would not be necessary.

Casanova had asked her what she liked to read. She refused to tell him at first, declaring indignantly that it would be like baring her soul. "Baring her soul" was how the heroine of a romance novel might have described such a disclosure, but Laura knew it was more a matter of what tickled her fancy. Her taste in books did not run to very serious works. When she finally confessed that she was fond of frivolous novels, Casanova did not express any disapproval, but embarked with her on a course of study that in the years that followed would make her a dangerously well-educated woman.

&N ot many evenings after that, when Laura had prevailed upon Gelder to put a few extra slices of trimmed ham and a whole ripe pear on the old man's plate, Casanova asked her to read aloud to him from the French translation of Boccaccio's *Decameron*. This book, which she had read together with the Baroness more times than she could remember, was as dear to Laura as a lover; indeed, it had served her better than a lover many times, certainly better than Gelder, whose brief, grunting exertions were over before she could recite a favorite passage to herself, which alone, she blushed to think, made his rapid intrusions bearable.

Seated at the library table, Casanova set the volume in front of him and invited Laura to sit on his knee to read. She refused, he cajoled her, she refused again, he insisted. There was a sleepy, ritualistic rhythm to these pleadings and refusals like the melody of a familiar tune, something by Mozart perhaps, and it made them both laugh. Finally Laura admitted that she wasn't worried about what he might do to her if she sat on his knee, but what she might do to him—the weight of a hefty wench could damage such a fragile-looking limb. Casanova reacted with amusement.

"I like you so much!" he exclaimed. "I could even love you! Ah, mademoiselle, you do not know what joy you bring to an old man's heart."

There seemed to be no deterring the old goat, so Laura sat her well-rounded bottom gingerly down on the Chevalier's knee, listening for the snap of bone, and sighing with relief when the skinny leg held. Casanova shifted her so that her bottom came to rest fully on his lap. She smelled on his person wig powder, cinnamon, and something else that might have been a subtle scent of death, or only the dust of old books. In his lap she felt no telltale stiffening, and so she relaxed and prepared to read.

Casanova opened the book not to the beginning, but randomly in the middle, and explained to her that any book of high quality, the Bible, for instance, or the histories of Herodotus, was capable of answering any question posed to it. He called this form of divination "oracular reading." All one had to do was ask the question, open the book, and voilà, the answer would be found.

"Ask a question, my dear."

Laura thought for a moment. "What does an old man want from a girl like me?"

The *Decameron* opened to the sixth story on the third day, the tale of Ricciardo Minutolo, who loved the wife of Filipello Fighinolfi. He tricked her into believing that Filipello would secretly meet her at a bagno, and then made love to her himself, she believing all the while that she was actually with her husband.

"How does this answer my question?" Laura was bewildered.

Casanova explained. "Clearly, an old man would like to do with you what Ricciardo did with Filipello's wife, but he must trick you in the dark and make you believe that you are with another man. A younger one, no doubt."

Laura bid the Chevalier to ask a question of his own.

"What does an old man have to offer a beauty like you?"

The book opened to the ninth story on the first day, in which the King of Cyprus is transformed from a weakling to a man of courage by the sharp words of a Gascon lady.

"You see," Casanova said, "a perfect answer."

Laura did see. An old man needed courage, and she could give it to him. Her face lit up at her own cleverness, and turning to Casanova, she told him that she understood, and she knew then that she looked more beautiful to him than ever before.

Courage, for Casanova, was the most noble human quality. Courage was synonymous with sexual conquest and intellectual daring. To possess a woman, to defeat stupidity, or to think thoughts fully, without fear of where they might lead, these were only possible through courage. In grasping this, Laura Brock became Casanova's partner in adventure.

⟡C asanova had always regarded women as fellow adventurers. It had been his good luck to meet courageous women.

"What does courage mean to you, Mademoiselle Brock?" he asked pedantically, sounding like his old tutor Gozzi.

"We can never know just how much courage we have until a situation arises that tests us. . . . I suppose there must be some other qualities, at least for men. Foolhardiness, perhaps."

"A splendid answer." Casanova beamed. "You forget, however, the two most important ingredients, necessity and imagination! Courage without those criteria is no more than foolhardiness, as you say. Self-defense demands a certain sangfroid but it is hardly courage. Do you know who is the most courageous woman I have ever met?"

"I will be much obliged if you told me her story."

"When I met her, she was disguised as a castrato named Bellino. She has since made a great name for herself on the opera stage as a castrato and no one knows that she is really a woman. I met her at an inn where she was spending the week with her mother and her three siblings, a traveling theatrical family. I conceived a passionate desire for her. I was certain that she was a woman, despite her denials and her mother's oath. Her mother was a bit of a procuress, as it turned out, because when she saw that I was mad with desire for Bellino, she sent me one of her younger daughters, who was only twelve and a virgin. I spent a pleasant night in the company of the child and rewarded her handsomely in the morning, but I could not get Bellino off my mind. I pursued her to no avail all day, begging her to let me see for myself if she was a man or not. I only needed some proof for my hand, I even promised not to look. But she only fed my fires by first seeming to give a little, then

7

drawing back. The next night, the wily mother sent me her other daughter, who was fourteen and just as delightful as her sister, though not a virgin and much more experienced. She pleased me very well, but I wanted Bellino. I was mad for her, so I laughed when the old fox sent me the last of her siblings, a real boy, about sixteen years old, who was completely effeminate and already trained to please men. I increased my pursuit of Bellino until, after much coaxing and some extraordinary conversation about the male and female natures, I was able to convince her to show me if I did not touch her. She allowed me to peek through her bodice from above and I saw what I thought to be a monstrous clitoris. I knew it could not be a male membrum because I had no doubts that Bellino was a woman. In any case, I had resolved that even if the giant clitoris turned out to be a membrum, I would possess her. An outward maleness did not deter me. After much, much pleading and more philosophy than I care to recall, I undressed her and found the truth."

"I can only guess that your unfailing instinct for our sex did not mislead you!"

"You understand me well, Mademoiselle Brock." Casanova fell, rather creakily, to the Oriental rug and kissed her pointed slipper, to Laura's embarrassment.

"Please, rise, monsieur, you might be seen. She was a woman then?"

"Not just a woman! Theresa. Theresa-Bellino! There were a number of qualities about Theresa that I will never forget. One was trivial, perhaps. Bellino had worn an artificial penis perfectly molded to her body, a contraption that, when she had first allowed me a glimpse, I had mistaken for a monstrous clitoris. Later, after I unmasked her, we delighted in playing with this artificial limb, making and breaking the illusion. There was something deeply satisfying in encountering her male organ, with all its potential menace and similarity to my own,

8

and then conquering it and revealing the hidden vagina. This game confirmed my belief that the universe is, in essence, feminine, and that the aggressions it evinces are merely a mask, removable like a false penis."

"You believe that the universe is a woman?" Laura was astonished. When Casanova nodded positively, she said: "This interpretation must gratify your maleness because in a feminine universe you must be the only man."

Casanova savored her insight for a moment, letting it melt in his mouth like a Dutch chocolate. Perhaps she was making sport of him. He studied his uncannily bright servant through lowered eyelids and decided that she was serious. Nonetheless, it would not have served him to acknowledge her remark, so he went on.

"The second thing about Theresa that has impressed itself on my mind forever was her courage. Theresa, in order to resist the entreaties of men, transformed herself into one, but not an ordinary man. She became a castrato, a man who was desired by other men, men who loved women and who would have had to have a great deal of courage to trespass on their understanding of what constituted a man or a woman. In the mirror of Theresa-Bellino all men were bound to feel troubled, none more than myself, who knew that I would possess her no matter what gender she turned out to be. I have never been unduly bothered by trifling with other men, but I fell in love with Theresa-Bellino, and love, as opposed to trifling, is what, in the end, unmans us. . . ."

"Forgive me, Chevalier," Laura interrupted, not quite following Casanova's logic. "Love is impossible then between people of the same gender?" She had loved the Baroness Stefania von Helmund and she defied anyone to deny it.

"No, that is not what I mean. Love between men is possible."

"And between women?"

"I don't believe so," Casanova replied firmly. "Sooner or later one or the other will feel the lack. Do not misunderstand me, I love the activities of women with that proclivity and I have been a willing participant in a number of such orgies."

"You are a conceited peacock, Chevalier, and I would challenge you to a physical contest if you were not a creaky old man!" She made a threatening fist and brought it down, in jest, on the Chevalier's jaw. She had actually landed a blow, despite herself, and was sorry to see Casanova wince.

"I do not wish to argue this, mademoiselle. Your lack of experience gives me too much advantage."

Laura held her tongue. Lack of experience, indeed. She had known her employer's body like the palm of her hand and had since explored other women's bodies, each one a mysterious island that she had delighted in mapping.

"In any case, it was a battle," Casanova said.

"How was it a battle? What was?"

"I had succeeded in removing Bellino's penis before Bellino removed mine. This, in my opinion, is the model for all the battles I have waged in the world. The world, as you have so concisely put it, is a woman, but it is disguised as a male warrior, wearing a false penis. With courage and charm one can pull off her mask and reveal the beauty and kindness that are its true nature. In my laboratory, I have often been astounded by the transformations which substances undergo with the help of mercury. Matter is always in a process of metamorphosis, a process that has served me as a means of reflecting about my feelings and experience. Mercury is nothing but courage."

Satisfied with his analysis, the librarian sighed. Alas. These days, his penis served only as the object of philosophical reflection. But he kept this thought to himself. Theresa-Bellino, the mercurial, had indelibly impressed on his mind the glory of courage.

Laura said "You are now speaking of Casanova's courage. What about Theresa's courage?"

"It is obvious. Think of the lengths to which she has gone in order to succeed. A great operatic voice like hers would have been lost irretrievably to opera when only men were allowed to sing. She could have become a singer in the theater, but her talent was greater."

Actresses, beginning with his own mother, Zanetta, were courageous women who let nothing stand in their way to success. Zanetta had abandoned him to the care of relatives and, blessedly, to his own devices, at a fairly early age. Yet he had always worshiped her and eagerly followed the news of her triumphs on the stages of the capitals of Europe. He was extremely proud of his mother. It had never bothered him that she had given herself to a succession of men and that his own paternity was a bit of a mystery. In fact, he rather enjoyed the idea that a man he admired, like the poet Baffo, might be his father. This uncertainty had given him the freedom to be who he chose to be, whether Casanova the lover, or Chevalier de Seingalt, man of letters. His liberty had been Zanetta's gift. She had held art above morality and had made pleasure seem an ordinary and necessary activity, even a right. But it was in Theresa-Bellino that art, pleasure, courage, and talent shone most brightly, making a unified blossom that represented everything that Casanova loved.

He kept these reflections to himself. Laura saw that the librarian had become visibly tired and sad. She caressed his cheeks and his forehead and could almost see his thoughts race behind the wrinkles like fish beneath a wave.

Alas, alas, Casanova thought. In his old age, he had the keys to understand what he had only intuited when young. Whether such reflections were of any use to anyone but himself was another matter. He didn't really care. Self-knowledge was its own reward. He doubted, in any case, whether anyone could benefit from somebody else's experience. Very rarely. And then, perhaps, only by negative example. Yet, Laura's hand felt good: it was cool, soothing, and, yes, somehow courageous.

Seeing Laura's face made beautiful by understanding, Casanova was reminded of the face of a woman in Tintoretto's painting of the Crucifixion in his beloved Venice. This woman, part of a group of grieving women at the foot of the cross, looked out of the painting instead of gazing like the others at the tortured body of Christ. She looked as if she couldn't wait to escape from the scene to make love.

When he told Laura of his memory of that face, she thoughtfully observed, "It is true that grief causes this reaction in some women."

"You are delightfully wise," Casanova agreed. "Grief is the secret of magnificent loving. In Venice women wear their grief with such grace that men are often overcome by lust just watching them in church. Gondolas are black, like coffins, and they are the best places to make love, especially when returning from a funeral on the island of San Michele, or from a eulogy at Santa Maria della Salute, constructed in gratitude for the end of a plague that nearly killed all the beauties of Venice."

The memory of Venice brought tears to Casanova's eyes which, falling, traced reddish trails through the white powder on his face. He looked like a tragic and ridiculous papier-mâché mask, with a black mole drawn on one cheek and red-rimmed, still-blue eyes. His eyebrows, drawn on with charcoal, made two triangles that sat like tents on his finely cracked forehead. The corners of his mouth trembled and he opened his lips to speak, but no words came out. Laura understood his silence as a wish to be alone. She slid off his lap, picked up the tray, and left the room.

  The next evening, Casanova had recovered enough equanimity to boast that in the old days, if she had set him on fire by sitting on his lap, he would have given her no rest until she had made him happy. Laura, though she feigned shock, was by now as sorry as he that she couldn't. But she could grant him the small favors he began to extract during their evenings of study. The old man was playing a sophisticated game that linked his love of the flesh with the more enduring—or so it seemed to her in the course of her education—affection for books. Soon she discovered that he was himself an author. He had also studied philosophy in Padua, at one of the oldest universities in Europe, had been a student of experimental physics at Santa Maria della Salute, and was a chemist, a poet, an actor, a playwright, a gambler, a Mason, and an economist who had organized a lottery for the French king.

  He had written many poems, mostly odes and satires, but also philosophical essays. At the moment, he told Laura, he was translating from English a scientific report about a race of people who live inside the earth. "They are," Casanova explained, "the descendants of a human being whom God created on the sixth day, a being who was both male and female, and who escaped the fate of Adam and Eve by obeying God and taking not one bite of the fruit of the tree of the knowledge of evil."

  Laura interrupted him. "Isn't it the fruit of the tree of the knowledge of good and evil?"

  "No. In Paradise all is good, therefore that fruit could only contain the knowledge of evil."

  Laura insisted. "But the knowledge of good can only come from the knowledge of evil. Adam and Eve did not know that Paradise was good, it just was, they were not aware of its nature."

  Casanova smiled. "Being aware of the nature of good is

only a subtle form of evil. Such awareness leads to the defense of what one believes is good and causes a great deal of evil in its name."

"This is entirely too hard for me to understand," conceded Laura, not at all convinced. "Please go on with your story."

Casanova continued. "The Micromegs' habitat is the lost paradise, from which God has banished Adam and Eve. That unhappy couple, whose descendants we are, were condemned to exile on the surface of the earth, a terrible place subject to floods and disaster, harmful solar rays, and suffering. The happy, unbanished descendants of the Sixth Day being, known as the Micromegs, live in the edenic interior of the earth where they pass their allotted forty years (with some exceptions) making love and using their reason to improve themselves.

"The Micromegs are not stupefied by religion and superstition, because they are still close to God, but they are nonetheless subject to errors and passions that lead them into trouble. They strive to achieve clarity and wisdom, difficult virtues even for them, and nearly impossible for the wretched surface beings. The Micromegs are short, standing only as tall as" (here he demonstrated, lightly cupping the beginning of her rump) "the top of your thigh where it rounds off into the 'curve of delight.'"

"Some Micromegs have no need of eyes. They touch in order to know and they talk with their hands, using each other's bodies like instruments. For instance, if they want to discuss a problem involving the brain, they literally open each others' braincases and tap out with incredible delicacy their arguments and counterarguments, plucking the nerves under consideration and pinching just those nodules and living cruxes that serve their conversation. Their speech is a kind of music that swells spontaneously when their senses discover something.

"For instance, if I were to tell you what is in my heart, I would speak like this . . ." He put his hand under her skirt and gripped her thigh with surprisingly strong fingers. Laura put a cautionary hand on his to prevent him from reaching what he murmured was "Aphrodite's Temple." She knew that place by decidedly less metaphorical names, though at one time she and the Baroness invented many playful pet names for it, intended to describe it in various moods: Caravanserai, Prince Ludwig's Jewel Box, Shark's Cove. Despite herself, her juices had begun to flow, and she was tempted to let his hand know whatever it was it wanted to know. She could almost hear some lovely, distant music—the language of the Micromegs perhaps—and, stirring in the gentleman's breeches, she could feel the awakening of something she had imagined long dormant.

"Is that a happy Micromeg squirming down there?" she laughed.

"Indeed, the Micromegs have the gift of changing shape, but the squirmer to which you refer must only be half a Micromeg, or no Micromeg at all, because he seems unable to achieve his optimum form. . . ."

That this instrument had caused trouble and given pleasure in some of the great houses of Europe excited Laura, and its present sad condition filled her with compassion. She desired to see it rise again, for her. Near the end of his life, Casanova speculated that his virile member had been prophetic, because it had ceased to rise at the time of the "dreadful revolution"—his scepter, like the French king, toppled.

"I adore routine," Casanova exclaimed in the morning, when she came to dress his hair. "When my routines are disturbed I feel a certain disequilibrium in the universe. I feel personally responsible for earthquakes and storms."

"Indeed, but for those times when you cause such things yourself, directly, as part of your routine."

The Chevalier laughed and patted her hand as it rested briefly on his wig. She then applied the powder, which always made her sneeze. A silvery cloud rose briefly, diffusing the colored light from the mullioned window before settling on the half-written page and writing instruments on Casanova's desk.

Every day, he rose at six, had his hair dressed, made his own hot chocolate, and gave two hours of his time to his employer's library before settling down to write at precisely nine o'clock. His job was not a sinecure—Count Waldstein was a kind man but not a fool. Approximately twelve thousand books and manuscripts waited to be catalogued. No one knew their exact numbers or their contents. Following the Emperor's 1770 edict liquidating four hundred monasteries and convents in Bohemia, rivers of books had poured out of the monastic libraries, ending up piled pell-mell in universities and private collections. Most of Count Waldstein's acquisitions came from Cyriak and Benedictine cloisters. Fortunately, eight homeless monks had come along with the books and were employed by Casanova arranging them in neat piles, that being about the only thing they could do, since only one of them could read. The count had taken pity on them, as well as on four Poor Clare sisters, lodging and feeding them at his own expense. The twelve clerics were housed in a dilapidated wing of the castle and were rarely seen except between eight-thirty and nine in the morning, when they trudged single file and silent through the busy central court on their way to the library. At first, Casanova had attempted to engage them in conversation, questioning them about their orders and the fate of their brothers and sisters, but he had given up when the permanently distressed creatures responded only in polite monosyllables. The

Cyriaks were a silent order, and the effort of speaking caused them such agitation they looked on the verge of collapse. Generous nobles like Waldstein had settled meager pensions on a few of the thousands of aimless recluses, but most of them returned to the villages they had left decades before, where their poor relations, if there were any, could barely feed them. Others begged in the streets of Prague, holding out their bowls with touching dignity. Every morning, the authorities removed the bodies of those who had died in the night, some of them still holding their begging bowls, with the coins still in them. A story circulated to the effect that Death herself, dressed as a young widow in mourning, made the rounds of Prague, dropping gold coins in these bowls, after which the beggars died peacefully where they sat. Casanova often thought that a student of Bohemian history might learn a great deal by speaking with Prague's destitute Benedictines, Trinitarians, Ursulines, Servites, Barnabites, Carmelites, and the dozens of other orders.

What could Joseph II have had on his stupid mind when he issued the edict shutting down the convents? Casanova had met the Emperor and he had no doubt that stupidity was at work. Joseph was a well-intentioned monarch who believed in the creation of an ideally productive state—he had no time for idlers. He had read only a few books in his life, but one of them had unfortunately been Lodovico Antonio Muratori's *Della pubblica felicita oggetto de' buoni principi,* a naive treatise about government, and like all such systems, good only for befuddling the minds of insecure princes. Casanova's compatriots, when not applying themselves to the fine arts, did more harm than good. Look at what Niccolò Machiavelli had wrought! Joseph was Maria Theresa's son, but he had neither his mother's intuitive understanding of the complexity of empire nor her passion. The lack of passion was possibly a good thing, since one of his mother's passions had been the

17

moral improvement of her subjects, which had made Vienna the dullest city in the empire. Casanova had spent as little time as possible in that city where women were monitored like nuns for signs of any public display of their God-given charms. It had been a matter of honor for any actress worthy of her profession to be banished from Vienna for lewdness. He remembered the tragic mien of his friend Rodolfo Armandi when he had confided in Casanova that his mistress, who was an actress, had not been banished from Vienna, a circumstance which, both of them agreed, cast grave doubts on her talent.

When Casanova met the Emperor, the monarch was in the middle of an audience with a fellow Venetian, Lorenzo Da Ponte, a witty but annoying character who was always turning up like a bad shadow wherever Casanova happened to be. That he should be in audience with the sovereign at precisely the time when Casanova was scheduled to be received was almost more than he could take. Obtaining the audience had taken months and the intercession of Count Waldstein. Da Ponte made it seem that he had just breezed in and was on close terms with the monarch, greeting his compatriot affably but with just enough condescension to set him on edge. Casanova mentally impaled the younger man with his sword, even as he bowed toward the Emperor, who looked pained. Casanova waited in vain for Da Ponte to vanish. Joseph seemed not to care one way or another, no doubt assuming that the two of them were together, representing the Venetian Republic in some fashion. Casanova suspected that Da Ponte may have, in fact, usurped his appointment by presenting himself at the palace and introducing himself simply as the Venetian. The secretary had probably looked it up and seen that a certain Chevalier de Seingalt, Venetian, had been scheduled, and let Da Ponte in. If that was the case, Casanova would not simply impale him with his sword, he would actually cut him into sev-

eral large chunks and feed them to Count Waldstein's greyhounds. Inwardly seething, he tried to ignore Da Ponte and
presented the Emperor with an elaborate scroll on which was
inscribed a magnificent plan for a Chinese-themed spectacle
that Casanova was convinced would be greatly appreciated by
the theater-loving populace of Vienna or Prague.

This spectacle had been conceived by Casanova as an
homage to the power and wisdom of emperors everywhere and
contained, in addition to fabulous costumes and music, many
lessons about the governing of empires, some of which fla-
grantly, but subtly, ran contrary to Joseph's own reforms. He
hoped that the flattered monarch would not notice the subver-
sion until he had endorsed and financed the project, by which
time, to save face, he might actually reverse himself. Casanova
was correct in assuming that Joseph would not notice. The
monarch shoved the scroll impatiently aside and told Casanova
to explain the project in as few words as possible because his
time was valuable. Under Da Ponte's evil smirk, Casanova proceeded to outline the spectacle, but he was far less eloquent
than the scroll. He ended up stressing the word "Chinese" far
too many times, to the Emperor's obvious confusion.

"Why would you make my capitals Chinese?" asked the
Emperor, wrinkling his noble brow.

"Your Imperial Excellency!" cried the frustrated Chevalier,
"everyone is fascinated by China now!"

"They are?" asked the genuinely bewildered Joseph. "What
is your name?"

"Casanova, Giacomo Casanova," he mumbled distractedly,
not realizing his mistake until he actually heard Da Ponte
laughing. Laughing! The little scoundrel! The nerve!

"Ah," said the Emperor, terminating the audience.

Ah. That had been the idiot sovereign's last remark. The humiliated Chevalier left the palace alone, while Da Ponte man-

aged to remain, stealing a few more minutes of the Emperor's time.

Later, Da Ponte relished telling the story and claimed that Joseph, after Casanova retreated, had exclaimed three times in a row: "Giacomo Casanova! Giacomo Casanova! Giacomo! Casanova!" When Da Ponte's version of events became known to Casanova his fury increased to the point of no return. Carefully considering his revenge, he rejected impalement and dismemberment. Instead, he decided to give Da Ponte a gift. He sent him a young prostitute infected with the pox, and was greatly amused when he heard that not long after, Da Ponte had taken ill and was suffering the hells of mercury treatment. Ironically, his revenge also embraced the Emperor, who was always sending his retainers to scour the streets for prostitutes. The same young woman infected Joseph as well, causing him to take to his bed, whence he issued some of the worst decrees of his reign. Casanova's audience with the Emperor thus had precisely the opposite effect from the one intended. His Imperial Highness would have been infinitely better off patronizing the Chinese spectacle.

"Ah," Casanova exclaimed, quoting the Emperor, amused by this memory as he sipped the last of his morning chocolate. "That is life. Ironic."

Ironic also that Da Ponte's mission in seeing the Emperor had been to continue a discussion initiated by the young composer Mozart for the underwriting of an opera in the German language. Casanova did see that opera, *The Magic Flute,* sung in German, and did not like it at all, partly because it reminded him of his embarrassing (and costly) assumption. Da Ponte's presence with Casanova in the imperial chamber had been purely coincidental.

The homeless monks, had they any sense, should have rejoiced in the Emperor's ill fortune—instead they prayed for him, beseeching God to bless the sovereign every time a coin was dropped into their begging bowls. Such people were good for nothing, Casanova reflected. Whatever information an honest student might glean from them would be no use whatsoever.

His own monks and nuns, besides not being much for information of any kind, were quite old. It bothered him to see their bodies bent like question marks. Seeing them shuffle along without energy or pleasure infuriated him. He had to control a perverse desire to kick the helpless creatures. He was nearly as old himself, but he didn't feel the kind of resigned weakness that wafted off these quasi-humans like the rank smell of disease. But then he admonished himself to be more kind, because these creatures had been made old before their time. When young they had chosen a monastic life that was old in essence. They had sacrificed their vigor in the mind-numbing rituals of shuffling, mumbling, and dozing. To think that at one time he had considered such a life! Idiocy! He laughed thinking how little he knew himself in those days. He who could barely stand to be in any one place for longer than a week without serious distractions, who had restlessly crossed Europe in every imaginable conveyance! He shut his eyes, imagining the map of Europe covered by the wheel marks of his carriages, from Venice to Naples to Vienna to Dresden to Moscow and countless places in between. The longest he had stayed anywhere had been when benevolent sickness had nailed him to his bed. This, he supposed, was nature's way of giving his body much-needed rest. It was during his illnesses that he had read and studied the thousands of books and the several languages that now formed an erudite but annoying barrier between him and what he loved most, raw life. Casanova dropped a huge incunabulum to the floor, startling the monks kneeling silently in the Latin, Greek, and Hebrew dust that came off the biblio-piles.

Actually, the Hebrew books were not quite as numerous as

they should have been, because the clever Jew who had facilitated the exchange from the cloisters to the castle had appropriated the most interesting volumes in that language. His name was Eliphas Emmanuel and he was well known to the Chevalier. Years before, he had met a learned Jew named Mordecai Emmanuel traveling with his beautiful daughter, Leah. Casanova had amazed the scholar with his knowledge of Hebrew, a language in which he could quote long passages from the Old Testament and the Talmud. Their long conversation resulted in an invitation to be the Jew's guest, an invitation Casanova accepted eagerly for both its intellectual pleasures and its erotic possibilities. Their discussion continued past midnight, while his successful seduction of the daughter continued past dawn. Leah, who was but sixteen, had a serious-looking younger brother, Eliphas, who participated occasionally with great shyness and gravity in the scholarly exchange between his father and the charming stranger. This brother eventually left Italy and took on a post as cantor in the Old Jewish synagogue in Prague. When not chanting in the temple, he collected Hebrew books and manuscripts, both for instruction and profit. When Joseph ordered the liquidation of monasteries, Eliphas traveled through Bohemia, buying books from their libraries and acting as agent for the orders that wished to sell their collections. It was thus, one decade after his seduction of Leah, that Casanova met again her brother, who, still a young man, resembled his sister to an uncanny degree.

Eliphas was a welcome and constant visitor to Dux. Talking with him, Casanova felt that he was continuing the conversation he had begun with his father many years before. It was too bad that Leah was not there to soothe him after the intellectual excitement. She had married a man her own age and together they had departed for the New World, where, Eliphas said, they were happy, though living in poverty in a Jewish area of New York.

Eliphas was deeply involved in the affairs of his community, which was one of the oldest in Europe and had, consequently, more than its share of misery and persecution. Maria Theresa had banished all Jews from Prague in 1744 because of their alleged collaboration with the Prussian armies during the Austrian-Bavarian wars. This unsubstantiated allegation led to the exodus of nearly one-quarter of Prague's inhabitants. The economic disruptions caused by the departure of the Jews were catastrophic, so the Empress relented in 1748, allowing them to return but only after paying the extraordinary price of three hundred thousand gold pieces, the so-called "toleration tax." No sooner had the community returned that a devastating conflagration, caused by arson, destroyed most of the Jewish Quarter on the night of the Sabbath in 1754, leaving most people homeless. After a long effort, the quarter was rebuilt, just in time for this new wave of homeless Christians to take the place of the Jews.

"Their Austrian Majesties are masters of misery," Eliphas observed.

"One can't judge them too harshly. Their intentions are nearly always reasonable," Casanova replied, with only a touch of irony. He was sympathetic to the plight of the Jews, a position that had earned him a good deal of hostility at the court of Frederick of Prussia, as well as being a point of contention between himself and Voltaire.

Eliphas changed the subject and pointed to the towers of books rising haphazardly all over the floor of the great library hall. "How many of these texts are you hoping to penetrate?"

"Good choice of words, Eliphas. If they were women, I would penetrate them all. Alas, I'm afraid that if I spent every remaining moment of my life reading I would not penetrate one-fiftieth of them."

"You certainly could not. But you nonetheless plan to add your own books to the already existing immensity!"

Casanova laughed. "Yes, a wise man would refrain. But what can I do? I am a writer, I produce words like the bee makes honey. I also have a need to see my words bound in fine skin and sold. I would be going against nature if I did not act on that desire."

"Yes, yet I suppose that when G-D made the word flesh he did not expect his flesh creations to turn the world back into words."

"We rarely respect His wishes in any other regard, why should we do less with this one?"

"That is blasphemy, Chevalier," Eliphas said quickly, making a gesture of mock horror halfway between spitting and covering his eyes.

"I am delighted. It is entirely too easy for me to horrify my fellow Catholics—all Christians, for that matter. Your religion is more difficult to offend because so much of it is based on argument. Everything the Devil might say has been covered in the commentaries."

"That may well be the case for scholars, but I assure you that the average Jew is just as superstitious as the average Christian. In fact, we have more superstitions than average Christians because we need them to get through the constant misery they inflict on us."

"What would you say," Casanova asked thoughtfully, "was the most useful superstition of your people?"

Eliphas told him the story of the Golem of Prague. One of the most learned rabbis of all time, Judah Loew ben Bezalel, known as the Maharal, the author of many books of commentaries, among them the *Netivot Olam,* which the Chevalier had certainly read, had also excelled in the magic arts. Despite his great learning and his eminent authority on ethical questions, he was repeatedly rejected from high posts in the community. Toward the end of the sixteenth century, when he was nearly seventy years old, he produced, using a secret cabbalistic recipe, a human being who owed his life to the secret name of G-D written on his forehead. This being, the Golem, would protect the Jews of the Old Quarter against further expulsions and attacks. The Golem was physically more powerful than his aging and frail protector. Rabbi Loew had to slip an amulet into the mouth of his creation every day in order to keep him calm and working for the good of the community.

One day the rabbi's daughter, Esther, fell ill and the old man spent the day of the Sabbath at her bedside. In the evening, terrified men came into the sickroom shouting that the Golem was loose and destroying the synagogue. Rabbi Loew left Esther's bedside and found the Golem, mad with grief because he was in love with Esther, causing havoc on the streets. The rabbi was able to slip the amulet into his mouth, but the Golem became despondent after that and did not leave his room. Esther recovered and tried to persuade the Golem to resume his sweet-natured duties, but to no avail. Finally, the rabbi became convinced that no amount of persuasion would restore the creature. He resolved to destroy it, but this was nearly impossible unless the Golem accepted his own death. Rabbi Loew persuaded Esther to take a flower containing the Essence of Death to the sad monster. With a heavy heart, Esther took the flower to the Golem, who knew only too well what the blossom contained. He loved Esther and took the flower from her, fully aware that he was receiving Death from the hand of the woman he loved. He inhaled deeply of the flower's scent and fell unconscious. The rabbi tiptoed into the room and erased the name of G-D from the Golem's forehead. The monster turned skeletal and his bones were taken to a room in the attic of the Old New Synagogue, where they rest to this day under lock and key.

Casanova was familiar with versions of the Golem story, just as he was familiar, perhaps more familiar, with the cabbalistic writings of the Maharal. The rabbi had written that the non-Jew is but unformed matter and that the Jew was form. The non-Jew was only an accident of matter, water, and history, while the Jew, made by God, was the only formed being. Matter, however, longs for form so that a non-Jew can become a Jew, simply by longing. Jews who convert to Christianity cannot remain formed and are soon dispersed into matter. These ideas had found few adherents anywhere, not among Jews and certainly not among Christians. Nonetheless, Casanova had considered the rabbi's ideas carefully in the context of the magical sciences that he had studied. The legend of the Golem may have had many superstitious elements, but the premise was sound. Human beings could be created, using the science of elements, just as life can be prolonged indefinitely by alchemical means.

"The remains of the Golem, have you seen them?" he asked the cantor of the New Old Synagogue.

"You toy with me," exclaimed the young scholar with somewhat feigned astonishment. "I said the story was just superstition."

"But my dear Eliphas, we are not among superstitious men here."

"My dear Chevalier," Eliphas said, taking from his pocket a large ring with several keys on it. "I am thirty-two years old. I have been cantor for ten. There are ten keys on this ring, one for each year, beginning in 1778. They are keys to ten rooms in the synagogue, which has twenty-four rooms, twelve on the first floor, eleven under the ground, and one in the attic. My ten keys open ten doors on the first floor. Ask me again in the year 1802."

"I will," Casanova said, looking deeply into the black eyes of his friend, which looked so much like the eyes of his sister. He felt for a moment that he was actually looking into Leah's eyes, and a wave of affection and regret seized him. Something nameless passed between the two men.

"One more thing," Casanova said, seeing that Eliphas was becoming anxious to leave, "what is your new name?"

Eliphas laughed. The viscerally anti-Semitic Maria Theresa had just delivered a huge blow to the Jews, the full effects of which had not yet been understood. She had ordered all the Jews in her empire to change their Hebrew names to German ones. At the same time, she lifted most barriers to their educational and professional advancement. In one swift, ambiguous, double-headed motion she had destroyed their past while seemingly opening their future. The Jews were horrified. They debated day and night the question of how to preserve their identities. The thing dearest to the Jewish heart, right after the supreme unpronounceable, was the name that each family had managed to maintain through history, thus ensuring continuity. Words were sacred to Jews, but the sounds of their names were sacred above all. Maria Theresa could not have chosen a more insidious weapon. Jews had recovered from every calamity known to humankind: exile, hunger, flood, fire, murder. They had survived all those things through the power of words, the act of naming. Now they were being stripped of the essence of their Jewish identity. In the end, the decision was taken to preserve Jewish names in secret, thus placing yet another grave burden on their battered historical memory. They chose new German names from a deliberately limited range of words denoting the essentials of nature. Thus were born Steins, Golds, Rosens, Perlmutters, Baums, Birnbaums, and Rosenthals.

"My name will always be Eliphas Emmanuel," Eliphas Emmanuel said, "but for the purposes of legal transactions you may call me Oscar Perlmutter."

After Eliphas's departure, Casanova thought for a long time about the Golem, his life, and writing. The deeper meanings of the story were not yet evident to him but he knew that the city of Prague was essential to his destiny. He had not been the first of his family to come to Prague. He had visited his mother, Zanetta, on his first trip to the city. Zanetta had fled to Prague with the Dresden court when Frederick besieged the Saxon capital in 1759. She had been acting in *La Pupilla,* a play by her friend Goldoni. His mother had been distracted by a new lover, a Hungarian officer, and Casanova had been preoccupied by a love affair of his own. Their brief encounter had taken place backstage after a performance. They had made plans for dinner for the next day, but neither one was able to attend. His last glimpse of Zanetta in Prague had been of her standing among old props, her powdered face streaked by tears, waving good-bye as if for the last time. Casanova had walked from the theater to the bank of the Vltava river, where he studied the lights of the castle in the dark water for a long time before returning to his rooms, where a lovely little party, arranged by his paramour, was already in progress.

He had not yet been to the Jewish Quarter but now decided to visit at the earliest opportunity. He would disguise himself as a Jew and attend Sabbath services. The thought of donning a disguise cheered the Chevalier as it always did, and he decided to send his monks back to their rooms. He would take the day off and amuse himself in some familiar but never boring way.

‽**C**astles are all much the same, but Bohemian castles have an added layer of dust and pungency, he mused, watching the timeless bustle below the library window. Peasant carts loaded to bursting with oats, stewards rolling beer barrels on the cobblestones, scullery maids rolling their hips as if they were underwater, an inkstained clerk rushing somewhere with a scroll under his arm, and dogs everywhere, running between legs and humping each other. Only a cat, curled on a gargoyle spout, fast asleep in the pale morning light of an autumn day, appeared to ignore the agitation below. I admire you, cat, Casanova said, feeling in his bones a joy that came only rarely now, but which had been his dearest companion every morning of his youth. This joy, he knew, was the beginning of mischief.

An hour later, atop a skinny nag that seemed to be the only available mount, he exited the castle gates and quickly gained the open country. He had no particular destination in mind, but when he arrived at a crossroads in the forest between two hills, he took the left fork without hesitation. The woods stretched thickly on both sides of the path and he could hear the birds making a huge racket in the trees. A herd of deer grazed in his path and scattered quite lazily when he was nearly in their midst. The Bohemian forest was a legendary place and Casanova expected a host of fabulous animals and, he hoped, a score of nymphs, to suddenly appear. A village did appear, not an hour after he'd left the castle; it was a wretched collection of huts huddled around a gloomy and evidently abandoned convent.

A girl in rags shooed a flock of geese out of his way. Soon an army of tattered children came running after him. He disbursed a few coins into the dust and they scrambled after them, fighting and shouting. The Chevalier dismounted at the convent gates and pushed them open, followed by all the children and the geese. The courtyard was empty, but a string of smoke hanging above a chimney betrayed some life within. Before he could go any farther, a mustachioed man dressed in the remains of an unidentifiable uniform, and wearing a quite hefty sword, barred his path. He spoke in Czech, a language that

Casanova had tried to master but, so far, to no avail. He tried German. The man answered him in that language, evidently displeased by having to do so.

"You are in a quarantined place, sir. There is disease here."

Casanova looked at the blue sky—golden light poured over the tiles of the building throwing in sharp relief the moss and weeds growing from the walls. It was hard to believe that sickness was raging within.

"I am a doctor," he said. "What is the nature of this disease?" He shook away a few of the tykes that were clinging to him, trying to go through the pockets of his breeches.

The guard looked stumped by his declaration. Casanova pressed on: "I am familiar with many illnesses, perhaps I can help."

At this point, two identical men tumbled out of the convent door and answered for him.

"We have a rare illness here."

"Rarer than coins in a poor man's pouch," his twin echoed.

The guard took heart from his helpers. "It is so virulent it kills on the spot anyone who as much as wants to know its name."

"That is indeed a horrible disease," laughed Casanova. "I have had some nameless diseases myself, but I was half cured when I learned their names."

The guard reached for his sword, but Casanova had already drawn his and, without thinking, slapped him on the side of his head with the flat of the blade, felling him.

"You've killed him," shouted a twin, and the other echoed, "You've killed him dead!"

"No I haven't." Annoyed, Casanova shoved his foot in the man's ribs. He opened his eyes and groaned.

"Show me in," ordered the Chevalier, politely.

When Casanova entered what had been the dining hall of

the convent, he knew immediately the nature of the illness. A dozen or so deserters from his Imperial Majesty's armies were lying about on straw mats in various states of undress. Some of them were reading, propped on one elbow. None bothered to rise when the Chevalier entered the dormitory. On closer inspection, he saw that almost half of the group were women, though it was difficult to tell in the gloom.

Sensing no menace, Casanova opened several of the shuttered windows and chill autumn air and bright light rushed in, invigorating somewhat the listless residents. Having gotten their attention, the Chevalier stood in the middle of the room and declared them to be cured.

"My fellow sufferers, I understand your ennui. Please rise from your beds and make yourselves presentable. Two of you will go to the castle at Dux to buy wine, beer, and hams. I will provide the feast, but not before you bathe, comb your hair, and sweep out this filthy room!"

There was general agreement with this plan, and before long, an energetic wind swept the assembled, who bestirred themselves from their mats and took to the cisterns outside, where they splashed each other with water, making childish noises of delight. The village children themselves were hanging from the Chevalier like monkeys from a tree. He didn't find this entirely unpleasant because, dirty as they were, they smelled young, like saplings, and the Chevalier, a connoisseur of scents, found them intoxicating. The goose girl sat gravely on his lap, her budding breasts a reminder that nature renewed herself at every opportunity.

Long before the provisions arrived, Casanova had already been briefed on the true nature of the quarantine and illness from which the residents suffered.

"We met in the forest," a thin young soldier explained in German. "We are deserters from several armies. At first, we wandered around aimlessly and survived by stealing. When the convent was closed, some of us moved in. At first there were only six of us—now we are sixteen. We have been in this place for two years."

A young woman stepped forward. Her dark hair was neatly braided in a long plait down her back, and she appeared to be their spokesman. "We have been reading many books, and have formed ourselves into a community that shares everything without regard for age or status. We have forsaken our former lives and have taken on new names. We even have a new calendar, from the day the first of us arrived."

"You share everything? Even your bodies?" Casanova looked directly into her eyes. They were very black, with heavy lids, and there was something both Slavic and Asiatic about them.

"Absolutely. We are in Paradise. We banished jealousy and greed." She said this plainly, but with weary conviction, as if subsequent events had put this belief under some doubt.

"You do not believe in original sin then?"

"We do not believe in *the* original sin," she said slowly.

"Or God?"

"We are deists," a man said angrily. "There is a God and he is good. We are followers of Saint Sylvester, who said, 'God is like an onion because he is good and makes you cry.' That is the entirety of our belief."

Casanova was quite astonished. He had heard of such social practices among the savages of North America. There had also been such beliefs among heretics long ago burnt at the stake by the Pope. He asked if they had modeled themselves on ideas from the New World.

"Not entirely." The young woman spoke with quiet authority. "We have read *La Nouvelle Héloïse,* as well as accounts of the noble savages. But those were not our models. There have been many communities in Bohemia in the last century that lived simply and in harmony, without any private property. Most of them emigrated to the New World to avoid being destroyed during the wars of the Reformation."

Casanova didn't know if he was more amazed by the mention of Jean-Jacques Rousseau's novel or by the principles of this Bohemian community. All that aside, he didn't understand why such a sensible arrangement was suffering from malaise. The place was filthy and everyone looked tired. He said so.

"It wasn't always this way," said the young woman, who had renamed herself Héloïse. "During the first year, we transformed this place into a true paradise. We hid all outward signs of our existence, of course, so as not to attract the attention of the authorities, but we were productive. Our bakery was superb—we brewed beer and cured meat. We had a flock of sheep and we wove woolen cloth. The men were carpenters and smiths. Everything was in perfect repair and there was such cleanliness!"

Everyone shook their head in agreement and then fell silent, as if drowned inside a black cloud.

"Your fires must have been noticed. You are no more than an hour's ride from Dux."

"There were visitors," agreed one of the twins, whose name was Pangloss. "But our guests were sworn to secrecy," added Candide.

"Two visitors stayed. They loved our way of life, and they kept our secret. Until six months ago."

"What happened then?"

Before anyone could answer, the doors swung open and the two men who had gone to Dux for provisions came in carrying a small barrel of beer, several bottles of wine, and four fat hams. The sight of the goods brought a spark of excitement to the group. A not too dirty tablecloth appeared from somewhere, and even some pewter mugs, plates, and knives.

The good feeling was contagious, but a persistent melancholy still pervaded the room. After a few glasses of drink, the company became more loquacious, though no less resigned. They told their stories in a rush, interrupting each other, in an outpouring that made the Chevalier suspect that they hadn't spoken even to each other in a long time. There were many nationalities represented in the room, though the group used German as a common language. There were Bohemians, Moravians, Austrians, one Bavarian, Croatians, and two Magyars. Each man had been kidnapped from his village and forced into the Imperial Army. The women, with the exception of Héloïse, had been camp followers who had fled with the men when they deserted. Héloïse did not volunteer her story, but it was clear to Casanova that she had come from a good family and had been educated. She was proud, but her eyes bespoke a great sadness.

"You did not have the opportunity to answer my question," Casanova reminded her. "What happened six months ago?"

"Two of our group deserted us."

"Was that fatal to the rest of you?"

She was silent for a moment, then lowered her voice and explained the circumstance in a near-whisper addressed only to him. There was no danger of being overheard anyway. The beer and wine had quickly done their job. Everyone was shouting at everyone else as if they had met for the first time.

"They fell in love. This was against the rules and everyone did their best to stop it. We forbade them to sleep together and we all took turns sleeping with each of them. Despite our efforts, they met secretly. One day they threatened to tell the children."

Héloïse bit her lip suddenly, as if she had said too much.

"Tell the children what?"

"I cannot tell you."

Casanova reached across the table and took her hand. A tear fell across her cheek. He reached for his handkerchief, but could not remove it because the goose girl had fallen asleep on his lap and her little bottom had pinned it in place. The Chevalier wiped away Héloïse's tear with his hand, then brought the hand to his lips and tasted it. That silly gesture unleashed a flood of tears. Héloïse bounded from the table and ran out of the room. Casanova lifted the child gently from his lap and deposited her in the lap of the hussar he had slapped with his sword, who had revived as soon as the drink had arrived. He followed Héloïse outside.

He found her crouched in the shadow of a ruined stable. He pulled her gently by the hand and she followed him wearily. They walked until they reached the top of a small hill covered in late-autumn flowers. They lay in the meadow side by side and Casanova spoke gently to her, holding her face in his hands. At last, she stopped shivering and crying.

"They threatened to tell the children . . ." he reminded her.

"The children from the village," she said calmly now in her flat, authoritative voice, "they are the children of the peasants who lived here before. They are not, as you can see, our children."

"The question came to mind," said Casanova softly. "What happened to their parents?"

"We killed them," Héloïse said simply.

That was the secret. This small paradise was founded on a crime.

"This is what you meant then when you said that you did not believe in *the* original sin?"

"Yes. We do not believe in *the* original sin. We have our own."

Casanova fell silent. It was a terrible revelation, but it was incomplete.

"How is it that the children did not know?"

Héloïse put her head between her hands. "We wanted to

protect their innocence," she said, looking at the ground. "The women promised to teach the children songs. We led them into the mountain there . . ." She motioned toward a blue ridge barely visible in the distance. "We walked there singing and in the evening we had a feast. We stayed in the mountains for three days. We had taken all the provisions of our group with us. We had roasts and cheeses and . . ." She couldn't go on.

"You took all the children?" Casanova insisted.

"All but the babes in arms."

"The babes in arms . . ."

"Died with their mothers." Héloïse couldn't go on.

Casanova could not deny being moved, less perhaps by the fate of those hapless peasants than by the bitter lesson of the utopian experiment itself. He had always thought that the world, bad as it was, should be left alone to the extent that it was bearable. Stoic philosophy stressed the acceptance of fate as long as one did not find its decrees too repulsive. The radical "utopian" transformations that were becoming current in the world would come to no good. If they did not begin in a crime, like this one, they would surely end in one. Ideas were spreading at such an incredible rate that it wouldn't be long before all people could have access to the most dangerous, poisonous, and silly ideas from the diseased brain of any lunatic with a printing press.

There was nothing to stop the spread of half-baked ideas—people traveled and read more than ever before in history. Casanova felt guilty—he knew that he himself was an agent of infection who had taken all sort of absurd and seditious notions from one corner of Europe to another. Most of these he had discarded along the way. He had, after all, plenty of common sense. Nonetheless, he had let plenty of dangerous stupidities into the fresh air. Of course, when everyone knows everything, he reflected, some stupid ideas will certainly lose their charm.

They will be kept in check by better ideas. Perhaps. A long time in the future, perhaps.

Héloïse shivered in his arms. He felt her hand between his legs, looking for comfort. He sprang to life like a young man, fondled by that dirty, eager hand. When he felt her weight on his body, he remained perfectly still while she guided him to her secret place. And as she fucked him, he watched with detachment her surrender. She collapsed on him, whimpering like a child who had been punished and then hugged. But when he thought of the ragged children in the village, he lost his firmness. He left her crying quietly.

Meanwhile, the party had reached a stage of drunkenness beyond conversation. The communards were dancing together while the twins sang a bawdy song and beat on the table with empty wine bottles. When Héloïse returned, the intense young man who had claimed that they were "deists" took her by the waist and swept her into the circle of dancers.

The doctor felt that he had done his job. He had cured them of their illness, albeit temporarily. He left the room without hurry, mounted his nag, and headed back to Dux at an easy pace. Darkness fell just as he entered the gates.

The library was brightly lit and Laura was waiting for him there, curled up in a chair, reading *Candide.*

"No, no, no! Not *Candide!*" shouted the Chevalier, amused and disgusted at the same time by the inevitable conjunction of events that formed circles around him.

Laura was laughing uncontrollably at something she'd read.

"What are you laughing at, you silly goose?"

"Paquette!" she managed to sputter, "got the pox from a learned Franciscan who got it from an old countess who received it from a cavalry captain who owed it to a marquise who had it from a page who received it from a Jesuit who obtained it directly from one of the companions of Christopher Columbus—ha ha ha!"

The inescapable circle again. Casanova sighed and sat in the rose chair. On the table next to him was his weekly packet of French newspapers. He always awaited them eagerly, though he dreaded what he would find inside. He was more than justified.

All the journals, from the *Mercure de France* to *Annales politiques civiles et littéraires* and the *Journal encyclopédique*, were dominated by news of a single momentous event. The American colonists had declared their independence from England. A revolution had begun, aided by the French. Long citations from the speeches of Benjamin Franklin and the pamphlets of Thomas Paine filled their pages. The ambiguous and contradictory attitudes of the French nobility and the silence of the Crown were ominous. Many younger nobles, like the Count de Lafayette, had been enthusiastically won over to the American cause. The effect on France was incalculable. Diderot wrote that, "we are on the verge of a crisis which will end in slavery or in freedom; if it is slavery, it will be a slavery similar to that existing in Morocco or at Constantinople. If all the parlements are dissolved, farewell any corrective principle preventing the monarch from degenerating into despotism." Such philosophical passion was shored on all sides by political cartoons of such novel degree of savagery they made Casanova, who was rather partial to the genre, wince. Madame Du Barry, the King's mistress, was depicted in flagrante delicto with barnyard animals while the King himself was being sodomized by his ministers. Things had certainly changed from the days when Voltaire had printed his essays abroad and denied authorship. The handful of censors in France were clearly incapable of containing the flood of seditious literature. Half the journals in Casanova's packet were ostensibly "forbidden," yet nothing stopped them from being written, printed, and shipped beyond French borders.

"Sooner or later such propaganda will reach the most distant regions of the earth. There will be revolutions everywhere," he said, mostly to himself.

Laura was attentive. "Many of these ideas have been discussed even in Bohemia these past two years. Everyone is familiar with the French situation."

"Familiar with what?" cried Casanova, exasperated. "Half-baked, half-heard, half-misunderstood rumors! Do not think for a moment that the good citizens of Paris are any more or better informed than your Bohemian tradesmen!"

"Precisely," said Laura. "Tradesmen understand even better, perhaps, what these ideas mean. They do not read for philosophical delectation. They know that their self-interest is at stake and are determined to guard it and increase it if there is an upsetting of the social order."

"You sound quite well informed yourself."

"I read," Laura said modestly, and blushed.

Casanova looked at his packet and saw that it had been opened and carefully tied up again. He said nothing.

"Bring your Voltaire over here."

Laura obeyed sheepishly, bringing her book, and sitting gingerly in his lap. At the Chevalier's request, she pulled up her skirt to let him view "the cornice and the frieze" of her "temple," but kept her legs tightly crossed. Her attitude, Casanova observed, was very much like that of Voltaire, always displaying his shocking philosophy, but keeping his legs tightly closed so that his emotional core remained invisible. Voltaire was wrong, of course, to do so, and he, Casanova, had refuted his arguments many times. During one of their visits, he had made Voltaire weep by his recitation in Italian of the poetry of Ariosto, a recitation that was extraordinarily pleasing to the swarm of women who attended Voltaire like the nursemaids of a royal baby. Voltaire had been very jealous.

"What did you do then?" Laura inquired, astonished not so much by the story but by the clear evidence of an extremely proud Micromeg poking between her buttocks.

"I devastated him. I criticised his interpretation of the works of Petrarch and told him that all French translations from the Italian were useless. The great man became brusque and petulant in the presence of all his women. He looked moribund his entire life, but he now looked positively dead! It was a victory!"

"Mmmm, mmm," Laura said, quite impressed, squirming to better position herself on the Micromeg, "and then what did you do?"

"I left that same evening and went to Avignon to visit the grave of Laura de Sade, Petrarch's muse, where I wept. One of my companions said that it was indeed sad and that my weeping was most appropriate. That truly made me laugh. I told her that I was weeping from happiness not sadness. I loved Petrarch's Laura with all the passion in my heart. I embraced the tombstone. Voltaire could never, never know more than a tiny portion of her inspiring person, a portion preserved in eternity by Petrarch's verses, but only in Italian, I'm afraid. Voltaire might touch only the little toe of Laura de Sade's immortal right foot! That little toe is my only concession to French translation!"

By this time, her nipples were attempting to escape her bodice and soon enough they did just that as the Chevalier began his Italian recitation of one of Petrarch's sonnets. When he began yet another sonnet she felt that milk would begin to flow from her breasts. She said so.

"This would not be at all surprising," explained the Chevalier, "since the true function of poetry is to induce the flow of milk, a function forgotten amid all the impractical uses attributed to it."

Laura squeezed her breast and when the drop of milk that followed her exertions drenched her finger, she put it in the Chevalier's mouth, who, interrupted in midverse, drank it deeply, rejuvenating in the process like a dry sea sponge drenched in water.

Casanova's infatuation with Laura de Sade was beyond literature. Laura Brock realized that Casanova did not wish her to surrender, he wanted only to prolong the readings and the games indefinitely until he had merged her, in some indescribable manner, with Petrarch's muse.

To her great disappointment, the Chevalier fell asleep just as she had resolved to take him inside her by any means at her command. The long day and fresh air had felled him. She left the library quietly, reflecting on the power of poetry over her sex. The Chevalier was wreaking havoc inside her. What did he want? She decided that he simply wanted her to be imaginative. But she was, at this moment, quite beside herself. A lonely guard was leaning on his musket in front of the castle gate. His manly shadow, thrown by the moon on the rough cobblestones, filled her with desire. She was before him in a thrice. By the time he had lifted his sleepy and startled eyes, she had already freed his membrum from his rough woolen breeches. And while he was still pondering whether or not he was dreaming, she lifted her skirt and embraced him. The soldier let the musket drop, put his arms around her, lifted her up. He spent himself soon after and Laura ran to her room without looking back, hoping that in the light of day he would not recognize her. It had been a dream, after all.

ℒaura indulged her naturally aroused imagination and began to think of a new game every day. It was not easy to surprise the old Venetian, born in a city of masquerades, who had written plays and acted in the theater, and had traveled the breadth of Europe playing erotic games with women of every quality. Laura raided the wardrobe of Count Waldstein for silk, satin, and velvet clothing that she used to transform herself—tonight an aristocratic girl, another night a boyish swain. Casanova always laughed heartily at her efforts, but never cruelly. He showed her the right way to tie a sash, the nuances of velvet, the sophistication of a belt, ways to conceal a dagger, and myriad uses for a swatch of cloth or a string of leather. He blindfolded her, tied her hands, and worshiped at her feet, kissing them until she felt that she was melting away into the air.

The reading and games alternated with fits of melancholy. Everything they did reminded Casanova of something from long ago. At those times, his worn, handsome face closed like a shell and his eyes no longer saw her. Laura would then prepare a mixture of opium and cocaine in a small pestle, just as he had taught her. She would place two little heaps of the mixture on a small gold mirror, one of Casanova's cherished possessions, which, naturally, further reminded him of many things, and watch as he inhaled the powder into his finely tuned nostrils through a short glass tube. Soon after, his joy would revive, the old youthful twinkle return to his eyes, and he would begin again the playful and suggestive patter that was part obscenity and part high learning. That patter, Laura began to think, was Literature itself.

Casanova was as particular about his mixtures and pomades as he was about his authors. He abhorred vagueness and was forever praising exactness, correct measurements, accurate observations. One of his trunks contained a chemical laboratory, complete with a fine scale and weights, as well as dozens of flagons and flasks containing colored substances. When he first allowed Laura to witness his experiments, she had drawn back in horror. She may have been a practical girl with a good deal of common sense, but a residue of her father's sermons lay like thick coffee grounds at the bottom of her soul. She had heard the old Lutheran preach so many times against the evils of witchcraft and alchemy, she still believed that the Devil might have a hand in it. Her years with the Baroness had nearly cured her of most superstitions, but the smell of mixing chemicals evoked a visceral reaction. When she confessed her fear to Casanova, he reassured her.

"My dear girl, I have made many fortunes using ignorance to my advantage. Beginning at a tender age, I made fools of some very wealthy and superstitious people. My very first patron so believed in my occult powers he turned over the keys of his treasury to me. Only my own foolishness, the braggadocio of youth, prevented me from being the heir to his fortune. In France, I was regarded at one time as the very Devil himself, as revered and feared as that charlatan Count Cagliostro. But I am not going to impress you in any deceitful way. These substances have natural properties, many of which are still unknown. I am merely attempting to discover the power of their combinations. Nature is a very great mystery that allows no prejudice in its study."

He gave Laura a chemistry text to read, but she had little interest in delving into all the tedious classifications and intricate diagrams that filled it. She was much more intrigued by his suggestions of his rich and dangerous past, when he had been mistaken for the Devil himself. She asked him to tell her more about the people he had fooled and the adventures he had lived. He refused, at first, and it seemed to Laura that their roles had been suddenly reversed. Once, he had asked her to grant him favors and she had refused. Now, her turn to ask for favors had come, and the Chevalier was suddenly coy.

"Don't you find it amusing that I have been seduced despite my resistance, and that I must now seduce you so that I might hear your stories? Is a view of my aroused nipples not worth one of your childhood memories?"

Ever gallant, just as she had thought, Casanova replied quickly, "Not one of my memories is worth as much as a single glimpse of your living breast."

It was only gallantry. Laura could tell that Casanova prized his memories very highly indeed and that her living breast would never arouse as powerful an emotion as some of the breasts in his memory. So be it. She was not upset. It is the prerogative of old men to be possessed by their past. After all, most of their lives had taken place there. She only wanted to share in some of those memories and see them through his eyes. She was aroused by his past adventures; they made her feel as if she were kneeling in the dark looking through a small lit window at scenes of color and beauty.

⊷C̓asanova regarded his memory with some of the same wonder with which Laura regarded his stories. He was amazed at the ease with which he could recall the details of a dress or the twists of a conversation from decades past. The faces of past acquaintances appeared in his mind's eye, and the words they had spoken were as clear as if they were standing before him. He remembered his thoughts and feelings and felt old wounds as if they still bled. He remembered his carriages and horses! He remembered street names and house numbers in a dozen cities! He remembered the bodies of his mistresses and, most amazingly, their scents. It was this, above all, that was the key to his remembering. Smell. He had little interest in recalling decor or landscape, but the memory of his nose was nothing short of profound. In the culinary wasteland of Dux, memory never ceased to serve him a bouquet of exquisite dishes. Cheeses and ragouts rose like nymphs from an endless fountain of oysters and champagne. Eel livers, anchovies, mushrooms, coquillages, bécasses, crostata, mushrooms, and anchovies released their secret essences across lakes of Refisco, Scopolo, Tokay, and Arak. He could see and taste the feast he had prepared for MM and CC at his secret apartment in Venice, the silver gleaming in the candlelight through twelve sublime courses. The taste of the girls' own juices mingled with the exquisite gravies and wines. He recalled dipping his quill in a small gold bowl filled with black squid ink and writing a long verse that circled both breasts of his Bolognese love, Signorina S. He could conjure up the wines of a dozen countries, waiting to be uncorked and tasted one by one, his tongue a fine instrument trained to tease out their deepest essence. A symphony of taste and scent had inscribed itself in his memory like a musical score, ready to be replayed by a conductor of genius. It gave him pleasure to imagine that his precise memories of meals might tempt someone, in the future, to reproduce them. Would that this future epicure could also conjure up the lovely women who had been the indispensible accompaniments to his gourmandise. Alas. That was both impossible and absurd. The great gift of his memory was joy.

"I write in order not to be bored; and I am delighted," he said to himself. "If I write nonsense, I do not care, it is enough for me to be amused."

Amused. The word contained the "muse," and all he had ever hoped for was the presence of the Muse. He had fought for her sake, and would spend his last breath defending her.

The first snow of the year draped the castle in angelic splendor. Count Waldstein arrived at the head of what appeared to be a small army, followed in short order by a troupe of musicians and a company of Venetian actors.

Casanova was overjoyed. One of the actresses was his former mistress Teresa Morelli, who, he observed, must have discovered the secret of eternal youth—it seemed she had not aged at all in the ten years since they had loved each other.

The manager of the company was the impresario Locatelli, now a very old man, whom Casanova had met many years before. Locatelli had brought opera to Russia and had become famous after joining the La Croyère expedition to Kazan, where he had been arrested and imprisoned. He had published his adventures in the *Lettres muscovites*, published in Paris in 1736, which Casanova had read, enthralled, many times.

Locatelli's imprecations against the "barbarians of Scythia" had the sublime rage of poetry. After returning from Russia, Locatelli had been opera director at the Elector's court in Cologne and married the Elector's mistress, Giovanna, whose portrait hangs in the Brühl palace. In Prague, Locatelli had directed Italian opera at the Kotzen Theater and was one of Count Waldstein's closest friends. The Kotzen Theater had gone bankrupt when a rival entrepreneur, Joseph von Kurtz-Bernardon, drew away audiences to his german comedies. Locatelli had gone into debt, disappeared again in Russia, where he was rumored to own a tavern, and had not been seen for years until Waldstein brought him to Dux.

Teresa was married to the brother of Locatelli's rival, Felix von Kurtz-Bernardon, but she was nonetheless greatly attached to the elderly impresario.

The meeting of these old friends became so boisterous, Casanova neglected to pay sufficient attention to his patron. That evening he hastened to his chamber to apologize.

"Do not concern yourself with trifles, cher Chevalier. I really didn't notice. I am preoccupied with certain other matters, but you must swear not to mention it to a soul."

Waldstein was lying in bed with a mustard compress on his forehead. He suffered from migraines, and to ease the pain he was massaged by a Moor trained for this purpose. He dismissed the masseur, and bade Casanova to come closer so that he might whisper.

"I am expecting distinguished visitors. They are traveling incognito, but their reception cannot be modest. The men-at-arms I have brought with me are for their protection. The actors and musicians will provide entertainment, but I am counting on you, mon ami, to put the spark of wit in the conversation."

"Perhaps I can start a conflagration. With whom am I expected to converse?"

47

"I fear that the guests are bringing their fire with them. Maybe we ought to provide ice."

Casanova's curiosity was now seriously piqued. He was like a child about a secret—he couldn't rest until it was secret no more. He himself loved to organize secret picnics, bring mysterious guests to parties and, generally, drive everyone mad with elaborate charades. But he couldn't stand it when someone else kept him guessing, which was apparently what Waldstein intended to do.

"You must tell me, or no remark, witty or otherwise, will I address to your guests."

"I am relieved, Chevalier. I fear that if you had threatened to hold your breath instead, you might have died from lack of air."

After much cajoling, Waldstein gave in.

"The guests are Maria Christine and her newest amour, the successor to poor Isabela."

This was momentous indeed. Casanova opened his mouth to speak but only a delighted gurgle came out. Maria Christine, or Mimi as she was known in family circles, was the daughter of the Empress Maria Theresa, and had been the lover of her brother Joseph's first wife, Isabela of Parma. Joseph had been very much in love with Isabela, and though she gave him two children, she carried on a passionate and quite open affair with Mimi. Isabela died after only three years of marriage to Joseph, and left behind two disconsolate souls. Joseph remarried but did not love again, and satisfied his carnal appetites with prostitutes. Mimi, who had also married, seemed to have followed her mother's advice and was thought to have dedicated herself exclusively to her husband and children. Among Maria Theresa's eleven daughters and five sons, Mimi was the favorite. And now this!

Casanova hated Maria Theresa passionately. That her favorite daughter was delivering a well-deserved slap to that prudish monster filled him with satisfaction. Twenty years before he had lodged at the castle of Don Ambrosio, where he met Ambrosio's daughter, the virgin poet Clementina. Casanova won her love after a glorious struggle. One day Don Ambrosio took his family and guests on an excursion to see a woman known as the Beautiful Penitent, who was shut up in a convent outside the city. The Beautiful Penitent, whose new name was Maria Maddalena, had been a prostitute in Milan with a great reputation for beauty. Her patron, Count Firmian, had her confined in the convent on the order of Maria Theresa, who could not forgive the girl her mercenary beauty. At the convent, Casanova noticed her immediately among the nuns. When she looked at him, the girl began to scream.

"Holy Virgin, come to my aid! Go, evil sinner, you deserve to be here more than me!"

This astonishing outburst had everyone looking at Casanova, who denied ever knowing her. It was true. He had never met her before. The girl had apparently gone mad in the convent. She was taken away sobbing and Casanova silently cursed the monstrous woman who had caused the poor girl's madness and suffering. If he'd had an army he would have taken the unfortunate girl away from that hopeless place that very moment. The Mother Superior begged their indulgence for Maria Maddalena's behavior, saying that the girl had been for some time in great distress. The day before she had asked that two paintings, one of Saint Anthony and one of Saint Louis Gonzaga, be removed from the chapel because their images distracted her. On their way back from the castle, his love Clementina had asked him why the Beautiful Penitent had addressed him of all the men in the room, and not her father or brother.

"Apparently she thought that I looked more of a sinner," Casanova replied, but inwardly he cried for the poor girl and wished Maria Theresa in hell.

It now looked as though he might have his revenge.

"You look devilishly pleased, Giacomo."

"Of course. We are going to eat well."

Casanova had his doubts about that, however, so he contrived to stay close to the preparations for the feast and inquired constantly about the food as provisions began to arrive at the castle. He was pleased when five hundred live trout were delivered. He monitored with some anxiety the butchering of twelve pigs, eight sheep, and two cows, and counted the rabbits and game birds that had been hung from hooks outside the pantries. He frowned when he was informed that there would be no oysters and was not happy with the bundles of herbs that he had observed, because he saw no fennel. He turned up his nose at the mountain of garlic cloves and let it be known that an excess of that vile condiment might ruin every dish. He had hated garlic ever since his confinement in a Venetian fortress along with a thousand Albanians, all of whom reeked of garlic. The only use for that substance was to revive listless horses, as far as he was concerned.

When he wasn't following the progress in the kitchen, he spent his time in the company of the actors and actresses. He had been ashamed, at first, of his threadbare clothing and general decrepitude, but it was, he reasoned, a reflection of the provincial world he was living in. But from the friendly company he received nothing but affection. Locatelli was an extraordinary raconteur, and for once the Chevalier did not feel the need to take center stage.

Locatelli described in delicious detail his tavern in Moscow, named Krasny Kabak ("Red Tavern") which served an excellent meal for only one ruble, not including wine. His customers included adventurers and refugees from all over Europe, Russian scoundrels and nobles in equal numbers and, now and then, a member of the royal family in disguise. He guaranteed absolute discretion to his guests and had a number of rooms set aside for private parties.

"Only you, Casanova, can truly appreciate the intrigue! I will not name names but it is enough to mention that a certain thirteen-year-old princess has now brought ten different handsome officers to my rooms. The princess is so enthusiastic that I have had to build walls of double thickness to contain her cries of ecstasy. Only one month ago, I have had the pleasure of hosting my good friend Count Keyserling, who brought with him an entourage of African boys." Casanova knew Count Keyserling, an educated man who loved music. The composer Johann Sebastian Bach had dedicated his *Goldberg Variations* to him.

While Locatelli told his stories, Casanova and Teresa Morelli took each other's measure discreetly. She had had two other lovers at the time they had known each other, but he hadn't been jealous. He had wanted to hear all about her other liaisons because the details excited him. Sometimes he rushed to possess her while she was still warm from one of her frolics, and slapped her buttocks hard while she confessed with the innocence of a bad girl in a confessional. Their games became even more provocative when Casanova asked to spy on her and her officer-lover from a closet in her bedroom. She arranged everything so that he could have an excellent view of the proceedings. Their lovemaking had been prolonged and exquisitely painful to him—it was all he could do not to spend himself prematurely and end up bored and imprisoned. But he had timed it perfectly, and the three of them erupted simultaneously. After the officer left, he had possessed her at leisure.

He did not doubt that Teresa remembered as well. She smiled crookedly at him and the Chevalier felt time fly backward. He wanted her. That evening, during rehearsals, he went to the room she was sharing with an ingenue named Trevice and left a rose and a note on her bed, asking her to meet him at midnight at the foot of the stairs just outside her door.

In the hours before the rendezvous he delighted in his

impatience, the sweet pangs of which familiar state he had not experienced in a long time. He listened distractedly to Count Waldstein's recitation of a dreadful scene from a play the Count had been working on since Casanova had known him. It was based on an immoderate Bohemian fairy tale that involved dancing witches and girls who lose their legs in the mirror. By the time he was able to say, "Bravo, Count," and "Bonne nuit," the bells had already tolled the quarter hour after eleven.

Moving as softly as a dream, dressed in black velvet breeches and dark linen shirt, the Chevalier arrived at the stairs as the midnight bell sounded. Not long after, the darkness parted gently and he felt the tender heat of his friend. Without a word, he put his arm around her waist—how extraordinarily slender she had remained!—and drew her to him. Teresa yielded without a word, hesitating only for a second when he pressed his mouth to hers. She pulled down his breeches expertly, then turned around and offered him her bottom, which was also amazingly small and firm. That afternoon she must have been wearing a dress that exaggerated those features. He remembered thinking that it had grown some. But it hadn't been this small in his memory, either. These confused thoughts were overcome by her offering, so he lost no time in entering her from behind, remembering well how much she had enjoyed the Turkish manner. She gave out a cry, and when the Chevalier put his hand on her breasts to hold her to him, he knew. The woman he embraced was not Teresa Morelli. He touched the outlines of her face and was certain beyond all doubt that he was embracing Trevice, the ingenue. Far from being disappointed, he allowed himself the luxury of slow and deliberate enjoyment and then only pretended to finish. As soon as he was done, the girl ran like quicksilver back to her room.

The adventure gratified Giacomo's vanity enormously. He assumed that he had left the rose and the note on the wrong bed. Later, it occurred to him that Teresa Morelli had given him a present, graciously excusing herself. No matter. He had been feeling old, but now he was Casanova again, eternally the same. In the morning he studied Trevice carefully for signs of recognition, but she kept her eyes cast down and glanced at him only once, with perfect innocence. He couldn't understand how he could have been mistaken. The girl was but half Teresa's girth, though quite well made. Which goes to show that old or young, a man is a fool when passion has him in her grip. Teresa gave him her crooked smile that meant everything wicked, but nothing certain.

The mysterious personages were expected to arrive in the early evening. It had snowed again but then the sun came out, and Dux looked magical under the sparkling blanket of silver. Some hours before, Waldstein's soldiers had returned through the main gate, looking dirty and downcast. Casanova was sure that they had been involved in some fighting, but could not find out what had happened.

He had borrowed a presentable coat from the Count and had carefully bathed, but he had some doubts about his wig. Laura, who was usually cheerful and careful in dressing his hair, did not speak a word to him and was brusque and inattentive. Did she know of his tryst? He didn't underestimate a woman's intuition. In any case, he intended to tell her all about the adventure as soon as they were alone. He expected her to be amused.

The closed carriage was preceded by mounted guards in splendid plumage. The heralds began their trumpeting and calling long before the mysterious calèche without any crests on the doors arrived in the castle court. Two veiled women descended and were immediately taken inside. Casanova barely had time to bow before the guests disappeared.

The great hall where the banquet had been laid was decorated with tapestries and Oriental rugs. A stage, complete with backdrops, had been built for the performance, and the actors, already dressed for their parts, waited silently behind it. They were to perform the opera *Alessandro nelle Indie*, based on a libretto by Metastasio. Casanova had seen a production in Württemberg with the famous castrato Giuseppe Aprile in the title role. Afterward, there would be the ballet *Orpheus Descending into Hell to Seek his Beloved Eurydice and Finding her at Last in the Elysian Fields Among the Happy Spirits*. Quite a title! He wasn't sure whether the company meant to perform the full ballet, but he knew that Teresa Morelli was to play Eurydice, while Trevice was, unmistakably, a nymph.

A number of local nobles and their wives and daughters had been invited to attend with a warning to be discreet. Casanova scanned the gathering carefully, but there were no great beauties among them. He sighed with relief.

The assembled guests rose when the ladies descended the great staircase, and everyone gasped. Maria Christine of Austria looked exactly like her sister, Marie Antoinette. Portraits of the French queen were circulating in every form, from engravings to caricatures, so there was hardly a man or a woman in Europe who did not know her features. Mimi's companion was a pale girl with large violet eyes and an unhappy look on her elongated, aristocratic face. They were dressed in nearly identical gowns. Ladies-in-waiting carried their trains. Resting on Mimi's bosom was a diamond necklace composed of stones Casanova valued at about ten thousand ducats each.

Her friend, who was addressed as Blanche by the princess, sported a more modest necklace of pearls.

Count Waldstein sat beside Maria Christine and Casanova had the honor of being seated next to her young consort. The orchestra struck the theme of Alessandro and the performance began. Casanova watched with increasing anxiety as a great variety of dishes began arriving at the table, each one bearing the unmistakable stamp of Hans Gelder's crudeness, despite the help that had arrived from Prague with the Count. It was useless, really. The only solution was to have the oaf killed. Happily, the royal guests did not touch their food. They were more interested in the wine that flowed without interruption. After some toasts and three or four glasses, the guests' attention to Locatelli's leaping nymphs began to wane, though, to the nymphs' credit, they kept the local gentry enthralled with their displays of white flesh.

"You are the dreadful Casanova about whom the most indecent stories are told," Blanche said without a preamble, fixing him with her limpid violet gaze.

Casanova did not like her mocking tone, despite its being tempered with a hint of irony.

"Dreadful things are said of many people, mademoiselle. *Nequicquam sapit qui sibi non sapit.* He knows nothing who does not draw profit from what he knows."

"I was only hoping to hear your stories, Chevalier. I have no doubt that you have drawn wise conclusions from your adventures. As for myself, I am incapable of wisdom."

At this candid confession, Casanova softened. "Your beauty is a foregone conclusion and your companion adores you."

Maria Christine looked anxiously toward them, trying to hear the conversation, but Waldstein was speaking insistently in her ear and the music was reaching a piercingly Oriental crescendo.

"My beauty is of no use to me," Blanche said bitterly, draining quickly her fifth glass of wine. "I am a toy who can compose poetry and music and then be ordered to walk dogs."

"Lovers have quarrels," he said cautiously.

"Do you have any idea what torment Provençal love is?"

Casanova tried not to smile. "No, my lady, I am a man after all."

"Such love is the ultimate interior, mon Chevalier. We come from the womb and return to it and never do we leave it." She held out her empty cup and more wine flowed into it. "I circle the interior of the earth."

"A line worthy of a poet. I have loved women who love women, but they were free to love men as well."

He recounted briefly some of his pleasurable memories in the company of women with the Provençal vice. He had loved several, who'd exempted him from the general run of men. In some respects, his passionate kisses on those places they most enjoyed were not inferior to that of their lovers. His account made Blanche blush violently and Mimi became truly alarmed. She said loud enough to be heard, "Blanche, my sweetest, that is a lot of wine!"

"It is," Blanche said, holding out her cup again, "I am an empty goblet. Fill me up!" She turned to him, "You know, Chevalier, your sleeves are shabby, and you have only two teeth, but you have what my royal mistress would give all her teeth, certainly her clothes and possibly one eye, to have."

"Mademoiselle," Casanova said softly. "There must have been a man."

Her violet eyes burned. "Not one," she cried. "Her Royal Highness can only pretend." At this, she burst into tears and put her head in her empty plate. The ladies-in-waiting lifted her from her chair and carried her up the stairs while everyone pretended not to notice. Shortly thereafter, the guest of honor left the table, too. The actors, who had seen such things and worse, redoubled their efforts and were greeted with thundering applause for their tact when the play ended.

The next day, more snow fell. The roads became impassible and the company was forced to stay for a week. The lovers must have reconciled because when they reappeared for dinner they were holding each other's hands and smiling bashfully. They asked to see the library. Casanova had an opportunity to display his erudition, though he could not suppress an impulse to provoke. He showed them an album of Persian miniatures that detailed the act of love between men and women in a great number of variations. Maria Christine regarded it coolly, but Blanche was quite beside herself.

"Oh, the poor women," she cried. "They must be suffering the pains of hell and worse. How could they allow themselves to be violated in so many ways?"

"Indeed," Casanova said sadly, "I feel for them."

"Le Chevalier's sympathy touches us," Maria Christine said coolly, "but I understand that men do such things to each other as well. Our cousin Frederick practices unnatural vice, it seems. It serves him right, too."

Casanova well knew the hatred the Austrian dynasty bore Frederick of Prussia. He had attacked Austria the very day Maria Theresa had ascended the throne. Frederick had conquered Silesia and had been attempting to tear the Empire to pieces ever since. Be that as it may, it had little to do with his proclivities.

"A number of Roman emperors did as well," he said mildly.

"The corrupt ones, no doubt. I have never had any desire to see such things. I have done my duty to my husband but I pray that my Blanche will be spared marriage."

"Madame, thank you," sighed Blanche, and kissed her hand.

Casanova showed them many rare books and manuscripts, but their attention wavered. Blanche showed some interest in the bound editions of Virgil and Dante, of which the librarian was particularly proud. He spoke to them of translation with great passion, recounted his conversation with Voltaire on the subject, and recited from Ariosto. He couldn't help recalling, again, how Voltaire, who had always looked at death's door, had become even more wan under the sunny assault of Italy.

Some of the actors, including Teresa and Trevice, wandered into the library during his recitation, and now Locatelli joined in. He knew Ariosto by heart. They performed a duet of verses and then Teresa brought in a viola. A harp appeared to accompany them. Before long, everyone, including the royals, were sitting in a circle around the fireplace enjoying the music. Count Waldstein had chairs brought in, but most of his guests preferred to remain seated on the rug. He took a chair because of an old back injury acquired at the siege of Prague while fighting the troops of Frederick. More candles were brought in, flooding the library with light, while the full moon and the fallen snow outside added their own light to the baroque hall.

Casanova was as happy as he had been in a long time, surrounded by actors and aristocrats. Even Laura sat in the circle, and her youth and beauty shone like yet another light. Casanova noticed Trevice stretched out like a cat at the feet of the royal guests. Maria Christine propped one of her feet on the girl's hip. A frisson traveled palpably through the gathering and Casanova imagined that the superb frivolity of the century had not yet waned, though this might be its last gasp. In any case, he let his hand fall on Laura's thick, soft hair and let himself be lulled by the illusion.

He woke up next morning, in his bed, with Laura in his arms. He had an inexplicable desire for a glass of fresh goat milk. He rose and dressed quickly and headed for the pen

where the goats were milked every morning. One of his childhood pleasures had been to watch an old woman in Padua
milking her goat and then drinking a mug of it still warm. He
walked over the snow, feeling like a child. When he passed the
garrison, one of Waldstein's soldiers greeted him. He remembered the soldiers coming in dirty and fatigued the day before
the arrival of the guests and thought to inquire.

"Were you in a skirmish the other day, young man?"

The soldier avoided his eyes. "We cleaned up a nest of bandits before their highnesses came."

"Bandits? You found bandits?"

"Yes," he said laconically.

"I would like to hear your tale. Let's go inside, it is cold."

"I would rather not, Chevalier."

"Let's go." Casanova pushed him bodily and the soldier
opened the door to the garrison reluctantly. The antechamber
was dim. The walls were covered with rows of muskets and
swords. In the middle of a long table at the center of the room
was a mound covered with a blanket. Casanova pulled up a
rough stool and sat.

"Tell me about the bandits."

"They were in the hills, sire, waiting to kill us. We surrounded them and surprised them. They were preparing to
attack us. We killed them before they had a chance."

"Who were they?"

"Deserters." The soldier glanced warily at the mound on
the table.

Casanova got up and pulled away the blanket. Staring at
him with only a hint of surprise on their faces were the heads of
Candide and Pangloss, the twins, and the head of Héloïse, with
its long braid still attached. Her expression was calm but
undecipherable. She looked beyond him, into the future.

ount Waldstein departed shortly after his royal guest, and Dux Castle sank again into the depths of tedium. Casanova had desired to obtain the head of Héloïse to preserve and display in his chamber as a memento mori, but the heads of the "bandits" were buried secretly by the priest who would not tell him where. The deaths of the utopians had made him morbid, so he forced himself to think of other things. Instead of dwelling on death, he became obsessed with fresh fruit. He craved ripe plums, and pears, and oranges, but there were only wrinkled apples in the cellar. He spent three talers, which he could ill afford, to order strawberries from a greenhouse in Holland. They arrived weeks later, rotten but for one, which he wrapped in gold tissue paper and gave to Laura. To entertain himself, he began to write a historical dictionary of cheeses; he also completed a complex mathematical treatise, an essay on Homer, and a financial proposal to Waldstein for a monthly journal of philosophy and dramatic arts. *L'Histoire des fromages* kept him occupied for a whole month, but in the end he could not go on with it because of the paucity of the olfactory vocabulary. He considered simply inventing new words, composed of the most likely metaphors, but the Herculean task defeated him. And Waldstein declined to finance a journal on the grounds that the stages of Europe were dismal at the moment and that philosophy had acquired a bad name thanks to the French.

Desperately bored and untenably poor, Casanova then fired off a number of proposals to the monarchs of Europe. He wrote Joseph II, who he hoped had forgotten the proposed Chinese spectacle, suggesting the establishment of mulberry farms and silkworms in Bohemia. But the Emperor apparently had not forgotten. Not quite defeated, he wrote to Princess Maria Christine, thanking her for the joy she had brought to Dux and to him personally and begging her to intervene with her brother on behalf of his silkworms, which would, he was certain, enrich Bohemia and the Empire. Maria Christina answered that she would love nothing more than to see the trees of Austria produce silk, but that her brother was a man of modest tastes, content with clothing made of the coarsest cotton.

Next he wrote to the Doge of Venice, proposing the construction of dye factories to produce Venetian red fabrics for export. He signed the letter as Casanova, a son of Venice. A reply from the Doge's secretary warned the "son of Venice" that his impertinent proposal had nearly caused the venerable executive to send him back a black rope, a traditional symbol and signal of death. Casanova laughed, remembering well the anonymous letter he had put secretly into the Venetian ambassador's diplomatic pouch in Trieste in 1783. The letter predicted an earthquake that would level Venice. The letter caused panic in the city, and many patricians had fled. His missives still had the power to rankle. He wrote back to the Doge, thanking him for his near-gift of the black rope and declaring that in his current position as Magus of the Montgolfier he had the power to turn a black rope into a poisonous snake with a taste for patrician blood.

Casanova was fascinated by the Montgolfier, and had once dreamed of riding one of these hot air balloons across the Alps. He had also envisioned ascending over Vienna as part of a spectacle celebrating an anniversary of the Empire. Crossing the Alps had been his idea of a thrilling adventure, but Vienna had been an afterthought. It had always been thus: an idea to satisfy his own curiosity and a shadow-idea to finance it. He now combined them and wrote to the embattled King of France, asking him to finance twenty Montgolfiers to float over France dropping polemics against such enemies of the crown as Montesquieu, Voltaire, and Rousseau, which he offered to write. He was convinced, he wrote the monarch, that such messages from the heavens would awe his subjects sufficiently to renounce their silly complaints.

He wondered, though, if the Montgolfier itself was not somehow tainted with revolutionary ideas. In 1783, attending the opening session of the Academy of Science at the Louvre, he had been seated beside the American ambassador, Benjamin Franklin. He had been surprised when Condorcet asked Franklin if he thought it was possible to direct or steer an aeronautic balloon, and had been even more surprised to hear Franklin reply, "This thing is still in its infancy, therefore we must wait." Both question and answer seemed absurd to him. He could not conceive how an airborne object might take a direction other than that of the prevailing winds. He had thought at the time that Franklin was merely being polite, but he read in the *Mercure de France* a discussion on the future of the balloon where Franklin explained his attitude toward the new technology. "Gentlemen, the balloon is a child which has just been born; perhaps it will turn out an idiot or a man of great talent. Let us wait until its education is complete before judging it."

Casanova's conversation with Franklin after the lecture at the Louvre had been unsatisfying.

"Do you believe, Monsieur Franklin, that the American republic will survive without help from France?"

"We are proud of our French brothers for their love of liberty."

"That is understood, Monsieur Ambassador, but your republican ideas may very well become a threat to the French monarchy."

"We are a young country, Chevalier. Our choice is an experiment. The French monarchy has roots going back hundreds of years."

Franklin was a good diplomat; it would have been rude for

Casanova to press the point. He knew that Franklin understood perfectly what he was insinuating, but he could not reply otherwise, no matter what his thoughts on the matter. That is why Casanova, far too concerned with clarity and truth, would never make a good diplomat.

Louis XVI, of course, never answered.

The Doge did answer his last letter, in a way. The Venetian republic may have been in decline, her mighty fleet a shadow of its former strength, her territories in the hands of Austrians, Germans, and Turks, but her machinery of surveillance was intact.

᭜He had returned to his birthplace once, in 1774, after many years in exile. The Serenissima was cloudy that winter morning. Walking along the Zattere, he saw a woman in a nightgown open her shutters. She stood there for a moment, looking over the water at Giudecca, then she yawned and stretched her arms over her head, her breasts outlined beneath the sheer silk. She looked for all the world like the beautiful Giulietta, with whom he had traded clothes one Carnival day, centuries ago it seemed. She wore the same expression of Venetian faux-indifference and displayed her divine body with the same certainty of one who knew how to be watched and who knew also that she would yield to the gaze or to the touch no more than suited her. He felt like a boy again, watching her. He desired her and let her see him, looking. Without the slightest acknowledgment she moved away from the open window, leaving him to dream into the empty but inviolate space.

He walked the streets of his city, amazed by how tiny yet infinite she was. Each of her narrow, twisting streets projected out into sea-lanes that extended themselves in imagination (and actuality!) far beyond the city's physical size. Venice was a lesson in the power of projection and self-confidence that alone moves the world. He was a son of Venice, her image and her ambassador. But what was the source of this arrogant power, this infinite self-confidence? It was in the knowledge that pleasure and beauty are one, the knowledge that the world is interesting enough to conquer.

He walked past the house in Calle della Commedia where he had been born and stood under the window beneath some stranger's wash, listening for Zanetta's silvery laughter. Here he had experienced his first literary success at the age of sixteen, in the company of his tutor, Dr. Gozzi, the divine poet Baffo, and a visiting English man of letters. The English visitor had written the following ancient distich in Latin and handed it to him:

Discite grammatici cur mascula nomina cunnus
Et cur femineum mentula nomen habet.

(Teach us, grammarians, why cunnus [vagina] is a masculine noun,
and why mentula [penis] is feminine.)

After reading it, Casanova wrote a line in pentameter in response: *Disce quod a domino nomina servus habet.* (It is because the slave takes his name from his master).

Standing in the Calle della Commedia, Casanova listened for the applause that had followed his witticism, but heard only the raised voice of a woman berating a child: "If you don't listen, you'll end up like your father."

Casanova laughed and moved on, past the house where Teresa Imer had lived in a corte just beyond Senator Malipiero's palace. There he had been caned by the Senator when he discoved him taking liberties with Teresa, his "protégée." Nearby was Teatro San Samuele, where Zanetta had first performed in a play written for her by her friend Carlo Goldoni. And there was the house of Angela, his unyielding love whose inflexibility led him happily into the arms of Marta and Nanetta. Calle delle Muneghe. Palazzo Malipiero. Palazzo Contarini delle Figure. Palazzo Bellavite, the home of Giorgio Baffo. His casino at San Moise, the first of his hidden pleasure nests; Giulietta Preati's house; churches and convents, more houses and palazzos, a hundred places in whose interiors the friends and enemies of his past had shaped his inner being. The map of Venice could be found inside him, distorted perhaps, but still recognizable to some doctor hundreds of years hence who might have dared to dissect him.

Thank you, cruel Republic, he told the indifferent and unreadable Lion of San Marco. Curiosity, you have been my wife and my mother, you have kept me alive. A girl's graceful legs or pretty back together with that look of sweet, surging power has been sufficient to make me abandon whatever I was doing and surrender to her particularity. I have suffered through hunger, thirst, despondency, and boredom, thinking it all an interim, a dark interval from which she might, at any moment, rise and relieve the bleakness and the melancholy. And she always has. She was Venice in many guises.

On the other hand, at dinner with some of the very men who had condemned him to the Leads for possessing "blasphemous and unauthorized" books, he experienced such a sense of unreality he could barely keep himself from laughing. He was only a small piece in the game these men had played all their lives. Looking into the falsely amicable faces of men like Procurator Lorenzo Morosini and Senator Pietro Zaguri, he saw an indifference as vast as the yet uncharted oceans. He would have liked to tell them as plainly as he knew: "Venice is no longer a world power. Your indecent attention to the lives of her citizens must cease." Indeed, Venice was living her last hours, and her decline was due only in part to the loss of territories. Her decline was fueled from within: corruption on a vast scale ravaged the city. The volume of denunciations deposited in the many stone lions' mouths that jutted from the walls of the great churches had increased so much the Inquisitors could not keep up. Brother denounced brother. The slightest annoyances became accusations. Fear and suspicion were written on every face. But he could not bring himself to confront these wily old men; they could have banished him from Venice again. He did not fear these men, he feared only losing Venice.

In childhood he had hovered on the border between life and death. His nose had bled continually, fertilizing the earth with that "sang" for which he later substituted his manly seed and his money, profligate from birth. He had been saved from death by the ministrations of a witch who wrapped him in herbs, enclosed him in a box, and watched over him until he crossed from a dim and warm unconsciousness to a life of celebration and action. Having crossed the border from death to life he had had no more fear, but he had known that in order to keep that early bargain in good order he had to reenact that crossing over and over. To stay too long on one side of any border would have betrayed the purpose for which he had been saved.

"I am not proud of some of the things I have been compelled to do," he had explained to his powerful dinner companions, "but I have never regretted them."

Then an extraordinary thing happened. The men who had condemned him to the living hell of the Leads demanded to be told the story of his escape, just as dinner companions everywhere in Europe. The story was famous and everyone wanted to hear it from his mouth. Casanova understood then that reality was composed of two unequal parts. One was comprised of those things that actually happened, and the other, the far greater part, was made of the effects those things had over time. If he had not told and retold his story and been celebrated for it, these patricians would not have requested an account that could only be humiliating to them. Literature, Casanova realized, rewrites the future. He proceeded to tell the story of his escape, requiring, as he always did, a full two hours. And for a full two hours he enjoyed tormenting his tormentors with every detail of his breeching their impenetrable fortress. Only they were not tormented, they were amused.

His financial situation being as precarious as it was more often than not, the Inquisitors proposed that he work for them as a spy. This was their revenge, so perhaps they thought that they had the last laugh. He was paid a monthly salary of eighty ducats. He wrote forty reports, and believed that he was fooling them. His reports weren't worth the paper they were written on. He denounced the gaming and whoring at the Ridotto, which was known to everyone. He thought of his reports as exercises in banality that mocked his employers. "The shadows of foreigners and corrupt women can be seen in the windows of the Ridotto from the Grand Canal," he noted with false conviction. His own shadow was among them, since he spent a good deal of time there. In his report-writing imagination he watched and denounced himself. More than providing useless information to the Inquisition, he enjoyed his reputation as a "spy for the Inquisition." It frightened people. The name he had taken, Antonio Pratolini, was a dramatis personae, a new character on the stage of his life. There had been many, and the stage was quite crowded. The principal character, Jacques Casanova, alternated with the more decorous Chevalier de Seingalt. The two of them were brothers when they didn't fight. Jacques was himself the son of Giacomo. Casanova was the name of his mother's husband, but his father's name may have been Bragadin, Baffo, or

Dandolo. Jacques Casanova, the son of Giacomo, was invincible, his initials were those of the Son of God. "Seingalt" had come to him, full of blood ("sang") and song, conceived fully grown, in warrior garb, lance at the ready. "Seingalt" was Don Quixote, the literary character he loved above all: one-of-a-kind, foolish, impulsive, generous. The last one-of-a-kind, perhaps. In the coming age of mobs, when the world was ruled by the masses, such a one would be an insect to be crushed.

His return to Venice, even under the conditions imposed by the State Inquisitors, had brought together all the characters on his inner stage in a rare moment of harmony. He sensed the purposeful hand of fate now, just as he always had when he reached a crossroads. But what was that purpose? Up to his fiftieth year he would have thought such a question impertinent. Hubris. Offensive to the gods. Paralyzing to himself. But he had lived long enough to allow himself the luxury of asking it. What indeed was the purpose of his longevity, this life given over to love and some witnessing, but mostly love. Love which burned bright and clean and left only its memory behind. Memory! Nothing. Less than nothing. The sorrow of a representation that was only a lie, the opposite of what he was. Each stage of his life had been punctuated by women. Indeed, they had been his orthography and his syntax. They had been his whole grammar. He had always had a rich vocabulary, but without grammar his recondite and vibrant words would have remained a shapeless flood, wasted on fields of painfully applied knowledge, always suffering from insufficient gravity.

He was a poet. From the very beginning, his compositions had been regarded indulgently. In Naples, one of his poems drew the attention of the ladies of the court, who treated him with great affection. In this regard, poetry has an advantage over the other arts. Being the cheapest of the arts and the least remunerated, its reward, often its only reward, is the affection

of women. He learned this very early, but while poetry can
arouse the maternal instincts of women, it is not sufficient unto
itself to make the important transition between maternal affection and the gift of their bodies. To obtain surrender one must
affect the brusqueness and self-confidence of a warrior. This is
why, immediately pursuant on his poetic demonstrations, he
had strapped on the sword and waded boldly into deeper
waters with brash impertinence. His conquests had been swift.
Much later, he realized that it was neither poetry nor brashness
that conquered beauties, but his willingness to try on so many
guises for the single purpose of bedding them. It was simply
the energy spent in pursuit that endeared him.

Returning to Venice, he had thrown himself into several
artistic and amorous pursuits. He brought out the first two volumes of his translation of the *Iliad,* on which he had worked
intermittently since 1764. He wrote Venetian news for Ceruti's
Ephemerides romaines. He also published a review of theatrical
essays and wrote yet another polemic against Voltaire. He met
an intelligent woman of modest means, Francesca Buschini, a
seamstress, who loved him. He was back in his beloved city
and his life was full. For a moment, life was a simple sentence.
The pauses dividing youth from middle age, middle age from
old age, old age from death, were suggested easily by the
rhythm of his days and by his professional successes. A good
woman, a wife, suffices for most men to write the clear sentence
of their lives. For many reasons, this had not been his story, but
who was to say that it couldn't be? In the first place, he had
been the repository of more desire than most people, like a
basin receiving the overflows of a fertile rain. He had noticed
that it was not just the destiny of certain people, but also that of
certain generations, to concentrate a surplus of libido. The age
into which he had been born had been frivolous, excessive,
overly refined, style-mad, and perhaps irresponsible. Philoso-

phers in the future might look back on this age and decide that revolution had been a cleansing necessity.

When he found himself complacently entertaining such thoughts, Casanova was startled, even indignant. He needn't have worried. Fate was not yet through with him. A quarrel over a debt had gone awfully wrong and he was denounced. Without much ceremony, his audience of benevolent Inquisitors terminated his employment and banished him from Venice again. His wanderings began anew.

These were Casanova's thoughts when the Venetian merchant Spinola called on him at Dux, three weeks after his impertinent reply to the Doge. Spinola, a cousin of the Genoan ambassador by the same name, was as slippery as an oiled bean. Wrapped in a black winter cloak, covered by a hat as wide as a Parmesan cheese, smelling faintly of horse, he brought a puddle of wet snow on his boots into the library.

"What news do you bring?" Casanova asked, without offering him a seat. "Or should I ask you if you have anything to sell?"

"Nothing to sell, Chevalier! I bring a gift."

Wary of Venetian gifts, Casanova moved to the fireplace and picked up the poker, under the pretext of stirring the logs. He held the iron poker casually in his hands.

Spinolo laughed. "I am not an assassin," he said. "I came to tell you that the Inquisitors have made your exile permanent. Some of your friends regret it, and I have been charged by Senator Grimani, your patron, to bring you two hundred scudi and this beautiful Asiago." He held out a small purse and a round cheese wrapped in cloth.

Casanova thanked him and asked him to sit at last. Spinolo put the pouch and the cheese on a little table between them, and sat wearily. He had ridden from Prague through sleet, and the cold weather was hard on his bones. They exchanged some gossip of little importance. Casanova sent a servant to ask Feldkirshner if a room could be prepared for his guest.

That night, Casanova took the precaution of changing rooms, leaving only some pillows and blankets on his bed, resembling a man under covers. It was an old trick; he had done the very same thing when he escaped from the Leads. He slept on a sofa in the library, making sure that he had a good view of the door, lit faintly by the moon shining through the mullioned windows. Despite himself, he fell asleep after the midnight bell, and did not wake until the morning.

His bedroom had not been disturbed. Spinolo had departed before dawn, leaving instructions to ask Casanova's forgiveness for not taking proper leave. Casanova thought that he had been mistaken. Spinolo hadn't known anything about any black ropes. He must have truly been only a merchant; there was no evidence that Spinolo had come with designs on his life.

Casanova dressed and Laura came in with his breakfast.

"What is that?" She wrinkled her nose and pointed to the Asiago.

"That, ma chère, is one of my homeland's proudest products. It is made from the milk of nymphs captured by Pan." He unwrapped the milky ball, broke off a piece, and handed it to Laura.

"Not on your life," she demurred. "There are certain things I will not eat. Red sea creatures. Pigeons. Horse. Venetian cheese."

"You insult the honor of the greatest naval power on earth."

Casanova raised the morsel of cheese dramatically to his mouth, but his beloved fox terrier, Cybelle, bounded from the sofa and snatched it from his fingers. Astonished, Casanova looked first at his hand, then at Cybelle.

"Bad dog!"

Cybelle raised a paw and then took an amusing bow, but she never recovered from the bow. She started gyrating instead, yelping in pain. Minutes later, Cybelle was dead.

"The black rope!" cried the Chevalier, cradling his pet. "Someone will pay for this." He could not abide cruelty to animals, any animals, and he had loved Cybelle dearly. This was no longer a matter of philosophy.

The pleasures of vengeance were not foreign to him. Ironically, Venice herself had been both the stage and the inspiration for his most satisfying act of revenge. He had been imprisoned in the fortress of San Andrea, having been accused by a brutish sbirro named Razzetta of selling the furniture in his own house. He conceived a brilliant alibi by pretending to sprain his ankle. A Slovenian soldier was sent to Casanova's room in the fortress to watch over him, since he pretended to be in great pain. After plying the soldier with brandy until he fell asleep, Casanova slipped out of the room and scaled the fortress wall down to the water where a gondolier he had hired waited for him. When they reached Venice he bought a good sturdy stick and waited for Razzetta at the foot of a bridge in Campo San Polo near the sbirro's house. He knew that Razzetta always returned home from the tavern after midnight. Shortly after the midnight bells, Razzetta appeared, walking unsteadily. Casanova gave him some violent blows that knocked him into the canal. There had been no light, but the sbirro recognized him and cried out his name. A watchman carrying a lantern appeared, but Casanova struck the watchman's wrist with his stick and the watchman dropped the light. He was back in the gondola in no time, rowing back to the fortress. He climbed the wall and was back in his bed without anyone having noticed his absence. The next day all of Venice was talking about the beating, sure that Casanova was the culprit, but no one could prove it. The Slovenian swore that he had been with him all night and the commander of the fortress was outraged by the suggestion that anyone might escape from his prison, much less return to it!

Casanova told the story to Laura and though she laughed, she was quite worried, perceiving that the Chevalier's delight in his story was not innocent. He was summoning the courage of his youth for some far worse revenge. Indeed, Casanova only recalled the tale to calm himself before reflecting on what retribution he would exact. Razzetta had merely put him in prison, for a short time at that. Spinola, and the Doge who had sent him, had intended that he die. This was infinitely more serious, and called to mind episodes in his life less charming than his revenge on Razzetta. He had killed a gambler in self-defense in Mantua, when the man tried to plunge a stiletto into his heart. There had been other poisoners, too. The mother of a whore named Carmella had put poison in his food; happily, not enough to kill him. It seemed she had poisoned three potential husbands who had refused to marry Carmella. When the woman was finally caught and executed, Carmella had come to him, asking for a job. Casanova, though not certain that Carmella was innocent of her mother's crimes, employed her as a maid and seamstress. One day she vanished with all his shirts and the contents of a purse he had left lying about.

He said nothing to Laura of these episodes, common in the life of an adventurer. After she withdrew, Casanova unlocked one of his trunks and took out a bundle of letters wrapped in coarse paper and sealed with his sigil. He had stolen them from the offices of the Inquisitors in the Ducal Palace during one of the rare times he had been left alone in the scribe room, waiting for his instructions. The Inquisitors worked at night, but many secretaries did not. They locked their files carefully, but one of them had been careless. Quite by accident, Casanova had stumbled on a packet of communications from rich Venetians living abroad to the State Inquisitors. Surely, among them there was one whose views of the world could be construed as traitorous. Such a man might help him in exchange for his silence.

Casanova lay the stack on the table next to the poisoned Asiago. He laughed. Asiago had been the first alphabetical entry in his *History of Cheeses*. No wonder he hadn't finished it. He picked up the purse of coins and pulled it open. Inside were twenty lead bullets. Spinolo had taken quite a chance. What if he had looked inside the purse? Then, obviously, Spinolo would have tried to kill him. Revenge is a dish best served cold, he reminded himself, yet at that moment he would have liked nothing better than to jump on a horse and catch the would-be assassin before he left Bohemia. Alas. He was old, old. But his mind was sharp, and he was grateful that life could still offer the delights of action.

He melted the twenty lead bullets in a tempered crucible, and molded a square tablet from the lead, on which he inscribed, "Here lies Cybelle, faithful terrier who did no wrong, killed by the last Doge of Venice." When Cybelle was buried next day in the farthest corner of the courtyard that could still be seen from the library window, Casanova gave a brief eulogy in Latin that only the priest would have understood, had he not refused indignantly to attend such a "mock rite." Casanova read it in the falling snow while one of the soldiers served as gravedigger. Laura Brock was a witness, and she was quite moved when she saw a tear on the adventurer's cheek make its way down his chin and drop onto the frozen ground.

It would be a year before Chevalier de Seingalt could put his plan of revenge in effect. First, he needed money. Everything else would follow.

&ℰ𝒲ords are words and money is money but words are money, while money is rarely words. In the matter of credit, money is only words. If the word became flesh, what can prevent it from becoming money, a trivial operation compared to that first, cosmic operation? Trivial, yes, but how difficult! Looking into his threadbare purse, Casanova was not amused. Mostly he was horrified. He was surrounded by millions of words, some of his own making, and none of them showed the slightest inclination to become money. He was missing, it seemed, the catalyst, the agent that would activate the transformation. He had possessed quantities of this agent when young. He had talked his way into fortunes, and squandered them as easily as they were made. There was a time when gold had seemed to tumble from his mouth—golden words that existed only a fraction of a second before becoming cash! Long ago when Madame d'Urfé had engaged his services to effect her rebirth, he had waved his magic wand of words, and jewels had flowed from her coffers into his pockets! That ancient lady had wanted to be reborn and Casanova had plotted her transformation step by step, weaving a glorious web of words. She desired immortality, and he had obliged her to the limit of human possibility. He had succeeded in making her immortal—not in the flesh, but in words. In the beginning was the word, in the middle was gold, in the end there was the word again. But now, in the twilight of his life, words weren't yielding their bounty.

&c "Mademoiselle Brock, have you heard about the Count of St. Germain?"

"No," Laura said, alarmed by the Chevalier's genuine cry of despair. "I mean, we did, but he never visited the von Helmund estate. The Baron was a religious man, he believed that such charlatans should be put at the stake."

"And Cagliostro? You know of him?"

"Only that he was in the same line of work as le Comte de St. Germain."

"Those two were magnificent," Casanova said enviously, "the greatest charlatans of our time. Do you know why?"

"Because they were skilled at card tricks and transmutations?"

"Not at all. Because no one could disprove them. When the Comte de St. Germain met Madame Pompadour he was wearing precious stones on his garters worth millions. Louis XV tested him by handing him a diamond with a flaw. 'This diamond is worth seven thousand louis,' the King told him, 'but without the flaw it can easily fetch ten thousand. Can you remove the flaw?' The Comte came back next day with the flawless diamond, weighing exactly as much as it had the day before. The King sold it. Don't think that it was Louis's greed that facilitated St. Germain's success at the court. It wasn't that at all, though he proved himself quite adept at increasing gold and providing mysterious remedies to ailments. It was his honeyed tongue and his sense of timing. The rhythm of his disappearances."

"I am certain that your own honeyed tongue did not perform badly," Laura said naughtily, remembering one such performance just the day before.

"Well, that's precisely it. We were both profligate with

words, but whereas I liked to think myself witty, learned, perhaps charming, St. Germain was merely pedantic. All he talked was scientific-sounding nonsense and everyone hung on his words. The extraordinary thing is that no one knows what happened to either St. Germain or Cagliostro, so their legends continue to thrive! While everyone knows that I'm at Dux, too far to care about, too close to become legendary! I must do something memorable!"

"Doing something memorable . . ." Laura thought out loud, "is that something one must do at regular intervals?"

"About 'one' I don't know. Casanova must. The problem is that it must be a profitable memorable, not just memorable. Something on the scale of Madame d'Urfé. . . . I am still not sure whether I duped that poor woman or whether at some essential level she obtained what she wanted."

Having made an occasional profit by using a number pyramid, a cabbalistic oracle that answered questions, Casanova had gained a modest reputation as an initiate in the occult. "To be sure, I was sufficiently modest about my gifts so that people would come to me, naturally, thinking that they had discovered me themselves. I obtained a number of introductions in Paris, thanks to the oracle. Madame d'Urfé was one of the greatest readers of occult nonsense in all of France. She had been the mistress of the Regent of France and was still quite a beautiful woman in her eighth decade. Her home had a magnificent library that contained thirty thousand volumes of esoteric knowledge, including alchemy and all the hermetic arts. Her salon was frequented both by St. Germain and Cagliostro, but never at the same time, which gave rise to the rumors that they were one and the same person. Convinced of her high standing as a priestess of Hermes she had conceived the idea of changing her sex and becoming a man by getting pregnant and giving birth to herself in the form of a boy."

Laura's eyes became quite big on hearing such an extraordinary conceit. She had seen and heard aristocrats claim the most preposterous things about themselves and have recourse to charlatans of every description, including astrologers, card readers, and mesmerists. The wealthier they were, the more exalted their ideas of themselves. There had been a few philosopher-princes and hundreds of fools, at least in the two noble houses where she had served. But this business, it was the worst she had ever heard.

"My good friend, the Duc de Bernis," Casanova continued, unimpressed by her amazement, "helped to draw the woman into my snares. I told her that my oracle was capable of quoting ahead of time the words that the King would speak to her in the morrow. I then arranged with Bernis to induce the King to greet Madame d'Urfé with a phrase we had concocted. Louis was quite amused by the whole charade and, by the afternoon of the next day, Madame d'Urfé was mine. There was also, I am not ashamed to admit, an attraction she felt for me, which had not been the case either with St. Germain, who was rich but ugly, or with Cagliostro, who was a hunchback. I told her that I had the ear of a spirit named Paralis, who was the ruler of a world of water spirits and some other realms. With the help of Paralis I was going to help her achieve her dream of giving birth to herself. But first, there had to be many preparations, all of which required a fortune in gold and precious stones. . . ."

"You are a dreadful man, Chevalier!" Laura cried out, flushing despite herself.

"Not at all, ma chérie. Dupes are there for the taking. I could not have convinced her that I had no magical powers if I tried. And if I had withdrawn, any of the charlatans at her salons, including St. Germain and Cagliostro, would have been only too happy to replace me."

"Well, that is one perfectly self-serving way of seeing the

problem, but go on, Chevalier, the story is quite fascinating."

"After two years of making diverse preparations, including invocations of spirits and placating Neptune with a trunk full of jewels for which I substituted lead, we arrived at the inevitable ceremony when Madame d'Urfé would be impregnated. I made various astrological calculations and I could no longer delay the ritual, because we were being talked about everywhere and we were beginning to be ridiculed. I had also nearly drained her fortune, something like a million francs, I believe, and there was nothing to be gained by waiting. The full-moon ceremony took place in her rooms, where I had ordered that a large copper tub and various screens be brought. At the last minute, I told her that a supernatural being, something like a sylph, would be assisting me. I was afraid that when the time came to perform the ritual penetration I would be incapable of it, despite my great imagination. D'Urfé was, after all, more than eighty years old. I arranged with Marcolina, a fourteen-year-old girl I had taken from my worthless brother, that she should appear naked but painted silver from behind one of the screens and that she was to caress both Madame d'Urfé and myself until I achieved a state of readiness. Marcolina turned out to be a very competent actress, enthusiastic about her role. She caressed the old woman in the copper tub, filled with pure moon-water, until she sighed with such pleasure you could have thought she had already been taken by Paralis. Marcolina had great talent for the Provençal vice and much more experience than one would have thought. And to think that the idiot abbé, my brother, ran away with her and wanted to marry her. He believed her a virgin! Anyway, Marcolina brought Madame d'Urfé to the very edge of the ecstatic precipice and also managed to arouse me with the sight of her well-shaped young body. I then entered the bathtub and allowed myself to be possessed by the spirit of Paralis, who used my organ of regeneration to do its job, making d'Urfé faint several times while crying out the required invocations between truly savage screams of pleasure."

"I think that you might be exaggerating . . ."

"There is an essay to be written on the subject of passionate noise. Forgive me, my dear fraülein, but women of your race, the English, and Nordic people in general, make the smallest possible noises in love, they are so faint they are inaudible at times. At first, I faulted myself, but then I realized that this is part of a certain coldness of nature. . . ."

When Laura tried to protest, the Chevalier added quickly, "This does not mean of course that you do not experience the greatest pleasure. It is only that you regard its expression as undignified somehow. But I assure you that giving in to screams of passion has the effect of doubling, tripling, quadrupling the pleasure. Venetian women have perfected the art of calling out the aches and sweet hurts of male vigor until they have made a music from it. And a rich orchestration it is, indeed. No man can consider himself a man until he has heard the full symphony of a Venetian's surrender to Eros."

Laura was quite angry. She had always thought herself fully responsive to pleasure and she remembered distinctly that she had responded to the Chevalier's trifling with more than appropriate warmth. Was it her fault that he had not yet gone to the depths of her secret chamber, where the entrance to her womb often wrenched cries of ecstatic agony from her? It was easy for him to generalize about "her people," without knowing a thing about her. She let out a piercing scream, halfway between the cawing of a crow and the breaking of a lute string. Casanova panicked, looking around for some unexpected demon.

"What was that?"

"That unsettling sound, mon Chevalier, is what you would like women to sound like."

He laughed heartily and apologized. After sulking for a minute, she decided to forgive him. "About Madame d'Urfé, then . . ."

"Nothing more. The very next day she told the court that she was pregnant and that she would have a son. Everyone thought that she was mad. Their suspicions were confirmed when she made a new will leaving her entire fortune to her unborn child, instead of her natural children and family. She named me guardian of her son, who was herself, until such time as he was old enough to take control himself. At that point, her family started to threaten me seriously and compromise my standing in Parisian society. . . . I resumed my travels."

"What a scoundrelly adventure!" cried Laura admiringly, despite herself.

"Is it? This is where I am beginning to have doubts. Yes, I made some money from the old woman's delusions. Not that much, really, because the greater part of the jewels she gave me was stolen from me by a real low scoundrel, my valet Costa. And I quickly exhausted the rest playing faro. I have always considered gains obtained by clever deceit to be mere play money. I never kept any. The greatest benefit of the adventure seems to be the story itself. But what if, I ask myself, what if Madame d'Urfé was playing her own game, much cleverer than mine?"

"What could she have wanted? She was rich, still healthy, and you said that she was still beautiful . . ."

"What did she want? She wanted Casanova, a man the age of her son, and she wanted him in a way that would seem mad and extravagant, which would excuse her perfectly craven appetite. . . . She may have wished for a son, as well. Maybe she was a little mad, but only in a perfectly reasonable way."

"She wanted your seed?" Laura asked with practical good sense.

"Yes, but in that I did not gratify her. She believed that I

81

had given her my seed several times, but I was only pretending. I have mastered the technique of fooling a woman. Without this pretense most women are unable to achieve complete satisfaction, so I have learned, for their sake, to create a credible illusion. In the end, they are all grateful because I did not inseminate them. But at their moment of pleasure they care for nothing on earth except the seed."

"You may be right, Chevalier, but you should have never told me this. . . ."

"Fear not, ma belle Laura, if I ever produce seed for pleasure again I will not withhold it from you."

"What happens then if you inseminate me?"

"I will give birth to myself and you must raise me until I am old enough to remember who I am."

Laura laughed, but it was the strangest proposition she had ever heard, much stranger than a proposal for marriage.

&ℰ After Laura left, Casanova wrote to his friend Henriette, in Provence:

My beloved Henriette,

Age is only a small part of the problem, if we are to be frank with ourselves, and we are going to be frank, come what may. I have discovered something that is setting my mind on fire the way women once did. Old age can be borne: a good wench and a good fire suffice. My capacity for joy is intact, though tempered by the inevitable slowing down of my body. My discovery is of another nature. I will doubtless consider this matter in more reasoned ways in letters to my literary friends and rivals, but I want you, my soul-twin, to know it in unadorned simplicity. I have lived my life with curiosity and, hopefully, some courage, and I considered the happiness of my lovers to be of the utmost importance. I have lived without a plan, though I have made many plans, and I have heard the vengeful laughter of the gods more times than I can count. The greatest portion of this adventure has been the work of my mind, engaged in understanding myself and the world. When I wasn't pursuing pleasure, I was writing. These were my two chief activities, the rest were only consequences of love and literature. I have had a moderate amount of success in my literary efforts, but never of the high order I had hoped to achieve and believed that I deserved. Pay attention, my dearest. This is not the defeated observation of an overlooked intellect. I know very well that success is not always the reward of talent and that it depends, in large measure, on flattery and deception and on the ability to promote one's cause. I am speaking of something else entirely. I will compare myself with someone who has been both a model and an object of contempt for me. Even you may find the comparison a bit exaggerated, but I assure you that it is not vanity which prompts me. I speak of Voltaire, my elder by a number of years, but my equal in many respects. We have much in common, but for the most important thing, of course, which is that he is dead while I complain only of stiffness in my writing hand. Not a minor ailment, mind you, when my entire raison d'être is writing, but not quite as radical as rigor mortis. Be that as it may, let's disregard this essential difference for the moment. I am speaking of our immortal literary fates. Voltaire and I were both born in relu-

*tively modest circumstances and made ourselves into
who we are, to the point of assuming new names.
Casanova became Seingalt, Arouet became Voltaire. Before I was born, Voltaire had already been imprisoned in
the Bastille for his satirical verse. I, in my turn, was imprisoned in the Venetian Leads for a similar offense. We
both lived the nomadic lives of exiles who earned their
keep by their ability to entertain their hosts. We have
both gambled and have been fascinated by the lottery,
from which Voltaire drew a great deal more profit than I.
We were both members of that fraternity which, these
days, influences the political life of Europe to a degree
unimaginable even twenty years ago. When I met
Voltaire, I felt that I was in the presence of a brother. We
discussed and argued the merits of Italian and French
poets, we shared his mistress, his niece and housekeeper,
Madame Denis, and we ended up exhausted, sleeping in
each other's arms. But the morning after our tryst I became keenly aware of our differences. His antechamber
filled with sycophants come to present him with their
plays and poetry, with worshipful essays and translations of his works, or just sickening displays of craven
adoration. I was ignored the entire day, observing the
business of fame. Naturally, I was jealous, but not of his
admirers. I was jealous of Voltaire's ability to awaken
something inexplicable in his contemporaries. This man
who never tired of proving the superiority of reason over
superstition was conducting a kind of religious rite. I
have thought about it for many years; I realized that the
religion initiated by Voltaire was new; it is the Religion
of Fame. At its center is neither a man nor his produc-
tions, but an inexhaustible superstition that feeds only
on its own subjection. This Religion of Fame has never*

existed in such pure form. Famous men and worshipful readers have existed before, but this new cult exists only in and of itself, regardless of the pretext that occasions it. Standing at the window in Voltaire's remarkable library, I watched the supplicants waiting their turn and had a vision of the future in which the Religion of Fame would voraciously consume all the intelligence of men like so much pig slop, in order to strengthen its rituals and expand its power. And his death, my God, what a powerful illustration of this nightmare! He returned from his twenty-eight years of Swiss exile in Ferney and was received with such festivities the strain killed him! At least he died a martyr to his own secret cause. What was there in the writing of Voltaire that made it hospitable to such horror? That, my dearest Henriette, is what I discovered next, after carefully rereading all his works. I found that Voltaire was not concerned with the mystery of his own mind, but with a desire to reform society, despite his many contradictory denials over the years. This may seem obvious to you or to anyone familiar with his work, but herein lies the seed of a nightmare from which it will take mankind centuries to waken. That a philosophical writer should be a moralist is really no surprise. What is surprising and, indeed, new, is that the morality implicit here is boundless and without God. In the absence of a faith that lets men concede their destinies to Providence, this morality becomes a hideous new God whose demands are far greater than that of an inexplicable Deity. Voltaire has taken God's merciful work of containing mystery and made it part of the province of Reason. The ostensible ideal of his reformist fervor may have been Liberty, but its effects will not be liberating. The unfortunate consequences of his arrogance will be our burden in

the future. Nonetheless, his hubris has found an exceedingly receptive world. Injustice and oppression are the order of the day and night and the call to Liberty cannot but strike the deepest chords in the people. Voltaire was not alone in this enterprise. I could make my point with even greater precision by the example of Jean-Jacques Rousseau, a sour little man who made my birthplace, Venice, the key to his political philosophy, while failing to notice even the slightest of her beauties. In a world where Beauty and even Truth must now take their place behind Morality, such men are gods. My own work has been entirely in the service of Beauty and, occasionally, Truth. But, my sweet and unforgettable Henriette, this will no longer be the case. I am too old for the games of literary success. I have decided to put myself entirely in the service of Truth, the truth of my own life, a life that was dedicated entirely to Beauty. I am not a man of the present. I have resigned myself to gaining no laurels whatsoever for my poetry, plays, essays, or translations. My own understanding of literature will be a gift to the future. Perhaps posterity will find me no more interesting than my contemporaries have, but I will write the truth of my life, which has, in so many ways, been a gift from you, Henriette. I will go even further to say that my view of life has been that of a woman, a view that rejoices in the unending mystery of particulars and seeks to convince no one to reform or oppress.
Your ever faithful pet, hummingbird, and arthritis-ridden satyr,
Giacomo

Casanova put down his quill and looked at what he had written. He had no doubt that Henriette would understand. He saw her as she had been when he first met her, disguised as a handsome young officer, traveling in the company of a gentle Hungarian. He had quickly determined that she was a woman and had fallen in love with her in the carriage that took them to Parma. The Hungarian had graciously ceded her to young Casanova, who worshiped her more and more as he discovered brilliant new aspects of his mysterious companion. Henriette, who said nothing about her past, was fond of music, books, and food, but above all she was a master of the art of love. She had taught him pleasures that he had not thought possible outside forbidden books. His body, always restless, now experienced the delights of repose after making love. For the first time in his life, his heart had been completely conquered. Not content to remain in the womb of their perfect happiness, he had persuaded her to go out to the opera where they could be seen and admired. She was admired indeed and, shortly after, they were invited to an aristocratic party where she was the only woman, in order that her beauty might shine alone. A concert was performed that included a symphony, played by an orchestra, and, following this, a cello concerto played by a pupil of Vandini. Overcome by the beauty of the music, Henriette seized the musician's cello and asked the orchestra to begin again. She astonished the gathering by the loveliness of her playing. She had revealed her mastery of the cello and she could not hide any longer. Her virtuosity became the talk of Parma. It was not long before her aristocratic Provençal family found her and compelled her to return to the ancestral hold which she had abandoned in search of adventure, dressed as a man. Casanova's pride and vanity had lost him his love! Heartbroken, he accompanied her as far as Geneva, where they parted at an inn. He fell asleep near dawn and when he woke, Henriette was gone. She had left only these words scratched with her ring diamond on a windowpane: *Tu oublieras Henriette, aussi.*

You will forget Henriette, as well. He never did. Decades later, he returned to that inn and found her words still legible on the window glass. The affection between himself and Henriette never waned over the course of their lives. She was his most faithful correspondent. In their letters, they bared their hearts and discussed everything and anything, no matter how trivial or seemingly livresque.

He had resolved to hold nothing back from her, yet, rereading his letter, he wondered if he had been fair. Perhaps he was nothing but a bitter old man, jealous of his contemporaries. His own fame had been quite great, but not on account of his art. The account he published of his escape from the Leads had been read in all of Europe. His conquests had been the delight and gossip of salons. Was this fame or mere notoriety? After all, it had not been the charm of his storytelling that had excited his readers, but the content of his adventure. They had fallen so deeply under the spell of the action that they had ignored its true nature. The writer Casanova had rendered himself invisible by his own mastery of the storyteller's art. Like a good actor, he had subsumed his art to the illusion he had created. Voltaire, on the other hand, had never let anyone forget that he was the writer Voltaire first and then, only then, the man Voltaire. Curiously, that very conceit had gained him more renown than Casanova could dream of. It was worth delving into this apparent contradiction by rereading once again his model and rival. There was another difference between them, important enough to consider. Voltaire had hated his mother. Casanova had not; he had loved Zanetta. He made a quick note of this on the margin of his letter to Henriette: "Do not trust anyone who does not love his mother!" Casanova laughed. Doubtless, Voltaire would not have considered him a rival, if he had thought about it at all. No matter. Their battle was not taking place on the field of the present, it was unfolding in eternity.

꿈C asanova was traveling far into the world of Micromegs, the interior paradise of his own making, but there was no end in sight and no publisher for his book. The Micromeg paradise was not without money. There were rich and poor Micromegs, but no one was unhappy. The rich were simply willing to work harder, while the poor preferred leisure. All enjoyed the unique pleasures of their world, particularly the Micromeg language, a divine music that caressed all the senses. Their language was composed of six vowels written in the seven colors of the rainbow. These seven-hued vowels, or tone series, had in combination forty-two different word meanings, or harmonies. Casanova had calculated that the use of sounded vowels in syllable combinations together with musical intervals allowed for the formation of nearly thirty thousand words. At Micromeg gatherings and feasts, the keynote forming the basis of conversation was established by the host. The inmost soul manifested itself in music when the euphonious words reached a listener. These melodies of speech touched the soul not merely through the sense of hearing but through every skin surface. The few Micromegs required by their official duties to wear ceremonial robes would tear them off to better hear the words of their fellows.

At their best, his own words had achieved that effect on the outer, nonparadisiacal surface of the earth. He regarded the transfer of words to the soul as the single most important activity of his life because the result of this activity had always been—well, almost always—his conquest of a woman. Though complete conquest often required an intermediary—money— which allowed him to lavish jewels, clothing, and fine edibles on his amours. His present poverty was trivial and boring. Money would buy him better food, equip a carriage, purchase medicines. The mundanity of his need was doubtlessly the reason why the once-generous fates were stingy and displeased. He was a toothless old man reduced to begging the world to buy his words! How crass! How undignified!

He paced the length of the library, cursing and beseeching the fates at the same time. The late-afternoon light composed an intricate pattern of shadows on the castle wall. Gazing at it, the Chevalier thought he could see a tissue of numbers, a spidery nest of cyphers in the shadows. All his life, things that could be counted or designated by a number were eerily significant, filled with seductive meanings. And though he had at times tried to resist, an inclination toward the cabbala and the undeniable evidence of numerical power had rendered hollow any protestation.

His favorite parlor trick, a pyramidal fortune-telling oracle composed of numbers, had served him so well among superstitious nobles and bourgeois, that he had been revered, feared, and spoiled from Venice to Moscow. Had he actually believed in the oracle, he might have been employed for a lifetime. Alas. The desire had been as strong to debunk his tricks as to use them. But skepticism did not diminish in the least the efficacy of his system of divination, or of any other for that matter. He believed not in astrology, or cards, or coffee grounds. Yet each of those systems worked.

In daily life he noted the insistent recurrence of certain numbers that defied the laws of chance. Even time, being quantified numerically, had mystical qualities. The story of his escape from the Leads, for instance, always took exactly two hours to tell—no more, no less. When time passed swiftly, as it seemed always to in the act of love, he knew that it all took but a "quarter of an hour." An inner clock regulated all his movements and he knew, always, how much time he had left. And if his timing had been occasionally off, it had been only for misguided love. Perfect love had perfect timing. The smallest slight to Eros, however, could have disastrous consequences. One would think that after so much perfect service, Eros might give a little, sighed Casanova. But no, Eros is without pity, he demands perfection and punishes the pretender.

That there is an underlying mystery in the universe is as obvious as it is mysterious. Of this he was certain, and the knowledge liberated him, though it presented him with puzzles that intrigued and infuriated him as a man of sense. In the end, perhaps the only currency worth anything may be youth. In his youth, he had conquered, played, consumed and wandered, trusting fully in the benevolence of the universe. In his old age, he had to eke out a living among barbarians, penning words that might never see the light of day, words that he might burn as soon as he wrote them. He imagined flames licking the thousands of carefully wrapped letters and manuscripts in his trunks and felt bitter satisfaction. Flames even now were consuming the world of his past. He offered the fire his letter to Henriette, a small token of the bounty to come.

The weekly post brought a letter from Henriette. When he read it, he was glad that he had incinerated his unbearably vain letter.

My Dear Prince, Swordsman, and Soul-Twin,

Your Henriette rarely reaches such poetic heights of address, but something in the light of this season and the unfortunate situation in our provinces makes me careless and exalted. Our strong affection for one another through decades is my most cherished possession. I feel the excitement of youth deeply in my sex when I think of the triumph of our love. I have remained invisible to you since our sorrowful parting in Geneva. You know that I have been close to you on several occasions but I never let you see me, wanting to keep intact in your mind the perfection of our young love. And yet, even without the bodies that made our love so incandescent, we have been able to maintain an unbroken link. I speak of this magnificent mystery only in contrast with the events which daily are overtaking us. Our love helps me to believe that the miseries of this time are transitory. But they are brutal, nonetheless, so brutal and so crass that I am certain there is little reason for me to be alive now. Our correspondence keeps me so. I also cherish the time when we corresponded through the body of sweet Marcolina, your companion in Aix with whom I spent the night. I sent her back to you the next morning with an invisible message, hoping that the knowledge of our love-play would be transmitted directly to you when you in turn embraced her. I asked her not to wash, so that my kisses, still lingering on her divine body, might touch you directly. She was my first and best letter to you. Sometimes I write you letters that I never put on paper. I compose them in my mind and I hear you answer them immediately. Our conversation has defied age and distance, my dear Casanova. I say these things to you now because I want you to know that your Henriette will continue speaking lovingly to you even when her letters have ceased. You must know the situation here is very grave. Two weeks ago representatives of the Estates General presented us with a heavy burden of new taxes. Our holdings are entirely in land and property. Our credit in Provence is based only on the ancient name of my family. We are on the verge of bankruptcy—these taxes will be impossible to pay. I had news yesterday that the castle at Vigny has been looted by a revolutionary mob and the en-

*tire family massacred. My nieces were raped and killed. A
proclamation is circulating through the province naming
the next targets of the mob's wrath and we are among
them. Many nobles are fleeing into exile, but this is not
our way. As long as the King and the Queen, for whom I
personally have little affection, remain on the throne of
France, we will remain. These are my ancestral holdings.
You may remember how, in our youth, we laughed at the
follies and pretensions of the aristocracy. In those
unimaginably peaceful days we thought the traditions of
the nobility antiquated and ridiculous. I now find myself
willing to die for them.*
Farewell, my light and my magic wand,
Henriette

Casanova was furious. Stupid, stupid Henriette! She must
flee at once! He understood her sentimental attachment to the
moldy relics of her ancient family, but he could not understand
the betrayal of her own life force. There were higher priorities
for a human being than an old castle and some bad paintings.
One had a duty to one's life, to the maintenance of the vital
force. He was old, but not old enough to be in love with death.
He had to do something, anything, to save her. He would get
her another castle, three castles if she was so fond of them. The
whole of Bohemia was dotted with magnificent empty buildings
since the expulsion of the monks and the Jesuits. There was
still a world of castles outside the madness of France! He
needed money, money. He would undertake a mission to save
his Henriette from her idiotic resignation. He would begin by
appealing to his friend, the Prince de Ligne, who was active in
the exodus of the French aristocracy. If the Prince made Henriette his personal cause, she might relent.

Casanova started writing to Henriette but he kept tearing

up the letters. Nothing he said seemed either persuasive or commanding enough. To calm himself he turned his attention to another letter on his desk, this one from a young woman he had never met. Cécile de Roggendorff was the daughter of an old friend, the noble adventurer Baron Ernest Roggendorf. She had fallen in love with his legend and had been writing him increasingly fervent letters. She was intelligent and well-read, though naive and quite poor. He had arranged for her to enter service as dame of honor to the Duke of Courtland. In her letter she begged Casanova for a fragment of his memoirs, which she had heard he was writing. She also wanted to know when his *Icosameron* would be finished and whether it was true that he had named his creatures in honor of Voltaire after that illustrious writer's novel *Micromegas,* and whether there was any foundation to the rumor that he disdained all human company in his retreat at Dux because she could not imagine anything more wonderful on this earth than making his acquaintance. She didn't want much, did she? For a moment Casanova actually entertained the idea of allowing her to come. But then he saw himself in the mirror. His toothless grin was so tragic he had to laugh. He was good enough for a serving maid and a half-savage utopist, but a young Baroness might find him a bit decrepit. On the other hand, he knew women well enough to realize that their love for a man's mind went well beyond his appearance. This was certainly not true the other way around. The real reason he did not want to meet Baroness Roggendorf was her inexhaustible curiosity. Such draining adoration would most certainly disrupt his work.

Money. It was inconceivable that he could not be of use to someone with the means to underwrite his needs. He was amused by his own calculations, which had begun with a modest assessment of his living expenses, only to end in desiring a fortune with which to save Henriette. And yet, what difference was there between a small amount and a great one when one had nothing? He could just as easily conceive of a great plan as of a petty one. In his experience, it was easier to obtain a great deal of money by daring than to beg the price of a meal.

As fate would have it, there was also a letter from the Prince de Ligne, alternately obsequious and arrogant in tone. The Prince groveled at Casanova's feet while barely hiding his literary jealousy. A typical nobleman for you, thought the Chevalier. He is furious that genius is not the sole property of princes and that it is given, more often than not, to men of the lower classes. If he had not such contempt for the lower classes himself, Casanova might be in France right now, leading the revolution. But he knew only too well the cruelty and stupidity of mobs. I am the opposite of a nobleman, thought Casanova. For better or worse I have been a trespasser, a transgressor, and a corruptor of borders my entire life, and the institutions for maintaining borders have always had a resolute enemy in me. Happily, the aristocrats whose job is to maintain the integrity of their little states have not realized it. My techniques for remaining invisible have varied. I sometimes astonish myself with the cleverness of my disguises, though the best are always the simplest. Of course, living as long as I have should have made trespassing as easy as a children's game, but, curiously enough, the science of borders has kept up with my longevity. It is nearly impossible now to fool the system as I once did. But perhaps I am wrong. Each man may be born with precisely the degree of brashness required to trespass over the borders of his time. Perhaps the necessity to continually learn new tricks has so layered my knowledge that I see difficulties that aren't there. Perhaps the energy of desire alone suffices to transgress. I don't know.

> *Mon cher de Ligne,*
>   *Your interest in the world of my Micromegs does me*

good. I am the prisoner of old age and penury and have retreated almost entirely into the realms of imagination. I am most cheered by such high praise for its ineffable worth. I say "almost" because I cannot help but keep up with the news from France. The cursed journals penetrate my solitude and I cannot shut them out though I have tried. I ignored them for a whole month only to be startled when I resumed reading by the ferocity of history that waits for no one in accomplishing its malignant work. There is no doubt now that all of Europe will soon be at war, and I only hope that men such as yourself might have a strong hand in events. In such times, one can hardly stand by, but my usefulness in the world is limited. However, I would like to offer my service to you. I know Europe intimately—how people in each country think and how their sovereigns think (or not). And I have had a great deal of experience carrying messages across hostile borders and in observing the fortifications of war. You have seen some of my sketches. I would also like to aid the unfortunate families now being wrenched from their ancestral homes. I fear in particular for my dear friend, Henriette de . . . , who has resolved to remain in France and perish, despite the inevitable defeat of the mobs in the future. I am unable to persuade her to leave, but I believe that it is in your power, my dear friend, to do so. In exchange for your doing so, I offer my acumen to you without any demands for recompense, save for the cost of a good carriage and the expenses of travel.
Your devoted Casanova,
Chevalier de Seingalt

He was offering de Ligne his services as a spy. Well, he had done it before. He doubted very much if de Ligne would accept his offer. Casanova was too well known. Once again, the irony of his position struck him. He was too well known to be useful and thus earn a living, while everywhere in the world men would kill for notoriety. The insatiable Voltaire had never had enough fame. The hungry young men now rising from the rabble of France dreamed of seeing their names in the newspapers. The celebrity for which they all strove was his already.

His reflection was interrupted by the arrival of an unexpected visitor. Abbé Josef Dorensky had traveled from Prague to make the acquaintance of the distinguished librarian and to ask for permission to peruse one of the great libraries of Bohemia. With a shock of red hair and wild, gleaming eyes, he resembled, thought his host, a hungry wolf.

Casanova offered him a seat on a corner of a divan piled with books and made a sweeping gesture across the disordered landscape of the library.

"Mon cher Abbé! What you see is but a fraction of this great collection. Twenty thousand volumes have been catalogued and shelved, but twice that many are waiting for attention. You are welcome to both the order and the disorder. I assume that you will stay a few days?"

The Abbé nodded gravely. "J'aimerais bien. I would like to. Unfortunately . . ."

Casanova had divined his answer. "Unfortunately, you don't want to presume on Count Waldstein's hospitality. I know nothing about you, but I see the hunger of the intellect in your eyes. I am happy to offer you the hospitality of the library, if you do not mind sleeping under rather restricted conditions on this divan. I will be happy to share my sumptuous meals with you and even my charming maid. . . ."

The Abbé laughed. "Sumptous meals?"

"If you use your imagination in addition to your mouth they will be sumptuous indeed. The maid is most charming, though."

"I will gladly accept your hospitality and your sumptuous meals, Chevalier, but I will have to decline the maid." He reddened.

Casanova did not press him.

Abbé Josef Dorensky was an erudite ex-Jesuit who had studied Oriental and Slavic languages and wrote in both Latin and German. He described modestly his studies in philology.

"You are then of the opinion that Latin and German are the best languages for scholarship?"

"Not at all!" The Abbé was startled. "Any language can accommodate any sort of writing whatsoever."

"I disagree. I believe that Italian is ideal for poetry, French for comedy, German for narrative, English for satire and law."

"What about the native language of Bohemia?" the Abbé asked softly.

"I do not know it sufficiently to have an opinion."

"I do. Czech is a rich language, subtle and nuanced, as are all Slavic languages. It is suited to the most sublime poetry, the most cutting satire, or the most profound treatise."

"Well then, why are there no great Czech works of literature?"

"The reason lies in our geographical position and the historic dominance of German and Latin. When a new generation of native writers who love their language is born, the beauties of literature will flourish in Bohemia, too. As it is, there is a wealth of legend and lore."

Casanova insisted. "Yes, but this new literature will not

have a great tradition back of it. In France, Montesquieu could not have existed without Montaigne and there would be no Voltaire without Rabelais. In England, likewise, no Swift without Chaucer, no Pope without Shakespeare. In Italy, no Petrarch without Dante, no Leopardi without Ariosto. And none of these greats would have been possible without Homer and Virgil!"

"All the eminent writers that you mention," the Abbé said, "belong to all of us now. They will be translated into Czech and also read in their original languages by Bohemian writers. The sounds of the younger literary language will add something new and perhaps profound to the classics. Time enriches our understanding of them and remakes them for each generation."

"That may be true, but I would prefer, if it were possible, to hear Homer the way his contemporaries heard him, or to understand Virgil as the readers of his time did. History adds layers of something, it is true, but the work of the translator is to remove these, not to add to them."

"That is quite an impossible task." The Abbé smiled. "And I am a scholar, not a poet. I try to study those added layers and understand them."

"What will happen when all the languages on earth have their own literatures, and translations, and all add new complexities? Will we not then live in a Tower of Babel? The din will be so great, the classics will be all but forgotten, with the exception of some complex translations."

"It is not my habit to look that far into the future, Chevalier—but wouldn't the point when we reached the greatest incomprehension be the very moment when we shed all our prejudices about the inferiority of some languages and the superiority of others?"

"If that is a desirable goal, yes. I see that you have been infected by the values of egalitarianism."

"Far from it. I was only following your reasoning."

"My reasoning is simply that we must not let it come to that."

"That will be impossible," the Abbé said seriously. "In Europe today, all people are reclaiming their languages and their history."

"Then a dreadful age is coming," Casanova said thoughtfully. "When all the small nations of Europe claim their so-called rights, they will necessarily go to war with each other."

"Perhaps. A reasonable solution might be to recognize the genius of each language without making any territorial claims over the areas where those languages are spoken."

Casanova laughed. "Ah, mon cher Dorensky, you are much more an idealist than you are willing to admit. How might one enforce such a reasonable idea when German is spoken in the Bohemian lands as well as in the Austrian lands, when Hungarian is spoken in Austria, and French, English, and Spanish in the New World?"

The Abbé was silent for a long time. "The solution will come from the universal triumph of reason."

"That is my fondest hope, as well. Unfortunately, I know my fellow man too well. He is not reasonable. Have you ever heard of the Society of Masons?"

"Yes, but I am suspicious of their secrecy."

"The masonic societies were established for the purpose of giving reasonable men a neutral terrain where they might present reasonable ideas and share discoveries in the sciences. Many of the members of the society are citizens of nations at war with each other, yet the brotherhood of Reason transcends their differences."

"Are you attempting to recruit me, Chevalier?"

"Indeed," Casanova said impulsively. He had conceived a tremendous respect for the Abbé's far-seeing intelligence.

"I will think about what you have told me."

The two men spent the rest of the afternoon in conversation about language and literature. In the evening, Laura came bearing their suppers and a bottle of Tokay wine. She poked at the fire, and then seated herself on a tower of books, her ankles bared.

"You are very naughty, my dear," Casanova chided. "The Abbé here has no use for women. You may excite his senses and some important philological insights will be lost to the world."

Dorensky blushed.

"In that case," Laura said, pulling her skirt even higher, "the world will be the poorer for it, but the Abbé might be led to greater insights by his feeling of guilt."

"There is your solution to war!" Casanova exclaimed. "Guilt that leads to greater virtue."

"There is more confusion in the relations of the sexes than in your future Babel, Chevalier," the Abbé responded, trying not to look at Laura's ankles.

"I infinitely prefer the confusion of intimacy to that of public sentiment. My dear maid's ankles do not confuse me at all. Neither do her nipples. Or her temple of Venus, to be perfectly honest. I experience desire and the need to worship when I behold them, but that is salutary to my poor circulation and stimulating to my mind."

Laura revealed a few inches more.

"We draw our inspiration from different sources."

Casanova laughed. "You must admit that you find the sight of Laura Brock's beautiful legs inspiring! I can see that in your effort to avoid them."

Somewhat freed by his third glass of Tokay, Dorensky laughed thinly. "You are forcing me to admit it."

"I propose an experiment in inspiration," Casanova said. "Let us pretend that we are painters, though we know that we are both wordsmiths. Let us gaze on our Laura and compose a poem inspired by her charms. Or an essay, Abbé, if you prefer."

"As you wish."

Casanova instructed Laura to light more candles. He swept the books from the divan and prepared ink and paper. He made two writing tables from stacks of books, and bade the Abbé to sit by him, at the foot of the rose chair. He then asked Laura to pose for them as the model for Venus posed for Botticelli. Laura took her time undoing her clasps and untying her stays, revealing herself with excruciating slowness. When at last she was as naked as Venus, one could have illuminated the room solely with the roseate blush of the Abbé's cheeks and forehead. The two men bent in silence over their sheets of paper, raising their eyes now and then to observe their subject. Warm silence fell in the room, broken only by the audible beating of the young scholar's heart and his involuntary sighs.

After an hour, Casanova rose from his chair and deposited his poem at Laura's feet. She bent to pick it up, her breasts swaying as she did so. The Abbé looked as if he had been turned to stone.

"May I get dressed now, or do you require more time?"

She winked at Casanova. "Perhaps I should read the Chevalier's poem now."

Without waiting for Dorensky to answer, she read:

In every work of genius hides an idea
For others to enjoy and imitate
When Venus gave herself to Botticelli
He merely painted words that said
Now you paint Venus, future genius
Be sure to add a coda for the next
Thus art will always be renewed
Though Venus is eternally at rest.

Both Laura and Casanova applauded. Slowly, as if moved by a mechanical force, the Abbé rose from the carpet and lay his sheet at Laura's feet. Written on it was a single word.

"Beauty."

⁗On Christmas, one year after Laura had walked into the library with ham and melon, Casanova gave her a present. It was a gold box with an engraved Pierrot on its lid. At the bottom of it was a mirror that lifted when the box was closed and opened again. Under the mirror was a miniature painting depicting two naked girls frolicking with a satyr who lay on his back. One of the girls was engulfing the head of the satyr's manhood in her mouth while the other held the root of it for her and kissed him on the lips. The girls' luxuriant tresses mingled on the satyr's chest. The painter had delighted in depicting the girls slightly open and inflamed as if they had just been penetrated. There were even small milky beads on their thighs, suggesting the aftermath of a successful coupling.

Laura was moved beyond words, particularly since she knew that Casanova only had very few jewels left, having sold most of them in order to buy paper, ink, and medicines. She spent long hours gazing into the mirror inside the box, pleased at her reflection, her hair more lustrous than it was in reality, her lips redder and fuller, her green eyes deeper and bigger, the bridge of her nose more elegantly drawn. The slightly tarnished mirror was a flatterer, but so subtle in its wavering that she could not tell where reality and flattery parted company. She gazed into it until she felt herself swell with the strength of her own beauty, and then she lifted the mirror and dreamt herself into the scene, becoming now one, now the other girl, savoring the satiny head of the satyr's tumescence with its taste of both girls' effluvia. At such times, sometimes with Casanova in attendance, watching her, she was possessed of a mad desire to feel his milk inside her, but he still refused to surrender himself. He mirrored her instead in his eyes, which only increased her desire. From the small mirror in the box to the mirror in his eyes there was a whole world of her, multiplied and reflected hundreds of times, as if the very air through which her gaze traveled from one mirror to another had been filled with invisible beings holding mirrors.

Mirrors, Casanova told her, were another secret of Venice. Look at any Venetian woman, holding herself haughtily as she sweeps past admirers an evening on the Zattere, and you see her reflection, not her true self, which stays hidden until a lover will coax it out. Women parade only their reflections in public, taking out with them images carefully composed in their mirrors. Only when the theaters are open and one can go out masked do Venetian women shed their reflections and hide instead within a costume. The costume is a mirror as well, but it is made of cloth and thread, so that it can be physically removed, an indulgence and licence possible only during the Carnival season. The rest of the year, the invisible masks women wear can be removed only by the most skillful. He, Casanova, had been one of the most skilled. Ah, tempus fugit.

After he told her this, a profound melancholy rose from him like a bank of fog over the Church of the Redentore, and Laura could only look and sigh and witness the sight like a tourist viewing a postcard.

"I thought," Laura said, "that women could never go out alone in Venice."

"To promenade, yes, a lady is always accompanied by her husband or *cicerone*, but such an attendant is only a mirror.

Women go to church alone, though, and it is there that veils partly lift, looks are exchanged, letters passed. There is such beauty in these transactions in the proximity of danger. Women are under the constant watch of parents, husbands, busybodies, but they know how to fool them under the cover of symmetries carved into stone, iron, lace, and glass by artisans who understand the magical theater of mirrors that is Venice."

The beauty of Venice's adornments, Casanova told her, is in the way they allow for the play of elements, of wind, sunset, lightning, and, of course, love, the great elemental thief that animates stone and paint. The masked satyr, on his knees before beauty, steals what he can, while husbands and parents see nothing.

Casanova made her see the many windows looking out into Calle della Commedia, near the church of San Samuele where he had been baptized. She saw the theaters, and his mother Zanetta's witty company, lovers of art and life, a world that had been privy to sciences of seduction and joy all but forgotten now. There was no shortage of brilliant men then, even men of the church whose habits by no means prevented them from enjoying the amorous dolcezze of Venice. God favored love in Venice and made sure that His churches praised life and that His painters gloried in the body. A few overzealous and dour senators, who were doubtlessly impotent, tried to stop the brilliance of that fusion of amor dei and amor personae, but, for the most part, failed miserably. Tiepolo painted with light, Vivaldi made the palazzos vibrate, and Zanetta held everyone's heart in her hands. The convents were full of well-bred, amorous girls who had adventures that seem quite impossible today.

There was, for instance, his great love, MM.

"As in the Roman 'two thousand'?" Laura asked with feigned naïveté.

"Well, yes, and my other great love of the time, another nun, CC."

"And that would make 'two thousand two hundred'? Is that a year?"

"Yes, mademoiselle Brock, that is the year when Casanova's books will be finally read and understood."

"That is a long time from now . . ."

"Time, trompe l'oeil," laughed the Chevalier.

He had met MM, the nun, within the walls of a convent on the island of Murano. She was the friend of his fiancée, CC, whose family had sent her to the convent to put an end to her relationship with Casanova.

"Tell me her real name," insisted Laura.

"Very well. Caterina Capozzi."

MM had seduced the younger girl (convents were no guarantee of chastity) and had found out from her all about the endowments and ardor of young Casanova. She burned for him and arranged for a secret rendezvous. Disguised, always disguised, MM sneaked out of the convent and they consummated their love. On one occasion, MM invited the French consul to Venice, the Duc de Bernis, to join them in a night of love. Finally, Caterina joined them as well, giving rise to an intricate pas de deux, de trois, and de quatre, that exhausted all the possibilities of such arrangements. Amazingly, the women always returned to their convent in the morning and were never late for their prayers.

"Convents are the greatest fields of passion in Venice. Concentrated there is the perfume of a thousand flowers that keep themselves open by trifling at night and praying ardently by day. At one time, the turbulent waters of religious and erotic fervor mingled so swiftly there, no one could tell them apart. I don't imagine God wanted to. A few priests, maybe."

Laura permitted herself to be skeptical. "The details of such liaisons would have made more than a few saints blush, I am sure. Certainly, Saint Ursula and her eleven thousand virgins would have dreamt of no such thing."

"There is nothing," Casanova said emphatically, "like the hand of a virgin taking firm hold of her lover's membrum from within the grille which separates them at visiting hours in the convent. While the older nun, the chaperone, looks away or perhaps touches herself. If Ursula's virgins had had this experience, they might have lived instead of dying."

"Nothing," laughed Laura, "only being touched, perhaps, by a shameless scoundrel through a grille and then begging God's forgiveness for a thousand years."

"Ah, those nuns of my youth begged only for more!"

How far from the strict village of Laura's birth where finery was frowned upon and religion was a matter of grim commitment! Her mother's sister had taken vows and her family had been allowed but three visits in ten years. Laura had been shocked to see her aunt in the convent, encased like a dried fruit behind the empty glass of her eyes. In her childhood she had known her as a woman who laughed easily, who scattered a kind of light confusion about her. In the convent, she had felt afraid of her aunt; her mother cried during the entire journey back to the village.

Casanova never tired of talking about his native city, even though she (for Venice is certainly a woman) had banished him three times. He told her how Venice, splendidly costumed in her jewels of gold and blue, floats above her canals like a mirror that reflects only herself. To speak her language, citizens must speak the language of mirrors. They fasten mirrors to their windows to see who glides by in gondolas or walks in the streets below. There are mirrors where two canals meet so that gondolas will not collide. In the privacy of their rooms, Venetians are always constructing or readjusting mirrored mechanisms to gaze at oth-

ers through their skillfully cracked shutters. The shutters themselves, which mirror each other on the intimate stages of the
narrow streets, are constantly adjusted to let in just enough of a
stranger's gaze to inflame the imagination. The secret of knowing just how much light one must let fall into a room or on a part
of one's body is as intricate and complex as the lacemaker's or
the glassblower's art.

"I was born in a city of secrets, of which the greatest secret
is the manipulation of one's mirrored reflection. Certain
epochs, when the light is just right, are gloriously Venetian. At
other times, the darkness falls." His silence again suggested
the meanness of the end of their century and his deep sadness
at the beginning of another, which he saw unfolding in unending stridency, bad manners, and vulgarity. Subtlety, the layered
work of centuries, was no longer in favor. This would surely
pass, if only he might live long enough.

Listening to one of these silences, Laura wished that she
could somehow prolong the Chevalier de Seingalt's life, now
nearing its end. She surprised herself by expressing just such a
sentiment.

"You are a man of science who knows subtle chemical
operations. Are you not skillful enough to prolong your life? Is
time not a substance to be manipulated?"

His answer was unexpected. "Certainly. The only difficulty
is finding a reason for living."

"Well, that's easy. So that you might see another age of subtle pleasures, when light falls on your mirrors just right."

Casanova laughed like a child and kissed her. He seemed
to become suddenly young, like one who had, in an instant,
turned back the clock. The moment lasted, it seemed to her, an
eternity, during which many years, decades, and centuries
flashed past like faces before a mirror. She was certain that this
was no fleeting impression, that time was indeed moving in

every direction, and that forever, eternity, existed in the dusk of the library at Dux even as the setting sun illuminated the last of the high bookshelves.

ᵉᔪ Laura was not at ease with the mirrored world described by Casanova. In truth, the city of mirrors repelled her. She imagined a place where everyone spied on everyone else, where eyes looked on at one's most intimate moments, where privacy was impossible. She knew how hard it was to wrest an unobserved moment, to spend even an hour without being seen, to spend time in the company of her unguarded self. She shared an attic dormitory with fifteen girls from all corners of the Austrian country, mostly simple peasants who were perpetually astonished at their good luck of having escaped miserable village lives. They devotedly washed linen and polished doorknobs, gossiped with undisguised awe about their masters, and did all their business in company, without shame or self-consciousness. They peed and washed in each others' presence, giggled inanely at the slightest sexual reference, and coupled indiscriminately on their day off with grooms and stable boys. On Sundays they went to church and prayed for a husband. Their lives seemed uncomplicated and transparent. In fact, many of them were not, and Laura heard them sobbing in the night for some childhood sweetheart or an abandoned child or another of the many misfortunes that befell women in that day and age.

For all that, Laura lived somehow apart from them, and the other girls regarded her with suspicion. Since she had become Casanova's maid, lover, and ally, they had surrounded her with a watchful silence within which no gesture went unobserved and unremarked. She would have liked to find a corner of her own—the castle was more than half uninhabited and abandoned—but her entreaties to the majordomo had so far been unsuccessful. When she imagined the city of mirrors, Laura saw that, for all her beauties, this was a place even less private than her dormitory. In such a place, one could not even hide one's thoughts, because watching had become so refined it penetrated even there. Among the simple girls at Dux, there was at least some protection because of their stupidity. In Venice, Casanova had told her, hiding from others was a game, the object of which was never to allow anyone to see or hear more than what one wanted to make public. Laura tired just thinking about the effort that must have gone into playing such a game. There could have been no life outside this game, one's whole life must have been dedicated to it. When she expressed this apprehension to Casanova, he was astonished. It had never occurred to him that there might be a reason to shun the game.

"Does one not live in society?" he exclaimed. "Unless you are a monk or a criminal, why would you want to escape the geometry of social life? Pleasure comes from managing shame, from striking just the right balance between exposure and privacy. What else might you do?"

"Read a book in peace," she said.

"Does it matter if you are seen reading?"

"Yes. People will see what you are reading and judge you for it."

"Then you can hide, allowing only those who'd admire you for it, to see what you are reading."

"Yes, but why should you have such concerns at all?"

She came close to being some sort of republican here, and Casanova regarded her thoughtfully. In order to gain happiness for himself, it was necessary to have access to good society, a society he might shock and amuse, and by whose graces he might grow famous and, hopefully, rich. He loved, equally, the company of actors, musicians, dancers, and men of letters, but they existed only by the grace of aristocrats. That had been his life. To think, as this young woman seemed to, that privacy was somehow superior to conquest, was a folly he had rarely entertained. There had been times in his life when, disgusted by his own excesses, he dreamed of a monastic life, a life entirely devoted to study, free of the inevitable disappointments of society. Even in those visions of alternative selves he had, however, seen himself from the outside, from the position of an admiring company which respected his choice and sought him out for his wisdom. At least, this was his polemical stand. He knew now that he was engaged in work of a different kind. While still beholden to the society he had sought in vain to join, he did not write for them now. Nor was he writing entirely for himself. Or for Laura. His project was one of uncovering, or discovering, a society where music and love were the highest principles. The Micromegs were creative and happy. They invented machines that filled their movements with grace. Such discoveries were going to be useful to the people of the future. But what if the chronicle of his utopia revealed only the frivolity of a man desperate for the approval of others?

Laura did not know that she had brought the librarian to a point of a crisis. Her interest in his stories was childlike and without suspicion. She loved the Micromegs and couldn't get enough of them, just as she loved his shameless reminiscences. He had lived a life of adventure that he was capable of sharing with charm. She was no moralist. In speaking of her own need for unguarded liberty, she was only protesting her condition, the dormitory, the stupid girls, the constant interruptions. Nonetheless, she had touched a nerve and she tried to undo the damage in the only way that might appeal to Casanova.

"There is a new girl," she said. "She is fourteen years old and I find her quite beautiful. She comes from a good family—impoverished aristocrats, it seems. She arrived at the castle last week and so far she has only spoken to me. The other girls don't like her because she sometimes wakes up screaming from her dreams, which are very unusual. I think that her family has sent her into service as punishment for some offense, some shame. I know that she can read. I think she'd enjoy your stories."

Casanova's gloom lifted visibly. "Yes, yes, you must bring the child here."

Laura complained to Majordomo Feldkirshner that her work for the Chevalier, which involved greater responsibilities all the time—she left them unspecified—required more help.

Next morning, the librarian was delighted to see a slight, blond girl with merely two rosebuds where one day, hopefully, some womanly endowments might appear, come into his chamber with the coffee tray, followed by Laura giving her instruction on precisely how the Chevalier liked his table set and his bed made. She had sapphire blue eyes that sparkled with a far-off light whose source must have been in the stars. Casanova sat on a chair, pretending to read Goethe's disturbing bestseller *The Sorrows of Young Werther,* and watched the bustling of the two women with delight. The girl, whose name was Libussa Moldau, bent over his sheets, without looking at him. Her skinny legs were bare. Her small behind, looking as if he could cup it in one hand, looked serious but not innocent. A stirring in his robe was most deliciously promising and was noted, as if telepathically, by Laura, who gave him a sly look and let her hand brush, as if accidentally, Libussa's serious and not so innocent buttocks.

In the evening, the women reappeared, dressed, it seemed to Casanova, with some care, though in reality they wore the same aprons and skirts they had in the morning. Laura was radiant, explaining to her shy new friend that the Chevalier's stories were hugely entertaining, even though they could be quite indecent. "When this happens," Laura told Libussa, "you can cover your ears and I will let you know when to uncover them again. You are among friends here, though, so do not feel intimidated and do not hide your pleasure. I, for instance, have sometimes been so transported by these tales, I have closed my eyes and touched myself to relieve the pressure."

Libussa laughed nervously.

"Don't tell me," Laura exclaimed in mock horror, "that you have never pleasured yourself?"

Seeing the girl suffused by pink-tinged embarrassment, Casanova laughed, too. "I have seen many beautiful things in my long life, but I have never seen anything prettier than a girl in the flower of her youth dreaming of love and abandoning herself to her hand and her imagination. You must know also that being watched by another while in the transport of such imaginings, increases your pleasure tenfold."

Thus warned and eruditely lectured, Libussa settled on a couch in Laura's arms, closed her eyes, and prepared to listen to Casanova's tale of the evening. Casanova did not begin right away. He wanted to discuss young Werther, who had given him a genuine nightmare during his afternoon nap. He had read Goethe's tale of desperate love three times, he explained to his small audience, but still failed to comprehend its popularity. He could understand the public's fascination with young Werther's pain as he was dying of love, but he questioned both the necessity and the veracity of that pain. He also felt just a bit responsible, but didn't know why. It was said that young men were committing suicide all over Europe, despondent after reading this book. It occurred to Casanova that love itself may have undergone a momentous shift, the intensity of it having increased somehow in these times. They were times of great human emotions, entire societies were being unsettled, dark forces were on the loose. Perhaps love, the most powerful of all emotions, was being affected most forcefully.

Laura hadn't read the book. She listened carefully, but with some impatience, to her mentor's synopsis, and did not agree with his conclusions.

"From what little I've read," she said, "there have always been tragic loves. Why would it be any different now? Because of a book?"

"Perhaps," agreed Casanova, "more people can read now. Such a book might exacerbate what are, after all, the eternal sufferings of unrequited love. But I feel that there is something else. The language sounds more like the perorations of a French rabble-rouser than the private language of a broken heart. Werther is in love with death, more than he is with Lotte."

That was it, of course. The novelty of Goethe's book was that the object of Werther's love was only a pretext, an obstacle perhaps, between him and his true love, Death. It was a profoundly antiwoman book. Casanova, who was fascinated by women for themselves, and who had often thought that three-fourths of his pleasure in love had been the pleasure of his women, found this new attitude disturbing. Such feelings must have been among the consequences of unleashed idealism.

"Your Goethe," he told Laura, "does not love women. He loves death."

"My Goethe? He is no more mine than he is yours. I haven't even read him."

"Well, he writes, quite beautifully I admit, in your language."

"I have read some of his love poetry. It is very beautiful and not very different, if you permit me, dear Chevalier, from those sweet flatteries that you whisper to your hoped-for conquests in your own stories."

"Well, that's it," cried the Chevalier, "I whisper such things knowing that they are exaggerated and hoping that the natural wisdom of women knows them for what they are. A path to bed by way of their ears. Women like sweets, flowers, and jewels. They are wise that way."

"Some of them, perhaps. Others kill themselves because they believe you."

"No," the Chevalier countered vehemently, "my words do not kill them. Their upbringing kills them. And the strictures of the church. And fear of their own power of love. Bad experiences in the past. No one can blame my words."

"Yes," insisted Laura, "but suppose someone took your lyrical fancies seriously, at absolute face value, and understood them as gravely as a sworn oath. What then?"

"The only person who might do this would be a dull-witted reader! This Goethe has no sense of humor. He writes for a dull-witted reader. He has taken the irony and humor out of chivalrous language, he has rendered deadly and melodramatic what was inflected and subtle!"

Perhaps, he thought to himself, there was a Germanic element of startling novelty afoot in the world. Something grave and humorless that corresponded to the radical seriousness of angry peasants and barely literate bourgeois. In that case, his own writing would be surely misread by readers weaned on the sorrows of young Werther. Casanova closed his eyes and had a vision of generations of solemn-faced, grave young men, marching grimly to their deaths, past rows and rows of beseeching women begging them not to go. The women were invisible to them. Pulled by a thread of heroic and desperate exaggeration that they mistook for truth, the men marched blindly on. The future. He shuddered.

"In any case," Laura said, "haven't you ever wanted to die because of unhappy love?"

115

"Yes," Casanova admitted, "but it was a sickness only brought about by unrealized love. I was made a fool, then I made a fool of myself, and I wanted to punish myself with death for what I had done. I became my own judge and condemned myself to death for behavior unbecoming a gentleman. Love was only the pretext. I nearly murdered my so-called love first."

Meanwhile, Libussa, bored by this conversation in French, which she didn't understand, had climbed a small library ladder and was awkwardly holding the large album of Persian erotic prints. They fascinated her. She had never known there were so many ways to couple.

Casanova motioned to her to come down. "Sit, child," he said in German, "and I will tell you a story."

Libussa came down from the ladder, settled back next to Laura on the couch, and closed her eyes to listen. Unfortunately, the story the librarian told was in French.

Libussa fell fast asleep, her head on Laura's lap. She gently pulled up the girl's skirt to reveal her beautiful legs to Casanova, who was pleased with the view, and urged him silently to continue.

He told that night the story of Leonilda, whom he had almost married, and marveled at how closely the sleeping Libussa resembled her. Leonilda's mother, Donna Lucrezia, had been one of the first great loves of his life, but when years later he encountered Leonilda, he had not known that she was his daughter. When Donna Lucrezia came to meet her daughter's fiancé, she was astonished to see Casanova. It was immediately agreed that the marriage could not take place—instead, Donna Lucrezia and Casanova made love at the request of their daughter, who desired to see how she had been conceived. Casanova asked only that his daughter disrobe in order that he might witness the beauty their long-ago love had created. The naked girl lay in bed with her parents to observe the mystery of her own conception. Casanova made magnificent love to the mother, but when the time came for them to achieve bliss, Casanova withdrew in fear of repeating the accident that had created his daughter sixteen years before. Delicately, the virgin Leonilda caught her father's effluvium in her handkerchief, while at the same time helping her mother achieve happiness. Years later, he encountered them again under extraordinary circumstances, not the least of which was that his daughter's powerful but old husband asked Casanova to father them a child.

This was quite the filthiest tale Laura had ever heard, and Libussa awoke to find her friend pleasuring herself vigorously. The girl looked dazed, but she quickly understood what was taking place. She looked shyly at the Chevalier, as if asking for permission. He nodded his encouragement, and the observant girl began to imitate the movements of her friend. It was soon clear that under the shy exterior of Libussa Moldau lay an unbridled colt. She quickly tore off Laura's garments as well as her own, and flattened herself on top of her friend, biting her lips and her neck. Laura laughed and defended herself as well as she could but Libussa, who was like a wolf from a Bohemian fairy tale, wrestled her to the Oriental carpet. Casanova felt that he was watching a speeded-up version of his past love games, and was not surprised that when he blinked, he missed a full change during which Libussa had revolved like a clock hand, burying her head between Laura's legs. She barely had time to give the Chevalier a sidelong glance before, overtaken by pleasure and geometry, she buried her own head between the girl's skinny legs. Libussa quivered like an arrow and shimmered like mercury. It was like watching trout in a stream. The girl's obvious talent and appetite delighted the old libertine, who let his robe fall to the floor and stood over the women creakily, his shadow falling over them like that of a tower over a square at high noon, or of the past over the present. He felt keenly the passing of time. I am an old clock, still keeping time. When they lift their eyes from their timeless tryst, they will study me for time, to see if any has passed and whether they have played too long. And this is just what happened. First, Laura looked up at him to see if the time had come for him to participate in their game, then Libussa looked up from her bliss with a kind of absent and hungry astonishment.

Casanova was content simply to keep time for them. He wanted neither to participate nor to express himself in any way, though he couldn't help noticing, as did the women, that his long-dormant love instrument had risen youthfully and was pointing at them like a grandfather's stern finger. When Laura reached up and took hold of him, he let her lead it to Libussa's lips, whose mouth opened hungrily for it. He did not reach satisfaction, nor did he accede to the women's invitation to enter them. Nonetheless, it was a most satisfactory experience and he was filled with creative restlessness and a sudden desire to study chemistry and write verse.

ᥱᏚOn certain days, Casanova called one or both girls and asked them to masturbate while he wrote. Sometimes he addressed Laura in a beautiful, nearly extinct chivalrous language that set every part of her skin to vibrating. Now and then, after inhaling one of his mixtures, the old man opened his Chinese robe—he had seven of them—and proudly showed her his half-aroused manhood that was, at those times, a source of pride to him. Laura admired its heft and its length, imagining it at full mast. Gelder's was short, fat, and ungainly. Casanova's was elegant like a swan's neck. She knew that even

such half-arousal was an occasion for celebration since it happened but rarely. She did her utmost to make him happy, but
this did not happen. She engulfed him in her mouth and tried
to guide him inside her. He allowed her to taste him for a few
moments, but he always wilted before her gate. When this happened, he stroked her hair and promised her that he would surrender himself to her before long. Laura did not mind. She
knew that her role was to encourage his stories, to provide his
memories with the living flame of her interest, and to model for
whatever sweet love of his past happened to parade before his
mind's eye. She had become a model for the memoirs of the
most interesting man she had ever met. Laura did what she
could to help and she was happy that her young friend Libussa
had found their company congenial.

       In the months that followed, Casanova was
brought many times to the brink of completion, but this did not
matter very much to him. The benefits of energy and renewed
appetite for work more than made up for that elusive pleasure.
He started taking walks on the castle grounds and struck a
friendship with the German gardener, whose designs reminded
him of the garden at Frascati near Rome where he had loved
Donna Lucrezia. He told the gardener about the splendid topiary beds that had been scattered through that magnificent garden, so placed that lovers might enjoy themselves without fear
of being seen. He found a book of topiary art in the library and
translated it from the Latin into French, a language the gardener
understood a little. Casanova had almost convinced the skeptical old German to begin training such furniture, but when the

majordomo found out, he prevailed on Waldstein to cancel the project. Casanova wrote to Waldstein in protest, but received no answer. This plunged him into gloom and, for a time, nothing his women did could dispel it.

Also, he had arrived at the end of the *Icosameron* and he had the feeling that paradise itself, not just his book about it, had closed its gates behind him. Instead of considering means to publish his book, he indulged instead in his bitterest memories. He remembered all the times when he had been destitute and friendless. Such times, quite numerous after all, made him reflect on his foolishness and his character and cause an unending stream of *if*s. If only he had done this and not that. There were only two ifs, as he well knew. If he hadn't followed the teachings of the Stoics, he might have made plans for his life instead of letting every wind blow him hither and thither. And the biggest if of all, of course. If he hadn't been who he was, Giacomo Casanova, lover of women and pretender to class and wealth, none of it would have turned out as it had.

When he was in one of these moods, Laura or, quite often, Libussa, would slip in quietly with his supper, and observing his grave countenance, slip out again, but not before depositing a kiss as light as a butterfly on his cheek.

W hat did not help matters at all was that Gelder had gone crazy. Jealousy was doubtless the catalyst for the insane vendetta he decided to carry on against the librarian, jealousy compounded by the fact that under the Chevalier's influence, Laura became magnificently aroused and that he, Gelder, was the unwitting beneficiary of her ardor.

But something else was at work as well. Laura came to understand that it was a clash, not simply between two men, but between two worlds, and that she was the bridge between them, a bridge that should not have existed in any reasonable scheme of things. The two worlds in question were breaking violently away from one another. Everything was changing. The elaborate dress of the aristocrats was giving way to more practical clothing. The will of merchants ruled the cities and the palaces without apology. Simple and rude speech had replaced the flowery expressions of the courts. The desire for liberty spread to all classes of people everywhere.

At Dux, Count Waldstein could be counted on to uphold the old values, but the servants, Hans Gelder foremost among them, were another matter. Gelder was a radical, a revolutionary, a foulmouthed drunk, a fierce hater of privilege, an ignoramus who despised finery and fancy learning, a superstitious peasant who liked to think that he wasn't, and a very bad cook besides. Not to speak of his amorous skills, which were somewhere below Waldstein's greyhounds, which Laura liked to watch couple. Nonetheless, he had become indispensible to the Count because, bad cooking nothwithstanding, he was the unofficial overseer of this country seat, more reliable than the titular overseer, the overwrought Majordomo Feldkirshner, who spent his nights buggering his adjutant Wiederholt, and his days drinking and railing against the church.

Gelder had "the common touch," as Waldstein had once apologetically written to Casanova, and was his "ears and eyes among those who would hate us simply for being better born." The truth was a different matter. Laura had witnessed Gelder in his milieu, mocking his master and making foolish speeches filled with ridiculous misquotations from the likes of Rousseau and Fourier, speeches which so impressed Feldkirshner that he wrote them down, whether out of prudence or admiration, it was hard to tell. Laura was quite astonished by the completely different uses to which Casanova and Gelder put Rousseau. Casanova, who had known the French philosopher, discussed him, despite his distaste, with intellectual rigor and knowledge of the work. Gelder, who was only aping quotations he had read in the badly printed radical journals from Vienna, thought that Rousseau was expressing his own (Gelder's) thoughts. How Rousseau could have known what Gelder was thinking was a source of great astonishment among the cook's friends.

Naturally, Gelder and Feldkirshner hated Casanova, who never misquoted anybody. But the injury the cook suffered when he realized that Laura Brock had betrayed him drove him into a rage. His spies reported everything the couple did in the rooms of the library. The addition of Libussa to their orgies exacerbated feelings among the Bohemian staff, who did not like to see another of their own corrupted. Their doings became the talk of the castle, and Gelder's self-regard suffered accordingly. Bit by bit he carried out a petty course of revenge. He spat on Casanova's food, he carved wormy slices of meat, he wiped his dishes with dirty rags, and let no occasion pass without showing his contempt. Laura stopped sleeping with him and protested strenuously whenever she discovered his vile tricks. She stole what food she could, but this was difficult because she had no allies among the staff. The time she spent with Casanova absorbed all her energies so that she had little effort to spare on her fellow servants, who all sided with Gelder. She now encountered shaded looks and expressions of disgust everywhere she turned. Her bed in the maids' quarters was often strewn with dirt, and her own dishes soiled by invisible hands. She bore these indignities without complaint, but was outraged on behalf of Casanova, who was now writing without surcease, barely stopping to eat. She feared that he would waste away.

Now and then, the Chevalier de Seingalt noticed the shabby treatment and flew into magnificent rages on the order of natural phenomena, veritable lightning storms. One evening, holding a piece of rotten meat at the end of his fork, he roamed the halls of the castle looking for Gelder, whom he promised to impale on the end of his sword just like the rotten meat. Laura trailed after him, half-amused, pleading with him to stop. Casanova was wearing only his Chinese robe, which had fallen open, and he wore no sword. When he reached the kitchen, he found Gelder surrounded by staff like the chieftain of a small, humorless tribe. The Chevalier flung the meat from the end of his fork directly at Gelder's stout figure, but it missed and fell at his feet instead.

"You mock me, Gelder, but I will have your soul!" Casanova patted his white belly. "I have eaten people better than you for smaller offenses! I am going to place a mandrake root behind your eyes!" With these words, Casanova gathered his robe and turned his back to the cook, who had begun a pompous harangue, the gist of which was that "the times had changed" and that "no one was allowed to speak to the people in such language" because "the day of the flaming sword of Damocles had come into the square of the Rosicrucians," or some such drivel, to which his attendants nodded in complete agreement.

Casanova wrote letters to Waldstein in Prague, fulminating about the cook. On the rare occasions that the Count came to visit, he upbraided Gelder and the others, but his heart wasn't in it. In the end, he fired Feldkirshner, who complained far and wide that he had been the victim of a "Francmasonic plot." But the persecution did not stop. The new overseer, Langerhoff, was quickly intimidated by Gelder. Additionally, he even looked like Feldkirshner, down to his excessively polished hunting boots. His sidekick Blauner was a replica of Wiederholt. Casanova had no doubt that Langerhoff buggered Blauner just like Feldkirshner buggered Wiederholt. Perhaps this was in the nature of the profession, but the resemblance was uncanny. One time, after Waldstein lectured the servants on Casanova's behalf, Gelder went so far as to suggest that the complaints originated entirely in the librarian's imagination. Casanova was not present and Laura had thought about speaking up, but she did not dare. She was in enough hot water already.

"I am having my revenge," Casanova told Laura one evening. "I am using the person of Gelder as a pig in the stable of the Micromeg king. Gelder will be forgotten, but my pig will delight people for centuries."

Even literature-loving Laura felt this to be a feeble response. Nonetheless, she believed him and felt disconsolate. "The pig will be remembered, but who will remember me?"

The old courtier was ashamed. "I will make you Queen of the Micromegs. Astute readers will see you in filigree in each story like a fine pattern in the embroidery."

Laura was wrong to believe that Casanova would confine the matter of his slighted honor solely to literature. After a particularly foul supper, the Chevalier gave the actual Gelder some thought. Suspecting that the cook was a superstitious fool, Casanova asked Laura to smuggle a small black doll into the pantry. She concealed the object in a sack of flour. When the cook set to the making of bread, he stuck his arm in the sack and was pierced by the doll's headdress of needles. When he pulled it out he let out a scream. The hardened wax face looked like his own. In addition to the needle headdress, a small arrow pierced one cheek and exited from the left eye. The breadmaking assistant, a peasant woman from a particularly haunted Carpathian peak, fell to her knees and started praying at the top of her voice. Gelder raised a fuss but no one could tell him where the strange doll came from. Next evening a playing card depicting a hanged man turned up on Gelder's pillow. This time, the maid who found it had a hysterical seizure and ran up and down the castle corridors shouting that the cook was cursed and that in a week's time he would be food for worms.

Some of the women went to see the priest to ask for some kind of exorcism, a procedure that Gelder, despite the icy terror that gripped his heart, rejected indignantly. Gelder knew very well where the objects originated, but he couldn't prove it. Casanova had been observed conducting chemical experiments and had been denounced to the priest before, but after a long conversation, the matter was closed. The priest declared that Casanova was a man of science. That didn't explain, of course, the presence in his rooms of the naked or nearly naked Laura Brock, and the addition of a young Bohemian girl in the same state, but this was more a matter to be winked at than condemned. The objects ceased appearing, but Gelder began to suffer from headaches brought about by a persistent voice in his head. The voice spoke French at a very high pitch and was alternately angry or mocking. Gelder spoke no French whatsoever. The presence of a foreigner in his head was quite unbearable. After a week of this torment that no one could either cure or comprehend, Gelder swallowed his pride and went to see Casanova.

"Dottore," he said, "I have come to you about my condition."

"Your condition, my dear man, is curable. You, on the other hand, are the symptom of a disease for which there is no cure."

Gelder was offended but gritted his teeth. "What disease might that be?"

"Modernity," Casanova answered simply.

They came to an agreement. Casanova would gradually cure the cook in exchange for decent fare and the occasional use of the kitchen where he, Casanova, might prepare his beloved Italian dishes, including the famous macaroni that aided his escape from the dreaded Venetian prison, the Leads. He would also, generously and without recompense, teach the cook how to make these dishes, thus bringing some civilized pleasure to the barbarically glum castle. Gelder then had to sit through a long and insulting critique of Bohemian cuisine, which consisted, according to the librarian, of nothing but boiled hunks of some of the worst parts of animals hunted in the Bohemian woods, drowned in a green, vinegary sauce, relieved by nothing except some indigestible lumps of dough that did not deserve the name "dumplings," though everybody insisted on calling them so. Casanova did admit that Bohemian beer was drinkable, but its bitter dark taste was absolutely necessary for relieving the palate from the assaults of the drowned meats. Gelder would have liked to take the frail neck of the Venetian between his hammy hands and choke the life out of this denigrator of his nation, but the French voice in his head kept up a patter that sounded no less critical than the Italian's. So, once more, he gritted his teeth and waited.

As it turned out, he had a long wait, because Casanova, finished with the critique, now turned lyrical and began to praise in language that sounded suspiciously like verse the virtues of the varied cuisines of Italy. He said that buttery golden macaroni captured the sun. At the other end of the spectrum (he actually used this word, making Gelder's blood boil), cuttlefish cooked in its own black ink in the Veneto captured the night. In between, there were stellar dishes such as ziti sprinkled with Parmesan, noontime zuppe de verdura, Tuscan cheeses filled with afternoon, fruits for every hour of the day that constituted a sort of paradisical clock, and sweets that corresponded to every emotion, from the sighs of a young girl in love as embodied in lemon ice cream, to the rich pleasures of a courtesan in the last glow of her youth, fully present in amaretto chocolate and peach liqueur.

The only cogent thought that Gelder could formulate between these baroque lucubrations and the Frenchman's ceaseless exposition inside his head, was that justice would eventually see to the guillotining of the Pope along with every papish Italian. Finally Casanova, satisfied with his comparative polemic, promised Gelder that he would see to it that the voice in his head would switch from French to German. This would, at least, give Gelder the satisfaction of understanding what was being said, though he may not like what he heard. In a fortnight, the German voice would soften. Eventually, it would become only a murmur, until one day, when Casanova was satisfied with the state of the cuisine at Dux, it would cease entirely.

Mumbling something that sounded like gratitude, Gelder took his leave. When the sound of his footsteps vanished in the corridor, Laura, who had witnessed this and had had a very hard time controlling herself, burst out laughing. Casanova joined her in hilarity and the two of them laughed until everything hurt and they had to stop before dying.

In the spring, Waldstein's uncle, the Prince de Ligne, came to Dux. The Prince brought him a present, a little fox terrier he named Melampyge, to replace his beloved Cybelle. Casanova and Melampyge loved each other at first sight. When Casanova wrote, Melampyge sat on his lap and looked up to him with a serious gaze that was part adoration, part thoughtfulness. The Chevalier was convinced that Melampyge shared his thoughts.

The Prince and the librarian passed many hours in conversation, discussing and debating ideas and amusing each other with salacious anecdotes. De Ligne, a dedicated libertine, was a resolute pursuer of young boys. His visit was marked by initial disappointment; the Prince's mission to find Henriette had failed. He described to Casanova the difficulties of traveling through France. Every province had set up watches for fleeing aristocrats and every coachman was a spy. He had reached Aix-en-Provence, but could not reach Henriette's château. People looked grave when questioned about the fate of the family, but would say nothing. Others awaited his help; regretfully, de Ligne had abandoned the mission his friend had entrusted to him.

Casanova was not satisfied with this explanation, and suspected his dear friend of lying. De Ligne hated disappointing anyone. Casanova would have preferred the truth. The truth was better than a lie and it served one well in the end, even if it caused immediate pain. De Ligne was writing his memoirs and Casanova hoped for posterity's sake that the Prince would tell the truth there. De Ligne's memoirs were entitled, as fate would have it, *L'Histoire de ma vie*. His lady wife, residing at the Court of the Elector of Saxony, was also writing a memoir.

"Everyone is writing their lives but me," laughed Casanova, "and I have had the most interesting life in our time."

"That is highly debatable, mon Chevalier. You may have been the biggest rascal in Europe, but your adventures would appeal only to our worst instincts. They appeal to mine. On the other hand, I have known kings and queens, brilliant generals, illustrious intellects . . . I can tell you what they wore, what they said, and whom they bedded."

"That may be so, but did you notice what they ate? If you have not, your memoirs are barely of interest. Do you also speak from experience about whom they bedded, or do you simply repeat gossip? Those are the enduring observations of the memoirist."

Irritated, de Ligne composed in his mind the unflattering portrait of the librarian that would endure in his memoirs:

He played the seigneur in a coat of gray lutestring flowered in silver, a very large collar of Spanish point, a plumed hat, a yellow waistcoat, and breeches of crimson silk. He was tall, built like Hercules, with an African tinge; keen eyes full of intelligence, but emitting at all times such irascibility, uneasiness, and spite as to give him an air of ferocity.

Casanova might have approved the description, though in fairness, he was only dressed in this singular fashion in honor of his guest. He would have been very angry if he had known that de Ligne would go on to write, "There was nothing he did not know, except the things he plumed himself on knowing, such as the rules of dancing, those of the French language, of taste, society, and savoir faire. He was a fountain of knowledge; but he quoted Homer and Horace till you were sick of them."

That was sheer spite, and untrue besides, but Casanova never suspected the depth of his friend's ambiguous feelings for him. He would have shouted with indignation and anguish if he'd read of himself, "He had made a bow on entering the salon such as Marcel, the great dancing master, had taught him sixty years before, and somebody had laughed; he had done his steps in the minuet at the late ball, and somebody else had laughed; he had put on his plumed hat and his suit of gold silk with his black velvet waistcoat and his paste diamond buckles on his silk stockings, and the company had all laughed. 'Cospetto!' he cried. 'You are all Jacobins!'"

He might have approved of the attention to detail, but would have decried the aristocratic malice. The Prince was no master of the newest fashions either, and was an old man whose only amorous encounters were those he paid for in gold. He was ugly, surpassed in homeliness only by his Princess. He loved young boys, he once said, because he could borrow their beauty for a fleeting moment. That was the apex of his poetic achievement.

De Ligne had brought Casanova a slender volume published in a very limited edition, containing the writing of the Marquis de Sade. It was entitled *Juliette, ou les prospérités de vice.* Casanova read it without drawing breath and when he was finished reading, he hurled the book into the fireplace, where he watched it burn to ashes. What infuriated him was the deliberate and logical method de Sade employed in defense of vice. The episodes of vice themselves were contrived and bore no resemblance to real human activities, all of which, even the most loathsome, are inspired by obscure and contradictory emotions, not logic. Madame Delbene's lectures to Juliette bore the ugly traces of the philosopher's love of bathos, and were inhuman in their relentlessness. De Sade hated the world and had set out to destroy it by mocking the very wellspring of its passions. He didn't care that de Sade's argumentation often agreed with his own: this unworthy descendant of Laura de Sade was a hateful worm.

De Ligne, who witnessed with astonishment the burning of his gift, managed to say only, "That was a valuable edition, Monsieur Librarian."

"The burning of books is as abhorrent to me as it is to you, de Ligne. Remember that I was myself arrested for possessing books condemned by the Inquisition. What I have done couldn't be helped. De Sade offends me profoundly; he offends the joy of physical love, he sullies innocence, he wallows in excrement, he incites to crime."

"Are you offended by his atheism?"

"Yes, yes!" cried Casanova. "De Sade is a true atheist, more so than Voltaire or Diderot. His atheism takes the absence of God to its most logical conclusions: murder and enjoyment of crime. I fear for the future."

De Ligne was of much the same opinion, though in his heart of hearts he found de Sade's perversity closer to his own than Casanova's sweet and often sentimental tales of love. If the future was going to be as horrendous as Casanova envisioned, one was better off armed with de Sade's uncompromising perversity than with tales fit for the salon. None of it mattered to him; in his opinion neither de Sade's nor Casanova's writings would ever have more than a limited number of readers. De Sade was in the Bastille, where he was going to rot, and Casanova was at Dux, where intelligent life had to include Waldstein's horses.

But the incident put a strain on the already ambiguous relations between the two men.

Casanova amused de Ligne greatly by reading from the *Icosameron*. The Prince did not stint his compliments, but he considered the writing the private privilege of men such as himself, who understood the numerous references, the allusions to Free-masonry and alchemy. He took pains to subtly convey his feeling that such a book, when it was eventually finished, could not be entrusted to the public at large. He warned him about backlash from the German Church. German Protestants, he warned, do not have the deeply civilized "modus vivendi of our Latin people." If any of them, in the midst of whom Casanova was living, were going to get a hold of his manuscript, his descriptions of the sexual habits of his gentle Micromegs might pose problems. And then, forgetting all about Casanova's writing, the Prince went on to delineate what was clearly his new vision of the postrevolutionary world. The Germans, he said, are going to battle for the soul of Europe against the Holy Church. Their pragmatic and morally inflexible natures, combined with fear of authority and horror of personal liberty, were going to make them formidable foes in the century to come. One had only to read their poets, such as Goethe and Schiller, to realize that the spirit of the Middle Ages, which had been tamed by the Roman Church, was alive in all its barbarity inside the Germans. The Prince railed like this for an hour, before mentioning again Casanova's novel, which he praised for philosophical depth, literary quality, and frankness.

Casanova understood the Prince's complex reasoning, but resented the attempt to curtail his literary liberty. The arguments about Germans made him thoughtful, though. Casanova believed that people of intelligence and reason were above such superstitions as nationality and religion. That had been the whole point of establishing the fraternity of Masons, at a time when petty rulers threw their people into war in the service of absurd local quarrels. He knew that the Prince was a victim of literary envy, but his feelings were couched in such philosophical confusion that Casanova felt both challenged and discouraged.

The Prince's fear of Germans was quite odd, given that his own family was more than half German, including his cousin, Count Waldstein. In Casanova's life there was a German girl who threatened him with nothing but love and was certainly not infected with barbarism. Still, the matter required thought. He associated German with the rudeness of the servants at Dux and was made uneasy by Goethe's sentimentality. Perhaps there was something to the Prince's reasoning, though the problem may lie in the language itself.

De Ligne departed after a sojourn of only four days, promising the Chevalier some sort of employment when the opportunity arose. Casanova knew that it would never happen. De Ligne felt that he had done his duty by introducing the Chevalier to Waldstein, whom he thought quite a saint to put up with the cantankerous Venetian.

After de Ligne's carriage disappeared in the Bohemian woods, Casanova, in an extremely bad mood, wrote to Mademoiselle Cécile de Roggendorf, advising her to be "moderate and proud, without ignoring her true nature," and to be "on guard at all times against old foxes such as myself who cannot but help, because of their nature, wanting to devour you." Since he placed her in the service of the Duke of Courtland, he worried about her. Courtland was an old libertine like himself and in a short time he would grip the juicy innocent between his talons and feed to his heart's content. Maybe Casanova was simply jealous. The vividness of the duke's talons embedded firmly in Mademoiselle Roggendorf's snow-white breasts was entirely too vivid. He had never met his enthusiastic correspondent but of the snow-bright roundness of her breasts he had little doubt. In any case, he wrote to Cécile's brother.

"I have cultivated in your sister a love of the truth, moderation, submission, a noble pride which is not to be confounded with haughtiness and, finally, all those virtues suitable to her sex and befitting honor."

Such refined sentiments, inspired to contrast with de Sade's scurrilous style, were exhausting. He asked that a coach be readied for a journey to Prague; he needed, he said, to attend a scientific meeting of great importance. The coachman went to Langerhoff, as he always did when Casanova requested a carriage, and received the majordomo's grudging approval for the trip.

Casanova began to feel better as soon as they were out of sight of the castle. He let himself be lulled to sleep by the memories of his many amorous adventures in coaches and calèches. Public conveyances had provided him so many opportunities for furtive, delightful encounters with girls and women of every nationality. One day he must write an expert treatise on the differences between women of different countries, differences so philosophically interesting he could base an entire history of Europe on them. He loved Venetian women because beneath their haughtiness lay boundless passion. French women, in contrast, were merely accommodating and dutiful, loving easily, but without great involvement. French women calculated and schemed even at the height of their pleasure, while Venetians and Russians were transported to indescribable heavens of delight and, occasionally, madness. For the purposes of coach travel, French women and girls no older than thirteen were best, in the first instance because they didn't disturb anybody by crying out at the moment of release, and in the second because they were afraid that someone might overhear them. Girls traveling with their parents were best because they would rather bite their lips bloody than let out a sound.

༄‎In Prague, Casanova stopped at the modest house in Old Town where Joseph Dorensky shared a room with another scholar. Taking the young philologist with him, they drove to the palace of Count Waldstein, where a masonic meeting was just starting.

Casanova had been made a Freemason when still a young man, during his first sojourn in Paris. He had been introduced to the order by the Duc de Bernis, and had taken to the brotherhood immediately. The official purpose of the society was simply "charity," but its development encompassed much more.

Casanova was a nineteenth-degree Mason of the Accepted Scottish Rite, founded by Chevalier Andrew Ramsay. Nearly every aristocrat with a library and every intellectual of note was a Freemason, though the order was also open to tradesmen and, at times, women.

"All the great men of our century are Freemasons!" Casanova had once declared grandly to the Prince de Ligne.

"And all the great scoundrels as well," replied de Ligne. "There isn't one American rebel that isn't a brother. They even apply masonic ideas to the governance of their new country. What do you make of that?"

"The laws of the order's governance are sound, based on English principles. If the Americans succeed in transferring them to the majority of their people, they will create a harmonious society."

De Ligne dismissed this. "They will all be hung for treason in due time."

Casanova admired the Freemasons' belief in absolute freedom of thought and the necessity for men of knowledge to share their discoveries free from the quarrels of their governments. He adored the occult secrecy that surrounded the brotherhood, a defense against ignoramuses that hid well the irreverence permitted within. Most of all, though, he admired the intricate structures of the organization itself, with its layers of representation within each lodge.

The Prague Freemasons were honored that day by a distinguished guest, the French metaphysician Claude Yvon, an author of the *Encyclopédie*, a document Casanova both loved and hated. Yvon began by addressing his brothers, reminding them that "this Temple, remote from the Profanes, would appear to be one of virtue. A multitude of honest men have been eager to join it." He then discoursed on the allegiance of Masons to their local administrations and said, "The Mason must be a moral man, faithful to the government under which he has the happiness to live."

This sentiment so distressed Casanova it was all he could do not to interrupt. The mission of the Masons as he saw it was to combat those tyrannies that punish free thought and persecute men for their ideas. Freemasons should be in a position to censure harmful ideas by their reasoned dismissal of cant and superstition, and by virtue of their constituting an extra-national body. Otherwise, they were merely theatrical puppets. It was a good thing that he did not interrupt though, because Yvon had interesting news to impart. He announced the formation of women's lodges in the Netherlands and in Austria, following the example of French women Freemasons who had been meeting for over a decade.

The open discussion concerned the role of women in the society. Count Waldstein took the position that such inclusiveness might harm their work in the long run, because it would be diffused, becoming no more than a salon of some sort. Casanova argued against him that women would find collegiality and friendship within the order and that they would have an opportunity to cleanse their minds of superstition, which they, in greater number than men, were prey to.

Count Nostitz, who had opened his palace to learned scholars of the Piarist order and to ex-Jesuits, reported that his staff was busy uncovering forgotten chronicles of Bohemian stories and making studies of the Czech language. He was an enemy of Germanization, though German himself, because he believed that "the true character and the community spirit of a nation" must join "the genius of all nations" in the future. His argument impressed Casanova, who could see its necessity, but he feared the pride that would be born along with the assertion of one's origins. It would have been better for all men to speak one language, the musical language of the Micromegs perhaps.

He had envisioned that musical language as possible in the *Icosameron*, though he doubted its practicality. Not all men were endowed with a gift for music.

The Abbé Dorensky was received into the lodge by unanimous acclaim after Casanova lauded him and listed his accomplishments. The Abbé and his sponsor were invited to stay for supper; it would be a fairly brief occasion because the Count was leaving in the morning for Dresden. But Casanova declined his friend's hospitality, and with the Abbé in tow, directed his coachman to an inn in Male Strana, where he took a room.

"Now, my dear Abbé, your sentimental education begins."

Ignoring the young man's protests, Casanova ordered a sumptous meal to be brought to his room, and they sat down to wait for the two Bohemian girls the innkeeper had promised the Chevalier.

The Abbé had the last laugh, however. When the girls arrived it became evident that they were at least as old as the Chevalier. One of them had no teeth at all, the other had a hideous black hair growing from the end of her nose, and they reeked of wine. Casanova dismissed them immediately, to the whores' great distress, even though they had been paid generously. The two Freemasons were left to eat the sumptous meal themselves and to drink all the wine, which suited both of them fine after all. When they went to bed, having consumed all that it was possible to consume, the Chevalier had the distinct impression that the young Abbé would not mind at all being embraced.

"Have you ever trifled with a man, Abbé?" he asked.

There was an almost imperceptible motion as the Abbé nodded affirmatively in the dark. But Casanova, not at all adverse to the idea, was soon snoring, though not unaware as he drifted away that the Abbé was stealthily masturbating.

In the morning, the Chevalier returned the Abbé to his student lodgings and continued to Dux without so much as a glance back at Prague. His outing had been salutary, if not entirely a success, and his creative energies restored. Upon arriving at the castle, he rushed to his study, intending to add a few details to the story of Edouard and Elisabeth's sojourn among the Micromegs. He was prevented from doing so by the untimely presence of the insufferable Lorenzo Da Ponte. Da Ponte had come from Prague just as Casanova had arrived there. This was not surprising. The two were always at cross-purposes.

The Italian had come to present his mistress to the Chevalier de Seingalt. Anna Cordini was in fact his wife, but Da Ponte was embarrassed to tell the great libertine that he had actually taken the conventional path and married her.

Anna was a buxom redheaded Jewess born in the Jewish ghetto in Venice. She and Lorenzo had known each other since childhood. Da Ponte had converted to Christianity as a young man and took the name of his Catholic patron, a fact that he did not hide. The Jewish ghetto in Cannareggio, the oldest such community in the world, was well known to Casanova. Like all Venetians he had conducted business there and had enjoyed several affairs with fiery daughters of Israel. In fact, Anna reminded him so much of one of his youthful amours, he found himself studying her face for signs of recognition, but of course, none came. She kept her black eyes pleasantly trained on his face and her mien was unperturbed.

Da Ponte had come to collect a debt, he said, and to present Casanova with an interesting scheme. It was all too true that the Chevalier had borrowed one hundred thalers from the librettist some months after their unfortunate meeting in the Emperor's chamber, only days, in fact, after the poor man had recovered his health. There had been a heated discussion of Casanova's "gift," but the Chevalier denied having had any knowledge of the poor girl's condition. He told Da Ponte that he had slept with the girl himself and that there had been no ill effects. Casanova had the good sense to declare himself insulted by Da Ponte's suspicions and nearly challenged him to a duel. In the end, Da Ponte had believed him; in addition to Casanova's "gift," he had treated himself to several dubious working girls at around the same time.

Sighing, the Chevalier showed Da Ponte the empty purse that had contained the Venetian lead bullets.

"Behold the state of the purse of a man of letters in our time!" He turned it inside out. "Empty like men's hearts. My dear Da Ponte, I am writing the very last additions to my novel about Micromegs, a book which I hope to publish before the end of the year. I solemnly promise that when this book sees the light of print I will be able to repay you with interest."

Da Ponte knew very well that further discussion was useless. Casanova would pay; he always paid his debts. He broached the other matter.

"Our compatriot, Tierno, has acquired a perfect building in Prague that he intends to transform into a glorious comedic stage. We are hoping that you would write a play for us and that you could convince Waldstein to be the patron of our establishment."

How many such schemes had Casanova been party to in his life? Too many to count. Dozens at least. This time, however, Da Ponte had arguments that were quite persuasive.

"Bohemia is already known as the music box of Europe, and Prague is a better town for theater than Vienna. There are five stages attended every night to capacity. Italian opera, tragic theater, German and French ballet; there is even a small establishment that presents plays in the Czech language. A new theater that presented only comedy would attract spectators from all of Europe! I have heard it said that many of the elites that come to take the waters at Karlsbad would love to stop in Prague to amuse themselves. These travelers to the spa are not interested in tragedy, or even opera and ballet. They would like to recover from their therapies with laughter."

Casanova had been to Karlsbad and had taken the waters and soaked in the hot springs, which were immensely beneficial, and had heard the same thing from travelers who said that they found no reason to tarry in Prague.

"And what else?" asked Casanova. He knew Da Ponte well. There was always a front and a back proposition.

"Well, there would be no harm if there was a discreet room at the back of the theater where a seeker of pleasure might venture for a game of cards."

So that was what Da Ponte wanted! Casanova had sworn to himself several times that he would never make a bank again. Of course, he no longer had the money. Never punt, always be the banker, had been his motto; if he had followed it he would not be destitute now.

"That is simply impossible, Lorenzo. As you have seen, my purse is empty."

Anna, who had been silent while the two men conducted their negotiations, now spoke up. "I have two thousand guilders, left to me by an uncle in Amsterdam. I am willing to give you a percentage if you run the bank."

Here once again was the demon of adventure. Just when fate had decreed that he should remain still and begin the work that his intellect had been preparing him for all his life, temptation reared her budding horns.

"You are too trusting, Anna. You must know that gambling is never a certain thing. In the long run, everyone loses."

"Not the house," she said firmly. "I am a student of mathematics. I have made a study of gambling houses in Venice and

Amsterdam. The house never loses, especially in the long run. I can show you my calculations."

The Chevalier was amused. He wished that Anna was his consort; he loved women who loved mathematics. He had always been jealous of Voltaire—when hadn't he?—who had enjoyed the companionship of one of the most brilliant mathematicians of the century, the wild and beautiful Gabrielle Emilie du Châtelet, known to the world as "belle Emilie" or "la divine Emilie." Emilie's numerous liaisons did not prevent Voltaire from loving her madly. He had dedicated a dozen poems to her.

"Where did you study mathematics, Anna?"

"My tutor was the great Maupertuis."

Casanova burst out laughing. Maupertuis had been Emilie's teacher and lover also. Besides being a mathematical genius, he had been a musketeer and a captain of dragoons. He cut such a dashing figure that all his pupils fell in love with him.

"And did you know the divine Emilie?"

It was Anna's turn to laugh. "Oh, the stories I could tell you, Chevalier!"

Da Ponte did not seem pleased by this turn of events.

"Perhaps we could conclude our business first?"

"What business?" asked Casanova. "The only business in the world is the telling of tales. Occasionally, one has to get up and stretch or take care of natural needs, but a story should not be interrupted for any other reason. You are a writer, Lorenzo; surely you understand this."

"Yes, yes, but we have been without a meal for hours; we need to bathe and change our clothes."

"Why didn't you say so? Those are all natural needs."

Casanova rang and Laura appeared, accompanied by two chambermaids. She showed Anna and Lorenzo out, and then returned to the library.

"Am I going to be treated like a simple servant from now

on? You must let me know, Chevalier, so that I can arrange my affairs accordingly."

"Oh, ma chérie," cried Casanova, taken aback. "You are always welcome here. When they are gone, our intimacy will resume."

"I am not so sure," grumbled the unhappy girl. "Lately it's been raining counts, monks, and Jews."

"How lucky we are! Think of all those dry weeks and months when not a soul came to Dux! Very soon, boredom will return, I assure you. There will be months, years of it. . . ." He motioned her to sit beside him. He encircled her waist with his arms and buried his face in her bosom. "Months . . . years . . ." he repeated softly into her flesh, and Laura was seized by tenderness. She could see those months and years stretching infinitely into the future, and was grateful for the slow passage of time. She felt that she was not only Casanova's muse, she was the guardian of his work; she could not allow him to lose himself in uncertain adventures.

When their guests returned, freshly bathed and dressed, Laura remained in their company.

"Where were we? Yes, charming Anna was going to tell stories about the great Maupertuis and Emilie du Châtelet."

Anna settled herself comfortably on a divan, and Laura sat beside her.

"Madame du Châtelet had such sensual intensity, Maupertuis ordered her to wear a shapeless gown and a veil when he met with his pupils. There were four of us, and we were all troubled by the sensuality that no shapeless gown could hide! Maupertuis tried hard in those days to resist her, out of respect for her husband, the Marquis du Châtelet, and admiration for Voltaire, her lover. One evening, distressed by the death of her son, she called him to her house and insisted that he comfort her. It was clear to us later that she had become his mistress. She was more beautiful than ever, and no longer wore those shapeless dresses. Finding it difficult to concentrate on our studies, we asked that our teacher do something. His solution was quite extraordinary. . . ."

Anna glanced at her husband, who looked uncomfortable. She sighed, but went on. "Maupertuis decided that the only way to conquer the disturbance that prevented us from concentrating was to conduct his lessons in the manner of the ancient Greeks. At first, his idea caused great consternation, but it was quite judicious. Bereft of our clothing, completely naked, seated on couches before the board he used for demonstrations, we found ourselves attentive and inspired."

"Completely naked?" Da Ponte asked incredulously.

"Yes, and curiously, there was no more excitement, or at least not of the same prurient, hidden kind. We tended to our studies with a feeling of pleasure and enthusiasm. There was never any orgy, though I must admit that when the lessons were over I was often overcome by desire."

"There is no need to describe what happened after that," hastened Da Ponte. "Anna and I met again shortly after that time."

"An extraordinary story!" exclaimed Casanova. "A story that proves once more the superiority of the classics."

"About our business," Da Ponte reminded him.

"I will ask my beloved Laura here what is the best use of my time. My dear, if I had to choose between an opportunity to become rich and the painful task of writing the books that I have always wanted to write, which should I entertain?"

"Writing," Laura said without any hesitation. "Getting rich is never without risks and wealth quickly acquired is quickly spent. Writing will remain longer after all the rich men you know have met their makers."

Anna shot her a hostile, though not unadmiring, look. Da Ponte sighed.

"I have never known the Chevalier to ask a woman what his course of action should be."

"You are mistaken, Lorenzo. I have always relied on women for my course of action, particularly when that course was them. I have done nothing in my life that has not somehow been willed by women. The only times I have not listened to them were when they wanted me to do something I did not want to. This is not the case now."

Unable to convince Casanova to run a gambling establishment, Da Ponte nonetheless extracted from him a promise to enlist the patronage of Count Waldstein. He made him promise also to think about writing a musical play for his theater. This, Casanova would do with pleasure. He had written nine plays, one of them for his mother, but none of them had singing parts. Da Ponte, of course, was a celebrated librettist who had written for Salieri, but was now infatuated with the young composer who was Salieri's enemy.

"You must hear Mozart's new symphony, Casanova. He is a genius. He will be the premier composer of our comedic opera! Will you collaborate with me on a libretto? Mozart adores you. He has been told stories."

Casanova was silent. He could see collaborating with young Mozart. What did Da Ponte have to do with any of it? Casanova had written plays and libretti himself and could easily use some selected incidents from his life to inspire Mozart's music. What need did they have of Da Ponte?

Da Ponte knew what he was thinking. "You wonder what my role is. I have asked Mozart the same question."

"What did he say?"

"He said, you will write the libretto, Da Ponte, with Casanova's help. You are the bridge."

"I have no ill feelings for you, Da Ponte, but why do we need a bridge?"

"Perhaps," Da Ponte said tentatively, "because your life is so rich and so full you might have difficulty selecting which parts to tell. I know Mozart, we understand one another."

"It is curious," Casanova reflected mildly, "that there should be a bridge between my life and his music. You and I both come from a city of bridges. It is impossible in Venice to go anyplace without crossing one. I understand the beauty and the necessity of bridges. And yet, I do not see why there should be anything between myself and Mozart. Our minds reside on the same shore."

"Suppose, then," said Da Ponte, "that I went ahead, using only rumors and legends about you to write Mozart's libretto. You would be most unhappy."

"Are you threatening me, Da Ponte? What 'legends' might you employ?"

Da Ponte recounted briefly stories he had told Mozart earlier.

"I told him that you once escaped execution in Spain by seducing the wife of his jailer. Another time, you won a fabulous amount in a card game at the court of Naples and used the money the same night to buy the favor of the King's mistress, who granted you what you desired and then asked the King to banish you. You penetrated the Sultan's harem at Constantinople dressed as a girl and had all three hundred of the potentate's wives before you were discovered; condemned to be drawn and quartered by four Arabian horses, you escaped in a fishing boat and made your way to a Greek island, where you enslaved the small population and took every woman on the island for your wife."

Casanova laughed heartily. "You are a monster, Da Ponte! All these stories about my life are exaggerated. The real stories are both more extraordinary and more believable. I have an excellent memory, and my philosophy does not allow me to lie about my own life."

"That is an extraordinary philosophy, indeed. There is no man who can say the same. How does it feel, then, to be presented with such stories about your own life?"

"It is like looking in a mirror fashioned by a madman."

"What is this philosophy that allows for no dissembling?" asked Da Ponte's wife.

"I don't know about dissembling. I was only speaking of self-delusion. Since that accursed uprising in France, with its slogans about justice and truth, the number of lies have multiplied so greatly in the world, I doubt if we will ever find our way back."

Da Ponte's own politics couldn't have been more amorphous. Generally, he tended to agree with anyone expressing a passionate opinion and admired most those people who declared that they were ready to die for it. In the cafés of Europe there were men willing to die for art, for social improvement, for the nation, for the leader—even for a horse and, certainly and always, for a woman. He had heard Truth pronounced with a capital *T*, but capitals were fashionable and attached without much thought to every abstraction since the Rousseauists started spreading their gospel. He had never heard an aristocrat speak simply about truth in the telling of one's life. Casanova was right, such a thing was unheard of now, when everyone wanted to appear in thrall to some grand idea.

"What is the philosophy of such truth-telling?" insisted Anna.

"It is the philosophy of the Stoics, which I have followed since my youth, but have often regretted because it has led me to accept unacceptable things, as long as I did not have a repugnance to them. My nature is generally sympathetic and empathic and, because of it, I have felt repugnance for very few things. Nothing human is alien to me. I have believed also that the truth, told directly and under all circumstances, is the best defense. Of course, it helps enormously to be young and handsome. The truth is charming then, whereas in the mouth of an old man it can be construed simply as suicide."

"Have you ever considered suicide?" Da Ponte asked earnestly. The question concerned him deeply. He had considered many times doing away with himself, particularly after desperate nights in the company of debauchees. At heart Da Ponte was a religious man.

Casanova saw his momentary anguish and felt sympathy for him. Casanova knew the import of Da Ponte's question well. His own near-suicide was strung like a necklace of black lights over the waters of his private Lethe. He had nearly succeeded in drowning himself in the Thames one night in London, but the angel of mercy, in the guise of an acquaintance, saved him. He had already weighted his pockets with lead when the young nobleman accosted him and, seeing his gloom, would not leave his company until the darkness passed. Casanova had made his bitter peace with the executioner who was no other than himself. He had been mad but not unreasonable. The madness had been born of his terrible passion for a young woman, La Charpillon, a madness out of which his reason saw no way out save suicide. He had come close to absolute self-disgust at other times, most often after facing a bleak dawn following a losing night at cards, but he had never been as despondent as he had been that night.

"Suicide is a reasonable option, Da Ponte. I feel that I have been the author of whatever I have done in my life, for good or bad. But I am also a Christian and it is a sin." Casanova laughed. "The only Christians exempt from sins are bishops, cardinals, and popes. When I was young, I believed that I would be Pope one day."

Having touched on such matters, Da Ponte felt entitled to ask a truly intimate question.

"After such a life of adventure, how do you grow old, Casanova?"

Casanova considered the question seriously. Far from being impertinent, it was a question worthy of the great philosophers. His beloved Montaigne had tried to answer it many times.

"It is hateful. Sometimes I feel it as a kind of punishment. I console myself, like Boethius, with philosophy. Still, when the mirror returns to me so many joyful images of the past, I do not feel old."

Da Ponte measured his next words carefully. "In that case, your life is entirely your own. What need have you of collaborators, even the genius of Mozart? Life, generally, is not accompanied by the sound of music."

"Are you saying then that I should not even consider your proposal?"

"Not at all. Consider our proposal as a work of fiction. Lend us some incidents of your life that will be sufficient to build a character that is not you. In that way your own character will remain entirely yours."

"You are saying that the man in Mozart's opera, as written by you, with my help, will be such that posterity will clearly recognize the differences? Though these two may share some experiences, they will be such different men, no one will fail to know?"

"Splendidly put, my dear Casanova. I will be the bridge separating the two men, uniting them only for the purpose of ferrying some anecdotes across."

The idea was appealing. The Chevalier considered for a moment who that man might be, so utterly unlike himself, though acting out the same experiences. It would have to be someone much colder and less vulnerable than himself. An anti-Casanova, who would be punished by the fates for his libertinage. Il Dissoluto Punito. Casanova's fates had, on the contrary, spoiled him. The Chevalier was amused.

"Tell Mozart," he said, "that I will write some scenes."

Anna smiled happily when Casanova agreed. Whatever else might be said about the scoundrelly Da Ponte, his taste in music and women was impeccable. Casanova would have very much liked to keep Anna at Dux; he knew that her conversation would be most interesting. Alas.

꿈 **W**hen they were alone, Laura asked if she had been wrong to try to prevent him from going into the gambling business.

"Not at all, my dear. If I hesitate, it's just that I cannot endure boredom. My mind interests me no more than five hours a day, and in the evenings, despite your charming company, I sometimes feel forlorn. But for the times in my life when I was sick, I went out every night. If I could not find charming company, I sought out bad company. The habits of a lifetime are not easy to break."

"Then we must make sure that your mind interests you twelve hours a day instead of five. I will endeavor to amuse you in more imaginative ways." She kissed him.

Casanova sighed and leaned back. He felt content, yet he knew the dangers of contentment well. He had been content, even happy, many times before. He had been rich, he had been granted the company of beautiful and intelligent women, and had scintillating friends and admirers. And yet, he always abandoned happiness in search of new and uncertain adventure. But he was now old, neither rich nor blessed with company and nightly entertainments. He only had his mind and one beautiful, intelligent woman. He was lucky, in truth, and only an ungrateful and miserable wretch might think otherwise.

After he made peace with his circumstances, he fell into a deep slumber. He thought he heard, somewhere above his head, the creaky turning of a huge wheel. The wheel of his fortune turned once again, setting him on an unknown course. He dreamed that his mother, Zanetta, and her friend, the divine poet Baffo, were with him aboard a boat carrying them on the placid water of the Brenta canal linking Venice to Padua. They floated as they had in his childhood, when he had said to his mother that the trees were moving. She had cried, "No, you fool! The water is moving!" Then he had asked, "Isn't it possible, then, that the earth moves around the sun?" His mother and his tutor Gozzi had laughed, but Baffo had looked at him gravely and said, "You are right, Giacomo. These people are wrong. Always think for yourself." That is when his mind had been born. In his dream he felt his mind being born once again.

Next day, Casanova wrote what, after many changes, became the third act of *Don Giovanni,* an opera by Wolfgang Amadeus Mozart, with a libretto by Da Ponte and Mozart. His help remained unacknowledged but he enjoyed himself thoroughly when he attended the premiere at the Nostitz Theater in Prague on October 29, 1787. The theater was filled with exiled French aristocrats who laughed and wept in no particular order, thus letting some of their tragedy seep unto the stage. Their overwrought state, together with the all-too-careful care they had taken with their fraying velvet coats and evening clothes, gave the performance more depth than it might have deserved. Casanova did not recognize himself at all in the rascally figure of Don Giovanni, a stock character who owed his existence more to the Spanish "Don Juan" or to Molière's character by the same name, than to anything he had given Da Ponte. The only recognizable character from his life was Don Giovanni's servant Leporello, who resembled Costa. Da Ponte had been highly amused by Casanova's stories about his rascally valet. The speech Don Giovanni makes to Leporello could have been his, but it was a very crude version of what Casanova might have said.

"The chief business of my life has always been to indulge my senses; I never knew anything of greater importance. I feel myself born for the fair sex, and I have been loved by it as often and as much as I could."

Casanova shook his head in disbelief when Leporello sang of his master:

> *Now among them were countesses,*
> *Servant girls and citizens.*
> *Princesses and marchionesses.*
> *There were ladies of every station,*
> *Every form and every age.*
> *With the blondes it is his custom*
> *To command their gentle manners,*
> *With the brunettes, constancy,*
> *With the fair ones, their sweet ways.*
> *He wants plump ones in December*
> *But in June they must be slender,*
> *While the tall ones must be stately*
> *And the small ones must be sprightly.*
> *Old ones, too, he has not missed,*
> *Just to have them on his list;*
> *But his favorite form of sinning*
> *Is with one who's just beginning.*
> *Whether they be rich or poor,*
> *Fair or ugly—one thing's sure:*
> *Just provided they are women.*
> *You know well what happens then!*

Fine music, but even as comedy, the story was all too final and certainly devoid of the love that alone had moved him toward women. It may have all been true in a general way, but Casanova's women had names. He had loved them. Da Ponte must have given Leporello his own sentiments. The rake! The Chevalier thought that the librettist needed another round of the pox.

At the premiere, he had seen Mozart but had failed to meet him. He simply did not feel like fielding questions about the character of Don Giovanni, sure to be coming from the crowd of worshipers that were going to surround the composer. Casanova left before the final curtain.

ᴅespite the fleeting amusement of Da Ponte's visit and the slight pleasure of *Don Giovanni*, the Chevalier became quite bored when winter came and there were no visitors. As the months passed, his boredom turned to despair. He read, he wrote, he told Laura stories, but the rain and then the snow were incessant. The lack of good society, despite his extensive correspondence, drove him to a dark place within himself. He was surrounded by barbarians, there was still snow on the ground, he was living at the end of the world. His own mind, on which he had always counted for surprise, was becoming paralyzed by a sense of futility. The forty thousand books and manuscripts at Dux weighed on him like so many tombstones, instead of stimulating his imagination as books had done his entire life.

"What good are books, if the living substance that created them has left so little of their fire in them? The dead men who wrote them were unable to transfer even a fraction of their living soul. . . . The most learned of these books seem also the most dead."

Laura argued, "It is not the books that are at fault, but that small portion of the reader's soul that animates them. To open them, you must have the key of your own curiosity."

That was the problem, precisely. He did not contradict her. The key of curiosity was missing. He was not curious about any of it. The fact that the universe was a mystery had always elicited in him an excitement that was identical to that of sexual conquest. He cared for neither now. He decided to die. He sat in the rose chair by the window and looked out at the thinning snow, watching the first flowers poke their pale heads from the ground, then the advance of the exuberant green waking from winter. The hills around Dux burst into color, the birds made an amorous and ecstatic racket, the peasant girls filling the courtyard below the window emanated the fullness of fresh bread, the animals pranced and called out to one another, matter vibrated, flesh was awake, but nothing penetrated the darkness of the Chevalier's soul, which lay like a dusty library in the twilight of his self-willed death. He refused food. Laura was in despair. She wrote to Count Waldstein.

My master—

The librarian has set himself on a course that will lead to his death. He takes neither food nor drink nor does he look at anyone. I do not think that he is physically ill, but he has refused to see the physician. Very few people here care about what he does. Please forgive my presumption. I am only the lowliest of servants, but I know that the Chevalier is a great man. I have seen that he corresponds with men like yourself and the Prince de Ligne. He used to, anyway. These days he merely reposes in the rose chair

*in his room like someone who has lost both his health and
his soul. I appeal to you to send a physician who will penetrate his silence.
Your most humble servant, etc. etc.—
Laura Brock*

Laura's letter had the desired effect, both because Waldstein cared for Casanova, and because he was astonished by
the depth of feeling evinced by his servant's unpolished letter.
He reflected that Casanova's magnetism had not abandoned
him, even in the decrepit state that he found himself. He might
have done well to reflect that a simple girl capable of taking
such an action was proof that there was hope for the emancipa-
tion of common people. Such a thought was, however, precisely
the kind of thought he needed to banish from his mind at a time
when the Rousseauists were set on annihilating the aristocracy.
Perhaps he should punish the girl for effrontery instead.
Nonetheless, he listened, and dispatched the famous Irish
physician O'Reilly to Dux.

O'Reilly knew Casanova. They had met in Vienna and
become friends. Their conversations had been heated, because
Casanova mistrusted the medical profession. He believed that
doctors had killed more people than they had cured, and that
their quack medicines were useless. He had availed himself of
their services only for their proven (one of the few proven)
cures for the venereal pox. Whenever he had been sick,
Casanova cured himself by fasting, drinking only water and
staying in bed. He had been nearly killed by a physician who
had attempted to bleed him against his will. Casanova had
fired his revolver at him, and then recovered all by himself.
Telling this delicious story soon after getting out of bed was one
of the delightful aftermaths of his close encounter. O'Reilly
agreed with Casanova up to a point. He believed that the path

of progress was strewn with cadavers and that, unfortunately, the only means to test the efficacy of procedures and medicines was on live subjects. He recognized Casanova's right not to be one of medicine's subjects, but he believed that one day great benefits would be reaped from tentative and even unfortunate experiments.

O'Reilly agreed also with Casanova's contention that a person's powers of self-healing were remarkable. In ninety-nine percent of all cases, O'Reilly prescribed palliatives. They worked as well as any medicines. He still had some faith in bleeding, a relic of medieval medicine that was widely practiced, but he knew that of all possible remedies, Casanova would reject this in the strongest terms. For the first years of his life, Casanova had bled continually from his nose. He had been cured by a witch, but since he did not believe in witchcraft, he thought that it was his own insurgent health that had finally stopped him from bleeding to death. The witch had been necessary, though, because the powers of self needed a ritual frame for their realization. But what to do now? Knowing him as he did, O'Reilly doubted if Casanova would pay any attention to him. He purchased a dozen splendid wines and two hundred oysters, just in case, and made the journey from Prague to Dux in his cabriolet in less than a day.

He entered Casanova's chamber with a burst of Irish good cheer, making sure the servant carrying the wine deposited the case right at the invalid's feet. He also dispatched his own man to the kitchen to oversee the preparation of the oysters.

"There is no sickness," he declaimed, "but sickness of the soul. Physician, heal thyself." He opened a bottle, and Laura, who was hovering anxiously behind him, held up two glasses. O'Reilly filled them to the brim, spilling some. He was gratified to notice that Casanova's nose, despite himself, rose into the air to sniff the vintage.

"Ah," O'Reilly cried out, delighted, "Casanova's nose is once again smarter than Casanova!"

Casanova smiled without wanting to. He saw the justice of the physician's remark. His nose, more than any other organ of his body, including his "verb," had been the leader of his life. He had followed the scent of women and viands from boudoir to dining table, and had always congratulated his olfactory organ for its unerring correctness. If he had been nothing but a nose, Casanova would have been a happy man. Endowed, however, with so many other detectors of pleasure, he had been very fortunate indeed. It was a reflection that did not suit his illness. The dark angel of his depression stomped his foot angrily on this inadvertent ray of sunshine.

The good doctor knew a good thing when he saw one.

"Remember, my dear Casanova, the smell of a warm woman after a good glass of wine."

The command had its effect. The complex bouquet of a memory invaded his body like the insistent thrust of a blade. He smelled the smoked tongue and the Cyprus wine he had smuggled in his pocket to the room of Nanetta and Marta, and was flooded by the taste of their kisses and the scent of their young bodies as they loved each other that night long ago. This time, the dark angel could barely hold down the lead roof of depression. A smile betrayed him. Both O'Reilly and Laura burst out laughing.

O'Reilly handed him the cup of wine, but Casanova's hand did not rise to take it.

"What," cried O'Reilly, "my wine is not good enough for the Chevalier?" He downed his own cup and closed his eyes. "It's quite fine. Perhaps the great Casanova no longer likes to drink from a cup." He turned to Laura. "Hold this, my dear."

The doctor handed Laura the cup and told her to take a

mouthful but not to swallow it. "Now, you must put your lips to the dear Chevalier's lips and make him taste my good wine."

Laura wouldn't have dared if she had not seen the glimmer of amusement in Casanova's eyes. She approached him gingerly and bent her head until their lips touched. His mouth opened slightly and, carefully, like a mother bird feeding her infant, she passed some of the wine into his mouth. Casanova swallowed and she gave him some more until he swallowed it all. She took another sip from the cup and fed him again. The old man passed from distant amusement to active enjoyment. He drank a full cup of wine from her lips. But still, he said nothing.

"We have passed," O'Reilly exulted, "the first hurdle toward the restoration of the famous sensualist's faculties. Now, for the oysters!"

The doctor had taken the precaution of bringing with him olive oil and bay leaf as well as the oysters. It had been a good idea, because, just as O'Reilly had suspected, Gelder's barbarous kitchen did not contain one drop of olive oil. Olive oil was to an Italian the culinary equivalent of the sun. Having read a bit of history, the doctor knew that the Roman legions had been known to execute their commanders for the crime of providing rations of bad oil. Nor was the divine bay leaf something to be seen in Gelder's kitchen. Despite the protests of the Dux cook, the doctor's servant, Marcellus, had held his ground and had prepared the oysters à la Vénitienne. He now entered the room with a splendid mound of lightly oiled and bay-brushed mollusks in their gleaming open shells.

Casanova's nostrils flared wide. He had eaten nothing in several days and to be assaulted now by a food that was as delicious in taste as it was rich in context, was more than his depression could bear. Cursing mightily at the frivolous man who'd give up his profound melancholy for a bit of flesh resembling the female sexual organ, the leaden angel wrenched himself out of Casanova's soul and perched on his head, furious, but curious to see what came next.

What came next is that Laura, under the doctor's careful indications, took one of the oysters from its shell with her lips and held it lightly between her teeth, without biting it. She brought it half dangling to the Chevalier's lips and he sucked gently from its flesh without pulling it from her mouth. The divine juice flooded his senses. He remembered eating oysters from the breasts and from between the thighs of two young nuns, Armelline and Emilie. His muscles tensed; he pulled the oyster from Laura's mouth and swallowed it. Laura had closed her eyes, so aroused that she nearly flooded her petticoat.

The comparison of the oyster with the female sexual organ was a commonplace, and Casanova did not agree with his dark angel. While it was true that the flesh of the oyster partook somewhat of the texture of the clitoris and resembled the slight secretion of women in orgasm, it was also reminiscent of sperm, and was thus a combination of male and female excretions, a truly androgynous taste. It was the desire to be precise on this point, more than anything else, that was the cause of Casanova's first speech in many weeks.

"My friends," he said slowly, "the oyster is the result of the pleasure of a tertium organum."

The two companions applauded, overcome both by the insight and by the pleasure of his having spoken.

"It is evident," O'Reilly said gravely, "that the memory of happiness has healed my friend."

"Yes," Laura said, like an earnest medical student, "but how does one maintain this memory? Even as prodigious an eater and drinker as le Chevalier cannot continually eat oysters and drink wine. There must be a way to stimulate the happiness of his memories without a constant influx of mollusks and spirits."

"You are a splendid doctor, Laura Brock!" cried the doctor. "What is your opinion?"

"I have observed," she said, as if Casanova weren't there, "that the Chevalier has been able to stimulate the happiness of his recollections with his hand."

The doctor lifted a shocked eyebrow. Even Casanova, who had not stopped smiling, looked at her in some astonishment. The doctor wasn't certain, but Casanova was, that manual self-stimulation was quite impossible in his current condition. He had dearly loved this sport once, particularly in the presence of others who were willing to stimulate themselves as well. It had been a long time since his "verb" had attained sufficient firmness for such manipulation. The angel perching atop his disarrayed wig dipped its sharp toes back into his brain.

"No, no," Laura hastened to explain, "I don't mean masturbation. I meant simply that the Chevalier has, with his own writing hand, called his memories back to him."

"Splendid!" exclaimed O'Reilly. "Writing then might work as well as oysters and wine and, might I add, your own lips, to bring on the happiness necessary to live, without the saturating effects!"

Casanova listened to them carefully. For a moment he struggled between letting the dark angel back in and shooing him off. Writing had given him pleasure, certainly. But it had always been a pleasure which followed physical contentment. He had written out of a happiness that was already there, installed within himself by success of one kind or another. He had never written when he had been despondent, poor, or loveless. At those times he had tried to sleep until he recovered enough of his appetite to have a real adventure. On the wake of an adventure that brought him love, money, or intellectual satisfaction, he had written, yes, he had filled hundreds of pages with thoughts and calculations that had swarmed free after the flesh had been appeased. But how to write without the ground of corporeal satisfaction?

He had fantasized many times of dedicating himself to a life of pure study in the confines of a monastery with a good library, but he had been unable to. He had nearly joined a holy order in Switzerland, but had been prevented at the last moment by the appearance of a young woman with whom he had fallen in love. Destiny had always intervened at such times. But he was ideally situated now finally to realize that impulse. He was in the perfect place at Dux, surrounded by thousands of books, possessing the luxury of time, free of debt or of the threat of a rival or a government. Yet he could barely move for horror and ennui. Perhaps what he had written had been too much directed toward the world, too conscious of its eventual reception, and too coveting of honors and reward. He had wanted to astonish the world with his mathematical insights, with the beauty of his verse, with his storytelling gifts, with his appreciation of art and theater. Perhaps it had all been too accommodating, too mindful of his readers, too nice. But if he considered his own pleasure first and foremost he might arrive at an understanding of his writing, he might make an accomplice of it that would console him at all times and in all situations. Such complicity would make it unnecessary to first satisfy his physical needs in order to be free enough to write. Writing could nourish his body by satisfying his spirit. Was he capable still of such writing?

He was. His own life provided him abundantly with the material from which to extract happiness, by recalling it in words. It was so simple. He had always enjoyed telling stories from his life. All his listeners, including an occasional priest who had heard his rare confession, became so enthralled by his tales that they forgot entirely what brought them there. The abbott whose monastery he had been ready to join would have forgiven him any sin on the condition that he go on with his tale. He was a master storyteller, but he had always told his stories in pieces, here and there, for one audience or another, never for himself. What strange patterns might be revealed if he set out to tell his story from beginning to end? He was certain that patterns would emerge, perhaps even some picture of his destiny. All he had to do was set down word after word, sentence after sentence, and watch the unfolding of a flower whose color, shape, or smell were utterly unknown to him, though made of the substance of his own life. Had he gone through all his experiences without drawing the profit of a deeper understanding of the symmetries involved? No, he had not, but he had noted these symmetries only in passing, taking them for granted, like a magician whose genii had always been at hand. Certainly, his genii had been there, but did they obey the will of a deeper geometry? He had no doubt. He had consoled himself until now by believing such design to be a mystery, worthy of worship and impossible to know. The time had come perhaps to advance his magician's career by moving on to a new understanding. On the other hand, simply reliving his life by remembering it was reward enough. Such reliving would be also an exquisite revenge for the indignities of old age and for the insults of the simpleminded world taking shape around him. Ah, yes. Simple. But how simple? The mathematician of chance that he had always been began to calculate. He was sixty five years old. He might live, if he was careful, another ten. Were ten years enough to write a life that had often contained in one day what took some people entire lives to experience? Yes, but only if he started right away and did not stop until he died.

"You are right, my friends," the Chevalier de Seingalt said gratefully, holding out his glass to be filled. "You have given me a task to fill the rest of my life." And he drank the glass to the bottom at once.

⟡And that is precisely what happened, though not at once. Slowly, but with growing excitement, Casanova gave in to his desire to relive the past and began to write. He began the *Story of My Life* with some firm principles in mind. First, he would write everything that he remembered. Second, he would write for his own and his closest companions' amusement, sparing no one and, above all, not himself. Third, he would write his stories in the same manner that he told them in company for many decades, that is to say with a sense of suspense and expectation. Fourth, he would never call his memoirs *Confessions*, for the simple reason that any association with the loathsome whining of St. Augustine and Rousseau made him sick. St. Augustine might be credited with a modicum of honesty, but Rousseau had gone to such lengths to hide the details of his life that he had succeeded in making his writing stink of guilt. Fifth, he would be true to his feelings at the time and examine his life with gratitude not regret.

Every evening, when the women brought him his slightly improved suppers, Casanova read them stories about his life, if he was not still writing. He was writing with great difficulty at first, hesitating with every word, but then the dam broke and he was immersed in his past. He began in the morning and was still at work when the midnight bells sounded.

The Chevalier de Seingalt extracted a playful price from Laura and Libussa for the privilege of reading to them. Before picking up a page still wet with ink and letting his raspy, suggestive voice carry them off to the past, he asked them to undress partly, or sometimes entirely. Laura faced him with her skirt pulled carelessly up, or with a breast spilling out of her bodice, or she lay on her back or on her stomach on a turkish divan. Libussa sometimes wore masks from the extensive

Waldstein collection, a collection that the librarian had been studying and classifying according to age and place of origin. Casanova then began his tale, lifting his eyes from the page now and then to look at them, and then beginning again, inspired by the sight of warm, flushed bodies.

His stories aroused Laura and, at times, it was all she could do not to give replies and upbraid their characters. She imagined herself in the place of his women and, sometimes, in his place, making love to the women, and she felt both his feelings and theirs, feelings that were as intricate as the baroque age. That fairy-tale world, of which only tattered remnants still fluttered about, was as strange and alien to her as the parrots and monkeys from the New World that had been brought to the castle by an itinerant performer. Casanova's women lived for love and they actively sought it, with great daring, outside their boring marriages or paying protectors. But she felt close also to those girls or women who had frustrated his desire.

She recognized herself in Bettina, who came to his bed one morning when Giacomo was still only a boy, and washed his thighs, allowing her curiosity to arouse "a voluptous feeling" in him, "which did not cease until it could become no greater." After this gift, Bettina tormented him to the point of madness, because she had another lover, an older boy. Laura had had a strangely similar experience. When she had been only thirteen, she had given a bath to an eleven-year-old pupil of her father's. She had touched him out of curiosity and the boy became irascible and unmanageable when she refused to do it again. At that time, she had romantic feelings for an older student who spent summers in Würzburg. Laura found that her memory of that event, which she had utterly forgotten, made its way to the surface like a buried spring bursting suddenly from under a rock. That night she had restless dreams.

She next thought that she was the haughty Angela, who had

made Giacomo suffer until he found solace in the arms of Nanetta and Marta, his two "little wives," for whom she also felt the deepest empathy. Laura's life became an excruciating series of transformations. Perhaps she was going crazy. She knew only too well that the old man's stories were only stories, but she felt that he had somehow uncovered her own hidden life. It was absurd and enchanting and she could barely wait for evenings. A new garden of the *Decameron* had sprung to life in the library at Dux.

Unfortunately, Libussa was still studying the French language and most of it was lost on her. She bore long, mysterious passages without complaint, knowing that when they ended, Laura would kiss her and the Chevalier would watch with his big, disturbing blue eyes. Libussa still fell asleep sometimes during the readings and had strange dreams from which she woke with a shout.

"Papa!" she cried one time, "Your horse has no head!"

Asked to explain, she said that she had been standing at the window in a room filled with bright light that came out of soft pine cones mounted on the walls. There was music everywhere, an eerie voice was singing in a strange sort of German, but there were no musicians or singers anywhere. She had started to look for the singer when a man's voice said to her in that odd German: "Libussa, you . . . something, something . . . good." He had used a word she had never heard before. Then she saw herself nine feet tall on a white canvas on the wall. Maybe glass, not canvas. She was walking around with a rose in her hand, completely naked, making silly faces. She ran back to the window and looked down at these moving boxes that belched smoke. Her father climbed down from one of the boxes which, she saw, was a headless horse. That's when she shouted, "Papa, your horse has no head!" and woke up.

Horseless carriages! They existed already in the world of

the Micromegs. Perhaps the child had gone to the interior of the world in her dream and had seen the Micromeg paradise. He instructed Libussa to tell him all her strange dreams.

&cC asanova interrupted his work only to attend the coronation of Leopold II in Vienna. Joseph died in the year 1790 and his brother Leopold decided to spare no expense on the ceremonies in order to reaffirm the glory of the monarchy.

Casanova studied himself in the mirror for many minutes before declaring himself satisfied with the state of his wig, his silk and velvet wardrobe, and with the weight of the Pope's cross lying on his chest. He then joined the crowd on their way to witness what the newspapers were hyperbolically calling "the Event of the Century"; the coronation of Leopold II, Emperor of Austria. It was, at the very least, the great event of 1790.

"He looks like a monkey," the Prince de Ligne whispered, catching sight of the jewel-encrusted monarch surveying his people from beneath his spiked headgear.

"The result of a prolonged experiment in in-breeding," Casanova whispered. "Where will it end, mon Prince?"

"It will end with the barbarians, fresh blood."

Casanova bowed and doffed his hat as the royal coach passed. He had breeched a cordon of crisp dragoons to reach the front ranks reserved for the aristocracy. On his way he had elbowed and stepped on the feet of scores of princelings and principessas and had to bow, shuffle, and apologize incessantly. After struggling to reach de Ligne, he had hoped to engage him in a longer conversation, over dinner, perhaps, but the Prince made a curt bow and turned to his right, where the Duc de Richelieu was making witty comments to a future queen of Sardinia.

Thus ignored, Casanova watched Leopold's back as it disappeared into the cathedral with his family and royal guests, including the embattled Louis XVI. In some ways, the spectacle of this coronation, intended to reassure Leopold's subjects that royal glory was not on the wane, mirrored that of Louis XVI. In the months preceding that lavish ceremony at the Rheims cathedral, there had been rioting against high flour and bread prices. There was talk of postponing the event and the approaches to Rheims were ringed with troops, and when the cathedral doors opened to reveal the young Louis holding the scepter of Charlemagne and annointed with the holy oil of Clovis, there were few spectators who didn't feel the chill of premonition.

The Chevalier watched until the doors closed behind Leopold and his entourage, then he made the painful way back through the crowd, stepping on toes, apologizing, bowing, and begging pardon. Finally, he reached the outer edges of the immense plebeian mob where he could finally step on toes without having to bow, but things got worse. The plebes, excited by the presence in their midst of a very tall old gentleman, began in turn to trip and elbow him, putting invisible hands in his pockets, pinching his behind and worse. This time it was he who should have been on the receiving end of apologies, but since matters seemed to be only getting worse, he felt that this might be the time to fight back, so he distributed a few blows in no particular direction. One of his blows landed in the pudgy middle of a giant idiot, the only man in the crowd taller than he. The idiot raised his hammy hands, closed them about his neck, and began choking the life out of him. The Chevalier gasped and thrashed about trying to get away, to no avail.

Just as he was beginning to turn blue, something made the brute loosen his grip. The man bent backward in pain, having been hit from behind by the hilt of a dagger. A hand encircled Casanova's waist and he was dragged with great force through the crowd. When he was out of danger, he turned to thank his savior and beheld the familiar smirk of his renegade ex-valet Costa, proud as a peacock.

The Chevalier's first instinct was to draw his sword and run the scoundrel through a dozen or so times, before punching his lights out with his fists. Costa, his servant and companion of many years, who had witnessed and even shared in some of his adventures, had absconded one night with a trunk of precious jewels Madame d'Urfé had bestowed on the Chevalier in gratitude for successfully (she believed) rebirthing her. Casanova had intended some of the jewels as gifts for influential delegates to the Second Congress in Augsburg, where Casanova had hoped to make an impression with his proposal for peace. Costa's defection had left him in an extremely precarious position, to say the least, and he had sworn that the thief would pay dearly.

"You bandit, you robber, you perfect garbage!" shouted the bedraggled Chevalier.

Costa shrugged his shoulders and looked innocently at his enraged former master, who had indeed drawn his sword. Profiting from the still thick crowd on all sides, Costa sprinted away down the stairs leading to the Danube. Casanova followed him with an agility he didn't think he possessed any longer, catching glimpses of the ruffian as he rounded corners and snaked through the crowd. Casanova soon lost him near Blutenstrasse and sat down to try to recover his breath. He smiled, thinking that Costa, who had been invaluable to him on so many occasions, still had perfect timing. He resigned himself to never seeing the wretch again and drew himself up, pondering whether to return and watch Leopold's exit from some safe distance, or whether to go back to the inn and ravish one of the innkeeper's saucy daughters. He decided in favor of the latter and was about to turn in the direction of the inn when who should stroll casually toward him? Costa! Looking pleased! Casanova reached for his sword again, but Costa handed him a piece of paper that the astonished Chevalier took without thinking. Costa bounded off again and ran into a coffeehouse. The nerve! Casanova looked at the paper. The scoundrel had penned this:

Casanova, non far strepito,
Tu rubesti, ed anch'io furboi,
Tu maestro, ed io discepolo
L'arte tua bene imparai.
Desti pan, ti io focaccia,
Sera meglio che tu taccia.

(Casanova, don't you get all heated.
You have stolen, I have cheated.
You're the master, I'm the student,
I learned your art only too well.
You gave me bread, I gave you cake.
'Tis better if you said no more.)

He laughed so hard he had to sit down again. Then he followed Costa into the café where he had taken refuge.

"Come, you miserable thief," he said amiably when he found Costa sitting at a table inside.

Costa had saved his life, after all. All was forgiven. They strolled out together and Casanova discovered that he was actually glad to see him. They reminisced and caught up.

"I have become a poet," Costa announced proudly.

"Where are my jewels?"

Looking sheepish, the poet extracted a cameo ring from his pocket and handed it to his former master. "All that is left."

Casanova took the ring and examined it. The cameo depicted Mercury, patron saint of thieves. How fitting! He slipped it into his own pocket and invited Costa to dinner at his inn. Later that evening, the Chevalier had several balls to attend.

Costa had traveled to a great many places (on his jewels!) since their parting and had quite a few tales to tell. He had been to Paris, where mobs were roused every day by some new proclamation. He had rather enjoyed himself during the revolutionary unrest; opportunities for seduction had abounded. Girls in loose dresses—a new fashion that suited him greatly—wandered the streets in a state of great excitement that could only be quelled by a vigorous poke every few hours. He had participated in the plundering of a few aristocratic mansions, whose layout he knew intimately from having frequented them with his master in quieter times. While the mob was intent on stealing trinkets and destroying large objects, he had actually saved some masterpieces of painting that ended up stored in a house he had rented on the outskirts of Paris. Among them were two battle-scene paintings by Francesco Casanova, the Chevalier's brother. If Costa expected thanks from his former employer, he didn't get any. Instead, Casanova said contemptously: "You could have let the mobs have them! The man has a good sense of proportion and color, but no passion! His scenes are as dead as his ideas!" Costa was indignant. He argued that the paintings were worth a great deal. Casanova was taken aback by his valet's acquired pretensions, but he made no comment. It was quite amusing. If the imbecile thought that he had served posterity by stealing the paintings, who could argue? There was something significant in the whole charade, a hint of the future perhaps. A time was coming when petty thieves with borrowed vocabularies would present themselves as saviors of culture.

Costa had also been to Venice. He had insinuated himself among some of Casanova's acquaintances and had heard a great deal while cheating at cards. He had overheard, for instance, a wager of one thousand zecchini over the question of who would get Casanova first: the Doge of Venice, or any of several powerful enemies he had made in Europe. To the Chevalier's credit, he had also heard flattering comments about the Chevalier's literary work, which was held in high esteem, particularly by women. The wager had as much to do with the hope that the Chevalier would outwit his pursuers as with greed. He was regarded as a figure of great courage and genius.

Listening to Costa, he could not help feeling both flattered and incredulous. The Casanova who still preoccupied these people did not resemble him in his present condition. Some days he did feel like that dashing figure, but most days his arthritis bothered him and he was driven insane by loneliness. The existence of a public Casanova warmed his heart, but did little to alleviate the chill at Dux. Laura Brock did a great deal more for him than his enthusiastic public.

He didn't confess these thoughts to Costa, but kept a frown on his face, except for the times when he couldn't help smiling; the scoundrel was quite entertaining and knew precisely how to amuse him. Costa recalled with great precision details of his encounters, most of which had been made in the course of swindling someone. He had used Casanova's name wherever he found someone who still held the Chevalier in high regard. After encountering Costa, those unfortunate souls held the Chevalier de Seingalt in high regard no longer, so he had Costa to thank also for dispensing with the tatters of his reputation. Waves of fury overcame him as Costa blithely recalled his swindles, but they subsided almost immediately. After all, he had no plans ever to return to those places. He found it interesting, if unpleasant, that Costa had somehow continued his journeys, impersonating him. He had a disciple of his life who, whether he liked it or not, had duplicated his peregrinations, reducing the Casanovian art of seduction to a simple skill. Was this also a hint of a future where everyone would have a double who transformed sincerity into parody?

Costa, having seen the violent disorder in France firsthand, was convinced that the destruction of the French monarchy was only a matter of time. He had met revolutionary French agents in every country of Europe, and had briefly but enthusiastically performed that function himself. But such agents, in his opinion, were hardly necessary since the ideas of the revolution spread with great rapidity on their own. A pamphlet delivered into the right hands could do the work of a provocateur. Liberty, fraternity, freedom from oppression, democracy—these ideas moved like airborne dandelion seeds and found fertile soil in thousands of hearts. Costa was getting quite carried away by his description. Casanova noted the irony of his servant's expressing the hopes of all the members of his class, an irony made poignant by the fact that Casanova himself, along with Voltaire, Rousseau, and other Freemasons, had been the authors of those subversive ideas. They had set in motion forces which could not be recalled.

And Costa was right about the power of propaganda. The police agents of the state could not keep up with the dissemination of revolutionary ideas. Casanova could not help feeling some excitement as Costa described the meeting of the French Estates General on May 5, 1789, and the fall of the Bastille on July 14th of that year. He remembered the extraordinary power of Parisian mobs. He had witnessed the insanity of the mob at the execution of Damien, who had tried to assassinate Louis XV, a brutal quartering by wild horses. Unable to watch the nauseating spectacle, he had watched instead one of his friends buggering a woman while she watched the execution. Her cries of ecstasy had mingled with the bloodthirsty shouts of the spectators; there was no discord between their calls for blood and her raptures. Costa painted a vivid picture of the storming of the Bastille that began, according to him, with the incitement of a certain Marquis de Sade, who excited the crowds by shouting through a rolled-up manuscript, as if it were a trumpet. He, Costa, claimed to have the title page of this manuscript, which had floated over the crowd as it surged forward.

"What was it called?" asked Casanova.

"The One Hundred and Twenty Days of Sodom."

"Very appropriate."

Casanova felt genuine regret when the time came for them to part, though he rejected indignantly Costa's proposition that they "team up" in a new relationship. Costa claimed that since "becoming a poet," a man who lived "for the enjoyment of his senses," he could not be a valet again. On the other hand, since he found himself in straitened circumstances, he could perform some valet-like services for the Chevalier while sharing in a more equitable way some of the profits of their enterprises. Casanova told him bluntly that he couldn't afford a valet, that the days of his adventures were over, and that he did not expect any profit from any new enterprises. In fact, he was in rather straitened circumstances himself. Costa did not believe this and he said so, pointing to the Chevalier's resplendent costume.

"This costume, my lousy friend, represents the last of my money."

Costa departed tearfully, swearing to uphold the honor of his master, the greatest of men, etc.

꒕ A̤t the balls that followed the coronation of Leopold as Emperor of Austria, Casanova cut a dashing figure. He had an opportunity to exchange ideas with important and influential people, including ambassadors of Venice who circulated among crowned heads collecting information about the unfolding events in France. The position of Venice was precarious. Antonio Capello, the Venetian ambassador in Paris, had reported as early as 1788 that an explosion was going to occur and that Venice must make an allliance with one or more of the great powers, in order to be in a position to resist the coming storm in Europe. His warning had been ignored. Few men in Venice, with the notable exception of Francesco Pesaro, saw the need to change the policy of unarmed neutrality that had allowed the declining republic to survive the past hundred years. Venice relied on its extensive spy network to keep it abreast of international complications, but the will for change was lacking. French revolutionary spies had been arrested in Venice, but their ideas were already circulating, as they were in the rest of Italy. Both Turin and Naples pleaded with Venice to enter into an Italian alliance that would guarantee defensive neutrality. Prussia and Austria offered Venice protection as well. The Republic decided to go its own way.

Pesaro was an old friend of Count Malipiero and an acquaintance of Casanova. At the banquet given by Count Nostitz, the two men had a serious conversation.

"I would like to put myself at the service of my country. It is time that our Inquisitors quit persecuting the citizens of Venice and turned their attention to the external threats to the Republic."

"I couldn't agree more, Chevalier. I fear that our government has become too lethargic to act. We have always been a part of the East and I suspect that a certain fatalism has now infected our policy. This is the worst time for you to offer your services. You are thought to be in sympathy with the French revolutionaries. Were you not an intimate of Voltaire?"

"Mi caro Pesaro! What nonsense! In the first place, Voltaire and I were enemies, not intimates. In the second place, I have written against the excesses of mobs. I should be first in line to fight for Venice. Instead, I have incurred the deadly enmity of the Doge, who sent an assassin to Dux to dispose of me."

Pesaro regarded him with a mixture of incredulity and repulsion. "I have always thought of you as eccentric, but never insane. Why would the Doge do such a thing?"

Casanova described the message about "the black rope" and the visit by Spinola to Dux castle.

Pesaro was thoughtful. "I beg of you two things, Giacomo. The first is to do nothing about this provocation until I have had a chance to make some inquiries. If the Doge is indeed responsible for it, I will see to it myself that he is punished. The new Inquisitors who have just been elected are not in a mood to tolerate such practices. Secondly, I would like you to write a declaration describing what you just told me."

"I am grateful to you, Pesaro, but I am not in the habit of leaving my business in the hands of others. But I will be happy to oblige you with a written account."

At the Imperial Palace, while the new Emperor was being assaulted by a crowd of admirers, Casanova had a pleasant exchange with Princess Maria Christine. He declared to her his joy at her visit to Dux and the liking he had taken to her companion, Blanche.

"Ah!" The Princess made a gesture that was half angry and half resigned. "She has married a man! She is gone and good riddance!"

"A man?" Casanova pretended to be shocked. "I hope he was an unspeakably low type, a horse groom perhaps, or a gravedigger . . ."

"You mock me, Chevalier. I was heartbroken, certainly, but the man was not the cause of it. He is a high-placed officer of the Elector's, I like him quite a bit. He asked for my permission, in fact, and offered to help maintain the relationship as it was before. Can you imagine? He offered to let me share my sweet goblet with him!"

"Unbelievable!" said Casanova. "That sweet small goblet no lips but yours had sipped from, now grotesquely enlarged and made to brim with an alien substance! Abominable!"

"I take it that you have always been impertinent!"

"I beg your forgiveness, Princess. I am a man who has had his heart broken many times."

"This is not what we hear."

"I will be forever indebted to know what you hear."

"We hear that you are an impostor and a seducer, Chevalier. We hear that you created yourself a title. That you are a radical like Montesquieu. That you have swindled fortunes and cheated at cards."

He couldn't have described Costa any better. It was not pretty.

"You hear nothing good?"

"Well, in all fairness, I have seen one of your comedies and I have read your verse. You are a better comedian than Voltaire and a better poet than most, but you are not as clever as Pope or as witty as Diderot. I have heard that you are, or were, an ardent lover, which would interest me if I cared for men. We hear also that you are a cabbalist and quite good at it, if one does not extend you too much confidence."

"That is fair, Princess. You have healed the nearly mortal wounds you inflicted on me by your first declaration. I would be very happy to construct a cabbalistic pyramid for you to inquire into the future. I want nothing in return but your indulgence."

"I have no need to know the future, Casanova. I am one of the very few people in this superstition-riddled milieu who does not believe in forecasts of any kind. One has only to look around. The future holds a devastating European war that will go on for the rest of our lives. My brother will join all his former enemies to fight France. And even if France is defeated, the doubts she has unleashed about the divine hierarchies of society will not go away. I will never have another love as sweet as Blanche. My future will be like that of my good brother Joseph. I will enter into liaisons with women of all classes and I will give my heart to none."

Casanova was genuinely moved by Mimi's evident distress. He kissed her hand with compassion and respect. She moved into the circle around her brother Leopold, standing next to her sister Marie Antoinette, the French queen. Marie Antoinette put her arm in Mimi's; the two of them looked equally sad, uninterested in the future.

Casanova wandered among the tables piled high with delicacies, but food, for once, did not appeal to him. He loved being in aristocratic society, but he felt that he was attending a funeral, not a coronation. The musicians were beginning a quadrille and the dancing began. He had once been a great dancer, but he was rusty. From the edge of the ballroom he watched resplendent couples moving mechanically across a stage that was only superficially serene. Beneath it seethed the anger of millions.

While meditating thus, the Chevalier felt the light touch of a gloved hand on his arm. Standing there smiling radiantly was Donna Lucrezia; next to her was their daughter Leonilda, now a middle-aged woman, on the arm of a handsome young officer.

"Chevalier, I would like to introduce my grandson, Guillermo," Donna Lucrezia said.

Casanova inclined his head as his son and grandson saluted him in military fashion. The boy looked very much like Leonilda's husband, the late Marquis, but for a certain twist of his lips and the unmistakable Casanovian nose.

The little group made its way to a small salon where they could sit and talk more easily. The young Marquis looked with some incomprehension at the delighted company, not quite understanding the easy intimacy among them. Now and then he gazed thoughfully at the old Venetian's nose, trying to fathom something that escaped him. Donna Lucrezia looked dignified and beautiful, and Leonilda, his daughter, was ravishing in her sapphire-blue gown. He was overcome by desire for her and became sillier than he had ever been in her presence, save for the time when he had asked her to marry him, more than three decades before. He was delighted to hear of Guillermo's successes and his love for literature.

"He is witty and full of charm," Donna Lucrezia said meaningfully.

"He is brave and the women adore him," Leonilda said, with a hint of equally meaningful naughtiness. "Say something witty and charming, Guillermo."

"Mother," the young Marquis said, "the Chevalier surely has no patience for my wit. I will be glad to give him my poems, though."

Casanova declared that he would like nothing better in the world, and asked him who, among the great poets, he admired most.

Without a moment's hesitation the young man said, "Ariosto," and Casanova knew then, beyond a shadow of doubt, that he was indeed his progeny. He had sometimes doubted that he had succeeded in impregnating Leonilda, but there was little doubt now. He laughed and began reciting in a whisper the beginning of *Orlando Furioso*, and was joined by Guillermo, who matched him line by line. They were able to conduct their joint recitation for a full twenty minutes, and a crowd gathered to listen, applauding when the two men finished. Donna Lucrezia and Leonilda beamed with a special joy that brought tears to their eyes. Guillermo, Casanova's son and grandson, was overcome by emotion as well, without quite understanding the reason for it. Casanova gave him quick instructions to send his poems to Dux, and made a rather abrupt exit, after kissing the ladies' hands. He did not want anyone to see his tears.

What an old fool he was! He had lovers everywhere in Europe, and quite a few children. He had no doubt that he could have made a good life for himself with any of the women he had loved. He had no doubt that some of them, like the extraordinary Lucrezia and dear Leonilda, still loved him sufficiently to give him refuge if the need ever arose.

What had always driven him from the arms of love and safety? He knew the answer; because it was simply the desire for liberty. It was this idea, in all its abstract and imprecise meaning, that had hurled him headlong, over and over, into the cold night in search of the unknown. He had defended fiercely his "liberty," and had suffered untold misery for it. His "liberty" had brought him loneliness, poverty, and physical deprivation. Yet he had loved this liberty most of all. Who was she—for he had no doubt that liberty was a she. Was his worth so insignificant that it had to be tested over and over? This Miss Liberty had made him try to be born over and over again, ever restless. And wasn't this Liberty the same goddess in whose name the wretched masses of Europe were now rising against their rulers? Perhaps he and freethinkers like him had so flattered and nourished this "liberty" that she had grown huge and hideously strong and was now in danger of toppling the ancient order of the world. Could his love of adventure, of danger, of new women's bodies, his desire for knowledge not written in books, his need to write down his thoughts, all of those things that constituted his sense of the word "liberty," be the same qualities that inspired revolt in all mankind? It was possible. He had no illusion that he himself, or his more illustrious contemporaries, were entirely responsible for the cry for liberty that now swept Europe. The desire for liberty was an ancient one, it had toppled countless tyrannies, it was one of humanity's oldest instincts. And yet there was a substantial difference between the impulse that had made Christians resist the might of Rome and the liberty that men sought now. People were seeking more than freedom from tyranny and relief from taxation; they were seeking to free something that was within their souls, something that had no name but was no less powerful in its demands than the desire to enjoy the benefits of one's labor. It was that nameless something which had jumped from his heart into the world. It might have been better to supress that spark. Alas. But for that spark he would not have been at all. He owed his existence and his presence to the urgings of that "liberty," which had left him bereft and cold in his old age, just another in a vast crowd of fools. He had seen nothing but crowds all day, both noble and plebeian crowds at the coronation, crowds at the balls, and crowds in Costa's stories of Paris. The people had arrived; it was their age being born.

&sO n his way back from Vienna, Casanova stopped in Prague.

Prague was a majestic and gay city, changing its moods with the weather, and as lively in some of its quarters as an Italian city. Casanova rode up a twisted cobblestone street and set up at the inn of Three Boars, a cheerfully painted house on

179

Golden Lane, in the outer bailey of Prague Castle. Through his window he saw the street washed in gold by the sun. Throngs of people went in and out of the small, medieval buildings, housing apothecaries, jewelers, glass makers, painters, and leather craftsmen. Once, legend had it, they had housed Emperor Rudolf's alchemists, an ever-changing cast, many of whom had met unfortunate ends at the hands of the impatient emperor for whom they searched for the elixir of immortality, and labored to produce gold from base elements.

Immediately below the street was the sheer drop of the dry moat, where hungry bears once prowled. After a particularly bitter dispute, following their inability to satisfy the emperor's desire, two dozen alchemists had been thrown over the wall into the moat and been eaten by bears. "Alchemist meat tastes metallic and sallow," pronounced a bear in a mediocre poem written to flatter the emperor. The emperor found the poem in such bad taste that he had the poet follow the alchemists into the bear moat. Rudolph "the mad" was particularly afflicted that day. But there were still some alchemists in the neighborhood, as evidenced by the acrid yellow plumes issuing from a number of chimneys.

Casanova was dreadfully poor and had absolutely nothing left to sell, with the exception of his *Icosameron,* the manuscript of which he carried with him. He needed to find a publisher. He had failed to attract enough subscribers to pay the expenses of printing. He had given away all that he hadn't sold. The necessity of obtaining money had always driven him to unexpected adventures, some of which ended up making him rich, at least temporarily, and, always, happy to be alive. Of course, on a few occasions he had landed in prison, but the good times far outweighed the bad. He felt some of that excitement now, but it was decidedly less pungent. He was no longer young.

Casanova unpacked the manuscript of his completed *Icosaméron: ou Histoire d'Edouard et Elisabeth, qui pasèrent quatre vingt un ans chez les Mégamicres habitans aborigènes du Protocosme dans l'intérieur de notre globe, traduite de l'anglois par Jacques Casanova, De Seingalt Venitien,* hoping to write a proper dedication to his patron, the Count Waldstein.

He ordered supper in his room and was pleased to be served by a naughty-looking lass of fourteen with a lascivious grin on her face. This lass, in one form or another, had been like a happy punctuation mark in his long life of travels.

"You're the innkeeper's daughter and you have a younger sister," he hazarded, as she lay out the cheese on his plate.

He had guessed right. The girl, whose name was Ludmila, did indeed have a younger sister, of whom she was jealous.

"Yes, I do have a sister. Her name is Tinka. Would you rather have her serve you? She has one bad eye."

"We will see." Casanova laughed and replied, almost as if reciting from memory, "Have her bring me my supper tomorrow, and then I'll decide. Perhaps you can take turns serving me."

How many times had this happened? The younger, with the bad eye, will prove to be more skillful and more ardent. Ludmila retired, but not before Casanova asked her to fold his breeches, which he took off quite unapologetically. As she was folding them, he patted her fullsome behind, and the girl giggled. Ah, all was in its place.

After supper, Casanova stopped at the first apothecary whose shingle drew his attention. It had a compass on it, indicating a Mason brother. He was a certain Pallius, who spoke five languages badly. His shop was none too clean and not very well lit. The shelves were crammed with dusty jars that looked as if their contents had spoiled a long time before. Pallius, who was so short he could have been a dwarf, leapt to attention when the tall nobleman, dressed beautifully but vaguely out of date, entered the shop, setting off the bell. They established their masonic bond quickly, with a secret signal. Then the Chevalier got on to business.

"What is your cure for impotence?" asked Casanova.

The little man rubbed his hands together, composed a thoughtful mien, then said, "Nature can certainly be corrected. . . ." He then began reciting the Latin names of certain plants, none of which was in the least efficacious.

Casanova laughed. "Those are all bunkum and you know it."

"Well, if the doctor knows better, I'll be glad to hear of it."

"Yes, the doctor does know better. What I have is the most certain formula for arousal. It is not cheap, but I am willing to trade it."

"How will I know it works?"

"I will mix up a portion for you in your shop, using your ingredients. Tomorrow, we may test it on one or more of your clients. You do encounter the question, don't you?"

"Yes, yes," Pallius hastened to affirm. He had quite a few clients who would pay very well indeed for a resurrection of their abilities. "How do you propose we test it?"

"You will lend your rooms to the gentlemen and their objects of desire. We will administer the potion and watch the results."

This was more complex than what Pallius had envisioned. He would have been quite happy to give the gentlemen the potion to try in the privacy of their own homes. Setting up an orgy was something quite different. He looked more closely at his guest. A mischievous smile played on his face. Pallius was instantly and inexplicably amused. His own preference ran to young lads and he had never had any problem becoming aroused—except for occasional fainting due to the disproportion between his phallus and his total size—but the idea of an orgy appealed to him.

"Very well," he said. "What is the magic formula?"

Casanova listed the ingredients and the apothecary searched his shelves until he found them all. These they carried into the cramped laboratory in the back of the shop. The remains of many abandoned experiments crusted the insides of a dozen glass alembics and beakers. Casanova made a gesture of disgust.

"This place is filthy!"

Pallius sighed. He had been quite an enthusiastic chemist at one time, but he had lost interest as his failures began outnumbering his successes.

"Failure is the heart of the enterprise," lectured Casanova. "The more failures you have, the more wrong possibilities you eliminate. Eventually, the right solution presents itself. The path to success begins with the recognition of your failures. Taking careful note of failure is in itself a tool of science."

"Oh," lamented Pallius, "you're a philosopher, too. My head is beginning to hurt."

After Pallius washed several containers, which Casanova inspected carefully for residues of any kind, he asked the pharmacist to measure and weigh the ingredients precisely as he called them out. To make sure that the little man did not steal the recipe, he called for many wrong ingredients in an idiosyncratic order, using some, discarding others, and, in general, creating enough confusion to baffle even the best memory. Pallius, as he suspected, did not have a good memory, and even if he had once had it, the little flask from which he continually sipped spirits had surely destroyed it.

They cooked the mixture and pressed the resulting paste into a mold to form tablets. When they had hardened, Casanova held one to the light: it was purplish with yellow flakes in it. "One of these," he said, "will ensure that interest will not flag for at least six hours."

He had made eight tablets. He gave Pallius six and kept two himself. "If you can find three gentlemen willing to test these, you will find me at the Three Boars."

Pleased with his work, Casanova promenaded down the hill toward the river and across the Charles bridge, lifting his hat now and then to young ladies and their chaperones. It was a velvety evening and he felt young and unencumbered. At the same time, he also felt old and eminent, and he thought with pleasure about the manuscript he would spend the next morning editing. He was having some trouble making the story of the marriage of the characters Edouard and Elisabeth, who were brother and sister, flow naturally. He had had a much easier time of it with his best scene so far, when the siblings, who had arrived into the interior of the world inside a huge lead coffin, demanded food from the curious and joyful Micromegs. Understanding their desire for nourishment, several Micromegs, who wore no clothes and were androgynous, lay at their side, feeding them from their breasts. The nourishing red milk they feasted on was such ambrosial food, it lulled them into a refreshing and deep sleep, which worried the Micromegs, who never slept and believed that sleep was the prelude to death. It was a masterful scene and Casanova smiled, imagining the astonishment of readers who would not know if he had invented this or not. He certainly intended that many of his readers would accept the *Icosaméron* as the report of a genuine voyage.

$\mathcal{S}$eeing the brightly lit windows of the Casino Savarin, the Chevalier fought the impulse to enter its confines for a game of cards. He had ten gold louis, which constituted his entire savings. The wise thing to do was to wait and see how his business with the apothecary and a couple of other things he had up his sleeve would turn out. If they did turn out well and he was able to increase his fortune by another ten or twenty louis, then and only then might he chance to tempt fortune. But the excitement that sets a gambler suddenly on fire is stronger even than sexual passion. He felt the need to risk his money physically, in his teeth, like a drug. All his senses came alive with expectation. He saw himself sitting before a pile of gold already. He would double his bet every time he won, until the cards stopped running his way. Then he would draw back and wager little until his next lucky run. He had no doubt, from long experience, that the first run of the cards would be lucky for him. His problem had always been that, having won a great deal right at the beginning, he had not felt satiated. He needed to play more and, as he did, he inevitably lost. There were ways to manage chance over time, but they required him to stay alert to runs of luck and not to bet foolishly.

When was this fever first born in his blood? As soon as he learned to count, no doubt. He had been so young and brash once, he had gambled away every penny he had somehow managed to save. The ease with which he won astonished him. Losing did not bother him terribly, it merely strengthened his resolve to find more money, a resolve that led to adventures and a sense of well-being. He remembered losing a small fortune to a cheat on his way to Rome at the tender age of eighteen, then having to travel on foot, begging, with an evil Capuchin for a companion. Many times after that, he had counseled himself wisely to never wager. He never could keep his own counsel. The fever was stronger each time than his reason. Besides, he consoled himself, he had won often and had spent the money on extravagant gifts for his mistresses. Money won through wagering never seemed real to him.

These thoughts accompanied him all the way up the grand, carpeted staircase of Palais Savarin, which reminded him of a Venetian palazzo. A profusion of angels occupied the cornices and lovely aristocratic-looking ladies winked at him from oval frames on the walls. The gilt candelabras blazed with hundreds of candles. Happiness coursed through his body as he clutched his purse with the clinking louis d'or. He'd have to get a larger purse when he left here tonight.

A hush pervaded the smoky room. Men in dark redingotes surrounded the roulette tables as solemn as gravediggers. Casanova noticed with pleasure that a number of young and beautifully dressed prostitutes sat at small tables drinking champagne from fluted crystal glasses. Roulette had never been his game. He preferred faro, a game requiring a certain degree of skill. But he felt confident tonight. He changed a louis into twenty-five silver pieces and distributed them on the roulette table over numbers significant to him. His own birthday, April 2, 1725—or 4-2-17-25. The roulette wheel spun. Casanova looked away and studied the women, imagining how many of them his winnings might buy. The wheel stopped and the little ball clinked into place. He did not turn until he heard the croupier's paddle brush the felt as it pushed a pile of coins toward him. The number four had won. He had increased his fortune by two louis d'or. He pocketed the money carelessly and headed for the card table. Now he had a stake to wager with.

The faro table was crowded, leaving only a single spot at the very end of the horseshoe. To his immediate left was a tipsy officer of the Austrian cavalry who had quite a pile of gold on the spot before him. Two of the other players had the desperate look of all-night gamblers who were deeply indebted. Their despair was familiar to Casanova. They were wagering all they had, merely to win back what they had lost. At this point in the game, it was too late. He recognized the signs of self-disgust, fear, anger, and greed written on their faces as plainly as lines on the palm. They were muttering to themselves, beseeching the cards, swearing on their mothers and daughters that if only they won back their money, they would never gamble again. Suicide was not an uncommon result of nights like this.

Casanova shuddered. At least he didn't run the danger of harming his loved ones. He had never married, partly because he knew the extent of his habit. If he lost, there was no one to blame but himself, and no one to suffer the consequences of his foolishness. He put a whole louis before him. The banker was an impassive and impeccably dressed German with waxed and up-turned mustaches. He dealt a ten to his left and Casanova drew a queen. His table companions received miserable sixes and fours. The next card came flying to the right and Casanova didn't look. The banker drew a nine. Casanova turned up his card. A king. He had won. So far, the game was proceeding as it always did when he had that certain feeling. He was lucky in the beginning, just as the mounting fever spread deliciously, reaching all the extremities of his body. If you win, his phallus promised him, I will make you happy by performing as I used to. It's a deal, Casanova said, and left his winnings on the table for the next wager. He was betting two louis d'or.

The banker went over on the next hand. Casanova had won four louis. He left them on the table. Casanova won the next hand again. Eight louis. And the next. Sixteen louis. He now had more than doubled his fortune. It was the moment to stop. With the sixteen louis he had won he could pay for the private printing of his *Icosaméron*, buy a calèche, and pay rent for a year's lodgings in Prague. He heard the voice clearly, calling him to withdraw. He acknowledged it, but didn't stop. He pulled back fourteen louis and left two on the table. He lost. He doubled the next bet. He lost. When he was back down to the louis he had placed on the roulette table, he returned there.

Once again, he wagered on 4-2-17-25. He lost. He returned to the card table and began what he knew would be a long night's work. He already felt within himself the signs of that despair that were so plainly evident on the faces of his table companions. As he watched the gold vanish from the table, each one stamped with the head of Louis, he had the impulse to shout that it was all a farce. Louis's bodiless head no longer had a life, but for these coins. Surely, these coins were no longer valid. The king who had lent this gold its legitimacy barely had any power left, therefore this was only a children's game, no longer true in the real world. He wanted to shout, "Stop, let's go back to the beginning!", and he was sure that every one of his companions would have seconded his opinion, becoming instant Rousseauists. The cavalry officer had lost everything and was now standing, with a bewildered expression on his face, watching the other players. He had probably pawned his pistols and had borrowed money against his horse. It would be difficult even to commit suicide in a dignified manner.

The night stretched hopelessly ahead like a sea of black ink. Casanova floated in it, almost drowning, then surfacing miraculously, then sinking again. All he wanted now was his money back and a chance to feel whole again. No one wagers with bad intentions. Everyone wants only to win enough to make a girl happy, to relieve the misery of a mother's life, to buy a better suit of clothes. Greed is a demon that enters the picture much later and only when one has won and is swollen with the arrogance of his good fortune. When the light of dawn began filtering through the high panes of colored glass, Casanova wagered his last louis. He was destitute. At his inn a pretty one-eyed servant was waiting to serve him breakfast. She would see his unslept-in bed and become sad.

Casanova started the long walk back to his lodgings. At least he still had his horse in the stable. He was the librarian at Dux.

And the apothecary was working on his behalf. But the surge of hope that he usually felt when he counted his possibilities after a night of losing failed to appear. He was getting too old for this.

Casanova slept most of the day, waking only briefly when Tinka brought him his supper. She waited for him to rise, but he turned his back to her and went to sleep again. In the evening, just as he rose from bed, a messenger came from the apothecary Pallius. The testing of his drug would begin that evening in the apartment above the pharmacy.

Casanova called for a basin of hot water, and Ludmila dutifully washed him. She kept her eyes averted while she poured the hot water, but when he asked her to soap him, she did as she was told. He lay back under the ministrations of her strong hands and felt himself stir. Why, he spoke silently to his phallus, did you promise me to rise if I gambled? It's all your fault, he upbraided the sheepish lingam, who did not feel like responding. Ludmila's breasts brushed his neck as she soaped his head. There would have been nothing easier than reaching behind him and taking hold of those hard peasant breasts with their fat nipples. Once, he certainly would have done just that, without even thinking about it. He promised himself that if his tablets worked as intended, he would reserve at least two hours of their effect for the two maids.

She helped him dress. He was very particular about his toilette and did not leave the inn until his wig had been dressed exactly the way he liked it, and his clothing delicately and perfectly arranged. He smelled good and looked like a fresh picture of another age.

allius had gone out of his way to provide a fresh repast for his guests. Viands, cheeses, oysters, pickled fish, and liqueurs surrounded a graceful vase full of fresh flowers on a long table. Casanova's tablets were displayed on a gold dish set discreetly next to the flowers. There were Oriental rugs on the floor and embroidered pillows on couches pushed along the wall. The guests began arriving shortly after Casanova had complimented the pharmacist on his arrangements. Pallius acknowledged his compliments and pointed to a young man, pretty as a girl, who was bustling about.

"Francis did it all, he has many talents."

The boy blushed.

Casanova was surprised by the first guest. It was none other than his friend Lorenzo Da Ponte. When he had first met Da Ponte in Vienna, the librettist had been a model of virtue. Of course, there had been little occasion for libertinage in Maria Theresa's puritanical capital. The two men had spent a good deal of time drinking thick Viennese chocolate and arguing political questions. Such discussions would have never taken place if Vienna had been a more joyful city, but in the absence of real pleasure, Casanova made do with Da Ponte's company. In addition to being something of an ignoramus in those days, Da Ponte's main passions were the poetry of Goethe and singers. They had discussed the sublimity of Petrarch compared to the dark agitation of the German poet. Da Ponte believed that a new age of profound and tempestuous feelings was at hand, accompanied by the rise from the ranks of common men of great heroes who would sweep kings from thrones and introduce a new age of liberty. Casanova had always disliked the kind of thinking that linked poetry and art to the issues of the hour. He believed that, while they may have fed from the same obscure yearnings of the human heart, politics and art were of different orders. Poetry was tied directly to the divine in man, while politics was mere clamor. He had predicted that Goethe, who merely quoted the grand clichés of Italian love poetry, would end up a politician, in the service of some petty tyrant. Da Ponte had vehemently defended art that might serve enlightened leaders. Perhaps they hadn't disagreed at all, since both he and Casanova had held political offices, and were admirers of power, patronage, and wit. It was possible that Casanova had simply disliked Da Ponte then.

Da Ponte was accompanied by a dark and athletic young man who could have been a light-skinned Moor. He spoke neither German nor Italian, and greeted the company in some kind of French patois inflected by Spanish.

"My dear Casanova!" exclaimed Da Ponte, "I had no idea that you were behind this lovely occasion! I should have known! Prague is not a dull town, but something this decadent rarely takes place. No wonder my dear friend Pallius referred so mysteriously to the 'noble alchemist' who created the great aphrodisiac!"

It was Pallius's turn to be surprised. He had known Casanova only as Chevalier de Seingalt, a name that meant little to him. Had he known that his visitor was none other than the famous Casanova, he would have invited a better class of customers. As it was, he had confined his guest list to two friends who also happened to be Masons.

"Casanova! I am greatly honored!" The pharmacist was flustered.

Da Ponte laughed. "We are certainly in for a great evening. We may even be honored by a three-hour recitation of his escape from the Leads!"

Casanova protested. "We are here for a different reason, my dear Da Ponte. Only a very attentive feminine presence can elicit that story from me. And speaking of the feminine, how is the lovely Anna?"

Da Ponte shrugged. She had run off with a Russian general and was now mathematician at the Czar's court. Casanova regretted not having been more forceful at the time of her visit to Dux. He might have persuaded her to stay.

"Fear not, Chevalier!" Da Ponte grinned. "We will have sufficient female company!"

As if to prove it, Pallius's servant opened the door and two laughing wenches of no more than fifteen came tumbling in, pushed by a curly-haired youth in high spirits, drinking wine directly from a Portuguese wineskin.

"Mozart! Mozart!" the youth shouted by way of introduction. "And this is Venice and she is Barcelona! I named them myself! I changed their awful Christian names! What were they? Grete and Helga?" He fell to his knees and pulled up the dress of the girl he called Venice, but she held on to it firmly, kicking him with her toe and laughing heartily.

The wenches were beautiful, lusty, and mad for love. Casanova liked instantly the shepherd who had herded them in with such style. Mozart fell on the food like a wolf and uncorked one bottle after another, taking a sip and then passing it on. His manners were appalling, but Casanova was overjoyed. He recognized in Mozart the kind of faun-like creature who had attended Zanetta's salon when he was a boy. Beauty and genius excuse everything, the poet Baffo, his mother's friend, and perhaps his father, had told him.

It wasn't long before Mozart discovered the pianoforte and sat on top of it, swigging from a bottle of Madeira wine, and playing with his toes something he had composed on the spot. The wenches, in various states of disarray, hung around him like bunches of grapes, improvising a song to Mozart's tomfoolery. Their white thighs flashed, their breasts fell out of their bodices, and they kissed one another on the lips every time they came up with an amusing line for their song.

It had been quite some time since Casanova had beheld such a carefree spectacle. Da Ponte's young Moor had shed his robe and was sitting naked on his lap, sporting an erection worthy of a Roman centurion. Pallius's boy-servant sat quietly next to Pallius, who had his arm around his shoulders. The two of them watched the Moor's erection with a fascination bordering on ecstasy.

Casanova understood that the sneaky little pharmacist had advertised his tablets as aphrodisiacs rather than restorers of vigor. It did not seem to him that any of the men present, excepting himself, needed help with achieving full manhood. One of the wenches was now proceeding to free Mozart from his breeches. She succeeded well enough, and then, with a practiced gesture, tossed back her tresses, and began to fellate him. Mozart did not stop playing, but his composition now took on an almost solemn air, as if he were watching birds in flight. The other girl circled the room like a tiger until she sat suddenly on Casanova's lap and joined her lips to his. She also took his hand and put it between her moist and heavy thighs, opening herself just enough for his two middle fingers to reach the greedy mouth below.

"Pallius!" cried Casanova. "The tablets!"

Pallius rose to pick up the gold bowl and went ceremoniously from guest to guest offering the potion, which everyone swallowed with wine.

The effect was not immediately obvious, and it was hard to tell anyway since the orgy was already in full swing. An hour later, however, a kind of hush fell over the room, like a thick curtain of incense. The lovers had found comfortable positions on the Oriental rugs and were performing with the dreamy seriousness that was the prelude to an actual release. Venice, or Barcelona, it was hard to tell, had settled herself on top of the

Moor and moved herself up and down with intent grace. Her friend was kneeling on all fours, receiving Mozart's thrusts from behind with sharp sighs of pleasure. Pallius's boy put his head on Casanova's lap and mouthed his half-erection a little too abruptly and too intently. Pallius and Da Ponte were masturbating, moving around the room from one couple to another. The love-scented air became thicker and thicker, the sighs and cries increasing and decreasing in a tempo that Mozart conducted with one of his hands, composing, no doubt. Everyone but Casanova achieved their first pleasure at nearly the same time and the room darkened as if a flock of fat birds had alit suddenly on the chandeliers.

While everyone lay langurously in a postcoital dream on the rugs, Casanova said:

"I will now tell you the story of my escape from the Leads. The story will last exactly as long as it will take for your potency to be restored. The potion will continue to work for the next six hours."

"I don't need a potion," sighed Venice, sucking her finger, from which dangled a thread of Mozart's vital substance.

"It is excellent medicine, Casanova!" exclaimed Mozart. "I want to have it every day!"

"Casanova is, as you know, the greatest lover in Europe!" Da Ponte complimented him. "But the greatest story is the tale of his escape from the Leads."

"Is he a famous lover then or a famous escapee?" Mozart wanted to know.

"Is there a difference?" Da Ponte said. "He has escaped from both jail and women."

Everyone laughed and Casanova admired his fellow Venetian's wit.

"Before you tell us your story, Casanova, maybe you can

tell us how many lovers you have had." Mozart was already stirring beneath Barcelona's lazy manipulation.

"Ah, I wish I knew. I can remember them all. I remember their names, their faces, and every detail of our loving. But I have never counted!"

"Make us a list, Casanova!" Mozart insisted, fully erect again.

"Yes, make us a list," laughed Da Ponte.

"Yes," Pallius added. "What a story to tell! Casanova's list of love!"

"Such a splendid list! From courtesans to princesses, he has had them all," exulted Da Ponte.

Mozart sang, "And he made a list. . . . Un catalogo gli è che ho fattio. . . ." This was, of course, directly from *Don Giovanni*.

Casanova complimented Mozart on the beauty of his music in that work and said that he was proud to have had a small part in its creation.

"And for that, I will be always grateful, Giacomo. I wrote the music in one night."

"That isn't quite how it happened," laughed Da Ponte. "It is true that he wrote the overture in one night, but we had to imprison him to do it!"

"Ah, you animals!" shouted Mozart, throwing one of the girl's shoes at Da Ponte's head.

"What happened?" asked Pallius.

Da Ponte told the story, ignoring Mozart's numerous interruptions, protests, and corrections. "A couple of days before the premiere a great party of people came to the Duscheks' house near Prague, including the impresarios Bondini and Guardasoni, and the three women singers, Saporiti, Bondini's wife, and Micelli . . ."

"I had them all," interjected Mozart.

Andrei Codrescu

"After many bottles of wine, Mozart wanted to go have a picnic in the woods. The overture had still not been written and we were all worried because our genius was quite happy and completely indifferent to our concerns. Signora Bondini told Mozart that she had left her gloves on the harpsichord upstairs and the ever-gallant Amadeo rushed up there to get them. When he couldn't find them, Bondini came up and kissed him and then ran out of the room and locked the door. Mozart was furious. Saporiti shouted to him from below the window, 'Mozart, you have been condemned to a night's imprisonment until you produce the overture!' Mozart came to the window and threatened to jump if he was not sent food, wine, and a woman immediately. His jailers agreed to his demands and Saporiti went up to him with wine and food. In the morning, the maestro had written the overture!"

Mozart smiled ruefully. "Every note of that was written in response to dear Saporiti's sighs! I was inside her the whole time!" He turned to Casanova. "That is the story of my escape. How about yours, my dear friend?"

"That story is going to take one thousand nights, like Scheherazade's," said Casanova.

"We put our nights at your service, my dear Chevalier," Mozart said seriously.

"I will be your scribe," Da Ponte said.

Casanova was annoyed. "You forget that I am a writer. I am the author of my own *Escape from the Leads*. I already wrote it."

"Of course, Chevalier," Da Ponte said, "you are a well-known writer. We would never dream of altering either your life or your words."

"But the music that might bring those words to life will be entirely mine!" Mozart said, without either arrogance or humility.

"We will meet again then," Casanova promised.

With slight gestures at first, then bolder ones later, the orgy recommenced as Casanova told the story of his escape from the dreaded prison of Venice, below the lead roof of the Doge's palace. As he detailed the long nights of preparation and the obstacles he'd had to overcome before he was able to slip away from the Inquisition's prison one night, the company reached for one another, in different combinations, and made slow and mindful love, rising and falling to the rhythms of Casanova's youthful adventure. This story, which he had told many times and had even published in a popular pamphlet, never failed to lift the spirits of his listeners. No prisoner had ever escaped the Doge's cells. Even if he had not been falsely denounced and unjustly imprisoned by the Venetian Inquisition, his escape would have been admired for sheer ingenuity. People love nothing better than liberty. That was one point on which no one disagreed, not even those among his past listeners whose lifework was to oppress others.

When he was finished, Mozart exclaimed: "That is how all stories should work! They should all accompany lovemaking! What good are stories if they do not increase love! That is also the purpose of music! It should be forbidden to enjoy any art without making love!" He then gave a short, surprised cry and surrendered himself to Venice, who tasted him full in her mouth before throwing her head back and swallowing languorously and demonstratively.

After the story was ended the company was ready for another round of love, but Casanova bade them good night. They made plans to meet again two evenings hence. The little naked pharmacist saw him to the door and they concluded their business. Pallius payed ten louis d'or for the recipe to the aphrodisiac, and threw in a quantity of medicines, including an extract of willow bark for arthritis. Casanova had been experiencing pain in his writing hand.

Financially, at least, Casanova was where he started the

day before. Spiritually and intellectually, he was much richer. He had enjoyed the evening tremendously. He found himself pleasantly tired in his room back at the inn, and he gave the two hours he had promised to the inn-keepers' daughters, an hour to each one. He did not achieve his full pleasure, but caressed and gave them kisses that brought them quickly to ecstasy, and their pleasure substituted satisfactorily for his.

&C asanova paid several visits to Count Waldstein's residence in Prague, but was told that the Count had left town and that no one knew where he had gone or when he would return. Each time, he was received apologetically by the Count's secretary, who inadvertently dropped a number of hints that enabled Casanova to discover the reason for the Count's absence. He deduced that Waldstein was away on a secret mission to try to rescue the French royal family. It was generally believed that the monarchy would not survive. The streets of Paris were in a state of extreme agitation. England, Russia, and Austria had begun preparing for war.

Casanova visited several Mason brothers who might have insight into the events. None of them was terribly sympathetic to the plight of the Bourbon monarchy, or to the fate of the aristocracy, for that matter. His doctor, O'Reilly, was even less inclined than the others to consider the malign consequences of a revolution. O'Reilly lived in the vicinity of the Carolingian University, where he taught anatomy and conducted research. He showed Casanova the anatomy theater, where some of his students were dissecting the cadaver of a beggar who had died in the street the night before. Not as grand as the anatomy theater at Padua, where Casanova had studied, it was nonetheless quite impressive.

"This was a man," O'Reilly said, pointing to the corpse, "who had, at one time, been a skilled carpenter. He lost one of his arms to a saw and was forced to beg because his guild had been dissolved. Do you see the injustice? When such decisions are made at the blind whim of a prince, men of value die. The people in France ask only for the abrogation of such arbitrary arrogance."

Casanova looked at the dissected corpse of the carpenter—what might have been, according to Christian belief, his resurrected body, mutilated after death.

"Was he a religious man?" he asked the doctor.

"Does it matter?"

"You were speaking of arrogance and arbitrariness. Is it any less arrogant to open him up like a toy, whether he wished it or not? Your students stole his body from some back alley, never asking themselves if he was perhaps a Roman Catholic who might want to preserve the integrity of his corpse."

"That may be so, but his body will help us gain knowledge that will save lives. The dissolution of his guild by a tyrant advances nothing but misery."

"I am not arguing for tyranny," Casanova said mildly, "only for the recognition that whenever men hold power, no matter how little, they will abrogate to themselves the right to do as they will with those less powerful than themselves."

"Human nature is flawed in that respect, but this is precisely the point of the French revolutionaries. Respect for equality will breed a better man. We can improve our nature through progress."

Casanova laughed. "People, my dear physician, will always be unjust, greedy, dishonest, and cruel. These defects grow larger when inspired by grand ideals. People will be even more cruel when they will feel that cruelty is justified by their ideals."

"This debate did not begin with us, dear Chevalier, nor will it end with us," O'Reilly said ruefully, looking with sudden interest at a hunk of viscera, which one of his pupils was holding in his hand and gazing at with evident bafflement. "Let us see what the boy has discovered."

They descended into the center of the theater. O'Reilly looked closely at the viscera, which were in fact the beggar's liver.

"Is it the soul?" asked Casanova.

"No, but it is strange enough to preserve in my cabinet of curiosities."

O'Reilly had the tumorous liver transferred to a glass jar, filled with clear alcohol, and sealed. They walked to his laboratory, a large room lined with shelves crowded with glass containers displaying inexplicable organic matter that awaited the future for elucidation. Casanova toured the collection, listening carefully to the doctor's descriptions. There were three-headed fetuses, floating in amber liquid; small hermaphrodites who reminded him of his gentle Micromegs; hooded, lizard-like creatures with human eyes; horned heads; hands with fins and fingers; sexual organs with several extensions; a winged human female the size of a large moth; webbed feet with ten toes each; miniature creatures with fins and crowns; furry insects with gossamer wings and human teeth; basilisks; metallic serpents; a mouth with small hands and feet, looking about to laugh; and a great many other strange creations from Nature's discarded experiments.

"Are these nature's mistakes or prototypes?" asked Casanova.

"All I know," answered the doctor, "is that there are many more such things in the world and I would not be surprised if we, ourselves, will not one day be displayed just like this, in some future scientist's cabinet of curiosities. Beginning with those kings and aristocrats you seem to be fond of."

"Granted," said Casanova, who was not daunted by such speculation, "but to what end? Men have collected curiosities since the beginning of civilization, but what have they learned from them? Only that Nature is a great laboratory, a place of ceaseless experiment where mistakes are made and discarded?"

"Precisely. But as we penetrate Nature's laboratory and begin to understand her secrets, we may soon find ourselves in her place, experimenting with the forms of life as adeptly as we now experiment with inorganic chemicals. And then such mistakes may not be mistakes at all, but whims. Our desire for beauty or strangeness may well take new forms. Or even strange ones. This may be a long time in the future yet, but the path that will place us in Nature's commanding seat begins in the freedom to think and in the struggle for equality. Today we cannot yet conceive the benefits of liberty."

"I have always championed liberty of thought. I have always believed that anyone can rise through his own initiative," Casanova said carefully, "but if the fruit of liberty is the creation of monsters, do you not see its dangers?"

"Better men will not create monsters."

"There will never be better men. There will always be the same men. Freer perhaps, but not better. The first thing they will do, when they finally have the means, is to make themselves immortal, thus taking all their worst flaws into the future. After that, they will change the people who have opposed them into more pliant beings. Spurned lovers may create perfect wives for themselves. These future men will not make interesting monsters like the ones you have collected here, I agree with you. They will make beings as banal as themselves, mirror images that will be monstrous because they will be eternally the same. Their freedom will empower them to reproduce what the good church has both encouraged and suppressed, namely ignorance and vice. They will never make better beings because they cannot imagine them. Everyone already thinks that they are the best."

Their discussion lasted long after they had settled in O'Reilly's apartments with several bottles of excellent wine and an Irish spirit, called "whiskey," that Casanova found most enjoyable. It was a discussion that they both knew had been held by many philosophers in the past, but their own time seemed to demand its reprise with the utmost urgency. They were not discussing abstract questions. Their world was poised on the sword blade of change. They both had the feeling that great powers, once belonging to God, were passing into the hands of men. O'Reilly saw nothing but good come of it. Casanova was doubtful. Years later, when O'Reilly became Rector of the medical school at the University in Dublin and a celebrated scholar of reproductive chemistry, he often recalled this conversation with Casanova and argued it still, though his interlocutor had long been silent.

For his part, Casanova was discomfited by their discussion. He did not want anyone to mistake him for a defender of tyranny, or even a friend of the aristocracy that had never really accepted him, but he felt profoundly that the old order, for all its faults, was somehow preferable to what was coming. He returned to Dux deeply troubled, urging his horse, without noticing the chill wind that blew the last of summer's beauties from the hills, or the trees that in one week had turned yellow and resigned.

&ℜ iding at a leisurely pace, Casanova felt once again the thing that most satisfied his soul, the freedom to move, to go to a new place, to conquer the world anew. This in-between state, after leaving one place, but before arriving to another, was his ideal state of being. He needed it like air, and wondered out loud why it was that he always forgot it when he had been in one place too long. He dreaded to think of a time when he would be simply unable to move. He would end his life then, quickly and without regrets. He found it impossible to conceive of a world where there were no more new places, where travel was as regular and boring as staying at home. The establishment of regular routes in Europe had already made travel something less than extraordinary.

This time, however, he wanted to return to Dux. He had left behind pages of the manuscript of *L'Histoire de ma vie* on his work desk in the library, with instructions for the maids not to disturb it. Laura promised that she would see to it that his desk remained untouched, but for a light dusting. He had finally begun the work that was going to consume the rest of his life. He calculated how many years of his life he might recall in the ten years or so that he guessed he had left, and arrived at the conclusion that, with a great deal of sustained work, he might reach the present.

Casanova was anxiously awaited at Dux by Laura and Libussa, who, in his absence, had continued their intimacy, though they missed him terribly. So much so, in fact, that they had fabricated a kind of mannequin dressed in one of his silk robes and placed it in his rose chair. They made love success- fully only when they imagined that Casanova was watching, a conceit that both aroused and amused them. They intended to disassemble this parody before the Chevalier's return, but he arrived without warning, in the middle of the night, and gained access to his rooms before the evidence of their charade could be removed.

In the morning, Laura found Casanova in a rage. She had rushed in early, hearing of his return, and found the Chevalier throwing books against the wall, and swearing in several languages at once. At first, she thought that he was so offended by the mannequin that he wanted nothing less than her head. She apologized abjectly and began to pull it apart, but Casanova stopped her. The mannequin was not the object of his rage. He finally calmed down enough to explain. The entire chapter of *L'Histoire de ma vie,* which he had left on his writing table and in her care, had vanished.

Horrified, Laura brought every servant who had the least business in his room over the length of his absence to Casanova for questioning. At last, a plump Moravian girl began to cry and confessed that she had thrown the manuscript into the fire, thinking that the used paper was dirty and therefore worthless. In her defense, she pointed out that she had not disposed of any of the fresh sheets of paper that were as untouched as virgin snow.

Such stupidity was nearly inconceivable and the Chevalier, despite a real, physical pain in his heart and stomach, burst into bitter laughter. These were the people on behalf of whom the French revolutionaries would destroy the educated classes! Here was a perfect representative! Casanova watched the sobbing, humiliated creature, and could not imagine how such an idiot could ever gain enlightenment, no matter the efforts of a hundred Voltaireans. The people! They were fine in the abstract! In practice, this is what they did!

Laura was sick with guilt. She had promised him to let no one touch his writing desk, except for a "light dusting." She remembered the phrase exactly. The "light dusting" had turned out to be a storm, violent enough to blow away the Chevalier's proudest accomplishment. She simply did not know what to do to repair his hurt. She apologized, she declared her love, she threatened to kill herself. She brought Libussa, trembling with fear, before the Chevalier, and begged him to give them the most degrading instructions possible. They would obey. But nothing could quell either Casanova's fury or the even more painful resignation that followed his intial outburst.

"A light dusting!" he spat. "Violent storms are upon us—nothing is light anymore!"

Casanova returned to his manuscript. He rewrote the destroyed chapter, confessing in it his fear of ever re-creating the inspired prose of the original. He worked at all hours and ate so little that he began to look ghostly. He refused to bathe or to dress and rejected all of Laura's offers to help with his toilette. He left unread the journals that he had once read carefully for news of the day. He even skipped those sections of letters from his friends where the dramatic events of passing history were being discussed.

He only evinced interest in a dream Libussa had during his absence. The girl had found herself inside a metal tube that hurtled through the bowels of the earth. Strapped in small metal chairs with thin leather belts were men with long, black coats, helmets, and newspapers in their hands. They looked sinister and mean. Whenever someone spoke, in an even odder German than she had dreamt before, a light flashed and their words appeared written on the walls of the tunnel they were speeding through. At the end, she had been ejected from the tube into a street where people spoke French in a whisper. Large metallic birds hovered over the rooftops and scared everyone. Finally, she had been snatched by one of these birds and taken into the sky that was made entirely of layers and layers of very thin paper. The bird dropped her on the paper and she crawled hopelessly in the immense paper sky, reading as she made her way.

"What did you read?" the Chevalier asked.

"Nothing but news, but odd news, I don't remember."

Ten months passed before Laura decided that the Chevalier needed fresh air and that time had come to let bygones be bygones.

Laura Brock held up the Chevalier's frayed silk shirt. The stingy autumnal light shone through it.

"It's a disgrace," she said.

Casanova shrugged his bare shoulders and looked at her quizzically. Whenever Laura held up an object as an example she was about to deliver either a verdict or a proposal.

"This shirt must be destroyed." It was a verdict.

"And what will I wear?" shivered the Chevalier, sinking deeper into the only comfortable furniture at Dux, his rose chair.

"We will make you new shirts." It was also a proposal.

For a mere tenth of a thaler Laura purchased cloth. She was a good seamstress. She taught Libussa how to sew and the two of them set to work and made Casanova two warm, serviceable shirts. Casanova was grateful, particularly since autumn turned very quickly to winter, but he did not like the style. All the women of the castle sewed, with more or less skill, whenever they had a little time for themselves. Casanova often noticed them with needle and thread between their teeth, bent intently over a piece of cloth. There was something very pleasing to him to see them absorbed in this activity. He never failed to make a flattering remark whenever he saw them at work.

"Ah, there is Ariadne, pity the poor labyrinth!" he would say, or "Voilà, Penelope weaving and unweaving the world," or, "What say you, lovely Psyche making swaddling cloth for Eros?" The women smiled, not having the slightest idea what he was referring to, but pleased nonetheless by his attention.

Occasionally, he would interrupt his work—which absorbed him now nearly thirteen hours a day—and would stroll through the village outside the castle to watch weavers and spinners. He questioned them about their wool, and ran his fingers through bundles of it after the sheep had been sheared. He liked to watch the shearing, and made a study of the sheep, who looked at him with patient eyes, as if aware that they were the subject of highly significant reflection.

Twice a month, cloth peddlers came to the castle to display their wares, drawing an admiring crowd of women; they fingered the bolts, and put the mostly unaffordable linens and silks to their cheeks, and exclaimed in awe at the fineness of their textures.

Laura noticed. "You admire the seamstress's art," she said.

Casanova said nothing, waiting for the idea hatching in his brain to ripen. He was beginning to think that Laura and the other women might be able to make better garments than those they produced in the traditional manner. He had had some experience in these things, and had even owned a factory near Paris for the hand-block printing of silk that employed thirty-five girls. It had been one of the happiest times of his life. Unfortunately, falling prices and his own imprudence had bankrupted him. And before that, he had employed twenty seamstresses on the wild island of Kassiópi; he had organized their brothers into a private army and had set the girls to making him shirts. Unfortunately, he had mixed the pleasure of new shirts with the benefits of a harem and was nearly killed by his disgruntled army.

Near Christmas, Casanova arrived in his writing at the sec-

tion of his memoirs recalling his silk-printing business. He re-
lived the atmosphere of the factory; the smell of silk; the girls
(each one of whom he had hired after a personal interview) bent
over their work at the long tables; the autumn light as it covered
everything with a fine gold; the colored inks; the rustling of silk.

How much of his life had been given over to clothes? More
than half, he felt certain. The dressing and undressing, both of
his own body and that of countless others, had been one of the
main joys of his existence. He knew intimately the art of fas-
tening and unfastening; he knew the details of intimate garments, of clasps, stays, bows, and ruffles; he had wrapped
himself in his lovers' pretty bodices, still warmed by their skin.
He loved to kneel and hold a small foot clad in a pretty shoe,
particularly if he could then have a view of the lovely's inner
thigh. He would have liked to freeze in this position, where
time was suspended. He had commissioned a miniature painting of himself holding the delicate shoe of the virgin O'Morphy,
who became the mistress of Louis XV. He had given the miniature as a gift to Teresa Morelli. And then there were stockings,
in many beautiful colors, that had imprinted themselves on his
hands and on his mind, whispering like a breeze, filling the
sails of his memory, urging him on to boudoirs past with their
velvet curtains, brocade bedcovers, tapestry-covered walls.
And feathers, my God! How many brilliant feathers had
caressed him, lingered on his body, flown past him in a whirl of
brilliance at the theater and at the opera! And how many furs
had wrenched sighs of pleasure from the women wrapped in
them! His life was one long unfolding of such materials, from
the most delicate to the coarsest. He could write an epic poem
solely on the versatility of a single bedsheet that could transform itself from a feast table of love to a twisted rope for escaping from prison. The love of cloth, leather, and fur, woven,
spun, or tanned, more than anything else marked him as a civ-

ilized man. He would have made a dreadful noble savage, no
matter how much nakedness such creatures enjoyed.

Nakedness interested him only as the end of an excruciat-
ingly pleasurable process of uncovering. The few orgies he had
attended had not aroused him, simply because when everyone
is already naked, there is no mystery, no suspense. Clothing
and curtained beds and hidden rooms made a mystery of the
bodies hiding within. The Micromegs were naked, but the variety of their skin colors, yellow, blue, and red, added mystery to
their nakedness. And since each individual was both male and
female, they were mysteriously self-sufficient and made complex by intricate folds. He imagined that when Micromegs
mated, the choice and variety of positions were as deliciously
provocative as a tangle of breeches and chemises.

He had always dressed the women he loved by guessing
correctly their measurements and surprising them with perfectly cut gowns. His transformation of Henriette from young
male officer into patrician lady had been his sweetest success.
Without her knowledge, he had ordered enough fine linen for
twenty-four chemises, cambric for handkerchiefs, dimity for
petticoats. He engaged a dressmaker and a milliner and a
seamstress, bought her silk stockings, and ordered soft leather
shoes from a cobbler.

In Venice, status was expressed by the color of one's cloak;
patricians wore red, a color forbidden to commoners. In
Venice, where the mask had been brought to heights of perfection, the mystery of Eros had been best celebrated. Casanova
wept, thinking of the changes that were sweeping Europe. The
looser garments, the modest coverings, the drab colors that
were making everyone more or less the same portended a
future he wanted no part of. The first effect of the egalitarian
revolution was to strip men and women of their mystery. It
would not be long before everyone, men and women, would

look the same, act the same, and share alike banality and tedium. And all in the name of Liberty, Equality, Fraternity!

One morning, Laura was surprised to find the Chevalier looking as though he had been crying all night. His eyes were red and there were deep, dark circles under them.

"Are you upset, Giacomo?" she asked, caressing the top of his head before placing on it his well-worn wig.

"Can you imagine a world where people are like ants? Everyone dressed in black ant-suits, going about the same tasks in ant-like rows?"

She laughed. "No, I cannot."

"It will happen," the Chevalier said gloomily. "I have decided to anticipate the future. If I allow things to unfold as they have, people will have no choice but to wear the ant-like garments their leaders will impose on them. It is clear to me that the future cannot be detoured. Therefore, it must be met. I am going to create a mode of dress that will appeal to everyone so much that no amount of persuasion will make them change it. If the future is going to be egalitarian, so be it. I will design clothes that both men and women can wear with pleasure. They will be simple, but hidden in them will be a classical beauty that will always remain."

"Have you drawings, mon Chevalier? Such philosophy may indeed be of some use. . . ." she said thoughtfully.

"Not yet. What I would like you to do is to ask some of the younger women if they are willing to sew for a small salary. They must be pretty. I will also need some young men and women to model for me so that I might take their measure and be inspired to create my designs."

Laura considered his request with some suspicion, but she didn't want to see her Chevalier unhappy, so she and Libussa went around that very day to ask some of the girls if they were willing to sew for a bit of money. She asked the girls to keep this assignment to themselves. They also asked if they would be willing to model for the Chevalier; this part of their assignment would have to be kept even more secret. Five girls agreed with some alacrity. Choosing the men was more difficult, but they eventually settled on three young lads, a groom and two soldiers. Laura explained to them that the Chevalier de Seingalt was designing new uniforms and that they would be the first to receive them, absolutely free.

That evening, after their chores were done, five women and three young men, led by Laura and Libussa, came to the library. They walked in shyly and stood awkwardly, not sure what to do with their hands. The girls kept them crossed in front of their aprons and gazed at the floor.

Casanova put them at ease. He was settled comfortably in the rose chair, dressed in bright yellow velvet tights and a red silk chemise without an overcoat. He asked them to sit on the couch and on the rug in front of the fireplace, and Libussa served them hot chocolate from the Chevalier's personal cache.

"What think you of the future, my children?" he asked them.

Since none of them said a word in response, Casanova explained. "You realize, I am sure, that people do not know their place in society anymore."

Everyone nodded enthusiastically.

"Some stupid and ill-advised people think that in the future everyone will be equal in this world. It is true that we are all equal before God and that we will all be naked on the Day of Judgment . . ."

The audience shifted uncomfortably. They hadn't expected a sermon. It was only Thursday.

" . . . and it is true that all human beings have the same feelings and are capable of great thoughts if educated properly and well fed. In the real world, however, that's not how things stand. Do they?"

Nods all around.

"In the real world inequality prevails in wealth, intelligence, and manner of dress. The people who will be the leaders in the future will try to hide such eternal injustice by making everyone dress the same. They will make men and women wear the same clothes, without any differences. They hope that by doing so no one will notice inequalities."

The groom opened his eyes wide in terror. "I have to wear leather breeches to groom the horses! Are they going to make me wear a dress?"

Everyone but Casanova laughed.

"It is possible," he said, "unless they make everyone wear leather breeches."

"In that case," a maid said judiciously, "I cannot do my job of making beds and cleaning rooms. I need a loose skirt so that I can bend and kneel without being bound."

"You can kneel and bend in breeches," said the horse groom, and everyone guffawed. "You can kneel and bend even better without a skirt at all," he grinned and then put his hand over his mouth, ashamed of his daring.

"Don't be ashamed," Casanova encouraged him. "You have made an important point. What will we wear in the future? Skirts or breeches?"

The women, with the exception of Laura, all thought that skirts would be the wear of the future. Libussa said that the men in her village already wore skirts and that she had seen Scotsmen wearing skirts. The men argued for breeches. One of the soldiers said that if women wore breeches it would be more pleasant for men, who could then see clearly what women were always hiding under their skirts. The argument became quite passionate.

"There is only one way to settle this," shouted Casanova. "Let's everyone trade clothes. The girls must put on the men's breeches and men should don their skirts."

There was confusion. There were seven girls and only four men, including the Chevalier.

Laura had a solution. "Let us extinguish the candles and exchange clothes only by the light of the fireplace. That way, those awaiting their turn to dress can hide in the shadows so that they won't be seen."

The candles were soon extinguished and only the light from the fireplace remained. However, since Laura had added more logs to the fire, the light was bright. The fantastic shadows on the library shelves, floor, ceiling and bodies made everything look like a tableau in Casanova's planned but unrealized Chinese spectacle. There was a great shuffling of petticoats, undoing of sashes, pulling of breeches, and unsnapping of belts. The Chevalier, who could see everything clearly (just as everyone else did), was filled with delight. It was a splendid performance, worthy of some the best in his past. He enjoyed the girls' round white behinds and the rosy glow around their nipples and their ripe country breasts. He enjoyed equally the sight of the aroused young men, who looked like satyrs ready to find the girls' secret caves that very instant. He traded clothes with Laura. Three of the girls, who had disrobed but had no clothes to put on, huddled in a corner of the fireplace with their arms around each other. He gave them a coverlet and they put it across their laps.

There was a great deal of laughter when everyone looked around and saw the others dressed awkwardly in the clothes of the other sex. The men's breeches were too long or too short, the girls' chemises and skirts hung badly on the men. The women went about arranging the men's clothes as well as they could, while shifting uncomfortably and adjusting their own.

"Now let us consider judiciously for a moment," said the Chevalier, "who looks better? Men in women's clothes or women in men's clothes?"

There was no agreement. Libussa said that women looked better in men's clothes because they were smooth between their legs and did not have the obvious problem that the men were trying to hide. However, she had seen some devices in her dreams that made the distinction quite difficult.

"Yes," said the groom, "but men are able to better hide their difference in women's clothes. You can barely see my difference and it is not negligible, I assure you."

Everyone laughed and one of the girls said, "All men boast of that. Show us!"

The horse groom didn't wait to be asked again; he lifted his skirt and petticoat and there was a majestic horn in full erection.

"Ha!" cried the provocateur, "I have seen bigger differences."

The other girls urged the men to compare their differences. Casanova asked the three girls who were waiting their turn to dress to be the judges. With a great deal of giggling and protest, the three naked judges took the men's measure with their hands and declared the groom the winner. They were rewarded by choosing the clothes of three of the other girls, which they put on with less hurry than modesty might demand.

Casanova now called for silence. Everyone sat as best they could and he spoke in grave tones about his project.

"It is unlikely that we are ever going to settle the question of skirts versus breeches. I am going to decree breeches the winner. My reasoning is that in the future both men and women will be working at the same chores. Both men and women will be soldiers and both sexes will clean house."

There were protests, but Casanova continued. "Equality will demand such redistribution of labor. In any case, if I am wrong, this experiment will come to nothing. I will say then that narrow breeches and a chemise will be the whole of the future wear. My intention is to design such elegant breeches

214

and beautiful shirts that anyone looking at their wearers will see more than equal beings. They will see beauty. Now, let's take some real measurements."

Laura and Libussa went about the room with a tape, taking the measure of each model. They enjoyed themselves, as the Chevalier could plainly see, lingering long in all the secret places and setting the company giggling more than once. The naked girls were measured the longest and the best and the groom was measured twice by both of them.

Afterward, they traded back their clothes, which had been modified in a number of ways by the differences between bodies, though the greatest alteration came not from the stretching of fabric but from the particular scent each of them had impressed on the others' garments. This exchange of perfumes had an intoxicating effect on all of them. The groom invited the whole company back to the stable, where a fresh load of hay had just been delivered, if they did not mind the smell of horses. He had a large bottle of a strong liqueur called Becherovka, made with aromatic herbs, that he didn't mind sharing, as long as everyone kept very quiet, because he didn't want the other grooms to wake up.

Casanova saw the advantages of this arrangement, but he declined, saying that he now had so many ideas about designing the clothes of the future that he needed to get to work right away. He urged Laura and Libussa to go along for the fun, on the condition that they would describe to him later everything that took place.

The Chevalier, sitting alone in the firelight, remembered the first time that he had traded clothes with a girl. Her name was Giulietta, and it had been her idea to surprise her lover at a ball with her disguise. She had allowed Casanova very few favors while they exchanged clothes, but in his youthful impatience, he had stained her petticoat. The exchange of their clothes caused a scandal and he had come close to being killed by Giulietta's wealthy and powerful lover. He had always been fascinated by women disguised as men. The master of that art had been Theresa-Bellino, the faux castrato, who had impersonated both a man and a woman.

He had donned disguises and designed costumes for himself and others; Venice, the queen of disguise, had taught him well. Years of intimacy with actors and stages had thoroughly familiarized him with the art of the tailor. He had seen illusions so skillful that one couldn't tell king from beggar or queen from harlot, not that they were separated by much! He laughed, remembering his self-designed uniform when, at age eighteen, he had decided to become a soldier. It was white and blue, with gold aiguillettes and sword knots. He had mounted a horse that didn't belong to him and that took off without warning, bolting through the middle of a battle between the Spanish and the Austrian armies, until he reached the Austrian lines, where he was promptly arrested. He insisted that he was a messenger delivering a secret communication to the commander, Prince Lobkowitz. Taken to the Prince under guard, he had confessed all. The Prince laughed and let him go free, only confiscating the stolen horse. Later, he paraded around Venice in that splendid uniform until Abbé Grimani, his benefactor, bought him an actual commission as an ensign in the army of Venice.

It was quite extraordinary, when he thought about all the successful or (mostly) unsuccessful adventures of his life, how many of them had hung, so to speak, on a thread. With the right suit of clothes, a man could walk unimpeded into the waiting rooms of princes and princesses. Once inside, his bravado and charm took care of the rest. But now, they were preparing a world in which such a life was no longer possible. They had not counted on his vision.

Next morning, Laura and Libussa came to his rooms, looking sheepish and less lively than usual. He noticed a bit of straw in Libussa's hair. He asked for details.

"Oh, nothing extraordinary took place," Laura said. "We drank the Becherovka, and then some of the girls were taken by the soldiers."

"Several times," added Libussa.

"How many times did they take you?"

"Only once," Laura said.

"Not me," said Libussa. "They took me two or three times. The groom had every girl, I think."

"Anyway, let's not think about it."

"True, that was the best part," blurted Libussa.

"Be quiet, you stupid whore," Laura said angrily.

"Now, ladies, please. What happened, Libussa?"

"The stupid girls couldn't keep quiet after they started drinking. All the other grooms woke up. And the horses, too. There was a lot of noise."

"The other grooms wanted to have the girls, too. I protested. Some of the girls ran out into the courtyard wearing nothing. The majordomo and his buggery friend came. The whole castle woke up."

"Curious," said Casanova, "I didn't hear a thing."

"The girls and the grooms were all arrested and placed in the stockade. Libussa and I escaped by burrowing in the hay and hiding there. I am afraid they are going to talk about you, Chevalier."

"You go about your chores as if nothing were wrong," Casanova told them. "I will take care of the two sodomites."

As soon as the girls had left, the two castle managers entered the library without knocking. They stood by Casanova's desk, where the librarian sat writing calmly.

"We heard that you incited an orgy last night, Casanova," sputtered Langerhoff.

Casanova blew carefully over the paper, put down his quill, and turned toward them. "Are you two drinking too much after *your* orgies?" he wanted to know.

They disregarded the question. "What we want to know," the majordomo said, "is what are you going to tell Count Waldstein and the curate when both arrive here tomorrow?"

"Who summoned them?"

"We did, of course."

"Then you unsummon them quickly. Send a messenger. I have been working with some of the staff for the purpose of designing a future uniform. I have been ordered to do this by his Majesty Emperor Leopold. Here is his letter!"

With a steady hand and a steely gaze, Casanova handed Langerhoff a letter on his desk, which he had just finished writing and was still wet. Blauner peeked at it over his boss's shoulder.

"It's in Latin!" cried the majordomo. "We can't read this!"

"I will read it to you. 'I, Leopold, order you, Chevalier de Seingalt, to design a uniform of the future for the common people of the Austrian empire. You may use for this purpose as many servants as you need for the experiments. Count Waldstein has assured me of his support by providing you with his staff. We look forward to seeing the brilliant sketches that we are convinced you will produce.'"

Casanova waved the letter furiously in front of their noses, trying to dry it. "As you can see, it is you who must answer for your impertinence!"

"The servants were involved in an orgy in the stables last night," the majordomo said more politely. "When we questioned them, they replied that they had been excited by certain exercises they were asked to perform here in the library."

Casanova looked at him sternly, without a word.

"It is true," Blauner said, "that they said that you were measuring them for clothes of the future or some such thing."

"So why are you still standing here?" shouted Casanova. "Make haste to catch your stupid messenger! Incidentally, please free my models and order them here at once! I will punish them myself!"

Somewhat doubtfully, the two men took their leave.

Not much later, the maids and the horse grooms, looking sleepless and scared, bearing the marks of gloved hands and boot prints acquired in the process of questioning, showed up. Some of them were holding their heads, which hurt from Becherovka and too many questions. Casanova harangued them with mock severity and made them swear to never again do such stupid things. He made them swear also to never whisper a word of their modeling for him and then ordered them to return to his chambers that night after supper.

Laura and Libussa witnessed this scene without comment, but when the servants had left, Laura asked, "Do you think that it is a good idea to continue this experiement?"

Casanova was angered. "I must dress the future. It is my mission, as much a mission as writing down my life, which is going to cause a great deal more trouble than these clothes."

Besides, during a short nap beneath the hay, Libussa had dreamt that she was living in a tall tower made of glass. The tower was on giant wheels that moved it from place to place. She was not allowed to go down to the ground because, a voice coming out of nowhere told her, the ground was covered with corpses. Everyone in the building wore opera glasses around their necks. These glasses were very powerful because she could see millions of corpses on the ground when she looked into the distance. "The reason why they died," said the voice, "is because they did not wear the uniform designed by the Chevalier de Seingalt."

Casanova dismissed the girls and started drawing. He threw one sketch after another in the fireplace. Frustrated by his lack of immediate success, he turned to his writing desk. Perhaps if he took his mind off the designs he would feel better inspired later.

⅋**S**everal letters awaited his response. One of them was of interest, concerning as it did his memoirs. Cécile de Roggendorf wanted to know how he was going to organize in one book the great wealth of material that was his life. Casanova wrote her an outline of his projected autobiography, entitled "Précis de ma vie," ("An Abstract of My Life"), that began thus: "My mother brought me into this world in Venice, April 2nd, Easter Day, in the year 1725. During her labor she had a great craving for crayfish (écrevisses). I love them very much." He misspelled the French word for crayfish: instead of "écrevisses" he wrote "écrivisses," that is to say, "écrit" (writing) and "vice" (vice). This purposeful misspelling illuminated the path before him. Those were indeed the basics of his life: writing and vice. They had been transmitted to him by his mother, who brought him into the world for those specific purposes.

He finished his brief to Cécile: "This is the only résumé I have ever written and I give permission to make of it whatever use one will. Non erubesco evangelium. Jacques Casanova." The Latin phrase means: "I will not blush before this gospel." And he signed it with the French of his name, initials J.C. He was a cabbalist and he was making a blasphemous joke. His life was his gospel and the hero of that gospel was its divine subject, J.C.

He then became fully immersed in the cabbala of his life, coming up for air only a few times for the rest of the day. An hour before his models were due to arrive, he began sketching again. This time, the Muse of Tailors and Seamstresses smiled more kindly on him. He drew a pair of blue trousers that fell simply but with ample room for movement. The chemise, the color of which he could not yet ascertain, was likewise simple, resembling an Athenian tunic. He then changed his mind and made the trousers black and colored the tunic blue. He would have these made that very evening by his girls. He looked at his drawings for a long time, imagining all the people of the future clad in them. He had already predicted some of that future in the *Icosaméron*. There would be horseless carriages on the road, ships that traveled underwater, foods grown in one's pocket, telepathic devices for communicating long distance, animals trained to deliver goods on their own, and many talking species created in the laboratory. His uniforms would be hanging from hooks at the corners of every street, so that anyone needing a fresh one could just take it, leaving the old one behind. Next day, freshly washed uniforms would be hanging from hooks in their usual place.

When Laura arrived, ahead of the others, he showed her his sketches and asked her what she thought.

She studied them and frowned. "They look Chinese," she said.

"What do you know about that?" he said, annoyed.

"You showed me plans for your Chinese spectacle."

He looked at them again. They did look Chinese. So what? Perhaps in the future everyone would be Chinese.

Jeremy Bentham, an English philosopher, designed the Panopticon, a perfectly transparent house that intrigued Waldstein enough that he thought of having one built on the grounds at Dux.

"Imagine, Casanova, a perfectly transparent house where everyone can be seen at their chores and in their most intimate moments! Nothing hidden, everything plain as day, and at night you can see the residents making love. This is clearly . . . ha, ha, ha! the way humanity will live in the future."

"In that future when everyone will wear my uniform!"

"Of course, there remains the question of who would want to live in such a house. . . ." The Count's speculation was tempered by practicality.

"At first it would be a prison. There would be no need for guards because everyone not living in the house will observe the activities of the inmates." Waldstein stroked his chin thoughtfully. "But eventually, everyone will want to live in the Panopticon! They will grow jealous of the inmates!"

"Jealous?"

"It is human to desire attention. People in a glass house will draw attention all the time."

They were silent for a time, pondering the momentous consequences of life in a transparent house. Every fiber of Casanova's being was opposed to it; his whole life had been an argument against the glass house. The entire century had been a long evasion of the glass house. But it seemed that the future led inevitably to the glass house. Mysteries were being rapidly dismantled by science; men were willing to relinquish their selfish pursuits for the sake of society. The glass house combined these ideas in a purely mechanical egalitarianism.

Both Casanova and Waldstein were fascinated by mechanisms. Waldstein had an extensive collection of automatons, some of which he had designed himself. Two more were being built by clockmakers in Dresden even as they spoke, and Waldstein impatiently anticipated their delivery. When he was in residence at Dux the automatons were activated, terrifying the servants. Waldstein envisioned the glass house as a place to store his mechanical toys and the few servants needed to service them.

"Automatons have no need of privacy; all their parts are hidden. Their outer activity gives no clue to the operations taking place within. It follows then that the people who will eventually live in Panoptica will have to internalize all their thoughts and feelings so that their visible activities will offer no clue to what goes on inside them. These people, my dear Casanova, will be a new kind of being."

"They will be automatons?"

"No, they will be inverse human beings. What is now outer will become inner and vice-versa. The only way to gauge what goes on in their minds will be to dissect them."

"That will not be necessary. Language will still make visible what's hidden, even if the relation to being observed is inverted."

"Yes, but which language? As you told me yourself not long ago, there will be so many languages, each one claiming superiority over the others, that it will be impossible to make oneself understood."

"Well, in this particular future, people who live in glass houses wearing uniforms will have to speak the same language. I would prefer the musical language of the Micromegs, but if that is too difficult, it will have to be French."

"Perhaps your seamstresses can live in the house, making uniforms . . . when they are not busy servicing you," said the Count, who had been kept informed of Casanova's little project, but had said nothing until now.

The Chevalier changed the subject. "I heard that the famous clock in Prague Town Hall has stopped working. This has only happened two times in history . . . when Jan Hus led his revolt and at the coronation of Maria Theresa. Both times it started working again on its own, because no clockmaker in the world today understands that marvelous mechanism."

"It was built on cabbalistic astrological principles; the clockmaker who could understand it would have to be versed in those arts first," Waldstein reminded him.

"It seems to me that philosophy and mechanical skill, which used to form an integral whole, are now dividing from one another. Can you imagine a world where mechanics ignorant of celestial and occult systems will design everything?"

"I have already seen that members of the different guilds often cannot understand each other. How far can such divisions go?"

"Until everyone will be king of one infinitesimal idea and will know nothing outside his small domain," said Casanova. "You won't be able to make a gesture without help from others."

In the end, the prohibitive cost of the glass house persuaded the Count not to build it, but the subject remained a topic of intense speculation between them for the entire month the Count remained at Dux.

The long-awaited automatons were soon delivered by the clockmakers and their assistants. One device took the form of an enormous Russian wolfhound, capable of barking ferociously while running in a circle. It was perfect in every detail, covered with real fur. Its eyes were made of black and blue glass that gave off light when it was in motion. Whimsically, Waldstein had had an inkwell installed in the animal's back so that when he was at rest he could be used as an inkstand. Casanova instantly named him Voltaire, which drew howls of laughter from Waldstein. The automaton found no sympathy from Melampyge. The fox terrier ran around him barking fiercely and it was a good while before Casanova was able to calm him. Even after the mechanical wolfhound was safely out of the room, Melampyge kept sighing and looking around suspiciously.

The second automaton was a woman, also perfect in every detail, who moved languorously and gave the impression that she was ready to give in to love at any moment. She was quite stunning, in her blue dress and silken dancing shoes, with blue eyes of Dresden porcelain and blond hair piled high on her head like Madame de Pompadour. Underneath that dress were perfectly round buttocks made of ivory and a fur-covered temple of Aphrodite that was minutely carved to resemble the real thing. Her builder assured the Count that the doll was a virgin, and that he had only to test her for the experience of deflowering her. The mechanism could be adjusted so that she could be revirginated after each encounter. The Count named her Thalia, after the muse of drama, a name that Casanova found distasteful, so he secretly named her Charpillon, after his ill-fated English love.

Thalia-Charpillon was prepared for her first ritual use the very night she arrived; it was to be performed before a select audience consisting of the Count's valet Corvus, his French mistress Claribelle, Casanova, Laura, Libussa, Eliphas Emmanuel, and Abbé Dorensky. Eliphas and the Abbé had been visiting and had found themselves invited to the ceremony before they could think of any reason to refuse.

A small chamber had been prepared to resemble a private dining room in a Parisian restaurant. The table was set with gold dishes, crystal glasses, and flowers. A Venetian chandelier of rose Murano glass gave off muted light. A baldaquin bed with open curtains was behind the table. The audience sat outside the circle of light on Turkish floor pillows, drinking wine. Casanova had also brought a small bowl filled with aphrodisiac tablets. Hidden behind a curtain, a harpist was ready to provide musical accompaniment.

Thalia-Charpillon was already seated at the table, looking attentive. She was smiling and her full red lips contrasted with her smooth pallor. The clockmakers had used real human skin to cover her body, eight thousand patches removed from sixteen corpses. Her delicate hands with slender, long fingers, were covered by a pair of embroidered gloves. Her blue eyes reflected the light so eerily, the audience shuddered. The thought occured to everyone in the room that this was a real woman playing an automaton, and that they were being made sport of. Even Casanova, who had been present at the unpacking of the mechanism, found the illusion compelling.

Count Waldstein entered the room in a combat uniform, his mustache shining menacingly beneath his frown. He had decided to look angry. He sat down without a word and addressed his table companion harshly, while his valet served soup.

"You have been observed consorting with revolutionaries, Thalia! Do not deny it!"

This accusation was so preposterous, given Thalia's perfectly aristocratic looks and attire, that the audience guffawed. Undeterred, Waldstein continued: "You were seen wearing nothing but a linen shift, singing their songs and shouting their slogans!"

"Liberté, égalité, fraternité!" shouted Casanova.

The Count's voice rose. "How can you maintain your innocence when I have witnesses here!"

"Yes, we have seen her!" said Libussa.

"She's nothing but a whore," cried Claribelle. "She has given herself to all of them!"

Real tears streamed down Thalia's face. She said nothing, looking straight into the Count's angry gaze.

"So you deny it! Let us sup and then we will have proof!"

There was a prolonged silence as the Count brought the soup spoon to his lips and made an exaggerated slurping noise.

"Eat! What is the matter with you? Have you lost your appetite or do you prefer bread and pig fat to this divine mushroom broth?"

Waldstein harangued her like this some more while a steady stream of tears fell from her eyes into the soup. Casanova sensed that both Eliphas and Dorensky were most uncomfortable.

"It is only a game," he whispered.

"It is a mockery of the Golem," Eliphas whispered back.

"A mockery of human dignity," said Dorensky.

"Nothing of the kind," Laura said. "It is a stupid game of men."

"She is no virgin!" Claribelle said heatedly.

Waldstein's angry voice rose again. "If you will not eat my food you will be tested, my daughter!"

This appellation introduced a new element to the play. Everyone but Casanova was quite surprised by this turn of events.

The Count downed his wineglass and began to recite plaintively: "You are my only daughter! When you were sent to the convent, you were only ten. A stubborn child! When you came home at the age of fifteen, I hired the best teachers in the Empire for you! You learned languages, geometry, philosophy, geography, and history! Imagine! History! When you went to Paris to stay with the Duke of Orleans, I had no fear of your future! And then, three months ago, you ran away with a gang of bandits! It is a good thing that we captured them! What have they done to you! Your friends! Would you like to see your friends?"

Waldstein waved his arm and his valet Corvus came bearing a big silver tray on which were displayed the heads of two wild-haired men atop a mound of gently quivering eyeballs. He placed it carefully on the table.

A gasp of horror escaped everyone in the audience, except Casanova, who had been privy to the preparations. The heads were also automatons, and the eyeballs were made of tallow and porcelain. To the viewers they looked inescapably realistic, even more so when the heads started moving their lips and a series of inarticulate groans escaped them.

Libussa fainted. Laura covered her eyes. Everyone felt chilled and nauseous, unable to bear the spectacle any longer. At just that moment, Thalia rose to her feet, moved her arm forward, and pointed angrily at her father. He rose also and, taking her by the waist, carried her to the bed and threw her down on the covers.

The harpist, who had been accompanying each movement perfectly, now increased the tempo of her composition. The stunned audience remained rooted in place, their feelings having changed quickly from revulsion to sexual excitement.

Waldstein pulled down her bodice and Thalia's snow-white breasts spilled out, looking warm and alive, her nipples erect. He then yanked up her dress, revealing first her white thighs, then, to the shock of the audience, her finely spun fleece and the tiny crack of her jewel box. It looked to everyone as if Thalia was resisting the brutal assault. Her arms moved up and down and she tried in vain to cross her legs. Once more, the feeling that this was not a mechanical doll but the Count's real daughter, swept over everyone with visceral certainty.

Waldstein turned her over and pulled the dress further up, exposing her buttocks. He stood over her and motioned to his valet, who brought him a short whip. The Count sat on the back of her thighs and brought the whip down with all the force he could muster. Thalia cried out in agony. Waldstein's speech became quite incoherent. He accused her again of consorting with revolutionaries and swore to beat her until she was hungry enough to eat her comrades' brains.

It was almost a relief to everyone when he dropped the whip, undid his trousers, and, lifting up her buttocks, thrust himself into her from behind. A trickle of blood flowed out and stained the cover. Waldstein collapsed on top of her and cried out with genuine feeling: "My daughter! I was wrong! You were a virgin! Can you forgive me?" He began sobbing, but his sobs soon turned into snores as he fell asleep on top of the unmoving Thalia.

Equally unmoving was the audience, which appeared paralyzed, even though the performance was clearly over. Casanova was the first on his feet, applauding hard and crying, "Bravo! Bravo!" He was followed in short order by Claribelle, who was decidedly less enthusiastic. Nobody else bothered to clap.

As they started rising from the pillows to make their way out, Waldstein woke up and shouted: "That was only Act One! Please do not leave! She can be readjusted as a virgin for another adventure!"

Corvus removed the platter of heads and eyes discreetly.

"How little you think of women," said Laura, forgetting her position.

"Ah," said the Count, picking himself off the bed and readjusting his trousers, "now we must have the opinions of servants."

"Remember the future," said Casanova. "When everyone lives in glass houses, all lives will be a performance. The opinions of a servant will be as good as anyone's."

"Very well then, fräulein. In the future women will benefit from such devices. The blind fury of men will be spent on mechanical dolls instead of living and perhaps unconsenting women. There will also be mechanical men, able to satisfy the desire of women when they desire no more than such contact."

"I must leave, I have an urgent appointment," stammered Eliphas.

The Count turned to him. "Do you feel that this has been offensive to the Jews?"

"I don't know about the Jews," Eliphas said softly, "but this particular Jew is quite troubled."

"Explain then," the Count said menacingly, "what exactly disturbed you?"

"Very well." His voice became more firm. "My religion forbids touching corpses. Your mechanism is a corpse. Creating, or even pretending to create life through artifice is expressly forbidden. One of our rabbis created a human being and nothing but grief came to the Jews."

Dorensky, who had not said a word but had become as white as Thalia's buttocks, spoke now: "Human beings speak. Without language we are not human. Your illusion is dramatic but there is no intelligence. I must leave as well."

Faced with such a general revolt, Count Waldstein turned to Casanova. "What do you say to such objections, Chevalier?"

"Our audience has taken this spectacle much too broadly. No one dares to comment on the scene from the vantage point of their own feelings. I was repulsed, but also aroused. I believe that these sentiments overcame whatever objections I might have raised intellectually. Admit it, you were also aroused!"

Laura admitted it. "When the count whipped the doll, I was aroused. I blame my weakness on being a woman. Degradation has a certain attraction to a humble servant who has occasionally been punished by being whipped. It is a learned response."

"I was not aroused," Dorensky said firmly. "Without language there is no pleasure."

"Yes, I was aroused," Eliphas said, "for the same reasons,

perhaps, that Mademoiselle Brock mentioned. One learns to gain pleasure when one is crushed underneath the foot. That pleasure is a form of resistance to the pain. It is also an entirely private matter that should not be made visible in theater."

"But Jews are against making anything visible!" shouted Waldstein. "You have an injunction against icons! You have no art."

Casanova contradicted the Count. "The Jews have art. They make their images from words." He then turned to Libussa and Claribelle, who had not spoken, but had retired deeper into the shadows where they lay interlaced, mouth to mouth, while their hands were busy under each others' dresses.

"Bravo!" applauded Casanova, followed in short order by the Count, who now saw them. "There are some people who understand the appeal of theater instinctually!"

The conversation continued for some time, as did the drinking. No one left, but everyone kept stealing anxious glances at Thalia, who lay with her buttocks exposed on the bed, a dry trickle of blood under her. The Count also noticed the indecent appearance of his "daughter" and personally straightened her out, smoothing her dress, propping her up against the bed pillows, and covering up the stain. Thalia appeared now to be merely resting, her face peaceful and sleepy.

Casanova proposed that they all remove their clothing, wear blindfolds, and join Thalia in bed. "We will see then who can tell the difference between a living body and the automaton."

Claribelle and Libussa consented immediately, but both Eliphas and the Abbé made their apologies and left. Laura would have liked to follow them, but when she saw Casanova's sad expression, she was suddenly amused. She decided to stay and immediately proceeded to roll down her stockings.

They all sat on the bed, not daring to touch Thalia, who watched them with an unperturbed gaze as if it was her turn to be entertained. Corvus brought more wine and the aphrodisiac tablets and, later, platters of oysters. Casanova was the first to touch Thalia. Her breasts were surprisingly soft and lifelike. At his urging, they took turns touching her and everyone marveled at the texture. As the tablets took effect, everyone became more daring. The revived Count paid close attention to Claribelle and Libussa, who had positioned themselves like the queens on a playing card and were kissing each other deeply in their secret places. He placed himself inside Libussa and remained still while Claribelle's busy tongue entertained both. Laura took Thalia, stretched her on the bed, and carefully spread her legs. Casanova reached behind the nape of the doll's neck and pulled a small lever that revirginated the automaton. Laura guided him inside the virgin, who cried out when he broke the hymen. The trickle of blood that followed was identical to the previous one. They laughed.

A number of hours passed in vigorous exercise, mutual intimacy, and exhaustive pleasure. The time came when no one knew any longer what gender they were, enjoying the illusion that they possessed each others' sexual organs. It was from such sweet confusion at the peak of an orgy that Casanova had drawn the dual sex of his Micromegs.

In Waldstein's opinion, Thalia had been a success in her coming out in society. She had performed as well, if not better, than the daughter of any aristocrat. For his part, Casanova judged the doll to be an integral part of that future for which he was designing uniforms.

They lingered in bed, discussing the philosophical implications of automatons, as if having such a conversation in the nude was the most natural thing in the world.

"My mind feels a great deal sharper in the postcoital state," Laura said. "I feel as if the release hasn't been purely physical."

Casanova nodded. "Now, ma chérie, you have stumbled on

a great Rosicrucian secret. On the way to the Rosy Cross, the body must be exhausted by either pleasure or pain."

"Most Rosicrucians prefer pain," laughed the Count, who, like Casanova, was both a Mason and a Rosicrucian. Masonry being, by far, the less secret of the two organizations, they rarely mentioned it.

"This is the rosy cross," Claribelle said impertinently, slapping herself between the legs.

"Not so inaccurate," Casanova said seriously. "Many of our symbols stand for both the lower and the higher realms. Your jewel box is equivalent to a certain mystical level; the mirrors of the Tree of Life, they occupy the same Sephiroth."

"Our cabbalist friend has spent much time in that Sephiroth," said the Count.

Claribelle became aroused again. "He has spent no time at all in this one." Since the Chevalier made no sign and was, indeed, judging by the state of his mast, not in a position to take up the offer, she continued, "I have spent some time in that Seff . . . how you say it . . . myself, and I can attest to the curative effects of its essential juice."

The company then considered the comparative merits of female and male juices from a curative standpoint.

"A woman's juices being the original ones which all human beings must drink on their way to this world, it is clear that they have a greater healing effect," said Casanova. "I can still remember the taste of my mother's juices when I was born."

"That is a great claim indeed," laughed the Count, "and I hope that you'll permit me to be skeptical. Such memory, even if possible, cannot exist beyond the age when you tasted other women's juices. Their taste would have confused you."

"Not so," the Chevalier argued, "there was a quality of sweetness combined with the shock of light that has always stayed with me."

"The angel of forgetfulness did not put his finger on the Chevalier's lips," said Laura. "He remembers everything."

"The juices of men taste best," Libussa said firmly, surprising everyone, since they had assumed that she was quite dedicated to the sapphic arts. "They have more energy, more potential, they are alive. They try to burrow into your mouth like tiny demons."

"What do they taste like?" asked Claribelle in full faux innocence.

There were disagreements. Like quail eggs rolled in salt. Like unripe cranberries. Like squid eaten still wiggling. Like Russian caviar. Like oysters. Here, Casanova drew the line, explaining his certainty that the oyster, being nature's perfect mollusk, was the sum of male and female juices. Then they discussed diet and whether different foods influence the taste of juices. Most definitely, they decided. Someone who eats only flowers has to taste sweeter than a glutton fed on boar. Eating liver and peaches would produce an extraordinary flavor, decided Laura.

The company then decided to follow different diets for one whole month to verify some of these assertions. The Count, who was a hunter, swore to eat only deer and boar he had killed himself, with only the slightest of sauces made from the blood of the same animals. Casanova committed himself to a diet of goat milk, oysters, and melon. Laura thought that she could live on bread, pears, and cow milk since her opportunity for choice was quite limited in her position. Libussa was likewise hampered by the diet imposed on the servants by Hans Gelder, who having become more careful with the Chevalier's dishes, had yet to improve the commoner's fare. She said that she would try to exist solely on chicken, apples, and cheese. Claribelle vowed to consume only champagne, pâté de fois gras, and strawberries.

"And Thalia," the Count said, inclining his head toward the silent and smiling mechanical virgin, "will conduct all the taste tests."

The Count had his servant Corvus bring paper and ink and they drew a contract to follow the course they had set for themselves. Should anyone waver, he or she would be dealt with by the group as they saw fit.

They had lazily began putting their clothes back on, when there was a hard knock at the door. Corvus, who had instructed everyone not to disturb them, shrugged his shoulders. He opened it slightly and listened to the man on the other side. He then turned to his master, who was still without a shirt, and said: "A messenger from Vienna!"

"Let him in!"

A hooded, tired horseman in wet clothes stomped heavily into the salon, leaving big wet boot prints on the floor.

"I have ridden straight from Vienna to bring the news."

"Well, out with it, man."

"Two days ago, on the twenty-first of January, 1793, His Majesty Louis XVI lost his life for France. He was executed by guillotine and his head was shown to the mob at the Place de la Révolution."

For a moment, Casanova could see Louis's severed head on the table where the mechanical heads had been. He recalled the heads of Héloïse and the twins from the Bohemian hills, and they took on the features of the French king and queen. The face of Maria Christine, who so resembled Marie Antoinette, also hovered for an instant before his eyes. In a matter of months, Marie Antoinette would meet the same fate as her husband, the King.

Waldstein sent away the messenger and sat at the table with his head in his hands. His mission to France to save the royal family, undertaken three months before, had failed. He had been able to arrange the escape of several noble families, but he had failed to save the sovereigns, and he blamed himself.

One by one, everyone tiptoed out of the room, respectfully bowing at the door toward the stricken Count. Casanova remained just long enough to put an arm around his friend's shoulders. He said nothing, then he left the room. On his way out he took a last glimpse at the rumpled bed that had sheltered their happiness. He made a small gesture of parting toward the serene Thalia, who lay on her back upon her trickle of blood, ready to revirginate again.

"It may be easy for you," he said to himself after closing the door, "but our world will never be new again."

The contract Count Waldstein made everyone sign came to naught. Such frivolity was no longer possible. All Europe was at war with France; the Count joined his regiment at Augsburg and marched into battle. Dux was not untouched, but remained an oasis of calm amid the hostilities. Casanova abandoned the project of making a uniform for the future, to the great relief of the seamstresses, who found the Chevalier's unpredictable imagination quite unsettling; he devoted himself instead to the writing of his memoirs. The soldiers and the groom who had modeled for his new uniforms went off to war.

When Casanova wasn't writing he would sit for hours in the rose chair with Melampyge in his lap, staring vacantly out the window. His friends and lovers were dying one after another, even as he made them live in his remembrances. Frederick the Great was dead; the Baron de Roll followed him; his sister's husband, Peter August; Signora Manzoni, who had foreseen his future and had sheltered him in Venice. Mozart was gone as well; he died a pauper in Vienna, buried in an unmarked grave. Ambassador Foscarini, his last Venetian employer, had passed away; his youngest brother, Gaetano, who had abducted Marcoline; Father Gozzi; Bettina; General Kettler; the Comte de St. Germain; Pocchini; Lady Harrington, all gone. A procession of the dead passed him silently as he wrote. He made them live again, but he tried to be unsparing in his self-examination and adherence to the truth. If the dead were looking over his shoulder, they must have been uneasy.

Sometimes he had a fleeting, fearful thought that in writing about the past he was somehow killing the people who inhabited his memory. Casanova had some respect, and a degree of faith, in the cabbala, which taught that an intimate relation existed between words and that which they describe. It was possible, if one knew the right combinations, to create a world or destroy one with words. For the cabbalists, words drew their power from sound, but Casanova believed that another secret spring could feed them, namely the vividness of memory. If memory was capable of recreating the scent and texture of the past, wasn't it possible that it could infuse writing with the very essence of those things? In writing, perhaps, remembering could become life itself, endlessly renewed.

He had no illusions about his own powers, though; he knew, alas, that experience was inevitably diluted in the transfer to the weak medium of the written word. What vividness remained was hardly sufficient to kill anyone, or his poison-pen letters to such monsters in his life as the ex-majordomo Feldkirshner and the (now subdued) Hans Gelder, would have destroyed those enemies long ago. His writing had the power only to present pale shadows, perhaps to persuade, but it could not achieve the crystalline strength of the cabbalistic God-force.

The act of writing, however, was hypnotic; he became so

deeply entranced by the past that he didn't quite know where he was when his pen stopped moving. He would squint in the stingy winter light that squeezed through the panes of the high window in the library and make an effort to remember his body. His body! He wished he could forget it! He felt like Villon's old whore: teeth gone, skin like thin pergament, and his once elegant hands gnarled with arthritis. Laura prepared his tinctures of opium more and more often, but the pain was lifted only briefly, then lingered, giving the words he wrote a gravity that came from the battle to hold them down on paper.

The memoirist thought often of death, but in spite of his pains, he did not find suicide as appealing as he once had. "Life is a burden to me," he wrote. "What is the metaphysical being that prevents me from slaying myself? It is Nature. What is the other being who enjoins me to lighten the burdens of that life which brings me only feeble pleasures and heavy pains? It is Reason. . . . Reason tells me imperiously that I have no right to slay myself, with the divine oracle of Cen: *Qui non potest vivere bene non vivat male.* These eight words have such power that it is impossible that a man to whom life is a burden could do other than slay himself on first hearing them."

He did not forget that he had promised himself to visit the synagogue where his friend Eliphas was cantor. Perhaps there was some answer to the cabbalistic riddle among the Jewish scholars of Prague, with their Golem in the attic. He went as far as having the calèche prepared for the journey to Prague, but at the last moment, he decided that the journey would be futile. What secret powers did the Jews really have? Their unfortunate history didn't recommend the efficacy of their magic. The cabbala gave them only an aptitude for abstractions: language, philosophy, mathematics. Those talents, Casanova reasoned, were not much use in the afterlife. But they certainly made existence for the Jews more bearable in the here and now.

Laura was under instructions to let no one disturb him when he was writing, but that became quite impossible when Libussa began entering his chamber at all hours of the day and night. At first, he had humored the girl.

"What troubles you, Libussa?"

"I had a dream that I was at the top of a round building naked on a big round bed."

"The whole world seems to like you in that state."

"The whole world, it's true. I had to stay there in bed and receive visitors from all the nations. They came to the foot of the bed and then disrobed and, I don't know how to say this . . ."

"They did with you what I have seen you do on occasion."

"Yes, but, I don't know, they spoke the whole time in their strange languages, and there were all varieties of men, black, white, tan, vermillion. Some preferred the straightaway, others had a taste for my behind. I was expected to judge them all and then say which language was the best for doing . . . what we did. There was a glass canvas on the wall that showed me everything I was doing and, this is the strange thing, I had to press a lever every time one of the strangers pleased me more. The lever made big numbers appear on the canvas, two sets of numbers, one for the language, the other for the act. At the end, eight men with beards added everything up and they decided . . ."

"Don't tell me. The winner was German!"

"The first time they added up everything the winner was German, but when they checked their calculations they found that the winner was the language of Madagascar."

"Thank God!" exclaimed the Chevalier, visibly relieved.

"Chevalier, I would like to discuss the matter of which language will be spoken in the future . . . my dreams are not just stupid dreams."

"I have to agree with you; it is an important question. You have learned French very well, ma petite. What sort of language would you like to speak in the future? Are you going to learn Malagasy?"

"We have been considering . . ."

"We?"

"Yes, some of us have been meeting to talk about things like that. There are Czech boys, two German students, a Hungarian officer, and two Moravian winemakers. We feel that this war is going to free us from Austrian servitude and that we must have a new common language. You yourself have spoken of it. . . ."

Casanova had lost all interest in speculating about the future; he was living in the past. But the girl was stubborn. She had taken to wearing a red bonnet that looked uncomfortably like a Jacobin headdress. Perhaps this was the source of her new dreams.

"We feel that Czech should be the language of Bohemia and Moravia. At least, until we can learn Malagasy. What do you think?"

He found himself thinking, despite his desire to ignore the subject. He had kindled a flame he did not feel like tending.

"My dear girl," he replied, with only a hint of irritation, "the only language for a happy people is Italian. To be happy one must improvise, sing, and dance. My own language is ideally suited for improvisation. Have you any idea what happy spectacles erupt in Venice all hours of the day and night? Stages are set up in the campos and on the fondamenti at a whim. People going about their business transform themselves without warning into poets, storytellers, acrobats, singers. Venetians sing and whistle and they are answered by the songs of others across the canals. Men who have never met respond to each others' songs from a distance, adding verses. The gondoliers can put great composers to shame. We laugh at Pantalone, the Dottore, Arlecchino, and Brighella. Such public happiness, my lovely, cannot be had in German and not, I believe, in your Czech, though I must admit that there are superb musicians in Bohemia. . . ."

"That may be a matter of climate and temperament," Libussa said judiciously, "not language. The best lover was speaking Malagasy, remember?"

"You are mistaken, fraülein, the Italian language created the people and convinced the sun to shine harder! The Italian is the world's best lover. He takes pleasure in prolonged worship of his lover's body, and he sings to her with the divine voice of Ariosto. Compared with such care, the Frenchman's performance is nothing but necessity, while Germans, let's not speak of them, do not enjoy pleasure unless they are whipped and made to do disgusting things with urine and feces." He was joking, but only partly. It was, of course, impossible to know what came first, the language or the people, or who was the best lover, though he did suspect that he himself was that person. Most likely, language and love engendered one another in time.

Libussa insisted that the Chevalier should speak to her friends at one of their meetings. He declined, and grew even gloomier. Peasants having philological discussions! In a fragmented future Europe, such questions would be decided by force of arms.

"What happened to the passionate, silent girl who didn't say a word and spoke no French?" the Chevalier asked Laura after Libussa had gone.

"She's been dreaming a great deal. She sleeps ten hours a day, and when she's awake she walks about in a white dress with her arms stretched in front of her like a ghost. All the peasants have been coming to listen to her, like she is a saint or an oracle. She has been learning all sorts of things at the feet of Abbé Dorensky . . . have you noticed how they look at one another?"

"Well, that's it. Our little Abbé has infected her with his ideas!"

"What a way to talk!" she admonished him.

"Ideas are infectious," Casanova insisted. "They are a form of pox, and I have had them all."

"You've had all the ideas?"

"No, dear lady, all the forms of pox."

Laura looked at Melampyge, whose dark eyes seemed to ask, "What can you do with somebody like that?"

"You should drink your tea."

"Probably. But now, please forgive me, I must return to Spain, where I left Pellicia singing on the stage. She is going to take me to a ball where I will learn the fandango." He closed his eyes and saw himself performing that passionate and complex dance, possibly his favorite after the Venetian furlana. He had danced every dance, the allemande, the cabriole, the contredanse, the hornpipe, the gargouillade, the pasacaglia, the polonaise, the seguidilla, the landler, and some he might have forgotten. His arms tingled as if they were still holding the warm, softly scented bodies of his dance partners. But when he got up and tried to take a few fancy steps, his legs felt like sore sticks.

Libussa burst in again next day.

"Grampapa!" she called impertinently and came to sit on the rug next to his writing desk. Melampyge made a small growl of suspicion. "Please teach me the musical language of the Micromegs."

"In the first place," he said, quite irritated, "I am not your grampapa. Secondly, I wish that you would abandon the study of languages because it will drive you mad. Thirdly, you will never know as much as the Abbé, who has been studying since he was a child. Marry him, make him children, and speak whatever language comes out of your mouth first. And please quit dreaming so much, it is making the peasants nervous."

Libussa blushed and started rocking back and forth with her hands around her knees like a little girl.

"What is it that's driving you mad?" The Chevalier was becoming concerned about his little protégée.

"I'm not mad," she said, without stopping to rock. "I want to speak the right language. I dreamed that the Emperor of Languages flew me to his square house in the sky. We were inside a silver bird that made a noise like water going over a millstone. He wanted me to meet his wife, Language, who was very beautiful and was wearing a dress of newspaper. She made me suck her breasts and I got ink all over my tongue. The Emperor then made me write my name with my inky tongue on his belly."

Casanova was sure then that the girl was deeply troubled. When Abbé Dorensky came to visit, he admonished him.

"Have you been driving Libussa mad with your theories? She is a sweet and simple girl, any man would be delighted in her company. Do you intend to marry her?"

Even as he asked this, he thought that he did sound like the girl's father or grandfather might sound. Still, he had always tried to make sure that young women who had been his lovers eventually married well. When he'd had money he'd even given them dowries. Now only diplomacy was left.

Dorensky looked confused. "Marry? No, we were discussing . . . well, there is a group of us. We have been discussing the merits of the different tongues spoken in Bohemia—"

"I know all about that," he interrupted him. "What I want to know is if you know that the girl is in love with you. You are making her unhappy."

The Abbé thought about this. "She is not a virgin," he said.

Casanova got up and picked up his walking stick. "No!" he shouted, "but you are one stupid scholar!" He raised the stick. "Which language would you rather speak? The language of blows or the language of love?"

When the Abbé didn't answer, Casanova brought the stick down on his head, missed, and hit him on the shoulder instead. The Abbé scurried to his feet, dodging the blows from the Chevalier's stick.

"One more time! Which language—"

"Love, love!" Dorensky shouted, trying to keep from laughing. "Please put that thing down."

Casanova did. "If you were a man of honor," he grumbled, "you would now challenge me to a duel and I would have to kill you."

"How did we get from the subject of language to dueling?" wondered the Abbé, catching his breath.

"The subject is never language," said Casanova angrily, "the subject is always love!"

"Still," insisted the Abbé, "why should I marry? The truth be known, I don't even like women. Not that way, anyhow."

"I thought as much." Casanova dropped the stick. "We are not talking about women," he said. "We are talking about a girl who may be your intellectual equal, certainly a great dreamer, who wants to marry you."

"I like her company," the Abbé said thoughtfully. "She speaks beautiful Czech and knows many of the legends and songs of Bohemia. But her dreams trouble me. I think that she may start a new crusade."

"You see? That's enough for a whole lifetime of amusement!"

Libussa and Josef were married in the chapel at Dux by the old priest, who looked with unconcealed disgust upon the Chevalier, giving away the girl as if he was her father. For the occasion Casanova had donned a brilliantly plumed hat and his best suit. Libussa looked like a white candle, and gave off a flickering light. The groom was suitably unmonkish, having conceded to wear Casanova's green silk coat to the solemn occasion. Laura looked wonderful in a blue gown embroidered with gold keys. Her bosom was nearly bare and she had piled her hair high and painted her lips. Casanova felt his inappropriate Micromeg attempt to rise during the ceremony.

Afterward, Casanova hosted a feast for which he had paid by selling the pharmacist Pallius another recipe, a worthless one this time, for making hair grow. He had chosen the menu and had cooked the ragout himself, leaving Gelder to prepare only the cold dishes. Of course, there were oysters, which the Chevalier hoped would work their well-known magic on the Abbé on his nuptial night. Eighteen cases of wine and fifty bottles of champagne sufficed to inebriate all the invited guests, which included all the servants, the grooms, the monks and nuns in the dilapidated wing, the majordomo and his boyfriend, and several lesser nobles from the vicinity.

Four musicians came from Prague and played, at Casanova's request, quartets by Mozart. There were also six Gypsy fiddlers and a Russian with a strange string instrument. Bohemia was full of mendicant musicians; all one had to do was shout "Music!" and gangs of them showed up. Casanova loved them. He had played the fiddle himself in Venice, the only real job he had ever had. And the worst paid, incidentally.

The bride and the groom danced together, then Casanova took Libussa into his arms and swept across the floor like a young man.

"Well, what language have you decided to speak?" he asked as they took another turn. "German, Czech, Loveski, French?"

"All of them!" cried the intoxicated girl, flying a foot off the floor.

I am the same man, thought Casanova, not old, not young. How many brides had he given away? Eight that he could think of. Some of them were carrying his child and all of them had been grateful in the end. How many times had he been on the verge of being married, escaping only at the last moment through the agency of miraculous intervention or through his own skills? He regretted only his parting from Henriette. He made a quick calculation. If he had ten children—he knew about ten—and if each one of his children had two children, that would be twenty new Casanovas during his lifetime. In two generations, Europe could be overrun by Casanovas. In the *Icosaméron*, Edouard and Elisabeth, brother and sister, become the parents of forty pairs of twins, each consisting of a boy and a girl. During their stay inside the earth, which lasts 324 Micromeg years, or eighty-one earth years, the couple and their progeny multiply to more than six hundred thousand earthlings who make themselves master of the Micromeg world. Casanova felt a pang of remorse. Did the earthlings really have to reproduce at such a rate until they overran Paradise? Wasn't there something obscene there? His ten children had been conceived despite his precautions. He had always carried lambskin gloves that he almost always used and he was expert at the art of coitus interruptus. Still, he had slipped. But he was no Edouard.

The Abbé and Libussa retired to a private chamber that the majordomo had reluctantly put at their disposal for one night. Casanova and Laura retired as well, leaving behind the guests and the musicians, who had no intention of leaving until all the wine was drunk.

Casanova did not feel well. The champagne and oysters had upset his stomach and he couldn't sleep. Every time he closed his eyes, he saw one of the loves of his past walking toward him with a book written in Greek, Hebrew, or Latin. These were, of course, the perfect languages, but he could not find a way to impose them on the future. The future, like a petulant whore, kept refusing his proposals and spit on all the books. The future, which he could not see, was standing behind a screen so that only her shadow was visible. The shadow looked like Arlecchino. Several times, the Chevalier woke Laura and asked her to take a look at the darkness in the room to see if she could discern the shadow of the future. She could not. She tried to reason with him, telling him that this future was only the consequence of an upset stomach and that, if he could sleep, he would find no trace of it in the morrow. At long last, the Chevalier slept, but not before the future did some awful gymnastic leaps and threw a little black book at him, which he caught in his mouth and swallowed. The book had a bitter taste, but once in his stomach, it calmed him.

In the morning, he realized that he had reenacted the biblical scene from the Revelations of St. John, in which the angel gives John a book to swallow that tastes terrible in the mouth but is sweet as honey in the stomach. Casanova, unaccustomed to biblical visions, began trembling violently. Only a great dose of opium made his trembling subside. He had lived with the classics, strenuously avoiding more than strictly formal contact with the Christian book. There had even been a time in his youth when he had incurred the wrath of the priests, including his tutor Gozzi, because he wrote a sermon quoting Horace instead of St. Augustine or any other six hundred approved apostolic writers. But he had gotten his way and had preached with the aid of the pagan, but the episode ended his ecclesiastic ambition. It had been some kind of secret test.

༄ With quill in hand, Casanova began rereading his memoirs, crossing out a word here, replacing one metaphor with another. While most of the time he was convinced that the work would be burned upon his death, some part of him envisioned a reader. It was for her sake that he never used a crude word to describe a woman's "secret flower," and he worked to concoct metaphors for that divine place, finding that in so doing he was also writing a parallel poem. He was fond of "the temple of Venus," which echoed widely, or "the field of battle," or "the flowering field," or "the arena of combat," envisioning the place as a battleground or an intoxicating garden, both vast and resistant, conquerable only by his "thunder," or "pirate," or "humanity's chief agent," or his "verb." And the vital fluid that was coaxed from that battle was, variously, "the nectar," "the liqueur," or the "radical humid," an alchemical term. He was quite astounded, in rereading, how much his story followed the course of the alchemical operation. Perhaps he was only dreaming that he was writing his memoirs when, in reality, he was writing an alchemical treatise on the Great Work. He envisioned the stack of pages on his desk sitting atop a stone tablet that was inscribed as he wrote on the paper, but the words he put down on the paper were not the ones that appeared on the stone. The inscriptions in the stone were in an unknown alphabet, a species of cuneiform. He could not read them when he closed his eyes and saw the stone. He knew that in order to read it, he would have to dream it, but he never succeeded. He wondered if perhaps Libussa could dream it for him.

After the wedding, Libussa had gone with Dorensky to Prague, but she had returned in less than a month, wearing an azure dress and a white cape and the Jacobin red bonnet on her head, as well as a pair of golden lace gloves and matching golden boots. Her appearance was quite startling, and Casanova had to threaten the majordomo with his sword and black magic before he would consent to hire her back.

About her time in Prague she said not a word, and Casanova did not inquire, certain that Laura would let him know if Libussa confided in her. Thus, he was not surprised when Laura, looking more serious than usual, told him that things had not gone well with the Abbé, who was either unable or unwilling to perform his husbandly duties. Libussa's dreams had become more and more bizarre, and she gained a following of ex-monks and ex-nuns, novice cabbalists, poets, and would-be mystics. They met at the U Radice Café in a back room where they would listen to Libussa recount her dreams. Then they would indulge in an orgy of interpretation, taking every element of the troubled girl's dreams to have profound significance. Some of her apostles claimed that she was an oracle whose dreams described both the near and the far future; others saw her dreams as a kind of new gospel that contained the founding doctrine of a new monastic order which would be open to both men and women; still others sought clues in her dreams for a new organization of society. Libussa herself was not interested in these interpretations, but had not disdained the attentions of young Count Radnitz, who had dressed her in azure and gold, like a Greek priestess. Or, at least, like a Greek priestess in the theater. Count Radnitz had enthusiastically taken over her husband's duties, as well. Unfortunately, the Count had been called to his regiment and sent off to defend Austria. Libussa had abandoned the Abbé in the middle of the night and returned to Dux in a Gypsy wagon.

Casanova explained to her the matter of the stone inscribed with the strange script and Libussa went to sleep immediately, happy to dream a solution for her benefactor. She woke up an hour later and told him what she had seen.

She had dreamed Casanova, dressed in a Greek tunic, sitting in the agora in an ancient Greek city. A group of boys, ranging in ages from twelve to seventeen, sat around him listening as he philosophized.

"That is Socrates!" exclaimed Casanova.

"I didn't know the philosopher's name, but I heard some of his speech. He said that teaching cannot exist outside love and that a teacher must sleep with his students and instruct them in the wisdom of both mind and body."

She had seen him making love with two of the boys in a white house set on a rocky cliff overlooking the sea. Afterward, the philosopher Casanova and the boys went bathing in the waves. One of the boys dove to the bottom and surfaced holding a stone tablet inscribed with runic characters.

"You have seen it then!"

"Yes, but I could not get close enough to read it."

"Well, go back to sleep." He prepared her a tincture of opium and Libussa went promptly back to sleep.

Watching the girl dreaming on his bed, Casanova laughed. If she hadn't been so innocent, he would be sure that he was being duped. How innocent was she anyway? The idea of the inscribed stone had begun as one of his fancies, a fancy that soon took on some sort of substance because he had seen it so clearly in his mind's eye. He had transferred that picture, drawn entirely by his imagination, to Libussa's excitable imagination. Now she had easily made that a reality with her dream. It takes only two people to make the most preposterous fantasy real, he mused. When a hundred or a thousand people share a fancy, its reality is no longer disputed. Laws are written to legitimize it, armies raised to defend it, palaces built to house it. How else could one explain the persistence of such doctrines as the Virgin Birth, or the Holy Trinity, or the seven-day creation of the world? If one was aware of the consensual nature of reality, one would indeed be a fool not to take utmost advantage of the human capacity for delusion. The world was a source of pleasure and wealth for anyone daring enough to milk its wonderments.

After comforting himself with this line of demystifying reason, Casanova was astonished to hear what Libussa brought next back from sleep.

"I held the stone," she said, "and though I didn't recognize the marks, the stone read its story into my mind. It said, 'Waking several hours later I saw, or thought I saw, a dazzlingly beautiful woman come down from the chimney, wearing a huge pannier and a magnificent dress, with a crown on her head set with a multitude of stones that gave off fire. She approached slowly, looking both majestic and kind, and sat down on my bed. She drew from her pocket some small boxes, which she emptied over my head, murmuring words. After making a long speech, of which I understood nothing, and kissing me, she left as she had entered, and I went back to sleep.'"

Casanova was shaken by Libussa's revelation. She had recited word for word the greatest single event of his life, the miracle that had brought him into being. When he was a very young child, his mind had been strangely slow to develop, and, suffering from continuous nosebleeds, he had been taken to a witch on the island of Murano, and she had healed him. As he lay in bed in the house of the witch, his mind fully awake for the first time, he had a profound vision of a beautiful woman, the queen of the night, the mother of all that was good, the perfect lover. He had already written the passage into his memoirs.

Convinced now that Libussa must have somehow read his manuscript, he did not know whether to strangle the girl on the spot or to punish her in front of the whole household. Even as unreasoning anger flooded through him, he thought; what if the girl had not read his manuscript? Impossible. Still, something in him sensed the truth. He had asked her to read the secret stone that he had inscribed himself and she had read on it the secret of his survival. And that secret contained a further secret, because in his childhood vision the beautiful lady had made *"a long speech, of which I understood nothing."* The words she spoke then were still as secret as the words of the stone had been before he sent Libussa to the depths of the sea of sleep to retrieve it. Doubtless, hidden in the speech of the beautiful queen who saved his life was yet another secret. And many others, inscribed behind that one. Nature, Casanova saw at once, was an immense unfolding flower in whose billions of petals the soul wandered. The joy of the flower was immense. Her secrets might never be fully known, but one could know the beauty of the infinite mystery.

He embraced Libussa.

Hearing German, writing in French, dreaming in Italian, Casanova had the sense that his intellectual world was being dismantled every day. These different languages not only had their own obvious character, but that character shifted subtly with each speaker. For instance, Laura Brock's German, when she spoke with Libussa, had a softness he recognized as an emotional quality of temperament; the sound was she. There was a plea for understanding in it and a vivacity that Libussa, in her turn, reciprocated with what seemed to him a single long sentence, a species of lullaby that a forest maiden might utter with water falling in the background. There was water in the women's speech, a quality wholly absent from the conversations of men. Casanova listened to Count Waldstein speak to Langerhoff and heard, instead of water, horse hooves tearing up dry earth. He asked Laura to read him some of Goethe's verse. It sounded almost beautiful to him, accompanied by the gurgling brook that was in her speech. Abbé Dorensky's recitation of the same verses produced an unpleasant sensation, as if a firm hand had wrapped all five fingers around his heart and threatened him with extinction if he did not bow down. There was more than a hint of coercion in the language.

The Austrian Emperor Joseph II had made German the language of his empire for practical reasons; the administration of the empire was a great deal more efficient if the bureaucracy used German uniformly. He had not counted on the resistance of every ethnic group to his brilliant plan. He certainly had no pan-Germanic intentions. The royal family spoke French, which was the language of the European aristocracy, and he had even picked up a smattering of Hungarian and Czech that he liked to trot out on various ceremonial occasions. The Hungarians, who had gone their own way many times, wanted equal preference given to their language. There was some discussion in the imperial council, but no one took this idea seriously. Hungarian was so strange a language no outsider could ever learn it or even pronounce it. One accepted theory about the origin of the Hungarian language was that it had been shouted on horseback by Attila's hordes and that the wind had snatched away the vowels, leaving only dense consonants capable of carrying a message even at great speed in a dust storm on the vast puszta. Hungarian was a passionate language, but not aesthetically relaxed like Italian, or fiercely baroque like Spanish. The sounds of Hungarian were like the sound of flesh rent by wolves, of glistening fangs crunching on bone under a bright moon. Such a language could never fit within the orderly forms of Joseph's bureaucracy. German, with its combinatory powers and seeming precision was infinitely better suited to the task.

French, a truly subtle and capable language, was entirely unacceptable to both the friends and foes of Austria. On this point, a great enemy of Austria like Frederick the Great and a Viennese café owner could agree without hesitation. German was the only possible imperial language, and neither Joseph nor his successor, Leopold, understood the irrational anger of the subject peoples made to use it.

Casanova suspected that the matter was quite primal, having to do with some message carried by the sound, if not the actual meaning, of German words, a message that made one's blood (if one's blood was Italian, for instance) boil, before reason had a chance to intervene. He had certainly not felt that about English, a language he had never mastered, but for which, despite his ignorance, he had conceived philosophical respect. He had been encouraged in this regard by Voltaire's *Philosophical Letters,* which had brought the ideas of Locke, Newton, and Shakespeare into French thought.

As he considered the secret, antagonizing message carried by the German language, Casanova wondered if the provocation might be an urging to suicide. The despair that animated young Werther or the poetry of Schiller were of an inhuman origin; something sidereal and demonic seemed to inhabit the language, and if this was the case, the empire based in that language was doomed to self-dissolution.

He was absorbed by these thoughts when the week's post arrived. The early successes of the French armies were being reversed. The Viennese papers were exultant, the French papers somber. After the execution of the monarch, a coalition put together by the British was finally resisting further advances and taking back territories. Other unprecedented coalitions were forming; rather than fight the Prussians, Catherine of Russia entered into an agreement with her old enemy and partitioned Poland. Prussia acquired Gdansk and a vast territory linking up

Silesia and the Baltic provinces. Austria was not included in this apportionment, to the embarrassment of Emperor Joseph, who fired all his ministers. Still, an Austro-Prussian alliance turned westward, recapturing Frankfurt and marching into the southern Netherlands. Spain and Britain blockaded the French Mediterranean coast. The days of the young republic seemed numbered, even as Danton thundered before the Convention, "You have thrown down your gauntlet to them, and this gauntlet is a king's head, the signal of their coming death," and Brissot declaimed in the same vein, "We cannot be calm until Europe, all Europe, is in flames!"

But it looked as if the Convention was beginning to make some overtures for peace, even considering the restoration of the Bourbon monarchy. Dumouriez threatened to march on Paris to release the Queen and the Dauphin from captivity and proclaim the latter Louis XVII, but his troops refused to budge. Even Danton, only months after his bloodthirsty speech, began sounding a conciliatory note, deflecting a motion from Robespierre that anybody advocating negotiation with the enemy should be guillotined.

This was all very well, but Casanova felt little satisfaction. No matter what the outcome of the conflict, old Europe had been shaken to its roots by the French Revolution. The eighteenth century was finished in every way. No longer would an adventurous man be able to go at will between cities and states, with only his wits and breeding to commend him. There would be defended borders, new and bloodier conflicts. The old gentlemanly rules of war were being abolished, not that they had been observed that stringently in his lifetime. Advances in artillery made longer and more devastating conflicts a certainty. Hollow-sounding principles would supercede agreements between men, and ambitions like those of Frederick and Catherine would render impotent the will of smaller nations.

Andrei Codrescu

Casanova could remember a time when Voltaire's pamphlets were not used as justification for murder and revolution; when Rousseau's *Social Contract* was read only by a handful of salonards; when Montesquieu's name was unknown outside a small coterie; when the words "liberty, fraternity, egality" had meaning for the Masons that did not resemble in the least their Jacobin translation. But what did that prove? The treachery of language? The ability of words to acquire the meaning of their most successful use? Did words themselves mean anything? Or did they mean simply whatever a majority took them to mean? Did words mean the same thing in England, France, Holland, or Venice? More often than not, the same words meant different things in different times and places, which was why there were lawyers and lexicographers. Despite such evidence, Casanova believed in an innate power belonging to the word itself, to its sound. It was his sole belief beyond the realm of Reason that clinging to words was some of the demiurgic substance that created the world. He had no opinions about the soul, life after death, or the ontological mysteries of religion which were a priori outside of Reason and could not therefore be subject to its dictates. His body, he believed, was the sole instrument for knowing the world. Beyond the evidence of his senses there was nothing to discuss. Yet one of his senses, possibly his ear, told him that words had an existence above and beyond their ordinary use.

A letter from Prince de Ligne lay on his desk, but Casanova dreaded to open it. The Prince would not have written from the battlefield but for dire news.

My dear Casanova,

Forgive my brevity. We have just taken Condé in France and there are sounds of dying men outside the window, mixed with some celebratory shouts by our men, who will be drunk shortly. A messenger from Provence

*came last night with sad news regarding your friend
Henriette de . . . The castle of your lady friend has been
burned and the entire family perished in the Terror. I will
spare you now, but will recall every detail to you when we
are face-to-face. I regret being the bearer of such news.
Be brave, my friend,
de Ligne*

Casanova stood at the window and cried. He had been
philosophically prepared for this when he did not hear from
Henriette, but the reality was unbearable. His past did not
simply fade away, it was wrenched from him. Now, more than
ever, it was necessary for him to review what he had written in
his memoirs, to make absolutely sure that Henriette's portrait
was etched in glass with a diamond, just as her words had
been, *Tu oublieras Henriette, aussi.* Not only would he not forget Henriette, he would make sure that posterity didn't either.

Rereading his memoirs, he was seized by doubt. A frivolous
man had written them. A man in a hurry, who had not taken
enough pains to explain his philosophy. Casanova tried to imagine his future reader, but could not. He could only envision
glum, bearded young men with tragic expressions, reared on
The Sorrows of Young Werther and the rantings of Robespierre,
pitching his volumes into the fire. Stern, moralistic young faces,
disgusted by their own bodies, looking on him with contempt
from their flag-draped perches in a solemn future. Well, he
would save them the effort, and burn the book himself.

Laura brought his supper and sat by his side, looking at the
newspapers strewn by his chair. She commented mildly on the
events they described, but Casanova made no reply. But then
she said something startling.

She said, "I much prefer your stories to theirs."

"Those are not stories, my dear. What you read there are

accounts of dreadful things taking place now. Mine are stories of happiness from the past."

"I prefer the past, then."

Casanova was overcome by affection for her; Laura had made bearable his years in Bohemia, and he could not imagine what his life might have been like without her constant presence and lovely imagination. The idea that she would voluntarily abandon the present in the flower of her youth and follow him willingly into the past moved him to tears. Old fool.

Laura smiled and wiped away his tears with her linen handkerchief. "I am sure I'm not alone in my prefence. There will come a time when the news of today will also be far in the past, and won't seem so important, but your stories will continue to give delight."

Casanova caught his breath. He felt obscurely that the girl had spoken a truth, and that she would help fulfill her own prophecy. He had always entrusted his books and other valuables to the women he had loved and he had never been disappointed. For one who traveled as much as he did, loss would have been inevitable. Invariably, however, the keepers of his trunks in far-flung corners of Europe had preserved and saved them. Casanova, the vagabond, who often left a city in desperate hurry with nothing but his coat and his sword, never lost anything. This was a miracle, but since he did not believe in them, he attributed it to his lucky star. He had two stars, a lucky one and an unlucky one. His lucky star protected his health and his possessions. His unlucky star kept wealth and prestige from his grasp. His lucky star had been the more powerful by far. He hugged Laura. He decided to put off burning his memoir until he could accomplish an urgent task, possibly the last he would ever undertake.

ᴏᴏ**O**ne day shortly after his seventieth birthday, which he had celebrated with a small party at which Laura arranged for the deflowering of a peasant girl by a mustachioed Hungarian, the Chevalier departed in his calèche without a word of farewell. He had ordered the horses harnessed at dawn, under the greatest secrecy, and had spent most of the night making neat bundles of his manuscripts and locking them in a big trunk. On top of the trunk he left a letter addressed to Laura in which he begged her not to worry about his whereabouts. It was entirely possible, he wrote, that he would not return. He had been given the opportunity for a position at an unnamed royal court, a position that suited his disposition much better than the job of librarian at Dux. He would establish himself, then he would send for her and his trunk. He also left a letter for Count Waldstein, thanking him for having sheltered him for so many years and for having defended him against the insults of an uncouth staff. Here a note of bitter sarcasm slipped into his grateful effusions, but he made no effort to temper it. Waldstein had been a good patron, but he was a fair-weather friend who had taken the part of Casanova's enemies more often than not. Casanova added that some of his bitterness was only the irascible temper of an old man. He did not reveal his destination, but he offered that from his new position he might be able to influence some of the events of the day. Was that too great a claim? Perhaps. But he had no doubt of it.

He had hired the Hungarian to be his driver, though he barely knew the man. He was taciturn and fierce-looking, with a mean-looking scar on his left cheek, but something told the Chevalier that the man was honest, and not without a sense of humor. As Dux castle receded behind him in the early morning mist, Casanova instantly felt better. Embarked on what was possibly the last adventure of his life, he felt like the young man who had always been happiest on the road, looking forward to an uncertain but exciting future.

His disappearance caused great consternation. Laura was mad with worry. Gelder spread a rumor that the librarian was a spy who had only come to Dux to search for a very valuable manuscript in the library. He had stolen it and fled. The priest said that it was an alchemical manuscript that contained the secret of the philosopher's stone. Casanova had most certainly gone to a hidden laboratory to produce gold and to make himself immortal. Others said that he had gone back to Venice to work once more for the Inquisition, part of a secret plan for papal troops to invade Bohemia. Castle emissaries left for Prague to report the Chevalier's disappearance to Count Waldstein.

Waldstein read Casanova's letter carefully, frowning and then smiling. It was the eve of his own departure for another campaign in France and he was in a reflective mood. "Mark my words," he said to no one in particular, "he will be back in a fortnight with his tail between his legs, full of extraordinary and improbable stories!" He was not so sure about his own return. He had heard worrisome news of a revived French army, strengthened by inexperienced but enthusiastic revolutionary fanatics who thought nothing of marching into death singing their accursed "Marseillaise." This new breed of soldier was fearless and foolish, without an instinct for self-preservation. Waldstein would rather fight skilled Prussian mercenaries, with their deadly but professional precision, than these suicidal idealists. He threw the Chevalier's letter into the fire.

Casanova's route took him directly to Germany, where signs of recent fighting were evident. For two nights, he was unable to find rooms in any inn; wounded soldiers lay in every available corner and food was scarce. Several times his carriage was stopped by the passage of ragged troops; and he got through by invoking now the name of the Prince de Ligne, now that of Waldstein, and waving a packet of sealed papers that he claimed he must urgently deliver to one general or another.

Seventy years old, and ill suited to the rigors of a long journey, Casanova was tired and beginning to catch a cold. Luckily, just outside Tübingen he found a small landowner willing to house and feed him, his servant, and his horse. The man's farm was within sight of the medieval wall of the city, on a hill that had once been carefully cultivated, but which had recently been burned. Casanova and the Hungarian driver were shown to rooms that were bare except for straw mattresses and washbasins. A lively hunchback, dressed in rags that made it difficult to tell whether it was male or female, brought in a bucket of hot water, and Casanova sponged off the grime of travel.

Supper with the farmer's family was a pleasant surprise. A long table had been covered with a linen tablecloth and was set with lovely dishes of Dresden faience. The family consisted of seven daughters between the ages of eleven and nineteen, and three younger boys. The farmer's wife was a neatly dressed frau who seemed still young and was anxious to make a good impression on the Italian gentleman. She smoothed her starched black apron over and over between serving hearty German dishes of sausages, sauerkraut, potatoes, baked beans, and dark beer. Considering the devastated surroundings, this was quite a feast. Casanova imagined that deep cellars dug into the hillside must hold enough food to survive several wars.

He ate like a wolf, raising his eyes now and then to consider the feminine company, which looked prettier and lovelier with each glass of beer. He noticed that his coachman had quite a grin on his face, sitting perhaps a bit too stiffly between two of the resident maidens.

"You have here a blooming orchard of beauties!" Casanova

261

complimented the farmer, who nodded without looking up from his plate. But the mother beamed.

"The seigneur speaks very fine German," she said. "Thank God that the war has passed."

These two sentiments seemed incongruous, but had the war not passed, appreciation of his polylinguistic abilities would have been moot. The woman had native intelligence.

"Has the war caused you very much hardship?" he asked.

At this, all the women started talking at once, to the visible distress of the pater familias, who piled more sausage onto his plate and kept his eyes lowered. From what the Chevalier gathered, all but the youngest girls had hid in caves while the French and the Prussians battled nearby. The farm had been requisitioned by officers of both camps, who had been nearly perfect gentlemen. Here, the frau lowered her eyes in embarrassment and her husband swallowed another sausage nearly whole. The girls interrupted each other to describe the tedium of hiding while being able to observe the battle from concealed openings. That had been their entertainment for an entire month.

"Not the *whole* entertainment," offered the seventeen-year-old, who was the prettiest. She looked significantly at one of her slightly younger sisters, who hung her head.

Casanova resolved to question the girls more closely, so he requested that the two of them prepare him a bath. He was in familiar and delightful territory and he could not resist the old game. The mother and father did not protest his request, though the other girls clamored for the honor. Casanova made peace by telling them that he would stay for three days so that they would all have a chance to tend him and his manservant.

But the rich chocolate cake that followed the hearty dishes decreed that the bath was not to be; Casanova fell into a deep sleep as soon as he lay down, listening to the throaty laughter of the Hungarian enjoying his bath.

On the second night, he did have a luxurious sponge bath that both girls lovingly administered, not the least embarrassed by his half-erection, which they touched, as if by mistake, several times. In the course of their ministrations, they told him the true story of the war, which they had spent less hidden, and more exposed, than their parents were led to believe. After hiding for a week, they had sneaked out. They met some friendly soldiers who, in exchange for their favors, protected them from harm. Indeed, their hideout became quite a place of merriment, though one night they were nearly caught by a patrol and were in real danger of being violated by many men instead of just their chosen sweethearts. When pressed by the Chevalier, they admitted that their sweethearts had often traded them among themselves, but the girls had not minded. While they recalled this part of the story, their hands lingered on him longer and longer, until, unable to stand it any more, Casanova asked to see their beauties. The oldest put her finger to her lips and pulled down her bodice with one hand. Her breasts were white and full and the nipples were purple and battle-ready. The younger pulled up her skirt, under which she wore no drawers, and showed the Chevalier a pair of well-formed lips lodged deeply within a soft nest of reddish hair. Casanova put his finger there and she sighed, moving on it, until he withdrew it and put it to his lips, tasting deeply the flavor that gave strength to his life. He trifled now with one, now with the other, feeling his age not in the slightest. They parted with sweet kisses on all their naughty parts and Casanova gave them a thaler each to buy themselves pretty dresses. They promised to return in the morning. The Chevalier slept as if it was 1775 in Naples, not 1793 in Tübingen.

Andrei Codrescu

꙳The square in front of Tübingen Cathe-
dral was bustling. A group of rowdy students surrounded a
longhaired youth who stood atop a crate making some sort of
speech. Casanova approached, without anyone taking the
slightest notice of him, and realized that the youth was not
making a speech, but reciting poetry. His eyes were closed and
there was an ecstatic look on his face. Prepared to listen with
some preconceived disdain, the Chevalier was surprised by the
profundity and clarity of the young poet's recitation. There was
something unpleasingly irregular about his verse, but it was
undeniably of superior quality. His references to Greek gods
were accurate, though strangely contorted. What struck
Casanova was the quality of the passion that made the words
sing, a quality that was somehow Italian, not at all like
Goethe's or Schiller's.

> *Jezt komm und hulle, freundlicher Feuergeist,*
> *Den zarten Sinn der Frauen in Wolken ein,*
> *In goldne Traüm' und schuze sie, die*
> *Bluhende Ruhe der Immerguten.*

> *(You come now, friendly spirit of fire, and wrap*
> *The women's delicate minds in veils of clouds,*
> *In golden dreams, and keep safe*
> *In them the blooming peace of boundless goodness.)*

The poet's audience was appreciative in a rather derisory
way, and seemed determined to gently mock him, though they
were clearly moved. One student pushed a mug of beer at him,
which the poet drank thirstily before continuing his lilting
recitation in a voice that was not entirely masculine. At last, he

fell off his improvised stage and landed directly on Casanova's servant, who held him up as if he was a dummy. Casanova took one of his arms and they half walked, half pulled him to a tavern, followed by the rowdy fellows.

Inside, they deposited the poet between them on a wooden bench and Casanova called for beer all around. In the hubbub that ensued, the Chevalier was able to ascertain a number of things. The poet's name was Friedrich Hölderlin, and he was assumed by most of his companions to be mad. He had been a tutor to the children of a rich banker and had fallen in love with the banker's wife, Susette Gontard, for whom he wrote all his verses. There was a general discussion of poetry, from which Hölderlin absented himself completely, drinking instead with great concentration. The other students were not so shy. One of them said that Hölderlin's obsession with Greek gods was something that had already been overcome by Goethe, Germany's greatest poet.

"Goethe has found our own German gods who live for us more than those dead Greeks!" he exclaimed.

He was seconded by another, who shouted, "Goethe has killed the Greeks! Our German gods have destroyed the Greek gods!"

The others banged their beer steins on the table in approval.

Hölderlin, though he said nothing, allowed a skeptical grimace to play on his face. It did not go unnoticed.

"I suppose you think yourself greater than Goethe!" the first one said with unconcealed hostility. "You think you are better than your fellow Germans!"

Casanova wondered why Germans had to be so loud. Whenever he had found himself in the midst of a discussion in that language, the level of the noise was deafening. Italians were loud too, but not in such a harsh, menacing way. He intervened. "A true poet does not need to assert his nationality over and over. The beauty of his language speaks for him!"

"You find his language beautiful?" another student shouted.

"You ask this as if you would mind my opinion no matter what it was," the Chevalier said gently. "I will tell you what I think if you assure me that you will not draw your sword if my opinion does not agree with yours."

Everyone laughed and the belligerent questioner looked away.

"I find his language beautiful indeed and for a reason that might not be to your liking. There is classical beauty in his verse, which reminds me of Ovid and Tasso. I like it precisely because it is so very different from your Goethe."

Even as he said these words, Casanova knew that he was coming dangerously close to heresy. These young men worshiped Goethe in a manner that was not rational and allowed for no measured critical response. Speaking ill of Goethe meant speaking ill of Germany, the German language, and whatever else their fierce hearts beat for at the moment. At the end of the century every heartbeat was engaged, it seemed, in something important. As if to reinforce this thought, the bells of Tübingen began to toll the noon hour.

The poet Hölderlin had listened to the Chevalier with great attention, and a look of gratified bewilderment spread over his face before his head nodded and hit the table with a thump. With the passing of his ostensible subject into unconsciousness, Casanova considered the discussion finished, and made an effort to rise from the table.

"Not so fast," the belligerent student said, laying a heavy hand on the Chevalier's thin shoulder. "You are Italian! And a ridiculous aristocrat judging by your silly feathers! Explain to us why Italian verse is superior to German!"

Casanova was tired of the discussion. "Goethe has himself

admitted that Italy saved his life. Without the beneficent influence of my country, he would have killed himself like that unnecessarily melodramatic young Werther, whose transports are beyond those of the most ridiculous Italian opera!"

This was not the most diplomatic response. The slap on his cheek was an unmistakable sign to Casanova that he had blundered into a situation from which there was no easy escape. In a response that was as much automatic as ineffectual, the Chevalier slapped the student back. It was only then that he noticed that every young man crowding about him had at least one dueling scar on his cheek.

Terms were agreed on for the traditional resolution of these insults, and a location agreed upon. The students followed the Chevalier and the grinning Hungarian, who kept inexplicably licking his lips, to an inn near the cathedral. They set watch in front of the place and promised that they would come for him at dawn for the short ride into the countryside.

When they had gained the safety of their room, Casanova turned to his manservant, intending to instruct him on the duties of a second, when the man, unable to contain himself any longer, burst out laughing.

"What's the matter with you, fool?" inquired Casanova, though he was beginning to be amused himself, without knowing why.

"All my life," the man said in broken German, "I see men fight over women or honor. Never have I seen a fight over poetry!"

"You don't know Germans." Casanova smiled, relaxing. "The question is, what are we going to do?"

"That is not hard." The Hungarian peeked through the window curtain. The students had started a bonfire and were drinking, shouting out loud what they thought were insults in Italian. "Soon they will be like this—" The Hungarian put his head on his hands and snored. "At that time, you will be in the

calèche and I will be making horses go fast." He picked up a
chamberpot from its place beside the bed. "Save your piss!"

"Save my piss?"

"Yes." The unexpectedly prankish servant mimed what he
had in mind. As they were taking off in the carriage, he would
empty the pots of piss on the sleeping hotheads.

Casanova pondered this and found it an entirely satisfactory plan. He had never shied away from a duel unless he was
certain that he could not win, and in this case he was quite certain. He had handled neither sword nor pistol for many years.
He had an aversion even for hunting at Dux, and pleaded illness whenever his patron invited him to kill foxes. Casanova
liked foxes. In this case, the stakes weren't worth it; to die for a
literary opinion was absurd. What was more, this student was
not of his social class, and Casanova had been taught that one
can never accept a challenge from an inferior. For all these
reasons, he was pleased with the Hungarian's plan and slept
soundly for two hours. The Hungarian crept out to harness the
horses when the students fell asleep, and when the carriage
was ready Casanova made his getaway, dumping his chamberpot on the snoring defenders of Germany's honor. They sped
toward Heidelberg.

In Heidelberg the streets were given over to more drunken
scholars, disturbingly similar to the scarred youths they'd met
in Tübingen. This proliferation of students with big ideas worried Casanova, who had anticipated a civilized metropolis run
by respectable burghers with sturdy wives and beautiful
daughters. He had no doubt that such abounded, but they must
have been safely behind locked doors.

Choosing what appeared to be a quiet tavern, the two men
occupied a table beneath a carved wooden arch overhung with
wilting grapes. Their seats as well as the table were carved
also, but not by any skilled woodcarver; they bore the marks of

restless young knives that are forever and on all occasions practicing the spelling of their owners' names, sometimes followed by obscene but ungrammatical phrases in Latin.

A serving girl soon appeared and Casanova ordered beef, broth, and beer in his best German. The woman slapped him encouragingly on the back, nearly sending him sprawling across the table.

"I can't stand this country!" the Chevalier hissed in French, straightening up.

"Oh, ho! Monsieur likes his *chatte* delicate," she observed in crude but serviceable French.

Casanova surmised that a French army must have been there not long before and that the woman's crude French had been acquired in the most practical way.

"I beg your pardon, mademoiselle, your French is quite lovely."

"Lovely, mon cou, but my *con* is." She laughed at her joke and strolled merrily away to fetch their food.

The Hungarian grinned, but Casanova was in no mood to laugh.

"There are jokes and there are jokes. I am not a prude. I love people, I have been with all of them. Something about this country and language, though . . . It is as if their principles are so very few in number, they are ready at any moment to kill you for trying to introduce a new idea."

Casanova sensed the chill of something worse than death around him, namely the advent of a future in which neither he nor his qualities would be of any value, a future so grim and fanatical that only the deadliest men could be at ease in it. Women would vanish in that future, existing like tragic ghosts behind savage men. He hoped the sour beef and beer would drown such presentiments.

Casanova could not help but overhear a young man with a

sparse beard holding forth at a table in the middle of the tavern.

"All the worth which the human being possesses, all spiritual reality, he possesses only through the State," the youth declared, "for truth is the unity of the universal and subjective will; and the Universal is found in the State, in its laws, its universal and rational arrangements. The State is the Divine Idea as it exists on earth. We have it, therefore, the object of history in a more definite shape than before; that in which Freedom obtains objectivity. For Law is the objectivity of the Spirit."

This was certanly the most articulate sentiment he had encountered in Germany thus far, but even with his poor understanding of the language, it struck him as a refutation of all the principles that he held dear. His personal freedom had been contingent on the weakness of European states, on their myriad disagreements and rivalries. This young man's philosophy of the strong state struck him as inflexible and inhuman, worse than any dogma of the Church, which was, after all, amenable to theological argumentation.

Before the Hungarian could stop him, Casanova was on his feet and walking toward the philosopher's table. He introduced himself to the students who'd been listening to the diatribe; the group barely suppressed their amusement at his colorful costume and old-fashioned manner. Their leader introduced himself without rising from his seat, offering only his family name.

"Hegel."

Casanova bowed in response. "I heard your little speech," he began, "and it appears to me that you mistake for objectivity that which can be safely attributed only to the deity. In your scheme, we will not have the freedom of thought that we need in order to exist as individuals."

Hegel laughed, followed in short order by his acolytes, who didn't understand in the slightest what Casanova's objection was. Hegel, however, did. He laughed because he knew that he

could demolish such arguments with a flick of his wrist. This
he proceeded to do—or thought he was doing—by first inviting
Casanova to share a tankard of German beer with them, which
he graciously did, then outlining a chilling theory of history
that almost caused the Chevalier to weep. In short, both
Casanova and Hegel's disciples heard for the first time the
story of the universal struggle toward the Spirit, which proceeded through stages of struggle and synthesis, an infinite cir-
cular striving from pain to a distant light. Casanova understood
that for the first time in his thinking life he was being presented with a view of the world that was no longer derived from
the world and directed toward it, but operated entirely within
its own self-created theory. To enter such a world was to abandon all the delightful contradictions of one's humanity, to shun
mystery, to reject the playfulness and humor that ran counter to
the logic of the argument. The Chevalier realized at that
moment that this Hegel's view was only the beginning of an
endless successions of theories, each one more internally
coherent than the other, theories that would eventually use
human beings only as examples and pawns in the display of
their relentless logic. This was the world that the rhetoric of the
French Revolution was bringing into being.

Casanova closed his eyes and wished that he could vanish.
He wanted no part of the future. The young people laughed
again, thinking him drunk, or overwhelmed by Hegel's exposition. He was neither, and without another word he retired to his
room. There he took a tincture of opium and glided into a world
of dreams where gaiety and inconsistency reigned and where
the likes of Hegel were not admitted.

"At least you didn't fight a duel," his Hungarian said, when
Casanova woke up from his long dream.

From that time on, Casanova began to suspect that his plan,
which had seemed to him—and in some ways still did—unim-

peachable, might be subject to some difficulties. When he had conceived it, he had envisioned a defined arena of combat, a lovely room perhaps, or outdoors like the Giardini, where two perfectly matched combatants would argue passionately and dispassionately, alternating appropriately, until the judge, a prince of the first order, would put an end to the combat by crowning one or the other King of Language. What gave Casanova faith in such an obviously unrealistic picture was precisely its lack of realism. He had behind him nearly three-quarters of a century of diplomacy, intrigue, and seduction, all of which he had employed in the service of Reason. For him, personally, Reason often coincided with both common sense and self-interest, but not always. He had watched with amusement and occasional dismay how superstitious, gullible, and foolish people were. There was absolutely nothing that they were not willing to believe in, particularly if it was unreasonable. This state of affairs was not all unbearable if one considered that humanity was in the same boat. Princes and peasants were equally afflicted and equally vulnerable. At some point, however, men like Voltaire and Goethe began to shame people about that which came most naturally to them, that is, superstition and wonder. Each in his own way made people feel stupid and small, unintelligent and selfish. All of a sudden, childlike wonder and sheer self-interest became sins greater than the Church had ever dreamed of making them. From that time on, natural men were harder to find than honest men. Everyone began pretending that they were following Reason rather than Superstition, and Something-bigger-than-themselves rather than petty and perfectly understandable self-interest. Perfect idiots became pretend idealists and denied their natures. Happily, such foolishness was slower in taking root among women, but judging by some of the French revolutionaries, women were not lagging far behind. As human beings began falsifying their natures in order to be something they were not, tyrants were having the best time. Any tyrant, no matter how small or how incipient, recognized the golden opportunities presented by such times. All they had to do was to invest themselves with the symbols of an Idea, any Idea, and the miserable masses would follow them to the grave. Casanova reasoned that in such circumstances, the falsity of an Olympian contest, ringed with the trappings of Objectivity and the wreaths of Reason and Ideas, might actually be taken seriously.

Casanova was not wrong. The only trouble, and he knew it, was that he was just a few years, no more than a hundred, ahead of his time. Was his journey doomed? It rained violently and the road was washed out. Forced to spend another night in the house of a peasant—this one without daughters or charm— he caught a chill and lost his voice. When the skies cleared, he had a high fever.

The fever helped; it restored to him the pristine perfection of his plan. His analysis was correct, even if a bit premature, but he had a vision that time itself was speeding up and by the time he arrived, he would be neither early nor late.

$\mathcal{T}$ hese were his thoughts as he arrived in the resplendent, ten-thousand-cupola'd, miniature fairy-tale principality of Weimar. Though he felt as if he was going to per- ish from the intense grippe, he felt also a surge of pride that he had come at last to the very lair of his nemesis. He put up at an inn not far from Councillor Goethe's house, and opened the windows wide.

He was not surprised to see a large crowd milling in the

street below and even less surprised to hear that they were all waiting to see the famous writer, a wait that sometimes lasted six weeks.

Many of those waiting were also staying at the inn. Among them were women of all ages who had traveled from distant countries to offer themselves to the disconsolate romantic, sure that their love would cure whatever ailed him. There were also functionaries of various governments, anxious to make his acquaintance, ostensibly for literary reasons, but really because they had heard that Goethe was on his way to a remarkable political career. There were also literary pilgrims, from pale young poets to princes consumed by poetic ambitions. The politicians and the princes had priority.

Casanova sent the Hungarian across the street with a letter and watched as he dropped it in a large urn outside the great man's door. The urn was filled to the brim with letters that were scooped up each evening at precisely nine o'clock with a long gold ladle by an unseen person within. After watching this ritual for three consecutive evenings and feeling his fever disappear completely, Casanova decided to make the acquaintance of some of the other supplicants.

He met a tall, lily-white girl, dressed in white to resemble a lily, who gave off a scent of lilies even as she clung limply to the arm of a sturdy black-clad frau. Casanova bowed to her and inquired if she was there to present the beauty of her verse or simply her beauty to the great poet.

"Both, my dear man," answered Countess Lotte von Herder, annoyed but not displeased by the attention. It was the first time any man had spoken to her since she had left the devastated city of Mainz.

"In that case," proposed the Chevalier, "I would be honored to have your company and that of your governess for supper this evening, so that we might discuss poetry."

Countess Lotte blushed violently, ruining momentarily the lily effect, and explained that the woman in black, who was indeed her governess, was known as Miss Mulgrave. She was English. Supper with the gentleman was another matter, one that she could not imagine deciding upon without the aid of her Tarot cards.

"The Tarot!" exclaimed Casanova, "My dear Countess! Your luck is indeed extraordinary. I am to the Tarot and to the Kabbalah what Goethe is to German verse. I am the only worthy competitor of Comte de St. Germain in occult studies! I would be delighted not only to read your cards but also to consult my cabbalistic pyramid on your behalf!"

That evening, in his sparkling room, which had been decorated with candles and flowers and laden with the best Weimar had to offer in food and wine—on credit, of course—Casanova received the two women. He was pleased to see that the sturdy Miss Mulgrave had changed into evening dress and that the only really large thing about her was her enormous bosom. As for Lotte, she looked more like a lily than ever, but transformed into a rose as the second glass of wine had its effect. The Hungarian served at table and, Casanova noticed, lingered long attending to Miss Mulgrave.

Casanova displayed his knowledge of the Tarot splendidly and revealed to Miss Lotte things that not even her mother or father could have known, such as the fact that although she was technically a virgin, she had experienced deep kisses on her temple of Venus from her best girlfriend, Augusta, whose temple she had in turn kissed from frieze to cornice to altar. When he drew the cabbalistic pyramid with its black Hebrew letters, Lotte nearly fainted with pleasure. She leaned close to the Chevalier, blowing the gentlest breeze of her quickened breath on his old, powdered cheek, and resting her hand like a scared small dove on his thigh. It was not long after that an inexplicable wind blew out all the candles and Casanova found himself defending the poor child from the darkness by peeling away her outer layers and pressing her warm, damp skin and scared small breasts against his bony body. A great deal of shuffling and excited breathing could be heard on the other side of the room as the Hungarian defended the English governess in a similar manner.

Countess Lotte von Herder liked to talk. Next day she praised Chevalier de Seingalt's Tarot skills so highly that by noon several young ladies, some accompanied by their governesses, some alone, came to beseech him to read their futures. These readings, in their turn, were so successful, that the Chevalier's enterprise became the favorite pastime of all those waiting to see the great poet. Some of them had been in Weimar for over a month and had been dying of boredom, particularly the virgins who were not even sure if the Councillor would receive them.

Such success is not without dangers. The great poet soon heard of the doings across the street and noted a decided drop in the level of enthusiasm of his young supplicants, particularly the virgins. Casanova was abruptly summoned to appear before the poet.

The leader was seated in a weighty, dignified, but fully present manner in a large armchair, his brilliant eyes burning in a powdered face whose cheeks had been described variously as "cherubic" and "stately." Assorted admirers, some of them permanent, others only temporary, stood or lounged about in the ornate salon furnished with couches and chairs upholstered in rose-colored tapestry depicting fleshy angels.

"Chevalier de Seingalt," the poet addressed him in French, "I believe that I have heard the name. My good friend Frederick of Prussia mentioned a civil engineer . . ."

"My dear poet," Casanova responded in Italian, "I believe that you have indeed heard of me. I am Casanova."

A smile that began in the tiniest corner of Goethe's mouth began to spread suddenly across his face and spread and spread until it overtook most of it.

"Casanova, dio mio!" exclaimed the poet in accented Italian, "You are a famous man!"

"You know my translation of the *Iliad* into Italian?" Casanova asked hopefully.

Goethe's smile turned into helpless laughter and his "cherubic" or "stately" jowls began to shake helplessly. "The *Iliad?* No. We know you for the man who drove more women mad than Louis XV . . ." Goethe made an obscene gesture by thrusting a finger in and out of the top of his fist. The company burst out laughing.

The blood ran out of Casanova's already pale face. Goethe hastened to correct his rudeness.

"Dear Chevalier, please do not feel insulted. You are among friends. You have heard similar things about me, I am sure."

The company laughed again, only a great deal more respectfully.

"In all honesty," Casanova said coldly, "your rudeness does not bother me. I have traveled all this way because I believe that you and I are two models for the future. If the world chooses you, I pity poor humanity. I represent a hope for happiness."

The salon fell silent. Goethe contemplated Casanova for a long time before speaking. "I don't know what folly brought you here. As for the future . . . the future will have use for genius, but not much use, I fear, for refinement."

"Thank you," Casanova said sincerely. "What will inspire genius in these future battles? Not love, certainly, which is both refined and inexplicable. What then?"

"Forces," answered Goethe, suddenly furious, "forces of mythology, images from the folk wisdom of nations, gods who have been abandoned and who are now ready to rise again."

"Are these gods present in the German language?"

They had been speaking in French.

"Yes," Goethe replied in German, "the gods are manifest in the language."

"I asked you about the German language."

"The genius of myth once resided in Greek. Tomorrow it will live in our German."

Casanova bowed nearly to the ground, as his dancing master Marcel had taught him in Paris many decades before, and took his leave without another word. Goethe watched him back out and was seized with anxiety.

"A virgin!" he cried, "I need a virgin! A German virgin!"

Casanova, who heard him, muttered, "Good luck!" after the door closed behind him. He was certain he had forestalled, at least for the time being, the satisfaction of Goethe's request.

Early next morning, a somber Chevalier ordered his equally somber servant to make haste to return to Bohemia.

Three weeks had elapsed since Casanova's departure and everyone at Dux, with the exception of Laura, was certain that he would not return. Every day someone heard a new rumor about his death in an accident or a duel. Libussa had a dream in which a smiling Chevalier, looking many decades younger, was sitting atop a tower of books, smiling down at her and holding out his hand. There was a halo around his head and a pair of black wings folded against his back. Libussa climbed the tower of books and reached for the Chevalier's hand, but she slipped and tumbled into a darkness stuffed densely with the black letters of the alphabet.

"The cosmic goosedown," explained the dream Casanova.

The black wings Laura could imagine, but the halo made Laura laugh. This wasn't the only dream Libussa had about the Chevalier in his absence; in her other dreams, he was always about to test a strange machine, such as a magnetic balloon that dragged in its wake soldiers stuck to their swords, or a pair of glasses that were "mesmerized" to make whomever he looked at do his bidding. Laura pointed out that the Chevalier hardly had need for such glasses, since he could mesmerize anyone quite well without them, especially women.

Both of them felt a little warm between their legs.

"Mesmer!" they pronounced simultaneously, and burst out laughing.

Casanova's enemies, headed by Gelder, Langerhoff, and Blauner, spread and invented malicious rumors in which the Chevalier ended up ignominiously hacked to death by pirates or rent by the claws of savage beasts. Gelder was certain that Casanova had run off to America to do some sort of occult business with Benjamin Franklin, and that he had been captured at sea by Madagascan pirates who had buggered him to death. Langerhoff claimed to have absolute proof of this from a one-legged sailor he had met in Prague. Langerhoff grimaced when he told this story, not from any sympathy with the Chevalier, but because the one-legged pirate had left a particularly painful splinter from his wooden leg embedded in Langerhoff's membrum virile. It had proven impossible to extract and the doctor had laughed at him. It appeared to the majordomo that this was just one more insult that Casanova had visited on him from beyond the grave.

Imagine the surprise when Casanova, looking none the worse for the wear—maybe a little bit thinner and gloomier—descended from the calèche, helped by his Hungarian, and headed straight to his rooms. Some servants thought that they were seeing a ghost and shrieked. Laura was not told of his return until he had already settled at his writing desk and had begun scribbling furiously.

She regarded him gravely for a few moments before he noticed her. He lay down his quill and looked at her as if he was seeing her for the first time.

"Don't you recognize me, Casanova?"

"I recognize you, Laura. Do I seem any different? I feel changed, somehow."

"You seem the same as ever to me, but I will not know for sure it's you until I inspect the Micromeg."

They embraced, but Casanova was preoccupied. Laura left him alone, thinking that he really had changed. In his absence, she had changed as well. She had done a lot of thinking about her life. She knew that she was no longer young. Her merriest days had been spent in the company of this extraordinary old man, who was surely not long for this world. What would she do when he was gone? She had come to the strange conclusion that she must obtain and preserve some of Casanova's life fluid. This renowned profligate had squandered who knew how many seas of his precious fluid inside princesses and whores, but he had been stingy with her. She had come to believe that his sperm contained his soul, more real than all the letters and words he scribbled. His world, she realized, would never be hers; it had consisted of people she would never meet. When Casanova had read from his life, she projected herself into a world beyond her grasp.

The idea took hold of her that these people, in their essence, lived in the Chevalier's sperm. It terrified her to think that those wonderful figures from his past were slipping from Casanova's grasp, and that his writing, attempting to recapture them, only held them for an instant, not long enough for them to live again. This was his tragedy, and it explained the melancholy that pervaded his reminiscences. It had also become Laura's obsession. Casanova had squandered his money, had spent millions of words in witty conversation and writing, but she wanted to conserve what was left: his sperm.

When she confided her weird desire to Libussa, the girl said, "I understand. You want his baby."

But Libussa didn't understand. She wanted his baby, of course, but there was something else involved as well. Laura wasn't sure what this was. She imagined a glass container of Casanova's vital fluid, and saw herself carefully smuggling such vial to some safe place in the mountains. The idea was so unnatural and inexplicable she was both ashamed and fascinated by it.

When she confessed her obsession to Casanova, he didn't laugh at her. "There are scholars who believe much the same thing. There is a great ice vault under the czar's palace in St. Petersburg where the sperm of great men is preserved. The late empress, who was my mother's protector, was persuaded by Terni, a notorious charlatan, to create the repository. He may have been quite wise in this instance. Secret researches are being conducted to see if the sperm can be used in some way to bring these men back to life. It is believed that the entire personality and all the life experiences of these masters are contained therein."

"Yes," said Laura, "but I would trade a thousand Russian ice caves full of the sperm of great men for a few drops of yours."

Casanova was touched. He researched the chemistry that might aid her in preserving his essence, which he promised to give her. Laura carried on a correspondence with O'Reilly, who did not criticize her obsession either, advising her instead on ways of preserving the fluid.

Casanova thought that Laura's interest in science was part of the general fascination on the part of the public with such phenomena as magnetism, balloon flights, mesmerism, and other popular marvels. While revolutionary politics had plunged Europe into war, many people took refuge in scientific fancies.

Most of all, the Chevalier wanted to be left alone. The *Icosaméron* had been published in Prague and been a resounding failure. No one was interested in the adventures of Edouard and Elisabeth in the lands of the Micromegs. A hundred and fifty-six copies, out of a total of three hundred and fifty, went off to subscribers and twenty-five more were bought by booksellers. Twenty of those twenty-five were purchased outright by Eliphas. Casanova suspected that this had been an act of charity rather than sense, but Eliphas assured him over and over that his customers were especially interested in utopian worlds.

"The potential readership for the *Icosaméron* is vast, Chevalier," he said with a frown. "The messianic people, and that includes all Jews and Christians, are fascinated by descriptions of paradise."

"Alas, my friend. Paradise is boring. If I had to live in the Micromeg world I would die of ennui. Why would others feel differently?"

"For the simple reason that most people are weary, they are exhausted. They imagine paradise as a place of rest and lovely gifts to the senses."

"Perhaps, but there is another consequence of such fantasies; people might try to reproduce paradise here on earth. It provides rich soil for charlatans and fools."

Eliphas laughed. "Have you never dreamed of being the leader of a perfect world, Chevalier? A world of beautiful women perhaps?"

"At one time, maybe. Now I am concerned only with recalling all the real women I have known. When I have recalled them all, I shall die."

Eliphas did not ask him if his recollections had yet included his sister, Leah. Both men thought of her at the same instant and smiled.

The Chevalier did not know that Libussa had been listening eagerly to their conversation about paradises. She had been dreaming for many nights about a white castle hidden in the Bohemian hills. This castle had no towers, only a series of glass domes under which lived pleasant men and women dressed in loose white linen robes. They spoke a singing language that matched their movements, whether they were spinning, weaving, building barns, shoeing horses, or teaching children. Libussa went back to the white castle in her dreams as often as she could in order to learn the language, which also produced colors that shimmered around the bodies of the speakers. She had not read the *Icosaméron,* so it was quite a surprise when she revealed her dreams and sang several phrases in Micromeg.

Casanova took this as a sign that his sojourn on earth was finished. When fancies intended solely for amusement took on material dimensions, it was time for their creator to retire. After all, God had done just that after his Creation. He had gone to a remote heaven that grew more remote every day. Casanova worked ever more feverishly on his memoirs, which had reached the year 1771, leaving more than a quarter of a century to go. The years of his childhood, youth, and even middle age, had flown effortlessly from his pen, rushing to be told. More recent decades were difficult. Happiness, which had been the guiding principle of his life, had been hard to find in these last years. He found it more and more difficult to extract nuggets of joy from a dreary succession of failures.

One morning, Laura found him weeping with his head between his hands. His inkpot had overturned, and a puddle of black ink in the shape of a star covered his pages. She led him to his chair, wiped up the ink, saving all the unstained pages, and sat at his feet.

"The Abbé Dorensky came for Libussa this morning. They left together to build a community in the mountains where the Micromeg language will be spoken. She asked me to tell you that the community will be called Icosaméron and that you are its founding father. She hopes that you will be proud of the world that they are going to create. The Abbé asked me to also tell you that they have purchased fifteen copies of the *Icosaméron* from Eliphas, for the fifteen initial members of their group."

Casanova didn't know whether to laugh or remain in despair. He laughed feebly.

"Explain to me, Fraülein Brock, what sort of mischievous god is at work here. I created a work of fantasy which is now becoming a reality. I then labor to write the reality of my life and despair of ever rendering it real to anyone but myself. I feel that I am being made sport of."

Laura was offended. "The life you are writing is delightfully real to me. I just wish that you'd get to the part where I come onstage."

Casanova promised her he would do just that and worked without pause for the rest of the month. He was still no farther along than the end of the year 1771 and the lifting of his second exile from Venice.

Venice seemed inescapable. She floated beneath and above the page with her magical lights. Whenever he tried to get on with the story and move his little marionette from one adventure to another, the city herself, like an insistent and slightly mad courtesan, took over and displayed her tired charms. Instead of following his own personage, he found himself pulled back through his childhood through the Calle della Commedia, over the Academia Bridge, through the brightness of the Ridotto, under the shadow of San Samuele.

"But I have already been through all that!" he complained with exasperation to his unyielding old mistress. "I have written your alleys, sung your bridges, let the shadow of your convents and churches fall on my memories, I have given shape to all my Venetian loves and rendered their scents and sounds. . . . What more do you want from me?"

She wanted more, but Casanova did not know what it was she wanted until news came that the Venetian Republic had ceased to exist. The "Corsican ogre," whose fame had reached every corner of Europe, had declared war on Venice. Bonaparte, after offering Venice several opportunities for peace, came to the end of his patience. On May 16, 1797, four thousand French troops under the command of General Baraguey d'Hilliers had entered Venice. Lodovico Manin, the last Doge of Venice, the man who had attempted to have Casanova assassinated, issued his last decree: "Hereafter the government will be administered by a provisional municipality, installed in the Hall of the Great Council. All Venetian military officers will report to the Council at noon to take the oath of allegiance to the muncipality." A thousand years of rule by the oligarchy came to an end. The president of the new municipality, Talier, entered the Basilica of San Marco, where the Te Deum was sung. In the piazza, Talier burned the Ducal Cornu and the Golden Book of the patricians. The ultimate outrage, ordered by Bonaparte, something Casanova could not bring himself to imagine, was the closing of the open end of Piazza San Marco with a new wing intended to be a ballroom for French officers.

In the end, Venice had mirrored his own fate, and was now an exile among nations.

The Chevalier's principal occupation for the next few weeks was staring out the library windows. He listened distractedly when Laura attempted to interest him in castle gossip or in the incredible events in Europe. Every time he heard the name Bonaparte, Casanova gave a snort of outrage, though in some measure, he could not but admire the French general, who was, like himself, a self-made man. He had come from nowhere and was quickly on his way to becoming the master of Europe. But the man's brilliance was conducted behind such a shield of bad manners, Casanova felt mostly contempt.

In September Count Waldstein came to Dux with worse news. Bonaparte had made a secret deal to cede Venice to the Austrians in exchange for the Ionian islands. Waldstein thought that this news might actually cheer up the Chevalier, not suspecting the depth of Casanova's hostility toward his German hosts.

"Venice and you," Waldstein said, smiling, "now both belong to Austria. You are reunited, strangely enough. You may even be recalled to service."

Waldstein didn't actually believe this, looking at the toothless, drawn, pergament-yellow old man, but the phosphorescence of a strange, stubborn will emanated from the phantom before him. Waldstein felt a mixture of compassion and disgust. He might have enjoyed probing deeper into the mystery of Casanova's new mood, but urgent matters claimed him. He was beginning to see himself in a leading role in the Europe now taking shape, a Europe divided between France and Austria. His uncle, the Prince de Ligne, was already conducting negotiations for the restoration of the Bourbon monarchy after Napoleon. Unlike Casanova, he had little respect for the Corsican and did not appreciate Bonaparte's political genius, but the crisis invigorated him as much as it seemed to sap the old Venetian's strength.

Shortly after Waldstein's departure, Casanova's beloved fox terrier Melampyge died. The dog had sat quietly on his lap for a week before succumbing to a final illness. Her death inspired him to compose a tender funeral oration in Latin. Melampyge was buried outside his window next to his beloved Cybelle, so that he could always see the stones under which they lay. The servants and quite a few townspeople attended the unusual funeral yet again, curious to see to what lengths the eccentric Venetian might go this time. He satisfied their expectations by weeping and carrying on like an overwrought diva. Laura stood by his side, not embarrassed by the display, but wishing that her co-citizens would be swallowed by the earth in front of them. She was relieved when the stone was in place, the guffawing crowd had dispersed, and the angry priest who had threatened again to excommunicate the Chevalier for mocking a Christian sacrament gathered his robes and vanished.

Princess Lobkowitz sent from Berlin a replacement for Melampyge that Casanova named Finette. She resembled Melampyge only superficially; Finette was just a puppy and lacked her predecessor's deep empathy with her master. Nonetheless, Finette's coquetry and antics amused him and he resumed work, this time on the mathematical problem of the duplication of the cube. The problem had preoccupied him since 1760, and he had published three pamphlets on the subject, which had long fascinated scholars. He was close to attaining a perfect solution, closer than anyone before him, according to his friend Charles Henry, the eminent French mathematician.

If duplicating the cube was an absorbing distraction, a book that arrived from Paris presented him with a problem of a different nature. *The New French Dictionary, Containing Newly Cre-*

Andrei Codrescu

ated Expressions of the French People infuriated him. This book documented all the new words and expressions born of the French Revolution, and though Casanova had often criticized the conservatism of the French language and the inflexibility of the Academy in accepting new words, the new words he had in mind were words actually used by people and which had gained legitimacy by spontaneous circulation and adoption. This Leonard Snetlage, *Docteur on Droit de l'Université de Goiettingue,* legitimized a whole other class of words, words born out of political rhetoric, journalism, and the new bureaucracies of the Revolution. Even the calendar had been changed, making 1789 the year One and renaming all the months of the year. Snetlage was continuing this "revolutionary" work.

Casanova began his lengthy critique of Snetlage's work with the letter *A. "Anarchiste,"* he wrote, "Nothing is new here except the form, which seems to indicate a professor or lecturer of anarchy, and anarchy becoming a profession. This is a necessary institution, metaphysically sanctioned by the legislative Assembly, to which France owes its happiness and without which she would have never become a glorious republic."

His contempt and sarcasm embraced equally the new, yet already overused "égalité": "I am sure that this constitutional equality, on which your new government is founded, is and will always remain a mystery for the reawakened nation, one which the forever happy-go-lucky citizens, despite the misery that oppresses them, will have no problem using in all circumstances. One must be continually amazed by the meaning of this word when one sees with one's own eyes only inequality."

Casanova slashed and savaged "comité," "incriminer" (which sounded to him like a sort of inoculation against crime); "motion," (as in "the motion carries"), and many others. He did not dislike all the new words and he wrote to Dr. Snetlage that he was rather fond of "urgence" (urgency), the noun derived from "urgent," but that he regretted the fact that it rhymed with "ambulance." He approved wholeheartedly of "immoral" and "immoralité," words which, though long in common usage, had yet to make a dictionary appearance of any kind.

The exhaustive letter to Dr. Snetlage took many weeks to complete and he enjoyed the exercise so much he hated to end it. He lingered over the new lexicon, giving full vent to his cultural, political, and personal opinions, allowing himself to be ironic, sarcastic, sentimental, and digressive. When he reached the letter *"M,"* he realized that he was writing another autobiography of sorts. The words he analyzed were like magnets drawing to themselves the iron filings of his intellect. He had always loved dictionaries and regretted more than anything not having completed his "history of cheeses." He was also a passionate list-maker who looked upon a list as the magical skeleton of a world that needed only a breath of life to animate it.

Casanova loved the structures of matter and of language; he could see them instantly. The structures of matter provided him deep satisfaction at the moment of mutual happiness with a woman, when something structurally magnificent was created in spite of apparent differences. It might have been difficult for anyone else to understand, and he would certainly never write down such a calculating thought, but the goal of coupling for him had been to achieve understanding. Happiness might also be achieved, but that was a transitory and insubstantial sensation. He would have never confessed his true aim to anyone; he might have been taken for a researcher, like O'Reilly, and never enjoyed the affection of women who prefer passion and poetry to science. In fact, Casanova told himself, seeing the mirror in his room reflect an image of pathos and decrepitude, I am nothing if not a scientist.

In matters of language, he felt that his nervous and circulatory systems were connected to Latin and Greek, which created the river from which Italian, French, and Spanish flowed freely and joyously, while the dark pulse of German and Slavic sounds made sluggish islands in his mind. Writing his letter to Dr. Snetlage he was able to access the deepest meanings of the new words with a visceral accuracy and organic acuity that delighted and aroused him.

Laura noticed that some new energy animated the Chevalier. Perhaps the time had come for him to fulfill his promise to her. Every day she dressed his hair, rouged his cheeks, and whispered gossip into his ear. She didn't need to invent things to keep him entertained. The castle, like the rest of Europe, was in an exalted and absurd state in which preposterous ideas and silly actions were continually born. The servant girls competed with one another to have the most vivid dream or vision, following the example of Libussa, who was spoken of with an awe hitherto reserved for the saints. Young men returned from wars where they had soldiered for glory but no profit, and could not remember whose side they had served. The flags over Dux changed so many times, no one could keep up with the colors, but these changes seemed to have few consequences. Women abandoned their corsets after the example of Bonaparte's Josephine, and their dresses flowed as freely as their thoughts. Casanova found the new style abominable. The science of stays, corsets, and laces was being lost and with it went centuries of exquisite and secret pleasure.

"Micromegs!" he exclaimed disdainfully. "They are becoming Micromegs! Soon everyone will be naked! Quelle horreur!"

One morning when Laura, assisted now by a boyish new Moravian maid named Zenka, was giving the Chevalier a long hot bath in his special copper tub, Casanova exclaimed, apropos of nothing at all: "I have decided what my favorite object is!"

"I think I can guess," said Laura, grabbing Zenka's behind.

The Moravian girl giggled.

"No, I am serious."

"Do you intend to suggest that I am not," Laura teased, squeezing lightly but menacingly the wrinkled sac where the eggs of his manhood hid trembling. "The 'temples' of a woman's body, as you call them, were once the object of all your attentions."

"Yes," the Chevalier said, shifting ever so slightly from her grip, but enjoying it in combination with Zenka's finger, which was washing his arsehole, "but I have changed my mind. The most ideal thing in the world is the head of a king!"

Laura almost dropped his eggs, but she could feel the rise of his long-dormant Micromeg. "This isn't such a good time for the aesthetic appreciation of kings' heads," she whispered.

"Au contraire, my dearest. I remember Louis's head well, while it was still on his shoulders, of course, and it always looked . . . detached. All by itself. A splendidly coiffed, authoritative, beautiful head, meant to be on a coin. I remember looking at I don't know how many louis d'or, usually in the process of losing them at cards, and thinking, what a perfect head! The head of a king! I have seen all the crowned heads of Europe, including the kings of Sardinia and Naples. Of course, some of these heads were handsomer than others. Nobody would call Leopold handsome. But all those heads, without exception, had a life of their own."

Laura had a brief vision of the balloon-like heads of kings detaching themselves from the royal shoulders and floating into an ethereal realm to be affixed to coins. She was pleased to note that her cupped hand was filled quite nicely with the princely head of Casanova's scepter, which was quite proud and tall when it deigned to stand. It stood. The Moravian girl, happy to demonstrate an expertise for which she was quite renowned, continued to tickle the Chevalier's behind. The water was still hot, there was plenty of soap, and the women's hands established a sweet rhythm to which Casanova succumbed with a sigh.

Laura was certain that victory was hers, when the door was flung open and Count Waldstein strode in, smelling like horses and snow. He also smelled of drink.

"Out, wenches!" he shouted. "I must impart news to the Chevalier!"

Laura and Zenka dried their hands slowly, with evident displeasure, and Casanova opened his eyes, equally displeased. The kingly head, which had risen above the soapy water, now sank beneath.

"All right, all right," Waldstein said with a hint of understanding, "dry him and dress him and bring him to me in a quarter of an hour. You . . ." he said, addressing Zenka, "you are tall enough to be a boy."

"Yes, your excellency." Zenka curtsied.

"Well, are you or aren't you?"

Zenka shook her head regretfully. Waldstein frowned. "Too bad. Quarter of an hour."

Efforts to revive the water king failed, so Laura and Zenka dried Casanova quickly. He was in an ebullient mood and had not yet exhausted the subject of the heads of kings. He babbled all the way through his toilette, describing each king he had met and noting their distinctions with the precision of a phrenologist and the enthusiasm of a court poet.

Perhaps the old man has finally gone mad, thought Laura, as she led the Chevalier up the grand staircase.

They found Waldstein sprawled in an armchair in the library, his feet propped up on an old metal trunk.

"I have just come from Paris, where I disguised myself as a rag man. It was extraordinary! You would not recognize the city!" Waldstein shook his head in disbelief.

"The streets are open whorehouses. Floozies offer their wares in alleyways and churches. The revolutionary committees pass every two hours, looking for aristocrats and whores or whatever the criminals du jour are. These committees are formed mostly of ugly and mean old women who hate everybody. In defiance, the Parisians are drunk all the time and all the aristocrats who haven't fled are either beggars or turncoats of the new bureaucracies!"

The Paris of the revolutionary rabble that made gods of bankers and grocers held no fascination for Casanova. He would not have returned there even if the Bourbon aristocracy managed to reverse its fortunes. It was clear that venal, barbaric men using the language of newspaper clichés and streetcorner speeches had destroyed the gracious and elegant Paris of his early manhood. He still had the beloved French language, that perfect language of love, and no revolution could take that away from him, no matter the efforts of Dr. Snetlage. Nonetheless, one had to make an effort to listen to Count Waldstein.

"And so," Waldstein continued, "I was finally taken to a foul subterranean workshop. I never suspected the existence of such hellholes. This particular cloaca is situated near the Pont Neuf and it is entered directly through a sewer hole on the bank of the Seine. After a maze of tunnels one arrives in a suite of relatively large rooms where creatures without rank or evident provenance process corpses for the medical schools. The stench was worse than anything I have experienced on the battlefield. My guide disappeared and I was taken in hand by a masked giant with one arm who sold me the trunk for a sum that would have been excessive anytime. Of course, I inspected the contents before paying. It is all so very ironic!"

Waldstein gave Casanova a fond look. "There is no man in the world I would rather share my find with."

"Enough already," the Chevalier blurted irritably. "What is it that you bought?"

Waldstein was not ready to show his hand and spoil the surprise. "Do you remember," he continued, undaunted by Casanova's outburst, "the day that we received the automatons and heard the news that Louis had been beheaded?"

"How could I forget? You cried like a child."

"You may remember that I had gone on a secret mission to France not long before to persuade their majesties to flee. They refused. After the news came of their beheadings, I thought for a long time about their prideful stupidity and forgave them."

Casanova looked for the first time at the trunk on which Waldstein's boots were resting, and in an instant he knew what it contained.

"Only this morning, before you came into my room, I was telling my maids that the most splendid object in the world is the head of a king."

Waldstein burst out laughing. "You have been my guest for thirteen years, Casanova, and we have always been able to communicate without words."

Casanova bowed his head gracefully, or gratefully, and suppressed a wicked urge to tell the Count that he had always been oblivious to his suffering at the hands of the monsters who administered his property; that he had never understood Casanova's true poverty; that many times he had been deeply offended by the Count's arrogance; that he, Casanova, hated Bohemian food and the German language: but he did not mention these things because the Count believed otherwise and, occasionally, it was true that they had a remarkable convergence of thought.

"Well, then, since you made the girls privy to your thoughts in this matter, shouldn't they be present?"

"By all means," Casanova said gladly.

The women were called in, and Waldstein pulled the trunk

to the center of the room and slowly opened the lid. Inside, nestled in a filthy old quilt, were the severed heads of Louis XVI and Marie Antoinette, somewhat ashen and drawn, but otherwise perfectly preserved, as if an artist had drawn their features in ink.

Zenka fell to her knees. Laura covered her eyes. Casanova looked into the dead orbs of the suzerains and smiled. "I'm sorry," he said to no one in particular, "the bodies were more important."

Waldstein closed the trunk. "Whatever do you mean, Casanova?"

"I admire tremendously your extraordinary purchase," Casanova said, "but when I declared a king's head the most beautiful object in the world, I did not explain why."

Waldstein looked annoyed. "These heads are priceless. Imagine, at some future time, the display that might be made of them. They have been preserved, by the way, with a substance found only in the New World."

"That makes a great deal of sense. A substance from the New World to preserve the corpses of the Old. No doubt your collection of books, automatons, and preserved curiosities will be the basis of many great discoveries. Not even O'Reilly's laboratory can rival it."

"Indeed," Waldstein said proudly. "And with the legendary Casanova a part of my collection, my name will never die."

"That is true," Casanova said with gravity, "but I must tell you why their majesties' bodies were more important than their heads."

"If you have to," sighed Waldstein.

"Their heads, my friend, ensured the absolute freedom of their bodies to achieve sensual happiness. Kings are great because they are the freest of beings. Their bodies behave freely because they are kings. The revolution missed the point entirely. Instead of reducing everyone to the rank of citizen, they should have elevated every man to royalty. They have made drones of potential kings."

Waldstein was suddenly tired. He had no patience with this absurd speculation. He had traveled six hundred miles with the heads of Louis XVI and Marie Antoinette, and all he wanted was praise and sleep. And perhaps the Moravian wench. He kept Zenka and dismissed the others.

Casanova was fascinated by the latest addition to Waldstein's collection, but Laura was horrified. "The aristocracy is decadent," she said, in all seriousness, "to get pleasure from such as that!"

Next day, Casanova had pain in his bladder. He took opium, but the pain did not go away. He was seventy-three years old, and he knew he was dying. He wrote to Elise von der Recke, whom he had met in Weimar: "Through a painful malady nature has condemned me to a slow death but, through the grace of God, the end is not far off. As I can take no nourishment my feebleness becomes more accentuated every day so that I no longer leave my bed."

Apprised of his illness, his brother Francesco, the painter of battle scenes, wrote from Vienna: "Your letter has afflicted me beyond anything you may imagine, loving you sincerely and, if I lose you, no one in this world can further replace in my heart the place you occupy."

The outpouring of sympathy amused Casanova. He joked with Laura, who nursed him with a heavy heart.

"Tell me, Mademoiselle Brock, what do you think of these last words: 'I ate all I could, I leave you very little!' Or these: 'Do not read me without your love nearby! You'll fall into onanism'!"

On and on he composed last words and epitaphs, to Laura's great distress. She knew that the end was now near and that her chances of obtaining any of the dying man's sperm were rapidly fading. At the end of May, Casanova deigned to receive the priest and take extreme unction, saying loudly so that all might hear: "I lived as a philosopher, I die a Christian!" He then closed his eyes, but he didn't die.

On the fourth of June in the year 1798, Laura entered his chamber and found him asleep in his favorite chair, a pen still clutched in his hand, and a sheet of blank paper at his feet. She unfastened his breeches with care, and Casanova's "verb," which had steered him joyously to the end of the century, was revealed to be fully erect. She closed her lips around it and drank the life that shot abundantly from it, careful to save enough to fill the vial she carried in her pocket. She sealed it as O'Reilly had instructed, rearranged the Chevalier's clothing, and then rang the bell so forcefully that the whole castle came running. Casanova was, to all appearances, dead.

The writer and lover, who spoke Italian and wrote in French, was buried in German. His tombstone read: JAKOB CASANOVA—VENEDIG 1725—DUX 1798.

Only Laura Brock knew that the tombstone was the cover of an empty book. The substance of the book had escaped. Those present at the funeral, including Casanova's nephew by marriage, Carlo Angiolini, didn't know that they were witnessing the burial not only of the Venetian adventurer, but of the eighteenth century. During the eulogy, Casanova's pup, Finette, tried to bound out of Laura's arms and run to her master, whose shadow just peeked out from behind the church.

In his will, Casanova left the memoir, *L'Histoire de ma vie*, to his nephew, who carried it back to Dresden, where his father, the husband of Casanova's sister Maria Magdalena, was court musician. Dresden was also Laura Brock's eventual destination. Her brother Karl had established a small publishing house in that city.

Epilogue

$\mathscr{F}$or the next twenty-four years Casanova's great work, the history of his life, remained unpublished, and the name Casanova all but forgotten. Much later, he read ruefully what the biographer Stefan Zweig had written about this period: " . . . no one could have seemed more hopelessly dead than this most living of all the men who ever lived."

Casanova never met Zweig, but he knew Zweig's niece, Rebecca, who patronized Casanova's shop in Paris in the early 1930s. From Chez Casa, he sold antiques and curiosities from 1800 to 1823; later it became Aux Plombs Rare Books, and was a fixture on the Left Bank, in what came to be known as the "Bohemian" quarter. At some point every young person who had artistic pretentions and stayed up past midnight began to think of himself as "bohemian," and the neighborhoods where rent was cheap "Bohemia." This was the fault of an overwrought Italian named Puccini, who had written an opera called *La Bohème*, ostensibly set in Casanova's former place of exile and filled with Gypsies and artists. The real Bohemia was indeed a pleasant land but it bore no resemblance to Puccini's fictional country, versions of which were sprouting up in Paris and New York. Casanova was quite annoyed by this fashion, particularly since the "bohemians" who frequented his shop had no money and had to be watched closely because, more often than not, they made things disappear in the large pockets of their threadbare coats. Their only endearing qualities were the love of costumes and pleasure, qualities Casanova had always prized. He was also intrigued by the proliferation of self-styled "artists" and "poets," a species of idler that had been quite rare in the last century, but was now threatening to overrun all of Paris.

During the rule of Napoleon, through the restoration of the Bourbon monarchy, and up to the time of the treaty of Vienna (his dear friend the Prince de Ligne died in midnegotiation), Chez Casa had very few customers. Casanova was quite content to read all day, ensconced in an armchair in the dim chiaroscuro of his little shop. Behind the shop was a narrow room with floor-to-ceiling bookshelves, a sturdy bed he had built to suit his large frame, a Dresden porcelain washbasin, and a stove. The door to Chez Casa was easily overlooked and the name itself was painted in minuscule gold letters on a mirror hung in the window. The curious peered into the window and were amused, baffled, or bored by the dusty junk lying about within. A large hat that looked as if it might have adorned the head of a lady-in-waiting at the court of Louis XV spread its limpid ribbons over a Russian samovar. Several garish enameled brooches were strewn around the hat as if someone had flung them there. Oddly shaped jars of uncertain color shared the display with the hat, the samovar, and the brooches. A stack of books with their spines turned away from the viewer stood behind these objects as if their owner forgot them there. The arrangement was arbitrary, and Casanova made sure that it was arbitrarily changed every month. He added and subtracted

objects, changed the random encounter of one object with another, and worked hard to preserve the appearance of careless-
ness.

One of his earliest customers was a rogue with an angelic
face whose conversation was a mixture of obscenities and lyric
interjections. The childlike youth, who looked no older than sixteen, would sprawl insolently on the settee clearly marked "for
sale" that sat in front of Casanova's overfilled desk and launch
into a merciless condemnation of every literary name he could
think of. For the most part Casanova indulged his sallies, but he
was made genuinely angry now and then when the arrogant
snotnose, who called himself Arthur Rimbaud, ridiculed
Horace or Tacitus. Predictably, the "bohemian poet" was fond of
Sappho, Catullus, and Ovid. Casanova had the pleasure of introducing him to the poetry of Baffo, which so impressed him that
from that day on he was never without it. Rimbaud memorized
Baffo's poetry and then translated it into such juicy and bawdy
French Casanova could find absolutely no flaw in it. The badly
printed, pirated edition he had given Rimbaud as a gift was one
of twenty he had had produced at his own expense. Rimbaud re-
payed him for the gift by stealing as many other books as he
could lay his hands on, but Casanova didn't mind. The poet
brought enormous joy with him into the shop, lighting up the
place like a swarm of fireflies.

He did mind when Rimbaud brought around some of his
older friends, shifty-eyed and dirty characters who differed
from professional thieves only in their "artistic" pretensions.
They worshiped young Arthur and conveniently used him to
gain entree to worlds opened by his charm. One of these older
friends, Paul Verlaine, was better dressed than the rest and had
a respectable reputation as a poet. He was a married bourgeois
who had published a volume of verse. He obviously adored
Arthur and said little during his visit, leaning forward on his

cane with eyes half-closed. At first, Casanova thought that he had bagged a real customer, but Verlaine was, like all poets, either penurious or stingy. Casanova felt that he ought to charge him something for just sitting there, basking in Rimbaud's aura. He had a bad feeling about the two of them and was not surprised to hear a year or so later that Rimbaud had shot and wounded Verlaine, who had become his lover.

Several times, Casanova had been tempted to show Rimbaud his real treasure, the manuscripts of Jacques Casanova, Seigneur de Seingalt, but each time something prevented him, as if the hand of literary fate had pulled a curtain between them, decisively keeping them apart. Rimbaud would have loved the *Icosaméron,* because he was a child who loved fairy tales, and he would have adored *L'Histoire de ma vie,* because he was a filthy-minded adolescent. Rimbaud read instead Casanova's literary rival, the Marquis de Sade, whose work unfortunately influenced the young poet.

Casanova was convinced that his works would never be published. There was little in the spirit of the times as it tumbled by the door of his shop, steaming the window with its agitated breath, that was hospitable to his work. People still clung to big ideas, spouted falsehoods supported by nothing but hot air, and gave themselves enough airs to fill Montgolfier's balloon. The nineteenth century was, Casanova thought, perfectly represented by the balloon.

Casanova's only connection with his past, besides the neatly tied bundles of papers that watched over him while he slept, was an occasional letter from Laura Brock, now Laura von Glass. After the Chevalier's funeral, Laura had followed Casanova's nephew, Carlo Angiolini, to Dresden, determined to buy the rights to *L'Histoire de ma vie* for her brother's small publishing firm, Brockhaus. Angiolini turned out to be an uncooperative idiot, which was not a surprise to the Chevalier, who regretted having bequeathed the manuscript to his nephew the instant he did it. In a fit of fever, he had been moved that Carlo had made the journey to his deathbed. He should have seen that Laura Brock, who burst into tears when he made the bequest, was the natural heir to his story. After all, he had tried out countless versions on her and preserved only those to which she had reacted with the most delight. He had been a fool, no doubt about it. For all that, Laura remained his faithful advocate, though at first, the manuscript nearly slipped from Laura's grasp. Carlo entered into negotiations with Count Marcolini, the Prime Minister of Saxony, who had once refused Casanova's plea to underwrite the publication of the memoirs. The Count offered Angiolini twenty-five hundred thalers for the manuscript, a considerable sum that Brockhaus couldn't match. Happily, greed and stupidity prompted Angiolini to reject the offer. A year later, Brockhaus bought the rights from a dejected Angiolini, who needed quick money to procure an abortion for his mistress. The price was only two hundred thalers, a negligible sum amounting to perhaps half the value of a gold zecchino in 1821.

It seemed now that nothing stood in the way of publication. Laura had married the much younger Baron von Glass, whose disinterest in his wife's literary preoccupations suited her fine. She could dedicate all her time to her lover's legacy. She had not counted, however, on her brother's caution and lack of conviction. After buying *L'Histoire de ma vie*, Herr Brock locked the original manuscript in his safe and only circulated excerpts among his friends to gauge their interest. His friends, with few exceptions, were solid burghers who were shocked by the Italian's frankness and his flaunting of their values, but they read him avidly and only afterward complained about his possibly nefarious influence on society. Laura argued fruitlessly with her brother and would have gotten nowhere if her uncle Herman, a quite erudite gentleman who was also one of the biggest investors in the firm, had not taken her side. After a heated discussion at dinner one evening, Herr Brock finally relented, and hired a translator, Wilhelm von Schutz. Twelve volumes entitled *Memoiren* appeared between 1822 and 1828.

The first two volumes, wrapped in rose paper, were delivered to the door of Chez Casa one rainy day in the autumn of 1822, together with a letter from Laura.

> *My dear Chevalier,*
>
> *What happens from now on is in the hands of Fate. My brother, who has no idea what he is bringing into the world, has done a creditable and professional job. The translation by Dr. von Schutz is good, though he has considerably sweetened certain passages and has passed over others in a hurry. All in all, the translation soon gives way to you, my dear friend, and I can hear your unmistakable voice as if I were sitting at your feet at Dux, listening to you talk. Let us each open a bottle of champagne one week from today and make a toast to life, love and eternity.*
> *All my love*
> *—Laura*

Casanova left the books wrapped up on his desk and busied himself all afternoon rearranging his window. A man stood in the rain, motionless under a black umbrella, watching the old antiquarian create an odd tableau. He saw him place a small portrait at the center of the window, and surround it with a jewel-encrusted cross, a stiletto, a cameo ring, a page of musical notation, a letter covered in old-fashioned script, and a garter. The stranger, who would later paint this vitrine from memory and display the painting in the first Salon des Independants under the title *Au Plombs,* could not know that the small portrait was that of Casanova's mother, Zanetta, painted by his brother Francesco, that the jewelled cross had been a decoration from the Pope, that the stiletto had been employed successfully in dispatching a Genoese card-cheat, that the cameo ring bore the image of Hermes and had been extracted by Casanova from his cheating ex-valet Costa in Vienna during the coronation of an Austrian emperor, that the musical manuscript was a page of notes for Mozart's *Don Giovanni,* that the letter was from a noble lady who persished in the Terror, and that the garter was Laura Brock's, removed the first time they met. Casanova lay back in his armchair and watched the man with the umbrella walk off into the night. He listened to the rain, Paris, the rumble gathering beneath the street as the nineteenth century gathered steam, and his own racing heart. He carefully untied the ribbon, held the book to his nose, inhaled deeply the aroma of fresh print, and began to read himself.

The annoyance of having to read himself in German was soon overcome by the relentless march of the black, printed letters that slowly left language behind as the story unfolded. Now and then he threw the book down in anger, having discovered the alterations Laura had mentioned. Professor von Schutz was occasionally prudish, or the German language simply could not accommodate the lyric temperature of some of his descriptions. To his credit, the professor had been punctilious about names and dates and had omitted nothing that could be of interest to an historian. Germans were good at that.

He did not stop reading until he heard the bells at St. Sulpice tolling the matinal hour. He closed the book and slept until noon. For the next three years, Casanova was gratified to hear of the great success of his *Memoiren* in German. Laura kept him apprised of all mentions of the book and sent him reviews and notices whenever they appeared. Casanova awaited anxiously the arrival of each new volume and was certain that when the original was published in French his reputation would be assured.

Imagine his dismay when a French edition, pirated from the German translation, was published by Tournachon-Molin, a Parisian house. This extraordinary attack on his work—which is the only way he could think of it—did not resemble the original in any way, except in gross outline. Chapters had been eliminated, spurious incidents had been added, and much of the careful detail was absent. It was nothing but a scandalous piece of trash.

Casanova strapped on his sword and headed at once for the miserable slanderer, whose offices, he learned, were located in a crumbling house near the Opéra. When he arrived there he was surprised to find an agitated mob in front of the place, fighting to get into the small bookshop whose window was filled with his book. The fortunate few who got in emerged triumphantly holding a copy of the abomination in their hands.

"What is the meaning of this?" he asked a dark young man with flushed cheeks who had just emerged victorious and had sat right down on the curb to read.

"Ah, monsieur," sang the young man, "these are the memoirs of Jacques Casanova, the greatest lover in Europe."

"You mean to say, 'the greatest writer,' surely!"

"I wouldn't know about that," the man said brusquely, "and now, if it please the monsieur, I would like to begin my reading."

"No, it does not please the monsieur," Casanova replied tartly. "I would be much obliged to you if you paid me a visit when you are finished with this trash. We will discuss literature." He curtly gave him the address of his shop, and strolled away in a dignified manner, conscious that the young man watched him for a long time, no doubt mistaking him for one of those prudes who make it a habit to protest every novelty.

He was surprised to see the young man walk in front of his shop later that same day. He invited him in and learned that his name was Beyle, that he was an aspiring writer, and that he did not consider Casanova's memoirs trash, but literature, perhaps one of the highest expressions of that art.

"It is not possible," Casanova said exasperated, "to base an opinion on this dreadful massacre of your language . . . You must, at the very least, read it in German. Failing that . . ." Casanova raised his eyes hopelessly to the ceiling where a plaster angel with a chipped foot winked at him.

"Failing that, what?" The young man followed the antiquarian's gaze and remarked, "This text may be a chipped angel, but one could well imagine it in full glory."

This remark, more than anything else, emboldened the Chevalier.

"If you promise not to tell a soul, I can let you read the original in French. For reasons too complex to explain, I have come into possession of a copy. You must return this to me in a fortnight."

Before he had a chance to change his own mind, Casanova sauntered to the back and returned with his arms full of bundles.

The young writer was overwhelmed. "You have such faith. You don't even know me."

"Go on before I change my mind." He could feel the young man's emotion and gratitude and knew that he was not wrong. Beyle, nom-de-plume Stendhal, was emotionally and intellectually transformed and his own work influenced by his reading of the Memoirs. He missed no occasion to praise the text, though it was not the praise Casanova might have expected. Like many readers after him, Stendhal was overwhelmed by the sheer scale of Casanova's amorous adventures and failed to appreciate Casanova's aesthetic qualities as a writer, despite what he had told him in the shop. Casanova was bitterly surprised to read, some years later, a remark made by the French critic Paul Lacroix, insisting that the memoirs could only have been written by a writer of the stature of Stendhal. But he was most hurt when one of his countrymen, Ugo Foscolo, declared that the purported writer of the memoirs had never existed.

At least Stendhal returned the manuscript. Casanova's disappointments did not end with the publication of the first bastardized French text. Brockhaus, hoping to stem the flood of pirated editions, decided to issue a French text and commissioned Jean Laforgue, a French professor at Dresden, to edit it.

If the Tournachon-Molin text had been a crude but transparent bastardization, the Laforgue edition was something infinitely more insidious, a sabotage from within that nearly caused the Chevalier to forsake the world forever. If Casanova had met Laforgue at a literary salon, he would have dismissed the professor as a conventional republican with small ideas and not given him another thought. Perhaps, somewhere along the way, he had met someone very much like Laforgue, and had dismissed him, causing the type to seek revenge. If that was the case, the revenge was successful.

Professor Laforgue was not content to falsify major episodes—in fact he left these quite untouched—but he entered instead into each detail and reflection, changing Casanova's very thinking to accord to his own. There was no detail small enough to escape Laforgue's effrontery. Where Casanova had written sensuously of foods, describing his taste for such strong sensations as the texture of crabs, oysters, ripe cheeses, breaking champagne bubbles, capers, and sardines, Laforgue had transformed all that into "delicious suppers." The good bourgeois could simply not understand that the richness of the world was in what it taught the senses.

Elsewhere, Casanova has removed his shoes and is walking with "naked feet" so as not to make any noise. Laforgue, offended by naked feet, replaces them with "slippers." Slippers! Casanova would have laughed, if he did not feel like crying. This Laforgue was a personage straight from Molière. He censured language about the sweat of women, the smells of food, the body. Where Casanova had written that "he feared marriage more than death," Laforgue amends the text to read that he "feared marriage more than fire." Why? Try as he might, Casanova could not understand a mind that would change the beautiful simplicity of death into "fire." Was Laforgue toning him down for fear of his wife? After an orgy, Laforgue attributes "disgust" to him. No such thing. Laforgue invented this "disgust" out of his own bourgeois sentimentality. Casanova quotes from a love letter from MM, in which she writes, "I make love to the air imagining it's you." Laforgue transforms this into, "I throw a thousand kisses that vanish into the air."

Worst of all, Laforgue's republicanism continually attributed to him sentiments contrary to the ones he held. He added a nasty irony to the word "Jesuit," where Casanova intended a simple statement of fact. In a Spanish episode, he put an entire Republican speech into his mouth. In talking about a women's theatrical production in Trieste, Casanova was made to express conventional feminist sentiments: "It is a generally known fact that if a revolution is needed in Italy it is in the field of education, particularly female." Even if Casanova had thought such a thing, and certainly he had never opposed the education of women, he would never have expressed himself in such pedestrian language. Casanova's references to his belief in God bothered Laforgue, who did his utmost to transform him into some sort of Jacobin.

Even his famous escape from the Leads was not spared Laforgue's penchant for hot air. The simple, suspenseful description of the moment when he found that a grating barred access to the window became a melodramatic lament in Laforgue. Casanova put his head down on the book, feeling Laforgue's hands around his neck, squeezing the life out of him.

He wrote desperate letters to Laura, who though quite old by now, lost no occasion to give heart to the love of her life. She pointed out that time, which is fatal to mortals, meant nothing to him, and that he must hold on, come what may, until the day that he was either satisfied by his reception or too bored to go on. She suspected that the latter might come before the former, but she did not confess this to the Chevalier. When she died she was majority owner in Brockhaus and left explicit instructions for the publication of the original French text as soon as possible. Amazingly, her wishes were disregarded for another century.

Despite such egregious treatment, Casanova's fame grew. He did not know what to think about it. In addition to Stendhal, many of the great writers of the first half of the nineteenth century paid homage to him. He was particularly fond of the neurasthenic but infinitely charming Flaubert, and of his younger relative Guy de Maupassant. He read with amusement the increasingly respectful criticism appearing in Europe. He laughed at the poet Heinrich Heine's statement that he would not recommend the memoirs "to a woman I cherish but would to all my male friends." He knew that women would love reading him as much as men. He was not at all surprised to receive praise from George Sand. But surprising questions about his identity continued. Rémy de Gourmont wrote, "But suppose by chance that the work is a romance? Then in that case Casanova would be the greatest novelist who ever lived; but that is impossible, one does not invent material of such prodigious variety."

Casanova reasoned that a violent rupture must have taken place between the eighteenth and nineteenth centuries for such doubts to exist. Not only had factual memory perished, despite the existence of a mountain of documents, but men's minds were somehow profoundly separated from the past. From the vantage point of his little shop, now renamed Aux Plombs, Casanova decided that with the exception of this inexplicable loss of memory, human nature was pretty much the same as ever. Greed, selfishness, guilt, and lust still ruled human behavior. He particularly admired a poem written by Charles Baudelaire, who was often in the shop complaining about the mediocrity of contemporary theater and music. Baudelaire described "boredom" as the greatest of vices. This revulsion against boredom seemed to Casanova a sign that humanity might soon escape the idealistic morass left behind by religion and revolution and return to the human measure.

Meanwhile, every year another pirated edition of his memoirs appeared, translated into every language on earth. For the next century Casanova collected himself in Italian, Hungarian, Croatian, Czech, Finnish, English, Arabic, Bengali, Lettonian, Norwegian, Polish, Slovenian, Turkish, Swedish, and scores of others. The little shop became too small for his collection, so he purchased the building next door near the end of the nineteenth century, at a time when real estate prices were quite high; the World's Fair was taking place in Paris, and the construction of the Eiffel Tower had displaced many people.

From the upstairs windows of his enlarged shop, he was able to watch the erection of the Eiffel Tower, a structure for which he immediately conceived a profound sympathy, though he was almost alone in his approval of the fantastic creation of Monsieur Eiffel. One day there appeared in his shop a preposterous personage of enormous bulk who immediately and effusively admired the view of the tower, demanding loudly to know if such a marvel did not, in fact, rank with the splendors of the ancient world.

When Casanova concurred wholeheartedly, this man, Guillaume Apollinaire, an art critic and poet with a scandalous reputation, embraced him nearly to the point of suffocation, and welcomed him into a fraternity of which he had never heard.

"You are henceforth a member of the Cubist movement!"

Casanova asked if he had ever read Chevalier de Seingalt's treatise on the subject of the cube. Apollinaire had not. Casanova found himself for the second time in a century digging through the shelves in search of a manuscript. As he had done with Stendhal, he instructed the poet to return it in a fortnight, and when the enthusiastic Apollinaire, who had a fair knowledge of mathematics, returned, Casanova was gratified to hear him praise the solution. Soon after, Apollinaire referred in a published article to the "astonishing illuminist Casanova who was much more than it is generally believed by those familiar only with Professor Laforgue's edition of the 'Memoirs'."

Casanova's reputation as more than a pornographer whose adventures appealed to the prurient and the overrefined began to grow. Around the time that the Eiffel Tower was completed, a new edition of the *Icosaméron* was published. Critics praised the five-volume adventure of Edouard and Elisabeth in the land of the Micromegs, but the book did not sell. A fantasy writer named Jules Verne had so utterly fascinated the reading public that the slower-paced *Icosaméron* did not appeal to them. Readers were interested in fantastic scientific inventions, and the subtle paradise of the Micromegs couldn't hold their attention.

To keep up with the times, the Chevalier introduced broken mechanical objects into the window display of his shop, things such as sewing machines with missing parts, or clocks with no hands. He imagined that these discards would put people off, and he was surprised when a dandified group of young men and women began turning up regularly to browse. On one occasion, they joined hands, closed their eyes, and began a chant that sounded very much like pure Micromeg. Casanova admired the slim bodies and well-turned legs of the women in the group. For the first time in a century he even felt the stirring of his old passion for the female sex and was flushed with delight.

The leader of the group, André Breton, explained that they were Surrealists and that they were interested in old broken-down things, particularly modern things. They had invented a technique for incorporating into their art and poetry everything in the world, a technique the artists called "collage" and the writers called "écriture automatique." Breton confessed that he was fascinated by lists, so Casanova loaned him the unfinished manuscript of the Chevalier de Seingalt's *History of Cheeses.* He was not surprised to read in a new literary journal an enthusiastic notice by André Breton, in which the poet asserted, "Casanova's reputation grows. The man we adore as the Herald of a Sincerity that has yet to enter our petty age, was also a Surrealist. His *History of Cheeses* is another *Chants de Maldoror.*"

To his great distress, the literature of casanoviana kept growing as well. The original French manuscript had still not been published, yet books about his memoirs and, what was more distressing, about him, kept appearing at a dizzying rate. There were literary studies, biographies, researches, and novels, all based on the dreadful mutilation by Professor Laforgue. In his worst nightmares, Casanova imagined that the Laforgue edition was the true one and that if and when the original appeared, generations of readers raised on the Laforgue would abandon him.

Casanova wrote several times to Brockhaus in Dresden, demanding that they publish the original. Each time, he signed his letters with a scholarly-sounding pseudonym followed by a string of degrees and academic distinctions. Each time, Brockhaus responded that the time had not yet come to release the original work. Casanova suspected that the success of the Laforgue edition, on which all the translations to other languages were based, was preventing the cowardly Brocks from doing the right thing. He decided to shame them by writing and publishing several articles in the magazines of his Surrealist friends, demanding publication of the original *L'Histoire de ma vie*. He was convinced that his campaign was having an effect when the First World War began, and such concerns were overshadowed by events.

The war, despite its new killing technology, was familiar to Casanova; it seemed to him the same war that had broken out in Europe after the French Revolution. He had predicted that Europe would be subjected to permanent war from that time on, and he was not wrong. The brief periods of peace between the wars were intense, as if young people, sensing the inevitability of another conflict, tried to cram as much life as possible in the few years they had left. Sexual mores had changed, women had become more bold and independent, while men, particularly writers and artists, were much quicker to speak of their feelings. For all that, there was an aura of weightiness and guilt about sexuality. Humanity still had a long way to go before it regained the charm and ease that had characterized the amorous liaisons of his time.

During the war, Casanova took in two young dancers, sisters, whose parents had been killed. They had wandered into his shop one day, so he gave them a small room next to his. At night he could hear them "trifling" with each other and was tempted many times to join them. But this he could not do if he wanted to live long enough to see the publication of his original work. Chastity was one of the conditions of the strange pact that Laura Brock had made on his behalf.

When the war was over, his "daughters" married young American industrialists and offered to buy him a larger building for his shop. They were prepared to help him in any way possible, but Casanova turned them down with a smile. He could have gotten rich many times, but he had abstained. Living within his means was another of the conditions of his strange immortality.

The postwar visitors to Aux Plombs were a new generation of young men and women for whom Casanova was a household name. One day a French girl accompanied by a handsome American military officer came into the shop. He had his arm around her and kept trying to kiss her on the lips, but the girl coquettishly refused him, throwing sidelong glances at Casanova who did nothing to help her. Finally she pushed away her boyfriend, exclaiming, "You are a regular Casanova!"

The Chevalier was pierced to the quick. He began seeing his name in newspapers, used in lowercase to denote impulsive romantic behavior. He worried that his name would become hopelessly corrupted before his true work could be published. He renewed his efforts to persuade Brockhaus to release the original, and formed a committee to help him, persuading a distinguished writer and member of the French Academy, Raymond Queneau, to head it.

Books relating to his work and person were beginning to overtake every inch of space. Only a very narrow corridor was not occupied by casanoviana. On his way to bed each night, he read the names of the authors on the spines and felt dizzy. Armand Baschet, Charles Henry, the memoirs of his friend the Prince de Ligne (a harsh and unfair portrait), Charles Samaran, Edouard Maynial, Ademollo, d'Ancona, Valei, Mola, Molmenti, Brunelli, Croce, Nicolini, Damerini. Zottoli, Edgecume, Symons, Havelock Ellis, Morris Bishop, Guy Endore, Edmund Wilson, Lawrence Powell, and many others. The jumble of names made it difficult to sleep and when he did sleep he dreamed that all these good people would hold a public book burning, an auto-da-fé, when his original work was finally published. These scholars were feeding on a phantom. They had never read the real Casanova.

A society of "Friends of Casanova" had appeared in England and was already recruiting members on the Continent and in the Americas. The society wanted to verify the names and dates Laforgue had used in his translation. Since many of Laforgue's facts were wrong, the casanovists were beginning to claim that he had invented many things from whole cloth. Casanova was alternately enraged and despondent when he thought of these people traveling all over Europe, retracing his steps, bothering the heirs of his lovers, disturbing the dust of his favorite churches and piazzas, invading with their heavy tread his beloved Venice, violating the delicacy of his childhood memories. He felt they understood nothing of his effort. He had remembered in order to give joy, not to open up his past like a restaurant to a drooling mob.

In 1937 Casanova acquired a pistol of the latest make and a modern suit of clothes and bought a train ticket to Dresden. In doing so, he was breaking another of the rules of his afterlife, which was that he could not travel. Having been a nomad in life, it had been decreed that his afterlife must be sedentary. He didn't care; he had to force Brockhaus to release the original manuscript. He got as far as the Gare de Lyon, but was feeling quite unsteady on his feet. At a newspaper kiosk he saw a huge headline: WAR WITH GERMANY. The station was swarming with anxious people. He dropped the pistol in a wastebasket and returned to Aux Plombs.

The Second World War was even more terrible than the first, yet to Casanova it seemed that it was always the same war. Instead of sheltering just two orphan girls, he hid an entire Jewish family from the Nazis who had occupied Paris. In order to accommodate his charges, he had to remove most of the casanoviana from the shop. With their help, he packed the thousands of volumes and had them transported by truck to the country home of his friend Gertrude Stein, living in the Vichy south of France.

The pater familias was one Eliphas Emmanuel, who was most assuredly related to his old friend Eliphas. A scholarly and religious man, he engaged Casanova in a discussion of the cabbala the first time they sat down for dinner. His wife and four daughters were courteous and proud. Casanova was not surprised that the youngest girl, Leah, looked uncannily like his love of long ago. Their eyes met across the table and a flicker of recognition passed between them. Time was suspended and there was nothing to do but sink into that immensity where past and present merge.

They also discussed the Golem of Prague. The legend had not changed much in the century and a half since the first Eliphas had told it to him. The bones of the Golem were no longer in the attic of the old synagogue, Eliphas told him. They had been removed before the Nazis occupied the city and taken to a safe place until a wise rabbi might revive the beast to defend the Jews in these terrible times.

They spoke in French, now and then lapsing into German. The family was originally from Dresden, where Frau Emmanuel had worked as a secretary for Brockhaus publishers and had seen Casanova's manuscript with her own eyes.

"What a rake he was," she said, rolling her eyes.

"That he was, madame, but a good man nonetheless."

"Good in bed, I hear," she said, covering her mouth when

her husband gave her a sharp look. But the girls started giggling and Leah said, "That's important."

Frau Emmanuel knew some of the history of the manuscript and had heard about the controversy surrounding it. It seemed that the house had been on the verge of publishing the original version several times, but each time something had interfered. She remembered that in 1929, Herr Brock Senior had declared himself dissatisfied with the annotations to the book, which seemed to him not scholarly enough. "There must be enough footnotes and commentaries," he told his partners, "to equal the number of Casanova's own words. This must be perceived as a serious scholarly work, to offset the inevitable criticism."

Casanova shook his head in wonder. Enough had already been written about the unfortunate Laforgue edition to exceed many times the number of words he had written. Such paltry excuses were beneath contempt. It had been simply a matter of greed, nothing else. And prudery. Such flaws were only human, after all. He did not fault Brockhaus for this. If Germans had only been greedy and prudish, they would have been like many other people in Europe. Unfortunately, they were also romantic.

"We hear quite often that Germans are practical and Jews are idealistic, but such ideas do not make sense," Eliphas said. "We were practical until it was too late for us. German idealism leads only to murder."

Casanova had realized this long ago. The seed of the irrational exaltation and love of death that had been cultivated by Goethe and Herder had become the common madness of the nation. And what had become of the romantic ideas of the smaller nations, ideas about their languages and identities? They had flowered for a time, giving birth to national literatures, and then they had settled into a murderous contest with each other. Once again, Germany was making a bid for supremacy, but this time, unlike the imposition of the language in the Austrian Empire,

Germany was seeking cultural and territorial domination by force of arms.

Casanova stayed awake at night, listening to the rumbling of Nazi tanks and trucks outside, wondering if the world would ever wake from this nightmare. Machines had overtaken the human capacity for forgiveness and laughter and were killing coldly and without surcease. Perhaps there was no reason to live any longer. Another kind of being inhabited the planet now.

But Casanova did not end his life yet. He lived to see Paris liberated, the Nazis defeated, and Germany left in ruins. During the allied bombardment of Dresden, the Brock family evacuated their headquarters, taking in a truck the family's most prized possessions, including the manuscript of *L'Histoire de ma vie*. Twice, bombs fell close to their truck. One made a huge crater only fifty yards in front of them, making it necessary to abandon the road and head out into the countryside. Another bomb fell behind them, covering the truck with mud and tearing the tarpaulin covering the manuscripts. Hans Brock, then owner of the firm, wrote later: "Our family stayed calm in midst of the terror, knowing somehow that our precious cargo protected us from the hand of Fate. The writing of the adventurer Casanova, who had been so lucky, so many times in his life, seemed to be defying the odds once more. The ghost of Casanova was doubtlessly with us."

Casanova wasn't so sure about that. The year 1950 rolled around, the Brock family moved back to Dresden into larger quarters, and still *L'Histoire de ma vie* languished in their vaults. In Paris, women were more daring then they had ever been. They laughed and smoked in public and took lovers as lightheartedly as Venetian courtesans in Zanetta's day. A serious-looking species of philosophe occupied cafés and wrote pessimistic books about the future of humanity.

One noontime, a gnomish man smoking a pipe strode resolutely into Aux Plombs, and said: "I have read about this admirable shop in an article by André Breton. There is something fundamentally paradoxical here."

Casanova offered Jean-Paul Sartre a chair. They discussed the relative importance of two men who had been contemporaries, the Marquis de Sade and Jacques Casanova. In Sartre's opinion, de Sade had been by far the more visionary of the two. De Sade's uncompromising vision of horror was better suited to the murderous fury of the modern world. Casanova, in his opinion, had been too sentimental a man, too ready to forget and forgive, too pleased with his fellow humans.

Casanova contradicted him. "He was a rational man, but also a religious man. Casanova believed in a Creator. Your de Sade was a machine. His reasoning was that of a machine."

"Precisely," said Sartre. "This is the time of the machine. One must act in any way one can against the machine, even if that involves adopting some of the machine's behaviors."

Casanova shook his head sadly. "Grace and happiness will return to the world."

Sartre smiled and said, "I wish it were true."

A few weeks later he brought over some of his friends and they drank ten bottles of Tokay that Casanova had been saving since 1798. Everyone talked at the same time. The women wore pants like the ones Casanova had imagined would be the uniform of the future, and the timbre of their laughter was familiar to him from his own carefree days. Things must not be as dire as the philosopher made them out to be as long as women laugh.

In 1960, under pressure from the Friends of Casanova committee and the personal intervention of Raymond Queneau and Jean-Paul Sartre, who had become very famous, Brockhaus published the first integral edition of *L'Histoire de ma vie* in French. It was heavily annotated and excessively footnoted, but its appearance was greeted with such joy, Casanova no longer feared oblivion.

He received the first volumes of his book by airmail post. Inside the shipping carton he found a parcel wrapped in rose paper, circled by a ribbon tied by the only hand capable of making such a knot.

Casanova opened the book, buried his nose in it, inhaled it deeply and let go of his fears.

About the Author

Andrei Codrescu is a poet, novelist, and essayist whose work is often heard on National Public Radio. He has written and starred in the Peabody Award–winning film *Road Scholar*. His previous novels include *Messiah* and *The Blood Countess*. He is also the author of such nonfiction books as *Ay, Cuba!: A Socio-Erotic Journey*, *The Devil Never Sleeps*, and *An Involuntary Genius in America's Shoes (and What Happened Afterwards)*. Mr. Codrescu edits the Web-zine *Exquisite Corpse: A Journal of Letters and Life* (www.corpse.org) at Louisiana State University.